LAND OF SINS AND PROMISE

A NOVEL

JAY G. GRUBB

North Carolina

Land of Sins and Promise

Published in the United States by BQB Publishing
(an imprint of Boutique of Quality Books Publishing, Inc.)
www.bqbpublishing.com

Printed in the United States of America

979-8-88633-038-0 (p)
979-8-88633-039-7 (e)

Library of Congress Control Number 2024942981

Book design: Robin Krauss, www.bookformatters.com
Cover design: Rebecca Lown, www.rebeccalowndesign.com

First editor: Caleb Guard
Second editor: Andrea Vande Vorde

To Mary, my swan. To Thomas, who made me promise not to do an *Assassins Creed* and have my main character personally interact with every famous person in history. And to Rusty the cat, who crawled up on me every time he thought my writing was going off track, forcing me to rethink.

To Begin With

She fell out of a second-story window. No one would call her lucky, but she got out of the hospital in twelve days, with the odd statement that she would "get hunk with" the man she lived with. That man, George Washington Johnson, was the first Black recording star of hit songs that generations later are trying mightily to forget: "The Laughing Song" and "The Whistling Coon."

She will shoot him in the ankle before dying under mysterious circumstances. Hundreds of White folks will raise thousands of dollars for Johnson's defense. And in the twin time of Jim Crow and the Gilded Age, that is all we'll ever know about her; a young mulatto with no family. Oh, and she liked gin too much and hung out where people talk with their fists.

We know more about the people who flowed around her. From George W. Johnson to William Randolph Hearst, to a conflicted young man from the north of England.

PART I

Embarked

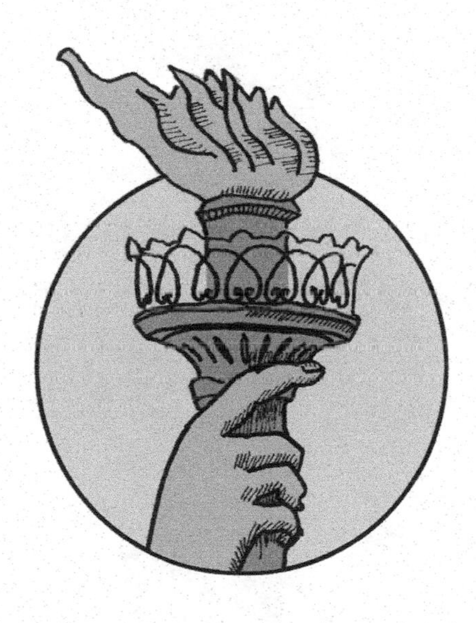

Chapter 1

No one made it to the dock to wave me off. Mother would have undertaken the journey to Southampton, but she was gone. Neither position nor gold had saved Prince Albert from typhoid, nor did they save my loving mother.

Father and my brother John, the favored, were far too busy at our Yorkshire estate. In their eyes, I remained merely a matter to be sorted out, this trip the latest in a line of bootless errands. After flirting with law and politics, I'd envisioned a heroic life in medicine, curing both court and commoner. Respectable. Independent.

Always helpful, my father had hastily arranged my attendance at the dissection of a particularly corpulent and hairy man. Bloody layer cake, green-blue sausage. I ran from the surgery so not to be shamed by vomit and tears.

After such false starts, I think my father was relieved by the prospect of my writing for a newspaper. He begrudged journalism, though the vilest of the writing arts, as necessary. The onion fields of our second estate in the Fens bordered on the country home of Sir Marshall Covington, the owner of a London newspaper of fine repute. My father's influence could secure me a solid, if not entirely dignified, position—credentials and experience be damned. He had one steady, successful son at his side. Because of John, he could play the chances with me.

Neither Father nor Sir Covington knew I'd already encountered Sir Covington's daughter Margaret in the Fens, where I risked life and limb to play savior to her damsel in distress. Sir Covington (whom I quickly rechristened the Old Man) remained baffled by how swiftly my relationship with Margaret went from formal introduction to plans of marriage.

I didn't know if Margaret was angrier at her father for offering me an assignment to America, or at me for my eagerness in accepting it. When the Old Man quipped, "It's also a universal truth that a man in possession of a good bride must be in want of a fortune," she responded with a silence so cold the words froze in the air.

A proper engagement, only a week away, was now postponed until I returned in two years. Extended engagements were disreputable, her father insisted.

As I boarded the German steamer bound to New York, a bellboy—man, really; we couldn't have been that many years apart—looked at me quizzically.

"Rest of your luggage, Sir?"

"Traveling light."

My camp duffel slipped and fell with a thud. I may have grunted. The sling on my left arm was complicating travel. Father had shaken his head sadly when he saw that I'd dug out the sling again. Hadn't the doctors declared my bones completely healed? John had given me a cold sneer. No matter, the pain was real enough. I managed to gently lower my leather-bound suitcase. Monogrammed with my full name, the case was my mother's final gift to me.

"Sir, don't see a return ticket on the manifest. Sure that's all?"

I tensed and the back of my neck burned. But I wasn't angry at the bellboy. He was only trying to be helpful. I was angry at my own deficiencies. Even my anger made me angry. No matter how much I papered things over with exaggerated refinement, I was little more than a courtly vagrant.

In any case, Father always preached about respecting all laborers and the folly of insulting porters, barbers, or waiters before they finished their jobs. I smiled, asked the bellboy his name, and handed him a tip to see my bags to my cabin.

My scant belongings were not due to rugged efficiency. Preparing for my journey, moving through the rooms of the estate, I had realized a hard truth. Except for clothes, tonsorial necessities, and the expected youthful memorabilia, little was mine. Even my beloved horse, Nike, belonged on my father's balance sheet and would pass on to my older brother, John. My mother had bestowed upon me one Banks family heirloom: a gold ring with a moon face featuring a spiral of Brazilian diamonds increasing in size like an imaginary constellation. Mother thought my sister, Aubrey, was too careless for rare jewelry, and John's wife had dismissed it as old-fashioned. I hadn't mentioned it to Margaret, since she insisted that a proper engagement ring be like the Queen's, with emerald and ruby.

None of that changed my situation. With neither title nor fortune, I had to make my own way or be trapped in the shame of living off Margaret's family money, a nest-cock. Or worse, begging for charity from my father and afterward, unthinkably, from my brother. Dependence breeds resentment, even in a child. I knew deep inside my bones that to live as a child, at someone's pleasure, would destroy my soul.

"Ugh." The bellboy hunched to one side, dropped the load, reordered the bags. "Small bag. What's in here, bricks?"

"Sorry. Books."

I fingered a lock of hair in my pocket. Before I left, I ran down at the last minute to the carriage house, where my prize steeplechase horse, Nike, was stabled, and snipped a lock of her mane as a good-luck memento. There was no time for a farewell ride. Horses had been the only constant in my life. I was told I'd ridden before I walked. I resisted the urge to kiss the lock and breathe in its familiar musk: old timber, warm dirt, cut hay.

Watching everything I knew slip from view reinforced how

unmoored I'd been since my mother's death. Her memory was as much distress as comfort. My champion was gone. What would she think of me now? My life was a dog's breakfast of beginnings left unfinished. I would return to England still young but never again so fresh as twenty-one. Even the wet metal rail in my hands vibrated awkwardly. I searched for pictures in the water as the ship sailed past the lighthouse and into the Channel.

Still early afternoon, I stayed on deck to watch England disappear. White clay cliffs of the Needles jutted up from the water like the back of a submerged sea monster. Torquay to Plymouth, and on to Penzance as the ship entered the Celtic Sea. The small German oompah band thought it clever to torture us with Gilbert and Sullivan's infernal Major-General tune. I escaped belowdecks to assess my first-class cabin, committed to record all that happened each day, when my memory was most reliable. I pledged to resist the temptation to rehabilitate my actions and words with staircase wit. Even so, I knew memory was an unreliable companion.

I pushed open the cabin door, then froze in place. A man stood near the foot of the bed, slightly bowed, hands on knees. I immediately recognized his Egyptian military dress. After the British took control of Egypt in 1882, Egyptian officers were occasionally among the troops near Buckingham Palace.

Startled, the man turned to face me with a look of annoyance that he struggled to erase from his features. His complexion skewed darker than other Egyptians I'd seen. His nose large but narrow, and his lips, neither full nor thin, sported a meticulously trimmed mustache. He wore no beard. Despite the shade of skin and slight wooliness of hair, he might have been mistaken for a particularly suntanned Frenchman returned from the Foreign Legion. Both a military and aristocratic air hung about him.

"Something I can do for you?" His English was perfect.

"I believe this is my cabin," I said.

"Then you're the second person today to make that mistake. A bellboy left minutes ago with, I assume, your luggage."

"I do not mean to be rude, but I am sure this is my room number."

"You English. Even your tall children assume they must always be right. I boarded a day ago, so I'm certain of my priority. In any case, the bellboy said he must fetch a superior to straighten this out."

On cue, a tired-looking crew member rapped on the open door. For some reason, perhaps since it concerned tickets and money, they'd sent the chief purser. Unlike the greeting staff, his English was tortured and heavily accented.

"*Guten Tag, mein Herren.* You would be Herr Joshua Clarke Banks, and you then are Doctor Abdel Qabash, no?"

"This man is in my room," I said.

Dr. Qabash replied stoically, "That man is in my room."

"Gentlemen, *bitte*. We have *eine verwechslung*."

"I do not understand." Other than a smattering of French, my language skills were limited.

"A, uh, confusion. The Doctor is only with us *zwei*, uh, two more nights. Then he transfers to sister ship so he docks in Baltimore, not New York. Herr Banks, you have copy of your arrangements?"

I'd left the arrangements up to others, again. "No."

"*Schon gut*. Herr Banks, you certainly have the cabin two nights from now for five nights, a full one-way ticket. But your agent neglected to arrange lodging for your other two nights."

"Can I just book another first-class berth?"

"No." The Purser shook his head wearily. "Before *ja*, now *vessel is extrem voll*."

"All right, then. Second class if I must."

"No, only *zwischendeck*."

"English. Please."

"How you say . . . steerage?"

I looked over at the Egyptian. He avoided my eyes and looked down at the floor. I didn't consider myself a fragile traveler, accustomed only to bed warmers, silk robes, and caviar. Father made sure we spent nights in the woods and wilds. We slept in rough-hewn sheds or simple tents, the bare ground for a floor. I tucked into shepherd's pie as well as French rabbit tureen with equal enthusiasm, but the thought of steerage horrified me.

As elegant and roomy as the steamer's first and second class were, steerage was part-prison and part-madhouse. Many thought it should have been abolished outright. Some British ships replaced it with a spartan, yet humane, third class. I couldn't imagine being jammed in with two to four hundred sleeping in one compartment on bunks—stacked above another, with little light and foul air. Food in second class nearly matched the delicacies of first class and were enjoyed in a luxuriantly appointed dining room. But in steerage, I'd face barely edible rations doled out with less courtesy than at a charity soup kitchen. The stories were well-known. Bread so rank that hungry emigrants threw it into the sea in protest. Poor travelers driven to steal water after midnight from second class. And no escape above. The hoi polloi packed tightly in a smoky, miserable fraction of deck. Even walking was impossible.

The Purser could see my distress. He stepped close to me and whispered, "Herr Banks, the Doctor appears more *afrikanisch* than Egyptian to me. I can ask if they move the schwarz instead of you. But the Captain has deep respect for the uniform, so I don't know he will cause such unpleasantness on a military man."

The Purser didn't talk low enough so that Abdel Qabash could not hear. The Doctor stared into my eyes as if searching for something, then beckoned me over with a wave of his hand.

"You know, my mother used to say two men in a burning building must not stop to argue."

"So?" I said.

"I've a proposal. Why don't we share the room? In my middle age, I've developed insomnia. More likely to catch an hour or two of sleep in the daytime than night. I'd much rather spend time in the lounge, or above, where I've rented a deck chair."

"And we do not know which one of us is to yield. I wish steerage on no one."

"All I ask is access for prayers." He counted them off on five fingers. "The *Salaat* is dawn, then just past noon, between noon and night, after sunset, and late night."

"I will not stop to argue."

We both turned to the Purser, who casually had been listening in. "This arrangement acceptable?" I asked.

The Purser shrugged. "*Das ist mir wurst*. I will have Herr Banks' bags retrieved. *Sehr gut*." At that, he clicked his heels and was gone.

Chapter 2

The door slammed shut, followed by an uncomfortable silence. I studied Abdel Qabash. "You are a captain?"

"*Yuzbashi*, what you call captain, yes."

"Should I refer to you as Captain or Doctor?"

"I'd like to be remembered more as Doctor than Soldier."

I nodded.

"Banks, as agreed, I need to restate my intent and start the *Zhur*, my prayer, all over."

"Why five?" I blurted.

"Excuse me?" The Doctor arched an eyebrow.

"Five prayers."

"Maybe if we have to come stand in front of God five times a day, we can't run so far away."

"Can I stay and watch?" I supposed it impertinent, but my curiosity overruled my courtesy.

"I'm not your Queequeg. Besides, you won't hear me, and if you did, I doubt you speak Arabic."

"Sooner or later, I will be in here with you, especially for your night prayer."

"*Salat al-Isha*."

"Right. Just trying to educate myself."

"Banks, I need to concentrate. Otherwise, it's meaningless ritual."

"I will be as quiet as a church mouse."

"No good. I won't perform for you. If you must stay, you may join me in prayer."

"Is that kosher?"

The Doctor smiled. "We're all children of Abraham, are we not?"

I saw no graceful way to decline without insult and so joined him in the widest part of the cabin. "Are we supposed to face Mecca?"

"Allah isn't so petty. I'm on a ship, so I'll face where it's going, not Kaaba. You, my friend, can face where you will if you'll just stop talking."

Chastened, I folded my hands and bowed my head to at least keep up appearances. Truth be told, I couldn't recall the last time I actually prayed. As a child, I was quite devout—evening and morning prayers and all that. In boarding school, I read Butler's *Lives of the Saints*, tempted by a forbidden Catholic track, and for the lists of gruesome demises. As of late, I'd become something of a Deist. I didn't know how much the Divine Watchmaker bothered to check in on his creation, but if God could not be bothered to part any modern seas, he bloody sure did not waste omnipotence fixing cricket matches. Still, I followed the advice of Ben Franklin in holding open the possibility of the rare hand of God interceding when truly needed. It allowed a touch of Thomas-Aquinas revelation to mix with my natural reason.

From the little I thought I knew, I expected the Doctor to be prostrate on the floor. Instead he stood, focusing himself. After some time, the Doctor brought hands to ears, then cycled through a series of movements. Hands front, then palms on knees; back bent, rising to bend again, slowly sinking to kneeling; and finally, prostrate, with forehead, nose, and palm touching the ground. I noted the elbows did not touch the floor.

The pattern repeated: sitting, prostrating, and standing. An elaborate, pious Simon Says. I checked myself for such a dismissive thought. The Anglican Church was no slouch as to ritual rising and kneeling during services.

Compelled to make some attempt at prayer, I settled on the Nicene

Creed. Making a show of crossing myself—spectacles, testicles, wallet, and watch—I genuflected, running the words of the Creed through my mind.

After what I counted as four cycles, Dr. Qabash remained seated for a time before he wiped his face with his palms and rose with me. "May God receive our prayers," he said.

"May I ask a question?"

"If you must."

"You were so focused. What was that glancing over your shoulders near the end?"

"Ah, actually a good question. I look over my right shoulder to the angel recording my good deeds, then over my left at the angel recording my wrongful deeds. I wish each of them the peace and blessings of God, for they're both with us always."

"I think I have a third angel recording a list of meaningless deeds."

Dr. Qabash laughed, a deep, open laugh. "You're a strange one, eh, Banks?"

I didn't think I harbored a need for older male companionship. Nowhere did I recall a particular childhood affinity for Merlin, or any of the other wise old men who haunted English fairy tales. The two uncles on my mother's side served more as furniture than friends, my teachers more menace than mentor. I was surprised by how much I enjoyed the Doctor's company. Unlike my father, Dr. Qabash listened to me. He asked questions rather than rushing to advise.

For his part, he appeared gratified that someone young might care to hear his opinions on politics and the news of the day. Despite obvious differences in age and appearance, if one saw us chatting away in the well-appointed first-class parlor or over dinner, they would mistake us for seasoned traveling companions.

While open and generous, the Doctor was guarded about his past. The reason why he traveled alone at this juncture in life appeared a sore spot. His wife had died in labor, his second son stillborn. His first son, grown and in the army, didn't have much time for his father. The Doctor also had a daughter, though estranged. When I moved to ask why, he held up a hand.

"Let's just say military training doesn't translate to the raising of headstrong girls." Then he changed the subject. I determined to press him on it later.

Heading back to our cabin, he asked softly, "Do you have any Scottish water we might share tonight? I caught a bit of the British habit."

I paused, confused.

"Water of life, I believe they say."

"Oh, yes, that water. Grand idea. I can get my hands on that particular elixir. Meet you in the cabin in a few minutes."

"And Banks, don't let them contaminate the purity of such fine liquid with ship's water."

While ordering the scotch, I paid a sympathetic steward to take extra jugs of water and boxes of biscuits down to the women and children in steerage. I didn't know if the gesture was for them or my own conscience. Back at the cabin, we stayed up a good part of the night talking. Eventually, the Doctor inquired about the sling on my arm. That led to a detailed account of the grim incident that had derailed my quest for steeplechase fame. John had blamed it on my rashness. Instead, the cause was John's one-upmanship and my father's favoritism.

"You know, I'm not to judge, but I've just the treatment for inflammation." The Doctor riffled through his medical bag and returned with an oddly ancient-looking bottle. "Real mummy powder."

"You must be joking. I'm to eat King Tut?"

"More likely a minor pharaoh or official, maybe a bit of mummified cat thrown in. Very old idea, bone cures bone. Let those believe who need to and can. Also, allow me to do a few muscle manipulations, and I'll instruct you on stretching exercises."

The Doctor insisted I take first use of the bed, as he'd no intention of sleeping yet.

I awoke the next day far past sunrise. To please Dr. Qabash, I packed the sling away. I discovered the Doctor topside on his rented deck chair, asleep. Knowing how dear such respite was to him, I went off in search of a chess set. The Doctor and a few others were to board a dinghy the next morning, transferring over to the sister ship bound for Baltimore Harbor. The Doctor had proposed we spend our last afternoon and evening playing chess, his favorite game.

My mission immediately ran aground. Timed chess matches were running in the state room, every visible board taken. After scouring the ship, I spied a set on deck between a matronly woman and an unfortunately whiskered man reclining on deck chairs. A single rose and vase sat in the center of the board, signaling disinterest in the game. When I asked politely about acquiring the board the man bolted up.

"What's it worth to ya?"

"Surely the set belongs to the ship."

"Possession's nine tens of the law, they say."

"Honey, don't be like that." The woman didn't look up from her magazine.

"Aw dear, just trying to recoup. Trip's cost me a fortune. This fellow looks like a young man of business." Turning back to me, he gave a conspiratorial wink. "Daughter married an earl, real bang-up romp, but I paid to have half our family steam over. Gotta get back to Chicago and make some hay. First the wife's making me stop at some big society shindig in Manhattan. Her little baby's a countess."

Ah, yes. The year 1895 was already shaping up to be a banner year for Dollar Brides. Another father pulling off the grand deal of acquiring his new-money daughter an old-landed title, punching his ticket to dinner with the Astors. How long before the new countess realized she'd traded cowboys and the frontier for hollow aristocrats still pantomiming wealth on huge, squandered estates?

Perhaps I was just envious. These parvenus managed to leapfrog up the nobility whilst my family languished at the modest rank of barons. Our patriarch had been modest indeed. Nathan Noah Banks, my great-great-grandfather, being the second son, had taken his small pension and run off to Montserrat in the Caribbean. There he took over an uncle's plantation and built it into an important exporter of indigo, tobacco, and sugar. If not for the convenient death of his childless older brother, Nathan wouldn't have eked out a barony. My father returned the family to the Yorkshire Dales, setting up a working farm of grain and sheep. The Bankses always earned their keep. Proudly, more pounds than peerage.

"What brings you across the pond?" The American was strangely sweaty in the cool air. I was tempted to grab the set and flee.

Frankly, I didn't have a satisfactory answer to his question. The idea of being the London newspaper's American correspondent came from Margaret's father—out of nowhere. Not my decision. I'd not yet made it mine.

"Work," I said finally.

"Honey, please, I'm reading." The woman still had not looked at us.

The man sighed and handed over the set. "More of a checkers man anyway."

Mission saved, but not before the man's barely covered sneeze mingled with the spindrift. I also didn't escape his insistent, bone-crushing handshake before I hurried off.

Not wanting to spy on, nor join him, I let the Doctor finish afternoon prayers in private before returning to set up the game. He was eager to engage. My hand tremored slightly. Chess was a frequent diversion during my stay at Cambridge, but like my studies, I'd never put my whole heart into it.

After matching his white pawn with my black, the Doctor regarded me with disapproval. “Hope you won’t merely copy my moves. You claimed to be proficient.”

“We will see,” I said with false bravado. I followed with a few awkward attacks and retreats.

As if reading my mind, he commented, “Short-term traps and threats. You need to think more than one or two moves ahead.”

All I could think was to guard my king with my queen. He moved his bishop to directly face mine. My concentration wavered. The king became my father, his queen at risk. Two bishops nearly touching, yet unable to interact, a pantomime of my brother and me.

“Would you please keep your head in the game.”

In a last-ditch effort to avoid defeat, I moved my king. The Doctor’s ninth move reinforced his bishop with the white queen for checkmate. I flushed in embarrassment.

“Well, I believe they call that a brevity,” I said.

“Hope you don’t intend to play miniatures all night. Only the dishonorable or the desperate enjoy easy victories.”

I pledged to focus, and my play improved. It could scarcely decline. The Doctor was pleased when a lengthy match ended in a draw, both our kings protected only by a knight or bishop. I took the opportunity of his good humor to ask a question.

“You never said why you left Egypt, which you love, to come to America.”

“No offense, my young friend, but I can’t stand another day under the heel of the British boot.”

“Surely English rule has been beneficial?”

“Sorry, no. Education, politics, all deteriorated under your empire. Our army’s humiliated. Even our noble white uniform has reduced to bland khaki.”

I thought it best not to argue with facts of which I knew nothing. “What will you do?”

"Open a medical office in Baltimore."

I lined up pawns for another match. "Doctor, I have read a lot of travelogues to the States. Not sure Americans—I mean, White Americans—will be your patients."

"What? I've papers from Qasr Al-Aini Medical School as well as being a field surgeon."

"They do not care if you studied with Henry Gray or Joseph Lister. In England your rank would allow you a certain access to society. An exotic for sure, but a known quantity. In America, they will see you as a Negro and will not let you touch them, and God forbid, especially not their women."

"That's insanity. I'm very good at medicine. I've saved lives." He moved his queen to take my bishop. "Besides, I'm Egyptian, not Nubian."

"I only know what I read. It may be too fine a distinction for Americans."

"It's a world of difference. No matter. Let's go dine. Your impulsive tactics weary me."

When we returned from dinner, I was finally victorious.

"That was an atrocity," grumbled Dr. Qabash. "You fluctuate between meanderer and berserker."

"Checkmate," I announced rather loudly.

"I became so amused by your insipid knight's tour, I let him take the prime square, becoming an octopus lashing out in eight directions."

"But I won."

"You sacrificed both bishops. *Zugzwang*."

"Pardon?"

"Forced disadvantageous options."

"Rather the point, yes?"

"It's impossible to respond to moves that are so obviously wrong. You must promise to visit me in Baltimore, where I'll teach you proper chess. You're like the prince and his three fates in the fable I told you at dinner. You escaped defeat too conveniently."

"The prince was inconsequential. His wife saved him."

"Ah, my mother said such fables are lovely lies hinting at truth." He shrugged. "Egyptians are superior in all things except mythology. Greeks and Indians may match us."

"Your military lost to the Empire."

"Momentarily. In Egypt and India, your empire will fall to a perfect nemesis popping from a pillar like Vishnu."

"Sorry. Vishnu?"

The Doctor shook his head. "British. Lording over a people, yet can't bother to learn their hearts and minds. You truly are like Hiranyakashyap."

"Completely lost now. You must tell."

"You're like a child, bleeding me of fables."

"I am closer to five than fifty."

The Doctor managed to sigh and smile simultaneously. "Last one. Lord Brahma granted the demon Hiranyakashyap a boon, to choose his death according to his wish. The demon desired immortality so to defeat Vishnu. Thinking himself clever, he set the terms of his death: He couldn't be killed inside a building or outside, not in day or at night, not on earth nor in the air or in water, not by man or animal, and no weapon, even mystical, could harm him.

"Armed with Brahma's boon, Hiranyakashyap troubled Heaven and Earth, and demanded all to worship him. But the demon's youngest son, Prahlad, continued to worship only Vishnu. Enraged, the demon tied his son to a pillar on the threshold of his palace.

"As Hiranyakashyap lifted his sword to behead Prahlad, Vishnu burst from the pillar incarnated as Narasimha, a chimera with the many-armed body of a human, and the head and claws of a lion.

Snatching Hiranyakashyap, the chimera eviscerated the demon with his claws, not weapons, and taunted him: 'It is dusk—neither day nor night, you're on my lap—neither earth nor sky, your threshold is neither inside nor out, and I am neither human nor beast.' "

"A tad legalistic."

"The point is, your empire believes it's immortal. It will fall to the perfect opponent beyond your imagining."

I suppressed a flicker of indignation, not wanting to spoil our remaining moments, and remarked on the weather.

I saw the Doctor off in the morning and immediately felt his absence. He'd provided a welcome distraction from my circling thoughts. Now past the initial excitement of leaving home, I was consumed only with self-doubt. I wrote in my journal all I could remember of the Doctor, certain I'd seek his counsel again someday. I considered our chess games. Did it matter more which pieces you moved or how you moved your pieces? Was it identity or action that defined you?

I spent day after day poring over the travel writings I hoped to emulate. Dickens, Kipling, Tchaikovsky, Oscar Wilde, Robert Louis Stevenson. One problem was clear. All of them were already public figures, the world curious about their impressions of strange lands. Even Lady Theodora Guest, whose recent North American travel narrative sold well, already possessed some renown from her biblical writings. How could I possibly compete with them? What if the European public was already satiated by the deluge of American travel memoirs? Perhaps I could bring a more nuanced view since I'd be a working newspaperman, not just a tourist. I took W.F. Rae's admonishment to heart, that most such books were "bundles of prejudices artistically arranged, or deliberate caricatures skillfully drawn."

Then again, some level of celebrity might be obtained by publishing newspaper stories, especially editorials. In persuading me to take this plunge, the Old Man led me to believe that as the sole English correspondent at the New York paper, I'd immediately have status on its pages. I let myself picture the byline on my own weekly column, perhaps my likeness imprinted. I imagined writing long, thoughtful articles on the state of American politics and society, my opinions quoted in halls of power and argued at corner pubs.

I tried to build my self-confidence by these hopeful thoughts, but I had to face facts. My qualifications for correspondent were scant at best. I knew not a soul in America and couldn't name all the states, much less tell their locations. My last encounter with Margaret hadn't ended in kisses or tears, but had been infused with an icy diffidence that still stabbed me. What was I doing? I thought I possibly made the worst mistake of my life. To top it all off, I began to feel a fever coming on.

As I leaned back in my chair, journal in one hand, a message fluttered out from the pages. Clever Margaret had chosen a London postcard emblazoned with "Wish You Were Here." No salutation, no valediction, only Margaret's meticulous script.

> I know it rude not to see you off at the dock. I can't summon the proper facade for the occasion. Father and you make no sense. What can you possibly achieve in America that you couldn't in London?
>
> Go slay your dragon and return at once.

Chapter 3

By the time the German steamer entered New York Harbor, the slight irritant of a kindling fever had become a raging furnace. My eyes ached in their sockets, my skin prickled, and I struggled not to pass out.

The riot of masts and steam stacks over the water echoed the confusion waiting on the dock. Heavy freight wagons crisscrossed dodging passengers and sailors rushed to catch their boatswain's last call. Oranges, fish, furniture, and more flowed out into the city without pause.

Passengers waited with luggage as two large drummers' wagons with teams clopped off first. When they were taken on and where they'd been kept, I couldn't suppose. Folding steel slats finally pushed aside for us to disembark. I'd no chance of finding my contact man in the pulsing masses. It was hard enough to see around the enormous hats of the women. Their wide brims protruded out like hotel awnings bedecked with flowing ribbons and exotic feathers. The women clearly feared the touch of any sun to skin. Many carried parasols, fancy and plain. Smells assaulted me from everywhere: rose perfume, horse flesh and manure, the soft aroma of fall apples, and the hard bite of seafood and manly sweat. My sea legs wobbled as the landscape seemed to rise and fall.

The wire I'd received said my driver, a Wyatt Brown, would take me to town. Having no idea of his appearance or how to find him, I clamored up on one of the shoeshine chairs shaded by large umbrellas. The shoeshine boy eyed me warily as I tried not to shiver or cough.

I'd have noticed Brown even if he'd not clutched a small placard emblazoned with "Joshua Banks" in Spencerian script. The man himself was unremarkable. About my height—just shy of six feet—average build, he moved like an athlete. A broad mustache spread over a not-unpleasant face. He could have blended into the sea of black and gray suits, but he did not.

He must have gotten dressed in the dark, I thought, trying to be charitable. His plaid lounge suit, what Yanks called a "sack suit," was an agony of orange, blue, and green with gutta-percha buttons. Underneath, he wore a regrettable robin's-egg V-neck sweater in place of a proper vest. His fold-down Eaton collar was more appropriate for a schoolboy, not a man pushing thirty. He lacked any necktie. All this topped off with a jaunty, high-crowned homburg. The hat, at least, was a respectful black with matching ribbon. I threw some coins at the shoeshine boy, grabbed my bags, and ran after Wyatt Brown.

"Hey! You there. Driver. I believe you are my servant."

"No."

"Are you not carrying a sign with my name on it?"

"Not your servant."

"You are Wyatt Brown, from the paper?"

"Don't work for Your Lordship." His tone was mocking.

"I mean no insult. There is no shame in social position."

"My employer is Mr. William Randolph Hearst. Been doing whatever he needs done for years, and far as he's concerned, I may be a rung or two up the pecking order."

My face, already flush with fever, turned hotter. "Look here, I am the chief American correspondent sent directly by Sir Covington himself."

"Let's get this straight. You're just the unfortunate end of a bargain to get our man well-set in London. Chief don't give a dead rat about you. May have to shepherd you around, but I'm not a servant, and I don't bow down."

"Don't have to get your Irish all up," I said, even as my fingers curled into fists.

"What'd you say?" The man looked suddenly shattered, his expression like a dog unexpectedly kicked. He grabbed my arm and pulled me into an alley. "Why'd you say Irish?"

I stared down Wyatt Brown. "You may fool the locals, you may have even been born here, but I grew up surrounded by Irish servants, field hands, and nannies." Unlike many Brits, my father had developed a fondness for the Irish from his days on Montserrat and leaned heavily on them for staff.

"The ghost of your mother tongue still haunts you. Why run from it, Mr. Wyatt Brown? If that even is your real name. No God-fearing Irish Catholic mother would fail to give her son a good Christian name. You pinch that name from a Buntline dime Western?"

I thought he might punch me. In my condition, it wouldn't have taken John L. Sullivan to knock me out. Instead, he moved his face mere inches from mine.

"You've got to keep this under your hat. You've no idea how hard it is for an Irishman in this country. Folks don't want to serve you a meal or let you a room. My mother, God rest her soul, jumped a currach from Inishmaan Island to a Galway steamer and brought me to New York in her belly. I'm true-born American, but they don't treat you that way."

"No?"

"Mother barely spoke English when she got here, spoke Irish at home. She'd be cleaning homes, and owners wouldn't even bother to learn her name, Breena. Just be Bridget do this and Bridget do that. Treated her like trash. We may have Boss Croker and a good many police, but you still see 'no Irish need apply' signs. To a lot of Americans, we're not even White, just brutes like the nigger."

"Mr. Brown, sorry we started down the wrong path just now. Fate's thrown us together, so we'd better make the most of the situation, but I need to ask two things of you. First, please back off. I am feeling terribly ill, and you should not wish to share this. Second, I must insist you never speak that word again in my presence."

"What? Nigger?"

"Please!"

"Why do you care?"

"The Banks family does not abide such insults. The African is God's creature, the same as you and me. I have seen my father nearly come to blows at someone's careless use of the word."

"Seems a tad extreme. It's only a word."

"Be that as it may, while I do not see eye to eye with my father on much, this much is incontrovertible. A word begets a thought, thought informs intent, and intent becomes the deed."

Wyatt Brown backed away a few steps. "Okay, but we're good on the Irish stuff, right? No spilling the beans."

"No beans will be spilled, but can we get to your coach? I think I may faint."

Relieved that I wouldn't need to walk far to our transport, I was taken aback upon seeing it: a gray Percheron, a rather large draft horse, harnessed to a spider phaeton, a small, speedy two-person coach. A snug little carriage for the sporting gentleman who liked to handle the ribbons.

Brown noticed me staring. "What'd you expect? A hansom cab with me stuck on top and you lording in private? You sit with me."

"No, no, this Brewster is top class. But might it not be better with a fine English Hackney horse?"

"Don't need some high-strung show horse. This boy can do forty miles a day at a trot. The breed's eager to please and got a heart to work."

"Not faulting the breed, it only struck me as an odd choice. A place for every breed, and every breed in its place. I have only seen Percherons pulling heavy wagons."

"Well, word is, this big fellow worked on a team pulling yellow Armor Meat Packing wagons at a circus when the Chief spied him. If Hearst wants something, he'll find money to buy it."

"Circus? Did he come with your outfit as well?" I should have held my tongue, but the fever weakened my self-restraint.

"Hey, maidens love this get-up. At least I don't look like the Queen's undertaker."

I didn't take offense. My tailor said as much when I picked the silhouette and fabric.

"Why would a young man need a funeral suit?" he complained. I thought it made me look older and more respectable, but it may have also reflected my mood.

"I fear I may be my first client. Mr. Brown, where am I to stay in town?"

"You don't know?"

"Things were rushed. London made arrangements."

"Huh. Lot of single reporters board with a family. Not too pricey. Feels more homelike, with meals and laundry. But you? You're staying in goddamned Washington Square right above Delmonico's. Right down the street from the Hoffman House where the Chief's staying."

"My father, of course." I sighed. "The Old Man, my publisher, Sir Covington, is way too tight-fisted to pay for frivolity. All right, take me to my flat before I pass out."

"No such luck."

"What?" I truly was starting to teeter.

"Your publisher, the Old Man you say, gave you an assignment right off the reel. Just enough time to stop at a cigar store and place a bet, then we're on a train to Atlanta."

"Is there nothing to do for Mr. Hearst's paper here in New York?"

"Hell, Chief hasn't really bought a newspaper yet. He's still shopping. Getting all his people set up no matter what paper it is."

My prospects appeared as shaky as my mind. I'd traveled so far to work with a newspaper that didn't exist. I'd run out my options back home. I felt I still had Margaret's love, but her respect? My own? Even a postponed marriage forced thoughts of children. What legacy would I leave them? A journalist could make a difference, exposing the sins of the powerful and the plight of the powerless. I had to succeed. By now I was fighting to stay on my feet. I felt myself stumble, half carried, into a private train compartment, saw blurs of red or green, heard the heartbeat of steel on track, and slipped completely into delirium.

I lost all track of time. Bells tolled, stations came and went. I floated in and out of consciousness, unable to tell reality from dream from delusion. I know I heard Wyatt, but also others. My father? John? Pictures of my life shuffled through my mind. The steeplechase championship played over and over, but scrambled and otherworldly. The last-minute switch of horses—my new mount turning to dust—me falling, falling. I felt no pain. My muscles no longer ached. Instead, I felt strangely numb.

A mirror rose above a mismatched vanity facing the bed I was lying on. My fever had broken, but my mind was still muddy. In the reflection I looked like a destringed marionette. The hotel room, for it could be nothing else, was overheated. I'd read the Americans were notorious for this, an environment more suited for orchids than peaceful recuperation. I kicked off the sheets and rose unsteadily.

"If it ain't Rip Van Winkle." Wyatt Brown sat by the window, clipping his fingernails.

"Where are we?"

"Atlanta, and before you ask, it's September 17th. You been out of it for three days, all the way down on the train. Been spoon-feeding you soup and oatmeal. You've mostly taken care of your own toilet—*mostly*."

I blushed. "Sorry . . . thank you. Not sure what I remember."

"You were pretty far gone, talking real weird."

"I have had fevers before, but it never caused such intense visions."

Wyatt Brown shrugged. "Could've been the morphine."

"What?"

"That doctor—at least, he claimed to be a doctor—looked a mite shady to me, but anyhow, he gave you a pretty fair dose."

"Good God, man!"

"Hey, they were going to throw us off the train if you weren't treated. That quack wanted to give you strychnine, Fellows Syrup or such, but I seen folks put down a dog with that stuff. So, morphine it was."

"My poor mother is spinning in her grave."

"No fan of it myself. Army pumped me full when I got banged up. Took years to shake it."

"I can hear my mother from the other side. 'My son the drug fiend.' Now I have disappointed both parents." I sat back down on the bed, my head in my hands.

There was a shadow of a grin on Wyatt Brown's face. "By the way, it wasn't only what you said that was weird, it was the way you said it."

"What do you mean?"

"You didn't sound so high-and-mighty. Sounded like, I don't know, a pig farmer. All 'ow do' and 'loup ower t'yat.' Couldn't understand the half of it."

"I . . ." It was a punch to my gut. Guard down, I'd fallen back into a thick Yorkshire accent. At boarding school near London, the other children had taunted me and called me a dim tyke. When time came to attend Cambridge, I wasn't having any of that again. I reported to university with a full-on Oxford accent. John thought it daft. He wore his Yorkie accent as a badge of honor or a cudgel, "God's own country," and all, but I never looked back. Even when I came home early, the accent remained. Only in moments of great anger or excitement did I ever slip.

There was no sense trying to explain or hide. My two-ness had revealed itself. I was a fraud, a social charlatan. "I suppose we both have truths we wish to hide."

"Yup, I suppose." Wyatt looked pleased with himself.

"Tell you what. Let's start over. I was a bit rude and imperious."

"Yeah, you *are* British."

"Yes, and considering the circumstances and our newfound intimacy of the last few days, please call me Joshua. Partners?" I offered my hand.

He hesitated for an uncomfortable moment, then firmly gripped my hand and shook. "Wyatt'll be the name if you're okay with that."

"Very okay, no questions asked. Actually, one question. What are we doing in Atlanta? I believe I passed out before you said."

"The Cotton States and International Exposition."

"We left New York for a cotton convention?"

"No. It's not the Chicago World's Fair, but still a big shindig. The President's coming, Liberty Bell, even got Buffalo Bill's Wild West Show, if you're into that malarkey."

I nodded casually but felt a childish glee. I was fascinated by the American West, or the west of grand legend. Shootouts at the OK Corral, stagecoach rescues, steely settlers and noble Indians facing off under an infinite blue sky. It was romantic fantasy, or even an outright lie, but with the Wild West Show, one could live the story without the blood and dirt of inconvenient reality. I had been forced to miss the show on its English tour because of the culling of the herd, and I'd sulked like a child.

Wyatt poured water from a pitcher into a washbasin. “But you’re not here for that. Your London paper sent you to cover Booker T. Washington’s speech.”

“The Tuskegee College chap?” I’d the barest familiarity with the name.

“The same. Word is he’s going to deliver a humdinger tomorrow. All the big papers are here. They’ll assign you stories for Hearst, too, once he’s set up. First, got to get you cleaned up and shaved. Look like you woke up under a sheep.”

Chapter 4

The next day, freed of both fever and morphine, my senses tingled with life. I was like a drowning man reborn to the surface now experiencing the simple joy of air filling his lungs. Wyatt accounted a similar experience. Years ago, after hatter's shakes and black-bile ejections induced by a cure of mercury-laced calomel, he'd finally emerged feeling near superhuman.

Wyatt and I bonded over a shared love of Ned Buntline dime novels, and horses. That morning, we had time to kill since the parade and speeches were to begin at one in the afternoon. Thank God for no more chess, Wyatt being more of a card-and-dice sharp. My father forbade us from dicc, citing thc Romans throwing lots for Jcsus's robe. For unspecified reasons, the prohibition on gambling didn't extend to cards. It may have been because in their youth, Father and Mother enjoyed putting a small wager on their neighborly bridge games. I blithely fancied I knew a thing or two about gentlemen's games. Wyatt proved otherwise, his mood greatly elated after taking a souvenir widowhead Silver Crown off my person while he introduced me to his favorite poker games.

In good spirits then, we approached the grounds of the expo, Piedmont Park—the very spot, Wyatt made known, from which General Sherman had shelled Atlanta into submission thirty-one years earlier. It was hardly time to grow a full, live oak, though a stranger would be forgiven for thinking there never was a Civil War. Here the once-vanquished South could strut and crow in a way it hadn't managed at the Chicago World's Fair. King Cotton would lead the way with a brand-new John Philip Sousa march to dance along to.

The park's hilly setup created an impressive presentation. A panoptic view of grand pavilions festooned with flags, domes, Moorish towers, and on high, a Romanesque temple to art. The effect heightened since many structures were reflected in a shimmering lake. Gondolas and electric launches plied the waters. Whereas the uniform, columned facades and classical porticoes of the Chicago Fair's famed White City announced a striving toward heavenly ideal, the job-lot gumbo of buildings and exhibits at the Cotton Expo spoke of the messy collisions of commerce down on earth.

We walked across a gently arching bridge up wide paths of crushed blue limestone to secure a good vantage point to observe the opening festivities. Wyatt led me to a scrum of reporters he'd recognized from the New York papers and introduced me to James Creelman from Pulitzer's *New York World*. Since Mr. Hearst hadn't yet bought a paper and we weren't yet competitors (my London paper being irrelevant to such men), Creelman greeted us as brethren. After some good-natured ribbing about haughty Brits and crude Yanks, we finally congratulated each other for not being French.

Events got off to a promising start, a rousing parade of twenty-five companies featuring five bands, including the second battalion of Colored Infantry and the colored guards from Macon. The revelry was brief, and a weary succession of speeches followed, a prayer from Bishop Nelson, an ode to Southern virtues, an opening address, and then the straight-backed Mrs. John Thompson, President of the Women's Delegation, spoke. All I could think was that Margaret would throttle the first person who introduced her as Mrs. Joshua Banks. It was bad enough I would steal her last name.

Around this time, the crowd became aware of a colored man on the speaker's platform. Creelman pointed out Booker T. Washington.

"Whoa, feel the chill on this crowd of crackers. They're all asking each other, 'What's that nigger doing on the stage?' "

I bit my tongue.

The crowd consisted primarily of Southerners mixed with curious Northerners, peppered with foreign and Black faces. The Whites held wary judgment as Washington started his speech, pro forma thanking the organizers for the inclusion of a Negro Pavilion at the expo. But when he suggested his people should have started dairy farms or a truck garden rather than seeking political power in Congress or the States, the White mass warmed to his side.

Then he stated, "The masses of us are to live by the productions of our hands . . . No race can prosper till it learns that there is as much dignity in tilling a field as in writing a poem. It is at the bottom of life we must begin and not at the top." The Southerners greeted this surrender of political power for bare economic existence with giddy enthusiasm.

After further suggesting the interest of Negroes and Whites best served by the interlacing of their industrial lives, Washington held up his hand and spread his fingers wide, saying, "In all things that are purely social, we can be as separate as the fingers, yet one as the hand in all things essential to mutual progress."

At that, the audience leaped to their feet, and a great wave of applause enveloped the stage.

By the time Washington finished, an ovation arose so violent and sustained that it appeared the crowd, especially the White crowd and the Southern crowd, thought they could cauterize the still open racial wound of America by the force of their clapping and cheers, and then go about their business. White Southern women plucked decorative flowers from the bosoms of their dresses and anointed the stage, and Washington.

Creelman tipped his hat and bolted along with the other reporters. Wyatt grabbed my shoulder.

"Why bother? Booker's going to talk to the local boys first. You're just some bloke from England."

"Suppose I have everything I need already." My notes were in the new Gregg shorthand I studiously committed to learn when I heard Dickens was an adherent.

Surveying the crowd, I was immediately confronted by a young Negro woman. Other than her race, she fit the uniform observed by young women at the expo: high-collared blouse with tight waist and leg-of-mutton sleeves, a long skirt that obscured what I imagined were street boots. She'd selected a simple unbrimmed hat set off with a raven wing instead of the elaborate piles of flora and fauna that overflowed the wide-brimmed hats of many ladies.

"Excuse me—excuse me," she said. "Where are the reporters who were here? I need to speak to them."

"He's a reporter." Wyatt pointed a lazy finger at me.

"Madam, they all ran off to interview Mr. Washington," I said.

"No. No. No. They need context. That man and his Tuskegee machine, the nerve. He doesn't speak for an entire race. 'Cast down your buckets where you are'? Foolishness. If there were, as he says, fresh sparkling water, the Southern man would steal it for his own and give us a poison well."

"Madam," I said, "to be fair, I believe he also called on the Southern White to cast their bucket—their economic lot, as it were—with the eight million Negroes in their midst."

The woman wrinkled her noise. "You, Sir, are obviously a stranger here, so I will forgive your naivete. The Southern man doesn't want to share economic power with our race. No. He wants to recreate slavery as far as he can manage. Did you know that 50,000 dollars of convict labor helped to build this exposition?"

"No, they do not trumpet that fact in the program."

"I can't abide Washington's message. Are we fit only for the plow or workshop, owing our daily bread to new masters? We need lawyers, doctors, scientists, businessmen, and, yes, politicians."

I hadn't invited this confrontation and didn't know what to say. "There is no need to be so harsh. Admittedly, I am new to these shores, but I believe he was only trying to reach an accommodation."

"What? By being 'separate as the fingers'? What a foolish analogy. Who buys a glove but cuts part away so that one finger is left to freeze in the wet and cold? Who would wash and manicure four fingers and leave one dirty and ragged? If we are separate, we are less."

I spied Wyatt first inching, then walking away, leaving me alone to negotiate my way out of the encounter. I always hated my brother's need to have an opinion on every subject, yet here I was, falling into the same trap. "Surely things have improved for the African Americans since the War?"

The woman paused. Up to now, her words had tumbled forth in unbridled bursts. I feared I'd unwittingly touched a nerve. She regarded me sternly. I noticed myself staring into her eyes. For one reason or another, I expected them to be at least as dark brown as my own. Instead, they were an enchanting green-gray.

"I, Sir, may be a woman of color, but I'm not African. I've never been to Africa. My family's been here since the early 1700s. When do we get to be just American?"

"I was told it was the preferred term," I said.

She sighed. "For some. WEB Du Bois and others are using the term 'Black.' "

"Ah, well, well, that makes sense." It struck me as elegant. "If one is white the other is black."

"Am I the color black?"

I decided to surrender and see if she would take it. "Madam, I did not seek to offend. You asked after reporters. I am at your disposal.

My name is Joshua Banks, and I write for a London paper, and soon a New York paper as well."

Her posture softened slightly. "Guess it won't hurt to mind our manners. I'm Eva Hope Moon, and I'll take you up on your offer. We must get out the word that not all of us are ready for such compromise. I, for one, fully intend to be able to spend a dollar in an opera house, or any other establishment. Mr. Washington can hide in a milkshed if he wants."

I found Miss Moon's forceful nature a refreshing break from the bloodless formality of high-born British society. I didn't mind her lecturing me.

Miss Moon's demeanor relaxed, but her voice remained firm. "Mr. Washington is of the past, he just doesn't know it. So afraid of losing the crumb, he's willing to give up the whole bread. I must put you in touch with the new voices of our race like Misters WEB Du Bois, William Monroe Trotter, and Pinckney Pinchback. I'm working with Mrs. Ida Wells-Barnett."

"You mean Ida B. Wells?"

"You know of her?" It was the first time I induced her to smile, and I was glad of it. "She married this year."

"Did not know that. She toured Britain last year, speaking on the lynching matter. Did not hear her myself, but she was in all the press. I believe she tried as much to shame your Northern newspapers as educate us Britons. I will say the British press has been denouncing this barbarism at least since that New Orleans mob broke eleven Italians out of jail and hanged them all."

"I assure you, Mr. Banks, as reprehensible as that massacre was, we people of color face a daily campaign of intimidation through lynching. In fact, I suspect what doomed those Italians was that the Southerners saw them as more dark than White, especially the Sicilians."

Miss Moon cataloged not only the primitive bloodlust of the

lynch mob (acts one could try to blame on uneducated White rubes, inflamed into spasms of mindless fury by stories of predatory Black men raping sacred White mothers and daughters), but she also described the everyday slights and degradation doled out by polite society and endured by even those Blacks who thought their elevation in economic class had made them immune.

Story ran to story. Charles Douglas, son of the revered Frederick Douglas, turned away from the Bay Ridge Resort on the Chesapeake Bay in 1890. The society matron, Mary Church Terrell, just last year, forced to engage a White friend as a straw man in order to buy a house near Howard University in Washington. Negroes were even insulted in death. Graceland Cemetery, where many elite Black families had members buried, announced it would not only prohibit new Black burials, but indeed, already interned Blacks would be plucked from the earth and deported to the inferior Woodlawn Cemetery.

As Miss Moon spoke eloquently and passionately, I found myself captivated. Her hair, though straightened into a pompadour with a fashionable Psyche knot atop her head, still hinted at a rebellious curliness. Her nose was pleasantly broad, which served to soften the otherwise angularity of her face. Unadorned by makeup, her color was neither particularly light or dark.

Miss Moon stopped talking mid-sentence. "Mr. Banks, are you listening at all, or are you making a study for a portrait?"

"I . . . I am sure I—"

"Mr. Banks, I've been a married woman. I recognize the carnal gaze and its intentions."

"No. Please. I am engaged to be married." I stretched the truth, since saying "almost-but-not-quite engaged" seemed weak.

"Well then, you should save such stares for your fiancée's wedding night. For a moment, I was afraid my clothes had evaporated."

Nothing is so awkward as trying to reassemble your countenance after such accusation. As I flickered through expressions of affront, embarrassment, and forced solemnity, Miss Moon saw my obvious discomfort and actually giggled.

"Not that a woman of color shouldn't be able to wed a White man. I certainly reserve that right. Just don't think we need to further dilute my race at this time. The slave owners did enough of that for now."

I steered the conversation back to Miss Moon helping me with her contacts to leaders in the Black community. She gave a phone number where I might leave messages for her. Embarrassed, I admitted not having the least idea where I was living in New York except for a hazy fever-memory of Washington Square being mentioned. I intended to write for Hearst's paper, but I didn't know which New York paper it was. If Hearst had bought one, Wyatt and I didn't rate a cable. I informed her I would check with Wyatt and give her my details later.

To make up for my fumbling, I offered to buy Miss Moon a tea. I was keen to try the brew advertised genuine at the Japanese Village.

"No," she said.

"Come now. I thought we had put that silly business behind us. I am no masher."

"It's not I would not, it's that I cannot. People of color are only allowed to dine at the Negro Pavilion."

"We shall see about that. Outrageous in this day and—"

"*No*. I'm not a damsel in distress awaiting your rescue. I have work to do at this exposition and don't need to be ejected. There'll be time for forcing the issue, for sitting down in restaurants and hotels and trains, but we must be strategic. When the *Comité des Citoyens* in New Orleans wanted to test the Separate Car Law, they recruited Homer Plessy since he was only one-eighth Black and looked as White as you. He had to go tell the conductor he was legally a Negro. We hope the Supreme Court will overturn the law when they finally hear the case. I can take care of myself, thank you. I'm older than you, after all."

"I highly doubt that," I said. "You do not look more than twenty."

“See, Mr. Banks, you are flirting. I’ll be twenty-seven come this Christmas Eve. Now I must get back to educating the public.”

She hurried away, me counting her footsteps until she was completely out of view.

Chapter 5

For the next eight days, Wyatt and I surveyed the expo. He proved a congenial companion and mostly humored my intent to visit every exhibit in every building, even the three pale yellow-and-white stories of the Women's Building, which Wyatt dismissed as boring. We both were awed at the electricity showcase. Still, I didn't think I'd ever convince my father to bring such a dangerous spirit as electricity into the estate house. Since I grew up around farming, the Forest Building's exhibit on the importance of the balance of trees and fields to prevent soil erosion fascinated me, but for Wyatt, much less so.

My suggestion that we ride the Phoenix, a lighter version of a Ferris wheel, brought a firm no.

"It will be a splendid view. You afraid of heights?"

"No, afraid of carnies and con jobs."

He harbored particular ire for the fortune tellers and the onion-towered Mystic Maze's hall of mirrors. "Fit only for children and the feeble-minded," he grumbled. What puzzled me most was Wyatt's extreme reluctance when I attempted to point us toward the white tepees of the Sioux Indian village. I wanted to ask Wyatt how Chief Stand and Look Back, a man who fought General Custer, now stood shaking hands and taking pictures with tourists. Wyatt mumbled something about an old leg injury acting up and quickly went off to the hotel. I checked out the Indians, then took the opportunity to shop for a present for Margaret. Overdue in writing her, I hoped to put her in a favorable mood. The Old Man was so insistent that I get here right away, and now it seemed I was killing time.

As the days passed, I found excuses to look for Miss Moon as she went about the promotion of her causes. I made sure Miss Moon received my address in New York so she might contact me with information.

Organizers declared October twenty-first Negro Day at the expo. As expected, I found Miss Moon around the Negro Building, which housed a wide array of industrial and applied arts along with magazines, patents, inventions, and musical compositions. Most striking was a sculpture of a Black man trying to break free of the chains that bound him. I announced it all first-rate, but Miss Moon shrugged, ambivalent at best.

"Why a Negro Day and a Negro Building? Shouldn't my race be represented shoulder to shoulder every day in every building?"

"I was informed that Black leaders lobbied hard to get this presence at the expo," I said.

"Well," she sighed. "I shall be traveling to Washington DC on the twenty-sixth to talk to some of those same Black elite. I believe their status makes them blind to what's really going on."

"How so?"

"They preen about the honor of this pavilion, yet yards away in Midway Heights, my race is mocked at a Village of Dahomey with so-called darkies pretending to be cannibals. Nothing but a bunch of New York minstrels paid to jump around like monkeys and yell like hyenas."

Luckily, Wyatt had steered us wide of Midway Heights earlier. What if I'd actually seen—and, maybe, enjoyed—such a spectacle?

"And you know what else they've got, to pile insult on top of injury? An 'Old Plantation' mock-up, right down to cotton pickin' mammies. I tell you, Mr. Banks, when some of my race demean themselves for the almighty dollar, it makes my heart cry."

I looked at her with sympathy but said nothing, afraid that my experiences left me ignorant of the proper words of comfort.

On October 25, the door to my hotel room flew open so fiercely that I feared the doorknob would lodge into the wall. Wyatt panted.

"Pack up. We go back to New York tomorrow."

I understood immediately. William Randolph Hearst had bought his newspaper. Once again, I would not see Buffalo Bill nor his magic history.

Wyatt shook his head. "Goddamn *Morning Journal*. Can you believe it? Doesn't make no sense. The Chief could've bought the *New York Times* or the *Recorder*. I knew he wasn't getting the *World*. Joseph Pulitzer, he's a tough old bird, and 'sides, the Chief wants to earn his own spurs, but the *Morning Journal*?"

"Is that bad?" I asked.

"It's just a scandal sheet run by Pulitzer's brother, Albert, and Albert ran it into the ground during the Depression. Hotshot from the *Cincinnati Enquirer*, John McLean, just bought it and is already unloading it. Now we're rushing to get out a first edition by November seventh."

"Then I work for said *Morning Journal*?"

"Just *Journal*. The boys said it looked better on the masthead."

The next morning, when we entered the train station, Wyatt was still fuming. More information from his mates up north hadn't pleased him. Hearst evidently bought the paper back in the beginning of October, but no one bothered to inform Wyatt—or me, for that matter.

Moving through the train station, Wyatt kept going on about how—compared to the *World*, *Tribune*, *Herald* and *Sun*—the *Journal* didn't stand a chance. I was distracted by searching about for Miss Moon. She said she was heading to DC on this day, but on which train?

I caught sight of her hurrying for the worn carriages at the front of our train. They stood out not only in their relative dilapidation, but also for their segregating yellow coat of paint. I ran to catch up to her despite the quizzical stares of onlookers and, without thinking, grabbed her gently by the shoulder before she could jump onto the train. Immediately, I realized my transgression as Miss Moon spun around, her hand already moving to slap me. I prepared to duck, but she pulled back her hand as she saw me.

"Mr. Banks, I hardly think you've the right to handle me like a farmhand."

"So sorry. I do not know my manners. It is just that the train is about to board, and I wanted to invite you to sit with Wyatt and me. We have a private compartment. There is ample room to stretch out." Thinking it might be a further inducement, I added, "I now have a New York paper to write for."

She gave me an unexpectedly hard glare. "Are you still such a pilgrim? I can't go with you. We're in the South. I must sit in the Negro cars."

"Nonsense. I paid for a private compartment and will not hear of such a thing."

"Though it wounds my soul to be segregated like diseased cattle, it isn't your choice." She stared into the crowded Negro carriage. Men, women, and children sitting on hard wooden benches, crammed in among luggage. We both knew that even though it was a fair day, the carriage would be stuffy with its windows shut tight, or if opened, Miss Moon's pristine green dress would be fouled by black coal dust and soot for being right behind the engine and fuel pile. "I've never ridden in a private compartment. I've never been north of the Mason-Dixon Line."

"So there it is, madam. You deserve it."

Miss Moon followed me as if walking in a decrepit house with a floor that might give way with every step. We encountered no such disaster, just a scowling Mrs. Grundy-type, who wrinkled her sticky beak and refused to cede us any ground as we passed in the train's narrow corridor, forcing us to the wall. Momentarily crushed against Miss Moon, the scent of lavender and sweetgrass escaped from her dress.

Wyatt looked surprised when we entered the compartment but rose to politely greet Miss Moon. "Hope you can elevate the level of conversation this trip. Mr. Banks wasn't too engaging on our way south."

"I'll do my best." She glanced about nervously.

We took our seats as the train lurched forward, me sitting across from Miss Moon so I might easily talk with her.

As I moved bags to make room for Miss Moon's case, Wyatt pointed at the fancy new box peeking from my bag. "What've you got there?"

"A present. For Margaret. A hat." It came out a stumble.

"Hey now, let's have a lookie."

For some reason, my hands shook a little as I lifted the white felt hat from its shelter.

"Lordy, ain't that putting on the dog. I mean, I get the snowy egret feathers, my Becca'd go for that, wispy and all, but what's those orangey-red ones?"

"Scarlet Ibis. The clerk at the expo talked me up from jungle cock or condor. What do you think, Miss Moon? You are better to judge than would-be Charles Worth there."

"Well . . ." She paused. "It's unique, isn't it . . . if a mite . . . forward. This the sort of thing your—was it Miss Margaret?—would fancy?"

"I—I do not really know." It pained me to admit.

"Sure she'll be pleased," Miss Moon said.

"They'll sure see her coming." Wyatt grinned.

I hurried the hat back into its box, slid it onto the shelf, and tried to change the subject. "I do not mean to pry, but you said you had been married. May I inquire what has become of Mr. Moon?"

"Not Moon." There was a solemn tone to her voice that made me regret the question. "Oscar Wiggins was his name. Moon is my maiden name. I took it back after he died."

"So sorry for your loss," Wyatt said. I nodded.

She gazed out into space and set her jaw. "Sorry is not sufficient, gentlemen. You should be morally outraged. You should be demanding redress and justice, but you're merely sorry. My Oscar was a dentist, a man of worth and substance. That made no difference. All that mattered was his resemblance, ever so slight, of another man of color, who may or may not have touched a White girl, who may or may not have wanted to be touched. That resemblance was mandate enough for the upright Dr. Wiggins to be torn out from his hearth and home, from my breast, and be hung from a random lamppost. It didn't even make the papers."

"I am so—" I started. "I mean to say, I assure you that you have my promise I will not hesitate in my efforts to call attention to such butchery. My pen is at your service, and now with London and New York—"

A loud rap on the door interrupted us. A short, rather small, officious conductor stuck his head and shoulders into our compartment.

"Been a complaint about a Negress passenger where she don't belong." He stared down his nose at Miss Moon, who, for the first time since I met her, seemed to wilt under his glare.

I started to leap up in furious argument, but Wyatt casually blocked me from rising. He flashed a huge smile at the little man.

"Good morning, conductor. Hope you're well today."

Taken aback by Wyatt's glowing cheerfulness, the conductor mumbled, "Thank you, fine, but—"

"Sorry you need to use your valuable time on us, but you see, this girl is exactly where she needs to be. Now, you might have heard this around the station. Mr. Banks, here, royal visitor from London town, took terrible ill on the train down here, thought we might lose him, and he can't travel without the constant attention of his nurse."

"Nurse?" The gears in the little man's head shifted.

"Yes, indeed. Imagine how awkward it'd be if Lord Banks had to go all the way from his private compartment up to the Negro car for an injection or treatment. What a humiliating way to treat a gentleman and honored guest."

The little man relaxed. "No, guess we can't have that. I'll tell that old busybody to mind her own business. You take care, Your Lordship." He punched our tickets and was gone.

Wyatt gave a deep bow, and I started to applaud when I became aware of Miss Moon. She had tears in her eyes.

"How dare you."

"What?" Wyatt looked puzzled. "We won that round."

"Won? You think your little cheat solved anything?"

"Sometimes you have to take what small victories you can," I suggested.

"I think I'd rather have been thrown off the train, like Mrs. Wells-Barnett, than be treated like my life has no value except in service to a White man."

The rest of the trip, Miss Moon read or looked out the window in stony silence until she disembarked in DC. She was right—I was merely sorry. I had no real comfort to give. I offered my pen as if a mighty sword. Vain poetry. I had no answers. The great American experiment appeared to be crumbling, at least for eight million, and I was only a tourist.

October 1895

My Dearest Margaret,

First, know distance has not dimmed my love for you. You are in my heart always, and in all ways.

You may think me hasty in accepting your father's assignment to America, but darling, how could I reject this opportunity without losing status in his eyes? Being a foreign correspondent is my golden chance to prove—not just to your father but also to my family—that I can, in fact, succeed on my own.

Along with my newspaper duties, I plan to write a travelogue. As you know, they are all the rage in Europe. Please don't say anything about the book to my family, especially my brother. John already thinks me a pie-in-the-sky dreamer, something about hearing hooves and expecting not horses but unicorns. I say, why not live life with the possibility of unicorns?

I am still settling into my rooms. Please write me at the Croisic, Fifth Avenue at Twenty-Sixth Street. The owner is a touch of a rogue, the Marquis de Croisic, Richard de Logerot. He was arrested a year ago for perjury regarding the failure of another property, the Hotel de Logerot.

No matter, the Croisic is posh with its first few floors taken up by what many consider this city's—maybe this country's—finest restaurant, Delmonico's. America is still recovering from the financial panic, but you could not tell by looking through the huge glass panels at the nobs and swells dining within.

You will be pleased to know the Croisic offers accommodations only to bachelors—no families, no women. I am surprised by the number of bachelors of all ages and stature in New York. Perhaps there is a shortage of eligible ladies, or American men are particularly chary about the rigors of marital bonds—I do not yet know. I have not made acquaintance with any of my flatmates.

I may need to overcome my English reserve and introduce myself. It appears Americans are open to that sort of intrusion, if not outright boorish imposition. I do have an associate, Mr. Wyatt Brown. At first impression brutish, he has proven to be a useful guide, perhaps in future, a confidant. He was especially helpful when I fell ill on my way to Atlanta. I did not want to upset you with such news. I am now recovered, but it is partly reason for the delay in this post.

By the time you receive my letter, I will have finally reported to the *Journal* for my assignment. I think I would be a natural for international affairs, the rebellion in Cuba is getting much ink here.

Wyatt thinks it unlikely that I will get to see Mr. Hearst, the owner, or even the managing editor, Mr. Chamberlain. More likely some assistant editor to begin with. Your father led me to believe he, and I as his representative, had some pull with Hearst, so we shall see.

In fact, I have already seen Mr. Hearst, but he paid no mind of me. He is temporarily in a set of suites at the Hoffman House right on Fifth Avenue, and he walks to Delmonico's for a substantial lunch nearly every day. I have been near enough to touch him.

He is easy to spot: tall with blond hair parted in the middle like a reasonably wayward schoolboy. After all, he is only thirty-two. I recognized the lordly air of wealth and privilege about him, but they say he is soft-spoken if not high-pitched, and his men are fiercely loyal to him in a way Mr. Pulitzer's are not.

You will also be receiving a fine hat I picked out at the Cotton Expo in Atlanta. The merchant guaranteed it an exclusive line, not available in London, so you will not have to worry about attending a function and encountering its twin. I once saw my sister Aubrey go to pieces at Christmas when a matron walked in with a dress identical down to every lace and button. Aubrey gave the dress to a maid the next day.

I am aware you are unhappy about the postponement of the engagement and wedding, but how much better will it be when I return on higher footing, not reliant on my father or yours?

The knowledge of your love gives me strength. To quote Lord Byron, "'Tis sweet to know there is an eye will mark our coming, and look brighter when we come."

I miss you with all my heart.

Joshua

Chapter 6

It was 6:00 a.m. when Wyatt banged on my door at the Croisic.

"Up and at 'em, Your Lordship."

Luckily, I was already up but not yet in shirt or trousers. I opened the door, irritated he hadn't done me the courtesy of remaining in the lobby and sending up his card so that I might be fully dressed.

"Why so early? My editor's assignment is at seven-thirty. This evening."

"I know who your editor is, and you're not ready."

"Who?"

"Nowak, a real tin god, and he's not going to like you at all."

"Why should I get off on the wrong foot with this Mr. Nowak?"

"As far as you're concerned, he only has wrong feet."

"What on earth are you on about?" I fell into a chair.

"How dost he hate you? Let me count the ways. What are the five boroughs?"

"Eh . . . Manhattan . . . Brooklyn . . ."

"Brooklyn is a town in Kings. Then there's Queens, Bronx, and Richmond County, what the old Dutch codgers still call Staten Island. Oh, and some folks call Yonkers the sixth borough, but they voted down the referendum last year, so they can go to hell."

"I accept it might be helpful to familiarize myself with my surroundings."

Wyatt shook his head and grabbed an apple from my desk. I'd taken to poaching apples from a display bowl in Delmonico's.

"Nowak will eat you alive." Wyatt started to play act with a gruff voice. "'What am I supposed to do with a goddamn reporter who doesn't know where goddamn city hall is?'"

"Actually, think I saw city hall, but point taken. You will help me?"

"We're taking the tour, all the stops." Wyatt repeatedly huffed on the apple, then polished it against his jacket.

"Let me get dressed."

"Yeah, about that . . ."

"What now?" I slumped back.

"If you go there tonight looking like the British ambassador, you might as well wave a red flag at a bull."

"Why should he get bent about my kit?"

"First, don't think he's any love for any English. Last time I saw him, he was ranting about some border dispute between Britain and Venezuela—"

"Guiana? There is no dispute. We bought that land. If they had not found gold, there would not be a peep. I do not see why your president is sticking his nose in British affairs."

"Joshua, I don't know what or where Guiana is, but don't start any of that with Nowak or you'll get an angry lecture about the Monroe Doctrine and how it's always Brits sticking their noses into everybody's business and how they think they rule the world."

"It is an empire, after all."

"Don't hold no water with him. Point is, we got to get you some American duds."

"I am not going to your tailor. I would rather wear a sack-cloth and ashes."

"You're not man-about-town enough to wear my tony gear. We'll go to Arnold Constable or Lord & Taylor. You can pick out a boring accountant suit."

"Reduced to ready-mades." I shook my head.

"It's not just Nowak. Those bespoke suits got you standing out like the fly on a wedding cake." He raised the apple for a bite but instead gestured with it. "Now, if you were interviewing J.P. Morgan, it might be useful, but most times you want to blend in more."

"I suppose there is some logic to that."

"Oh, and we should replace those drawers of yours. You look a little sissy to me."

"Am I to undress for Nowak as well?"

"No. Just helping you out. Women expect to see a manly union suit, not that frilly stuff."

"Women? What women? I am almost married."

"Joshua, you're here for what, least two years? There's going to be women."

I put up a passionate defense of my pure intentions, but Wyatt only laughed it off.

"Reminds me. Don't ask anything about Nowak's wife. No how's-your-family small talk," Wyatt said. "She ran off not too long ago, took their little daughter with her. Touchy subject."

"A lover?"

"If only. Celibates."

I looked back blankly.

"Koreshan Unity, you know, utopians, Dr. Teed, Hollow Earth."

I shook my head. "Not in the British papers."

"Nowak should've been keeping tabs on his young wife. She already ran off before, to follow that Ralston Health Club."

"Have heard of them. Breathing exercises and diet, not eating watermelon, that sort of thing."

"No, much odder. Shaftesbury tried to set up some paradise down in New Jersey. Wanted to castrate any male who wasn't their kind of Caucasian. He fleeced her for overpriced books on Higher Magnetism. Anyway, she showed back up but was always on the balls of her feet and wouldn't walk in a straight line. You'd think after that, he'd known she was susceptible to crazy notions.

"But wait—it gets worse. Not much later, Mrs. Nowak attends a mighty powerful lecture by Dr. Cyrus Teed about how God is both male and female, and all that's keeping women down is sexual desire. Poof, she's gone. Nowak hires private detectives, reaches out to his newspaper contacts. Nowak's a bulldog, he's going to bite and not let go. Found two husbands already tried to sue the good doctor for alienation of affection—out in Chicago, I think. Rumors spread that despite the talk about celibacy the Unity was more harem than holy order. Finally tracked her down to sweaty nowhere in south Florida on the Gulf of Mexico, the Koreshan were calling New Jerusalem. Did everything but kidnap her, didn't get her back."

"Why would she want to leave and live like that? Was he cruel to her?"

"Naw, he acts the tough guy, but he'd never hurt a woman. Against his code. You'd be surprised how many married women might find celibacy attractive, especially if it came with equal rights. My Becca is nearly there, marital relations only for procreation. How many children do I need to accept gladly? She's been preached to that if I pull out it, it changes God's plan to the Devil's hand."

"Stop. Please. I do not need to picture the Devil's hand." I reflexively closed my eyes.

"Delicate, huh?" He took a bite of the apple. "Going to have to loosen you up. Let's get cracking. Got a lot of ground to cover."

Wyatt was true to his word. He dragged me all over four of the boroughs. Staten Island would have to wait. The clothing mission started poorly. The clerk appeared intent on making me look either a dandy or fruit peddler. At last, the store tailor, an old Italian kept around for alterations, saved me. He helped me find the suits of better-quality fabrics and in gentleman's designs. For a small fee, he not only fixed the trousers and sleeves, he tidied up the shoulders and waist. Not handmade, but three serviceable suits for less than the price of one from London. The old Italian even put cuffs on one of the trousers, swore cuffs were coming back in style.

I soon realized Wyatt's ulterior motive for my geography lesson. Borrowing Hearst's fancy coach, he was set to fulfill his own doings all over town.

Most of his business took place in various pubs or saloons, many illegal, which Wyatt referred to as "blind pigs." At first I took them to be only inferior distributors of embalming whiskeys and day-old wine, but to the common man, they were bank, office, and social club. As bank they cashed checks, held savings on account, and extended credit. As office they were mail and message exchange and a clearing house for employers and job seekers. As social hub they provided space for all forms of fraternal and political orders, labor unions, and more. Whilst you didn't ask a bartender to set a broken bone, he probably could dress a laborer's wound and dispense medication, a balm for those who didn't have necessary coin for doctors.

At two such saloons, Wyatt ordered a five-cent mug of ale, and in each instance, he threw the contents down his throat as if his stomach was on fire. I, anxious about my meeting with Nowak, drank a newfangled concoction of brown syrup and fizzy water called Coca-Cola. I couldn't relate the flavor to anything else that I've imbibed in the past but suspected that it contained caffeine, or a similar stimulant in quantity, as it left me jittery. At another saloon, we merely grabbed two abandoned beer mugs, which were our tickets to gorge on a plowman's nightmare of cheese, sausage, smoked herring, pickled onion, radishes, and, to settle the mix, chunks of pumpernickel and rye.

Our last stop was a cigar shop, not to purchase products but to place bets. I followed Wyatt inside. I always found the earthy smell of tobacco shops much more pleasant than the act of smoking. With a few head nods and gestures, the bets were placed.

"Wyatt, may I ask you something?"

"Go ahead, shoot."

"I am surprised, and must say pleased, you do not chew tobacco. Since arriving on these shores, I have been disgusted by the overwhelming prevalence of men—nay, even young boys—spitting vile tobacco juice like consumptives coughing up bile. Spittoons are everywhere: staircases, lobbies, train carriages. I have witnessed men spitting directly on sawdust spread on the floor."

"Lord knows I've broke many a promise made to my dear mother." Wyatt nearly teared up. "But I've refused to chew."

"Ah yes, departed mothers. Mine had no fondness for tobacco, but indulged father his occasional pipe by the fire. My father deeded me one of his fancy panel-bent billiard Barling pipes, but I prefer a simple white clay pipe whilst walking the fields."

"Pipe's too fusty. I'd rather smoke cigars, but the ones I like are pricey and Becca won't let me smoke at home. She read that it's poisoning the children. I told her it's natural—wards off disease. She makes that awful face if I try to kiss her after a cigar. What about Margaret? She mind the pipe?"

"Never came up."

Wyatt let it drop. He pointed at a display of rectangular packs. "Got these back home?"

"Pre-rolled? Looks a bit tatty. Does anyone really smoke these?"

"Used to be street boys and down-and-outers. Lately, noticed some of the girls at the clubs picking up the habit. Say it keeps them thin. Few old Jews in my tenement told me they used to roll cigarettes for Buck Duke down in Durham. Real pro could roll three, maybe four cigarettes in a minute. Then comes this Bonsack machine, which rolls two hundred a minute. Businessmen love their machines."

"I do not see it catching on. Seems crude."

"Yeah, coffin nails. Some states want to ban the things. Doubt my grandchildren will ever see a cigarette. Still like to smoke, but everyone knows nicotine is outright poison."

In the early evening, Wyatt returned to my lodgings.

"You coming with me to the *Journal* tonight?"

"No, not a good idea."

"But why?" Wyatt was becoming a welcome crutch for me.

"Nowak's got a bug up his butt about me, not sure why. He can't touch me. I work for the big chief, but there's no sense in stirring him up. Anyway, I put a big bet on a fight. Want to be there to collect my winnings."

"Please tell me it is not a dogfight. I abhor that evil practice."

"Give me some credit, Joshua. I'm not a beast. Love dogs. Had a cute little bull terrier, Oro, as a boy. Don't even like the cockfights. Went once and felt so bad for the dead bird I gave half my winnings to thc ASPCA."

"Good to hear. I have no respect for animal blood sport. It is a poor farmer who squanders livestock."

"No, this is a backroom bare-knuckle brawl, big boys. Have to run or miss the action. Probably be a knockout."

Running late, I threw on a simple blue herringbone suit and dashed outside. Wyatt was right. I now blended into the noisy crowds. Of course, the avenue was strangely bereft of hires.

My hopes momentarily rose at the sight of a trolley but quickly cratered. I'd no idea of the mysterious routes or schedules of New York trolleys. Mine had been a life of cabs.

Hurrying on foot, I recalled stories of stern employers who would lock their office doors minutes after the appointed time of a meeting, the latecomer cooling his heels for an hour or two before being sent home.

Then a curious possibility came into view; a double-deck horse-drawn bus fashioned from polished wood, much finer than the London omnibuses plastered with signs for Yorkshire Relish and Pear's Soap.

Seeing no other option, I flagged down the driver and inquired if he might be headed in the vicinity of Park Row. He sensed desperation in my voice and said he wasn't, but for the right fare he might make a detour, then quoted an amount equal to robbery, but of a sort gentle enough to be tolerated. I paid with the understanding we would head there directly before he resumed his usual route. Climbing the rear staircase to the last available seat, I heard a chorus of barely muffled curses from my fellow passengers. I sat and stared at my knees.

Minutes later, standing in front of Park Row and Spruce Street, I couldn't help but be disappointed in the *Journal*'s home in the remarkably unimpressive Tribune Building, its mediocrity emphasized by the Maine granite of the sixteen-story New York Times building and the graceful steel dome atop Pulitzer's twenty-six-story World building.

My feelings on this entire endeavor had become mixed after seeing the first few issues of the *Journal*. The layout was smashing—rivers of text broken by meticulous, first-rate illustrations. The content, however, too often wallowed in sensation and melodrama. I cringed in embarrassment at a November 19 headline: "KILLED BY HYDROPHOBIA . . . Both Lads Barked and Snapped Like Dogs, Suffering Terrible Agonies, Little Ralph in His Struggle Bit Through His Tongue and Lips Again and Again."

Perhaps the Old Man erred in making a pact with Hearst instead of the respectable *New York Times* or the Pope of American journalism, Charles Dana at the *New York Sun*. Perhaps the Old Man saw more in the hungry young Hearst (and what he'd accomplished with the San Francisco *Examiner*) than I did.

I ran up the stairs and approached the open doorway of Nowak's office at "exact o'clock," in my mind hearing the incessant drone of my old headmaster: "There is no on time! Only early or late." Outside the office, at rows of desks, reporters, staff—I wasn't sure—labored over text.

Immediately, a sharp tenor shout belched out to no one in particular: "Where's that damn London cub? He was supposed to be here ten minutes ago."

Hat in hand like a schoolboy arriving for detention, I ventured in. "I was waiting outside, Sir."

"Poppycock. Sit down."

Behind a nameplate sat Adam Józef Nowak, chair leaned back, feet propped up, fingers laced behind his head, elbows wide as if trying to claim every inch of space in the room. He continued to peer down at a file like a bird of prey, his nose a sharp beak, the tips of his untamed mustache piercing diagonally down past his cheeks like two talons, his hair short on top like a bristled crown.

"Let's get this straight, Cub, right off the bat. Only reason you're here's so the Chief could get our man settled in London. My druthers, you'd be down in the mail room, but we can't afford to insult Sir Covington. Put you on obits, but young Willie Gibson loves the morgue beat too much to yank it away from him."

"I thought I might be of use covering foreign affairs. I have more of an international perspective."

"Listen, you pompous Anglic, you're not stealing one drop of ink from my local boys, and frankly, we don't need your international perspective. We've an American perspective, thank you very much."

Nowak's intense eyes, framed by heavy down-turned eyebrows, began to dissect me. I thought surely he had to blink eventually but didn't wait and looked around the room instead.

There wasn't much to see, and I took it in quickly. As to business, maple **in** and **out** trays, contents meticulously stacked, flanked the right and left sides of a large steel-tanker desk. Nowak sat in an incongruous shield-back petite Louis XVI chair, its front-fluted legs hanging in the air like the claws of a praying mantis. A chalkboard covered one wall. On it, in surprisingly elegant script, were story ledes and assignments.

Of personal items, even less was divulged. On a shelf sat what I knew to be a baseball, even if I remained mostly ignorant of the game. Its pitted-leather cover hung frayed and loose—a totem of youth, I surmised.

No other indications of human connection appeared except one. Handsomely framed on the wall hung a flag. At boarding school, my roommate and I had spent hours quizzing each other over the Flags of the World, yet I couldn't place it precisely. A horizontal band of white sat over a bold band of red. Centered in the white, a coat of arms featured a thin white eagle and a mounted white knight.

I did recognize the white eagle from an old Russian flag, the Congress Kingdom of Poland, but there, the noble eagle had been confined in a red canton in the corner of the blue Saint Andrew's saltire. But Poland, we'd learned, existed only as Russia's Vistula Land. The flags we memorized carried the czar's standard black double-headed eagle, or more likely, displayed the white knight. An engraved brass plate on the frame read only: "November 1830." I racked my brain for the importance of the date but only recalled Earl Grey succeeding Wellington as prime minister, or—more imprinted on a schoolboy—the last hanging for piracy at the execution dock in Wapping.

During the minute or two that all this flowed through my mind, Nowak watched me studying the flag and respectfully said nothing. Finally, he cleared his throat.

"Listen. Got to stick you somewhere, so here's what. You're on the music beat."

"I will do my best, sir. My family maintains a box at the opera, and I am not opposed to a light musical."

"What? Hell's bells kid, no. We've got the celebrated James L.

Ford for all the highfalutin stuff. No, you'll be covering the crap he won't: coon singers, low vaudeville, the greasy stuff."

A roar of protest rose in my chest but choked off in a weak groan. The ghost of a smile flickered over Nowak's lips.

"Oh, and Cub, this is America, see? Don't want any Brit stuff, no "c-o-l-o-u-r" or "fairy cakes," or "lifts" instead of elevators. My copy editors don't have time to fix that claptrap. Look, you'd better not just toe the line. Better keep two, three feet behind the line. Any excuse, and your rich, royal a-r-s-e is on a packet ship back to merry ole England. Got it?"

For a moment, I thought about arguing my position. How could I make any mark writing trash about throwaway amusements? I came here to dive for pearls, not wallow with entertaining swine. I felt like a nail arguing with a hammer, so I said nothing, for now.

"See, you at least got yourself a regular reporter's suit. That's Wyatt's doing, right? Yeah, well, watch yourself with that swordsman. Thinks he's an eighteen-carat sporting man, leaves his wife with those kids at home while he's gadding about. Okay, not thrilled young Hearst is out late with those chorus girls, but he isn't married. Listen, don't be taking lessons from Mr. Brown. Keep your nose clean and out of my way, and you just might make it through your assignment. Maybe."

Nowak didn't even bother to dismiss me. He merely glanced at the doorway, then returned to his files.

The bitter wind slapped my face as I exited the building. Not again, not already. What the bloody hell now?

December 1895

Dear Joshua,

I first want to thank you for your letter, no matter how tardy. I do want you to write. Sorry to hear you were ill. A relief to know you're well again. I do care for you and miss you. There.

What on earth were you thinking with that monstrous hat? Are you not aware of the cruel and barbarous manner by which the snowy egret feathers are harvested? Ruthless murder during nesting season. Eggs and baby birds were left to starve. Two generations were wantonly destroyed.

You obviously didn't know I've long been a member of the Plumage League, now the Society for the Protection of Birds. Our rules prohibit wearing any feathers other than ostrich. They aren't killed. We're petitioning the Queen to decree a stop to osprey feathers on military uniforms.

Joshua, really. Have you ever seen me wear anything so garish? So foolish? Since you say the price was dear, I didn't destroy it. I gave it to your sister Aubrey. She is a sweet girl who enjoys such frivolities. I don't require gifts. If you must, then be more pragmatic.

You make the same mistake as father. That I'm a child-woman suitable only for keeping house and ushering children into the world. Do you know what his current excuse is for preventing my continued studies? That additional education might exceed what is required for a "marriageable mind." That while men admire gifted women in public, they don't desire them as wives.

Why do men insist on treating all women as though we resemble the most fragile flower among us? I don't swoon. My father encourages my brother Ted's physical activity.

He built a gym for him above the coach house. Ted has to smuggle me in and keep watch so my father doesn't know I'm exercising.

Joshua, you should know that purple ink is all out of favor. Black is now recommended. By the same measure, I don't care for flowery talk from afar. Save your poetry for when you can whisper in my ear as you hold me in your arms. You quote Byron when you should have talked of his daughter Ada, who, though married and a mother, wrote of the romance of numbers, mathematics, and computation. That's what I wish to read.

Write to me of my interests, not love or gossip. You know I enjoy anything about sports, whether racket or rugby. I want to know everything of science. That's what I'll study if allowed to attend university. I joined an observatory club. Please don't dismiss it as stargazing. We're meticulous in our record-keeping.

I'm afraid you may think my anger at your leaving and the postponement of our wedding was due solely to my wanting the status of marriage or the liberation from my family. My desire is baser than that. I'm soon to be twenty. Your actions have condemned me to two additional years of virginity.

Don't think me too forward or crass. If we're to be husband and wife, we must be free to speak boldly of such. I've read much, including Dr. Virgil Primrose English's *The Doctor's Plain Talk to Young Men: Anatomy, Physiology and Hygiene of the Sexual Organs*, as well as James Aston's rather extensive *The Book of Nature: Containing Information for Young People Who Think of Getting Married, on the Philosophy of Procreation and Sexual Intercourse, Showing How to Prevent Conception and Avoid Childbearing; Also, Rules for Management During Labor and Childbirth.*

All to say, I'll not be a frightened innocent running in tears from the conjugal bed. I know what's to come, and I intend to take my full measure of pleasure. How much easier for you to forestall our connubial society when you've already sated your hunger before. Don't think I don't know you had your hand on Carvel's ring with that maid Jenny. Then, when the scandal became the talk of the servants, your family got rid of the problem. So con-venient.

It wouldn't have been the same for me if I'd fallen into the lusty grip of a stableboy. Society excuses sin in men; in women, never.

Do not misread my affection. You are still my rescuer, my white knight. But romance is built on a hundred gestures, not just one gallant act, no matter how heroic. Don't stay too long in the field. Perhaps it's possible to abbreviate your quest and return to my bosom?

Yours,
Margaret

Chapter 7

"Jackpot!" Wyatt nearly danced around my sitting room.

"Why are you so gay?"

"Why are you so glum? We get paid to hang out all night listening to hot new music. God save us. Thought we'd be stuck at the morgue, or city hall, sleeping through speeches. Hey, you review theater shows too?"

"Only ones so low or shabby that James L. Ford will not raise his pen." I slumped even deeper into my chair.

"Perfect. They're always the best. Not all that moral uplift."

"You do not understand. I am not here to paint the town red. This is not a game. How can I establish a career as a serious journalist if I am covering the hoi polloi and their disposable merriments?"

"First, you don't understand. Life's all a game if you play it right, and I'd rather paint red than cry blue. Second, that Dane, Jacob Riis, did right well covering the lowest of the low. *How the Other Half Lives* is a big hit and may have done some good. Those photos, men stuffed in cheek to jowl, women and kids barely clothed and fed, it melted some hearts, or at least, embarrassed the hoity-toity you want to cover."

"Now you are making me feel a toff."

Wyatt lowered his voice and leaned in close like he was telling a secret. "Joshua, this is the ocean I swim in. I know all the singers, dancers, and comics in town. We can hit shows that aren't on the respectable citizens' social calendar. Grab a pad and pencil; I've got a nice first story for you. This stagehand, Sammy—a light rig came right down on his head. He's in the hospital. Don't know if he's going to make it. Bunch of artists are throwing an impromptu show. Raise some cash for the little lady and his two girls. There'll be acts you never see together. My buddy Len Spencer's got a brand-new song from Chicago to debut. Won't be released in sheet music for months."

I made the effort to get to my feet. "All right, Wyatt. It sounds better than sitting here, searching for faces in the wallpaper."

"That's the ticket. Don't let that bastard Nowak wear you down. Maybe you can't make a silk purse out of a sow's ear, but you can't eat a silk purse."

"That makes no sense." I grabbed my coat and hat.

"Okay then. If you wind up with sow's ears you can at least make bacon."

"Wyatt, I grew up around livestock. The only thing sow's ears and pork belly have in common is the pig."

"You know what I mean. We can make it work."

"What choice do I have? Take me to the phaeton."

"Wow, I didn't even think I'd make the show tonight. Becca was really riding me for being out so much this week, but hey, sorry honey, now it's business."

We arrived at the small variety theater just as the houselights dimmed. A hat had already passed by for the wounded Sammy. Although not a major hall, the plush mauve drapes aspired to velvet, and imitation-gold gilt set off the stage. The smell of old wood, cigar smoke, and spilled whiskey had taken up permanent residence. On the platform, a large chair—a throne, really—presided at the center of a semicircle of simple spindle-back chairs and three-legged stools.

"Good, didn't miss anything," Wyatt said. "My buddy Len's up first."

At that moment, a voice offstage boomed. "Gentlemen—and

I don't see any ladies among us tonight—for your pleasure, the Imperial Minstrels featuring Len Spencer, Billy Williams, and Dan Quinn."

Three men shuffled onstage. Caucasian, their faces blackened by burned cork, their lips grotesquely set off in frozen white grins. A man, still young, powerfully barrel-chested, whom Wyatt pointed out as Len, stood in front of the suddenly comical throne and addressed the crowd.

"Before we get into character, I want to thank you all for coming out on short notice. Please be generous with folding money in the hat. Not going to soft-pedal it, give it to you fortissimo. Sammy's in bad shape, and this cash could turn out to be a widow's boost.

"As you see, we failed to wrestle up an orchestra, and all I've got are my two endmen for the minstrel meeting, so we can't do a full-blown parade and all. We do have the fabulous Edward Issler on a mighty beat-up piano. Eddie, don't think we're going to hear the D above middle C tonight. And the Banjo King himself, Vess Ossman. We'll do a minstrel first part—as best as we can—we've marvelous acts for the olio, including, if I may be so bold, a song I'll be singing. It's so spanking new that the umbilical cord isn't cut. Barney Fagan sang it over the phone to me just this morning with the ink still wet on the staff paper. The boys and me rehearsed it only an hour ago, so you can look forward to a debut instead of another chorus of 'The Frolicking Coon' or 'Nearer My God to Thee.' Now without further ado . . ."

Here his attitude changed, his shoulders stooped, and he shot a shifty glare at the audience, who responded with immediate delight.

"Gentlemen! Be seated."

With that, the three made a fussy show of sitting, Len in the center throne, the others at the far ends of the half-circle. Banjo and piano played a quick snatch of a two-step, after which the three men on stage nearly fell from their seats, clapping and whistling.

Maybe I should have expected what came next: a series of jokes that drew hearty laughter not so much from humor but from derision. The naked racism, however, shocked my conscience.

Len: "What ya say, Billy?"

Billy: "What do, Leonard?"

Len: "Money's mighty cheap now."

Billy: "Why, how's that? I can't get me none."

Len: "Why, you can get silver dollars for forty-five cents and fifty-five cents almost anywhere . . ."

Billy: "Ah, go on, nigger, I don't believe ya."

Len: "Now every dern fool nigger knows that forty-five cents and fifty-five cents makes a hundred cents, and you can get a silver dollar anywhar for dat."

All dialogue came accompanied by an embarrassing display of exaggerated loose-limbed mugging. The performance turned more cruel and derogatory as the end men took over their roles, one as Zip Coon, a vainglorious uppity-city Negro, and the other as Jim Crow, a lazy country dullard. Jokes turned to razors, rape, the sexual, and the scatological. I felt disgust and embarrassment at the resulting laughter—laughter partly driven by the infectious chuckles and guffaws of someone offstage. Wyatt saw me searching the wings for the source.

"That's Len's shill, George Johnson. You know, 'The Laughing Song' guy."

"Do not know it."

"Been under a rock? Well, you'll meet him after the show."

"Wyatt, is it always this profane?"

"No, they're getting pretty raw tonight, like old times. Think they're taking advantage of no women or young'uns in the audience to reach back to some of that antebellum stuff."

"I do not know how much more I can bear."

Fate intervened as the two endmen retreated to their seats, and

Len rose and walked forward to debut Fagan's new ditty. Piano and banjo started a strange syncopated rhythm. The steps, slow-slow-quick-quick were for a dance not yet invented. The lyrics, sung in demeaning dialect, were not entirely insulting. Not at first.

> Thar' is gwine to be a festival this evenin',
> And a gatheren' of color mighty rare,
> Thar'll be noted individuals of prominent distinctiveness,
> To permeate the color'd atmosphere.
> Sunny Africa's Four Hundred's gwine to be thar,
> To do honor to my lovely fiancé,
> Thar' will be a grand ovation of especial ostentation
> When the parson gives the dusky bride away.
>
> My gal is a high-born lady
> She's Black but none too shady
> Feather'd like a peacock, just as gay
> She's not color'd, she was born that way.
> I'm proud of my black Venus
> No coon can come between us
> 'Long the line they can't outshine
> This high-born gal of mine.

On the chorus, I relaxed. If you swapped out the word "coon" with "man" or "dude," it was mostly a love song. Without the dialect—acceptable. Then came the next verse.

> When the preacher man propounds the vital question,
> Does ye' take the gal for better or for worse?'
> I will feel as if my soul had left my body, gone to glory,
> And I know my heart will make an awful fuss
> I anticipate a very funny feelin'
> Nigger's eyeball, like a diamond sure to shine,

> But I'll bask in honeyed clover, when the ceremony's over
> And I press the ruby lips of baby mine.

As the refrain began again, bewildered anger seized me. Why? Why the Negro slur? Was the debasement of the word "coon" not enough? It didn't really fit the meter of the song. Was there a requirement, lest anyone missed its purpose, that the song must be defaced, splattered with black tar? How was I to write about the merry cruelty of this?

After a thunderous round of applause, a comic named Charley Case was announced. An unassuming man ambled into the spotlight. Heavily corked up, difficult to guess his age, he appeared on the cusp between youth and middle age. Once in place, he moved very little with no exaggerated mannerisms, no shuffling, nor wide-eyed buffoonery. His only motion was the absent-minded winding and unwinding of a piece of string around his fingers. I braced myself for the onslaught of "de's" and "dats" of mocking dialect. Instead Case spoke in clear, casual prose.

The blackface was superfluous. He could have been any ethnicity—Roman, Celt, Romanov. Stories of his good-for-nothing father might have sprung from anywhere on the globe, but one thing was certain: the American unspeakable underlying it all: class. Charley's ne'er-do-well father was the working-class layabout looking for an angle. Charley went on with his stories, dryly playing his own straight man.

> Father was always a great drinker, but he always knew when to quit. He never drank more than he could stand, whenever he saw he couldn't stand anymore, he'd stop for a while. Then when he could stand again, he'd take another drink.

Father only struck my mother once in their entire history, and even then, he felt so sheepish he wouldn't look at anybody for weeks. Of course, he could only see a little out of one eye, but never less . . .

I looked around the hall. After the brutal broadness of the Zip Coon and Jim Crow routine, how well would Case's droll, dry humor go over? At first it seemed the audience had missed the jokes, but soon they were caught up in the tale of the rascal "accidentally" stealing firewood and paying for it with a punch in the mouth, with Charley insisting, "That didn't amount to much damage at all, because those four teeth had been troubling Father for quite a while anyhow."

I relaxed, grateful the next comic, Russell Hunting, performed without blackface, instead serving up a broad caricature of pugnacious Irishman Michael Casey's ignorance of how to use a telephone. Wyatt wasn't amused.

"Who doesn't know how to use a telephone? He's making all Irish look angry and stupid. These Mick routines are just not funny."

"Mick?"

"Yeah, you get all flavors here: Mick, coon, rube, yid, wop."

Was this an adolescent America trying to consume and absorb its diversity? It wasn't a pretty sight. The next act, WC Dukenfield, someone's visiting cousin no older than fifteen, signaled we finally escaped minstrelsy into plain vaudeville. He silently juggled cigar boxes with a skill surprising for his youth.

After Ossman plucked a rousing banjo instrumental of John Philip Sousa's "Washington Post March," Len Spencer reappeared, face scrubbed clean.

"We've a special treat for our finale tonight. Also, there's a new hat passing now that the liquor hopefully loosened your purse strings. If you've heard our next singer, maybe with Lew Dockstader's

Minstrels, you know he's the voice of an angel. If not, get ready to shed a tear. Born in England, but he's all ours now. Here he is, Richard Jose."

I whispered to Wyatt, "So glad we left the blackface behind."

"Oh, Richard won't touch it, not even when he was in the minstrel show. Told Birch and Cotton he had a skin allergy."

Jose was corpulent but seemed always to have been so, and he wore it comfortably. He was the most well-dressed of us all, with a sharply pressed evening jacket and vest, a long watch chain across his broad belly, its gold glittering in the stage lights.

That a sparkling tenor voice should issue from such a body is, of course, no surprise to any frequenter of the opera, but Jose went a step further. His voice floated up to E above high C, a countertenor, the range of female altos, and not by falsetto or headvoice, but full chest. He used every bit of his range to wring the emotion out of "Softly Now the Light of Day," but when he launched into the hopelessly sentimental lines of the next number, "Darling, I am getting old, silver threads among the gold" and "Oh, darling you will be, always young and fair to me," I detected a glint of tears in some men's eyes.

I thought myself immune to such sentimental piffle, sure, until Jose pulled the wings off all eight verses of "Abide with Me." The last time Lyte's hymn of defiant supplication bathed my soul occurred at my mother's grave, and I was transported there immediately. By the time Jose proclaimed, "Where is death's sting? Where grave thy victory? I triumph still, if thou abide with me," hot tears ran down my face.

Wyatt led me into the backstage room, where performers draped about on couches and chairs, including several who had not been onstage. I recognized Len Spencer, Jose, and Vess Ossman. Charley Case, now stripped of blackface, was clearly Charley Case, but the others, I couldn't tell. One man stood out conspicuously, the lone real Black man: short-cropped hair, eyes twinkling above a broad nose and bushy mustache.

Our entry didn't interrupt the conversation.

"So, how'd we do?"

"They coughed up 'bout 140 bucks, if you believe it. Richard, you really killed there at the end."

"Did my best, gents."

"Hey Jose, you oughta record that 'Silver Threads Among the Gold.' It'd be a hit for sure."

"Canned music? Not sure I'm up to singing into a horn."

"Ask George. He's the master."

All eyes turned to the Black man.

"Well, it's not so bad. Just got to be real still and clear."

"Len, that 'High-Born' song, that was some crazy rhythm."

"Yeah, if you believe Barney, and he's an Irish storyteller, he composed it to the flippity-flop of a broken bicycle pedal. Now if I know him, it won't be long before he claims he was down to two nickels on his wife's birthday and sold it to the publisher for her present."

"Wouldn't mind playin' some more raggedy stuff like that. Didn't know Barney was much of a writer. Always thought of him as a buck-and-wing dancer."

With that, Vess Ossman wobbled his knees out and in, and stomped a clumsy clod dance.

"Plunk, what'd you do with the money your folks gave you for dancing lessons?"

"Billy, I never claimed to be a dancer. Got all the work I can handle right on this banjo."

The Black man joined in. "Plunk, better watch, heard Gibson company's selling guitars cheap as taters."

"George, now don't you worry 'bout me. You know those guitars aren't loud enough for recording clear, and with a band of horn players? Forget it."

"Yeah, George, what Plunk's really got to worry about's that Van Eps boy. Hear he plays twice as many notes and drinks half as much whiskey."

"Speaking of whiskey, where's the good stuff?" A man called Fred rifled through the bottles as he talked. "Don't let Graham pass off any of that rectified swill."

"What is rectified?" I whispered to Wyatt.

"Who knows? Heard it's straight ethyl alcohol diluted with water, tinted brown with tobacco juice and iodine, and flavored with burned sugar and prune juice."

Charley Case, standing near, overheard us. "Well, at least it'll keep you regular."

George, the Black man, was studying me. "A Brit's here, fellows! Sounds like we're visited by royalty tonight."

"Hey, what about me? I'm English." Jose exaggerated a stage pout.

"Ha, you washed up from the moors in knee pants. You don't count."

"I am barely royalty," I said. "My father—"

"He's being modest," Wyatt stepped in. "This here's Joshua Banks. He's a baron, or some such. Anyway, he's the *Journal*'s new man covering you reprobates."

This information was greeted primarily by nods and grunts. Charley Case raised his hand like a polite schoolboy.

"How you think I'd go over, over there?"

"Honestly?"

"No, dear man, lie to me."

"Frankly, fine in London, maybe Manchester, but the countryside, they would be scratching their heads," I said.

"Yeah, Charley. You should wait till they build that bridge."

At that moment, a tall man whom I didn't recognize stuck his head in the doorway. Len reacted.

"Polk Miller, as I live and breathe, what are you doing down here with the riffraff? Aren't you at the University Club or something?"

Miller strode in. "I heard about Samuel. Thought I'd make a contribution."

"Better be a big one, you with all that animal medicine business." I didn't catch who said it, but they sounded agitated.

Miller ignored the endman but handed several bills to Len.

"I was told there's a London newspaperman here tonight."

Len pointed to me. "Gonna give him the lecture, professor?"

"I don't want him thinking some blacked-up White stage Negro, playing the monkey, is any way like the real, natural Negro music of the plantation days," said Miller.

"Well, you should know." One of the end men—I think it was Billy Williams—seemed intent on riling Miller. "Your daddy owned a mess of Negroes, didn't he? You act so smug singin' 'In De Middle ob De Road' and 'Watermelon Party' to the Arts and Literature Club, but your biggest number is 'The Bonnie Blue Flag' of the Confederacy. Well, you fought in that war and lost. I'll take my coon with a razor over your happy-slave-plantation nostalgia."

"I'm trying to preserve real Negro music." Miller drew himself up like a preacher giving a sermon. "Not that mockery concocted by velvet-waistcoated gents from the fields of West Forty-Seventh Street, or the fancied-up and whitened University Jubilee Singers. Those High Church folks are ashamed of the true spiritual.

"And don't accuse me of lobbying for the re-enslavement of the Negro. I consider the deep-seated prejudice against the Negro as a race to be cruel and foolish. I intend to form a Black quartet to help me accurately portray the Old South, though I fear my fellow Southerners might not accept a mixed-race presentation. But I make no apology that it's been my aim to vindicate the slave-holding class against the charge of cruelty and inhumanity to the Negro of the Old Time."

Len stepped in. "You only saw what you wanted to see. You may have thought those slaves were well treated and content, your daddy may even spared the whip, least in front of you, but if you'd unlocked the door, and they'd a way to escape, you bet those slaves would have hightailed it out of there."

"Here, here!" Jose chipped in. "Not human nature to desire servitude. Even in a gilded cage, the bird wants to fly."

"God, now you sound like my sister," one of the end men groaned.

Vess Ossman tried to play peacemaker. "Now, boys, you gotta give Polk credit. He plays the clawhammer style as authentic as it comes. You heard what Uncle Remus said: 'There's a live nigger hiding in Polk Miller's banjo, and you look for him to jump out and go dancing when Miller strikes a string.' "

I'd tried to stay a fly on the wall through the performances, and now here, but could take it no longer.

"Gentlemen, you must explain to me why you insist, even in the presence of this African American, on using the slur for negro.

The sound went out of the room. The other end man, the one who had played Jim Crow, pointed at the lone Black man.

"He ain't no nigger. We don't ever think of him like that. He's George Washington Johnson, a fine-colored gentleman. He's sold more records than all of us, a legend. The 'Laughin' Song' will be around long after we're all pushin' up daises. Hey, George, what'd you think about old Confederate Polk?"

Johnson wiped his brow. "I guess he can't be blamed for what he's born into any more than I can. He reminds me of my best playmate when I was a little child, Samuel Moore. He was a son of the plantation owner."

"See, the sweetest man you ever want to meet."

The second end man, recently Zip Coon, popped around his companion to face me. "Yeah, and where does Prince High-and-Mighty come off berating us? I don't remember English being famous for their kind treatment of all the darkies they colonized."

Len slapped a strong arm across my shoulders. "Hey, look, I got a great story idea. George is recording tomorrow. Why don't you tag along, write it up nice? Maybe we can get some sales in England."

Everyone stared at me like Len had thrown me a lifeline. I took it.

February 1896

My Dearest Margaret,

My deepest apology for the hat. Please put it down to my lack of taste in women's fashion, not an inference of yours.

It does, however, drive home a point. Our interaction, our conversation, has been vastly limited by tired convention and meddling chaperones. I propose we take these posts as an opportunity to learn each other's wants and ways without the judging eyes of our families.

Glad to hear your brother Ted is granting you access to his gymnasium. There is also a small gym in my building, and the trainer highly recommended Indian clubs as a companion to women's calisthenics. I have sent a set to Ted so as not to raise your father's suspicions. The trainer did warn me you should not overdo the heavy clubs lest you go from lithesome to burly.

Your letter surprised me. While I knew you enjoyed tennis and badminton, I would not have supposed you cared for rugby. I once was a serious student of the equestrian arts, and also a decent fencer, though in fencing, John will best me. I can play cricket, though fall asleep watching it played. But rugby, rugby gives me uncomfortable memories—too much knees, elbows, and blood. I have to say I prefer Queensberry-rules boxing to the mayhem of rugby.

I believe the Americans have done rugby one worse with what they call "football." Imagine if rugby players could run down the field interfering and blocking the other team, not just singularly, but in mass formations like the flying wedge. Flesh and bone flung at each other in a knight's melee without armor. Last year's Harvard–Yale game is being called the Hampden Park Blood Bath because almost every player was injured, and four players permanently crippled. That series and the Army–Navy game are both suspended. Many, including the president of Harvard, are calling for the elimination of football before a player is killed.

My friend Wyatt tried to explain the rules, scrimmage lines, and downs. All made no sense to me. I think he likes it mostly as a jolly-good betting scheme. Why five points for the relative ease of kicking a field goal through uprights on the goal, but only four for taking the ball all the way to the goal line for a touchdown? Wyatt said this October, the officials allowed a team to throw the ball in a forward pass. For the win. Bedlam.

I would call it another passing fad, but Mr. Hearst paid one of the best writers here, Richard Harding Davis, to fill a full front page on the Yale–Princeton game, and it sold out the Thanksgiving issue. (Thanksgiving is basically a harvest feast: turkey with stuffing, cranberries, pumpkin pie, surrounded by hokum about pilgrims and Indians.) I must admit, I envy Mr. Davis. Not just that he cuts a dashing figure. (He is the model for the clean-shaven escort on those Gibson girl prints.) He is a relatively young and well-respected journalist with several books to his name.

Meanwhile, I have been condemned to covering the most common of entertainments. How am I to be noticed? At least I may send London stories of more weight, bypassing my masters here. I understand the London paper did publish my piece on Booker T. Washington's speech. Good, but it is hard to keep faith in the future. You called me your white knight. I feel more the Knight of Infinite Resignation. I have made the leap, but I fear I may never land.

Before signing off, I feel I must comment on two points in your last letter. As I would come to your defense, I also take up for my sister Aubrey. I love her dearly. Aye, she does fancy the bright lights, and dreams of the sophistication of London, or that failing, Manchester. But she is not frivolous. Did you know she personally collects coats for the needy and helps distribute them as well? She also uses her charm to raise moneys for the Widows and Orphans fund. I know you meant no harm but felt I had to make that plain. She and I regularly exchange light notes.

That brings me to the difficult subject of, as you say, the maid, Jenny. First we did not get rid of her. My father procured her a better position with a family in Tunstall. Second, I did not prey on some inchoate damsel. Quite the opposite. I was barely seventeen and she ten years my senior when she "happened" into my chamber whilst I was rising from the bath. Not to besmirch her good name by determining who was seduced and who the seducer, except to say, was she who knew the path and pointed the way.

That happened years before I heard you cry out for help in the Fens, and I will not disown my experience. You may, in fact, be glad Miss Jenny absorbed the first fumbling of unleashed lust so you might inherit a lover capable of delivering the pleasure of which you wrote.

As you request, I will not quote poetry. I will only say that I hold your beauty and grace in my heart always.

With my love,
Joshua

Chapter 8

Alone, I plodded through a rainy Saturday morning, trying to find the recording studio. I wanted Wyatt along, but he'd begged off the night before.

"You absolutely must take your wife and children to visit your mother-in-law this particular Saturday? When did you become such a family man?"

"Promised Becca," he said.

"That has not stopped you from doing as you wished before. I really could use your help. George is practically a stranger to me, and thc studio is in a strange neighborhood."

"You got to understand, Becca's mom is cooking a *rijsttafel*. Only does it once or twice a year."

"What in bloody hell is a rijst—"

"Everything. Fish, meat, pickles, relishes, nuts, and fruits. And Oma, Becca's ma, does the East Indian Dutch colony sides—spicy blado, peanut sauce, and rendang, special crispy for me."

"Oh, you promised your belly."

"Joshua, come on. Oma's right-off-the-boat Dutch and cooks like she's feeding an army. Can't get Becca to even cook a Hachée stew, says she's no time. We live on sausage and potatoes, and no matter how much grocery money I give her, I'm always hungry after dinner. I swear she's stashing cash."

So, I had no one to complain to while the wind blew rain under my umbrella as I hurried to make my appointment with George W. Johnson, with one step eager and the next anxious. I gladly skipped the American suits for a speckled Donegal tweed, right as rain, yes, but wet is wet. As expected, the morning downpour scattered the cabs that normally loitered outside Delmonico's. All had run off for fast trade in the business districts.

I entered the studio, dripping wet. The room was both stark and crowded, with unnecessary furniture or pictures stripped away, all the focus on three large funnel horns pointed at George Johnson's head like an array of cannons bombarding a fort. Each horn fed sound acoustically down into the talking machine, extending a mechanical finger to etch a brown wax Edison cylinder.

Recent memory flickered. A traveling phonograph exhibit in Washington Square Park. A nickel in a slot to hear a Sousa band march. The machine safely enclosed in glass, sound escaping through rubber ear tubes tentacled out from the enclosure. The operator asked how I liked it.

"Magic," I replied, but altogether different than hearing a marching band in the flesh.

A bit miffed, he explained how the full Marine Band was fifty men. On a recording, they could only use twelve.

I couldn't imagine any more than five or six musicians crammed in here in this recording room. Behind George an upright piano sat upon a makeshift riser about four feet high, hobbled together from worksite scraps. Chairs at various heights encroached upon the singer, and a trombone and tuba sat patiently, awaiting their practitioners. There was no space for music stands, so sheet music dangled on wires pinned to the ceiling.

Trying to squeeze into position to view the proceedings, I brushed my elbow against a wall hung with all sizes and shapes of recording horns: wood and metal, long and narrow, short, rounded, square. A tulip-shaped aluminum horn rattled as I passed, which drew an angry shout.

"Hey, idiot! Who the hell let you in?"

"Now, now, Mr. Alex," George said. "Mr. Banks is with me."

"George, you know I hate visitors. They can't keep their traps shut and bump into everything."

"Mr. Banks isn't a tourist. He's from the *Journal* and a London paper. He's going to write us up real nice. Len thinks it could boost sales. And Mr. Banks is a baron."

"I don't care if he's Bonnie Prince Charlie. If he messes up a take, or breaks one of those horns, he's out on his ass. We want to put down least two rounds of each song before we can wrap for today."

"Don't pay him no mind, Mr. Banks. Mr. Alex's always grumpy when we start, especially when he's not got his coffee yet. You can sit in that musician's chair over there. The only accompaniment is Frank Banta on piano today."

Mr. Alex glared at me. "Somebody toss him a rag. He's dripped all over my wood floor."

Work commenced with the cold precision of battlefield surgeons. No motion wasted. Wax cylinders were quickly loaded into the machines. A bell would ring a warning—hand signals, three, two, a pointed one. George carefully announced, " 'The Whistling Coon,' rendered by George W. Johnson."

Soon I learned a round equaled ten times through the same song, each time the engineers resetting the machines and slipping on new cylinders. What was George feeling, singing take after take of self-demeaning lyrics?

> He's got a pair of lips, like a pound of liver split
> And a nose like an injin rubber shoe. . .
> With a cranium like a big baboon

I was repeatedly relieved when the song got to "but he's happy when he whistles this tune," and George launched into a flitting birdlike whistle. Scant reprieve as the song turned wicked for the last verse.

> He'd whistle in the morning, thro' the day and thro' the night
> And he'd whistle like the Devil going to bed
> Why he'd whistle like a locomotive in his sleep
> And he whistled when his wife was dead
> One day a fellow hit him with a brick upon the mouth
> And his jaw swelled up like a big balloon
> Now he goes along shaking like a monkey in a fit
> And this is how he whistles that tune . . .

George then whistled comically and finished with a snatch of "Way Down Upon the Swanee River."

Through it all, by necessity, George stood still as the Sphinx, turning neither right nor left, always staring and singing into the protruding horns. He sang stripped to shirtsleeves, the receiving instrument so sensitive it might pick up the sound of his suit coat rubbing arm against side. He mastered his breath lest it spoil the recording, even closing his lips on the last note until the little whirl within the horn ceased.

Twenty times, each note and whistle identical to the first, I understood Jose's reluctance to record. At least Mr. Alex, fortified with copious cups of coffee and seeing progress made, gladdened considerably.

"Okay, George, that's nailed down tight. Everyone, we're switching over to 'The Laughing Song' now."

The song revealed the true secret to George's success. Other whistlers promised serious competition (some even covered "The Whistling Coon,") but George's arsenal of all manner of gleeful laughter was beyond imitation. Its infectious nature was precisely why Len Spencer had used George to seed the audience response to the weak jokes of the minstrels.

George laughed his way through the jaunty song twenty times, each time as hearty and genuine as the last. And each time I grew more perturbed at the lyrics. Unlike "The Whistling Coon," written by some White man for a minstrel show, George W. Johnson, by his own hand, composed this object of laughter, "The Dandy Darkey" with his heel "like a snowplow, his mouth like a trap," who "when he opens it gently, you will see a fearful gap."

It was, after all, really a silly nonsense song, not unlike the Edward Lear poems of my childhood. Any words might work as long as they sounded right. So, why must the object of derision be a dandy darkey? The last verse of the song made no mention of Blackness, yet worked as well as any.

> So now kind friends just listen, to what I'm going to say
> I've tried my best to please you with my simple little lay
> Now whether you think it funny or a quiet bit of chaff
> Why all I'm going to do is just to end it with a laugh
> And then I laughed . . .

Was George trying too hard to please, or was he doing what he needed to sell the tune? Would America ever let its Black artists write songs not chained to racist buffoonery, or trapped in Black exotica?

Finally, the relentless recording stopped, setting me free to move around without consequence. Absentmindedly examining a violin lying on one of the other chairs, Mr. Alex surprised me at my shoulder.

"Do you play that thing or are you looking to eat it? God knows I'm 'bout hungry enough to."

"The violin? Yes."

"Can you play it as a fiddle? Not Paganini stuff, more 'Turkey in the Straw.' Then again, if you actually could play Paganini, well . . ."

"I actually prefer folk music, jigs, reels."

"I mean popular music."

"I know 'Daisy Belle.' "

"Can you play loud? The violin's a bear to get on wax."

"Are you seriously proposing I record?"

"Not sure how serious you can get with a novelty about getting hitched on a bicycle built for two, but yeah. Got two cylinders left and—no offense, George—you're a real pro, but if I hear either of those two songs again today, I think I'll shoot a hole in my head."

George let out a rumbling laugh. "No offense taken, believe you me. That'll make a story for you, Mr. Banks. Tell you what, Mr. Alex, I can whistle a duet while he plays."

Mr. Alex clapped his hands then set the machines. No time for nerves. I knew the tune by ear, as it was a favorite of my sister, Aubrey. I stuck close to the melody and let George dance around it with warbling harmonies. The song flew by, and when done, I felt sorry there were not more cylinders. I doubted ever getting the chance again, so I purchased both cylinders right there and then. I wondered if that was Mr. Alex's dodge in the first place, but I didn't mind.

George put on his coat. "Let's go rustle some lunch. Know a place that makes a top-notch ham sandwich."

Walking out of the studio, phonograph recordings tucked into my coat, I smiled for the first time that day.

No longer raining, sun pierced the clouds, and we set forth walking to the village. Though we traveled abreast, I felt George keeping a half step behind.

"I call you George. Why not call me Joshua?"

"Don't really know you too well. I could call you Mr. Joshua if you want."

"Why not just Joshua?"

"Dangerous to get in the habit of taking informalities with White folk. Even if you don't care, some other fellow might."

"What about Spencer? You call him Len."

"That's different. He treats me like his long-lost favorite uncle.

It'd be like using Mister on family. Len's been aces with me. I'll call him whatever he wants."

"Well, then I will call you Mr. George."

George gave a weary grunt. "Wouldn't do to sound uppity. Call me plain old George, or good old George. As long as the checks don't bounce, that'll be fine."

"All right, George, I have a question I really want to ask. Does it insult you to sing those coon songs?"

"Not singing about me. When Billy does a rube song, he's not thinking he's a rube himself."

"You do not think it reflects on your whole race?"

"Hold on now." For the first time, George's mask of affability cracked, and I could see he was angry. "You trying to make me spokesman for the whole race? I'm no Frederick Douglass. You carrying your whole race on your back? I'm only one man, and all I know to do is whistle, laugh, and sing. Anyway, a White man already let Sissieretta Jones get that fancy education, singing opera to the president. She done filled up our quota. They're not letting in another.

"If the Moore family hadn't taken in their heads to educate a little slave child, even though it was illegal, I probably wouldn't know how to read and write. And if they hadn't made me little Samuel's playmate, despite there being ten children, I wouldn't have heard him play the flute so pretty it made me want to imitate it with whistling. Sam and his mother were kind of like Polk Miller. They don't hate Negroes like some Whites, but they don't know what to do with us either."

George was talking himself down, and his voice regained a matter-of-fact tone.

"Now some traveling minstrel men, you can tell they hate niggers more than they love their mamas. They do everything to make us look less human, less than apes. Got no use for us. Shoot half of us and ship the rest back to Africa and they'd never sing a coon song again. But folks like Polk Miller are in a fix. He grew up waist-deep in Negroes. He'd rather play an old slave tune than Mendelssohn or Dixie. But he loves his daddy and poppy. They weren't evil men to him. So, he thinks of the Black race as talented children, and slave owners as noble caretakers. Even now he can't admit he just likes the Negro songs better than the popular White songs. Has to make an educational exhibit of it."

"Might you sing other songs? Ones that are more uplifting?"

"I didn't pick 'The Whistling Coon.' When Victor Emerson took me clear 'cross the river to record at New Jersey Phonograph Company, I thought I'd whistle 'Listen to the Mocking Bird,' or 'Litle Annie Rooney.' Mr. Emerson insisted on the Devere song. But he was smart, and he knew the public, what would sell.

"As far as me writing 'The Laughing Song,' it's not as bad as some. You know that fine Black songsmith Sam Lucas?"

"Of course, played Uncle Tom. He is of some renown."

"Well, he writes such nice tunes. 'Down by the Sunrise.' That's a jubilee song, and regular tunes like 'Jeremiah Brown.' I'd sing those on the streets near the Hudson River ferry terminal, maybe get fifteen, twenty cents. Then I'd try 'De Coon Dat Had De Razor' and, oh my, nickels would fall like rain. Poor Sam Lucas, he's so ashamed that on the sheet music he only claimed the music, credited 'Words by Prof. W.F. Quown.'

"Okay, George. Give the people what they want. All this talk of accommodation, but it is not a two-way street. I do not perceive a concerted effort on the other side. My friend Miss Moon informs me that your people lose ground every day. How long before the Negro in America demands equality by any means necessary?"

"Damn easy for you to say, Guvnor. Isn't near enough of us on our own. How many John Browns you think we got out there? We could maybe appeal to White man's religion till he truly believes we're all God's children, and God don't make no trash. I'm making more money singing coon songs than many of the White men buying them, and you expect me to run through the woods like Bras-Coupé."

"Who?"

"Everybody knows that story, least some version. It used to scare little White children into doing their chores and getting to bed on time, or Bras-Coupé was going to get them."

"Not in Yorkshire. We had Awd Goggie. Kept me from stealing apples, I can tell you."

"You're going to make me tell the story, aren't you?"

I nodded.

"There's a bench. Got to sit a spell anyway. My rheumatism is aching me, and the alkali ain't done me no use."

The wooden bench had seen better days, and I had to take care to avoid splinters. George just plopped down. The increasing shabbiness of the buildings announced we were on the cusp of a low-income neighborhood. I unconsciously checked my coin purse and swiveled toward George.

George's face took on a serious cast. "Going try to tell it the way my mother—folks called her Ann Pretty—memorized it, then passed it to me, not the way that White man Cable messed it all up. Mother got the story right from slaves brought from New Orleans. Wasn't no voodoo girl with a wax arm in a tiny coffin, and Bras-Coupé wasn't any royal African prince like Oroonoko, just a plain slave."

George closed his eyes for nearly a minute, composed himself, and began in sonorous tones. "In New Orleans the city guard declared absolute authority to practice violence upon any citizen who stepped outside the Code Noir. 'How are we free,' reformers asked, 'if officers parade, pistol and sword, to beat or maim at will, each guard a judge, a jury, an executioner?' "

"Police agreed to warn three times before resorting to sword.

Reformers and city councilmen allied to disarm, if not disband militarized rule. Police to justify their might spread fear and alarm. Escaped slaves, 'maroons,' became the fearsome foils. Chief among them was the 'Brigand of the Swamp,' a Creole slave named Squier."

"What's this got to do with Bras-Coupé?" I asked.

"Hold your horses. Only know it one way. Got to set the stage." George closed his eyes again, reset his pose.

"Squier fled General DuBuy's plantation but was caught in a fight, his right arm shot, his bone shattered. At the hospital, doctors amputated his arm while police set guard. After dysentery sank Squier into a state of feebleness, the city guard withdrew. Snatching the opportunity, Squier rose from death's bed, leaped from the window, and was reborn as Bras-Coupé. No arm, no matter. He'd foreseen his future long ago in dreams, and so he practiced pistol and sword in left hand as well as right.

"Off he ran to the cypress swamps around Lake Pontchartrain to form a raider gang, and in many gunfights, both maroon and city guard moldered lost among the cypress.

"Legend grew by post and poster. He became a demidevil with mystical powers. Bullets ricocheted off his iron torso. His stare made policemen disappear in smoke. With magic incantations in his native tongue, he floated muskets into the air. Children were warned that Bras-Coupé may be a cannibal, so they'd better mind their parents."

"Surely people did not truly believe such rot?"

"Do you believe in Robin Hood and King Arthur?"

"Touché. But the police must have eventually apprehended and tried Bras-Coupé."

"Not really. That lying book writer had the police lasso Bras-Coupé while he bounded around Congo Square. Don't make a lick of sense. A one-armed giant, wanted posters all over town, leading a ring dance surrounded by half the city guard? Mother was told the police actually signaled the start and end of Congo Square dancing with a pistol shot."

"The city guard did not succeed? Did he stay free, a rebel hero , as you say, like Robin Hood?"

"No, reward's what got him. Whether two thousand dollars or only two hundred, that's a lot of money. Bras-Coupé lay healing from wounds in a shack in the Bayou Metairie. Francisco Garcia, who'd been his friend, waited till Bras-Coupé slept, then bludgeoned him to death with a club."

"Betrayed, eh?"

"That wasn't the end of it. To set an example, Mayor Prieur demanded that Bras-Coupé be hung within the Place d'Armes, body rotting in the broiling sun. Thousands came to gape. Masters forced their slaves to gaze upon him lest they should think to stray."

George's belly growled. "That's all of that story. Best be going before they stop serving lunch."

George didn't speak again until we entered the village, an area called Little Africa.

"Finally. About ready to eat my belt."

George gestured to a particularly dodgy building, more suitable for an opium den than a restaurant.

"Hold the dog back, George. You mean to enter this establishment?"

Years surely had passed since the storefront felt a paintbrush or any touch of care. A canvas awning hung as much absent as present, sun-bleached of color, threadbare and torn. I knew these kinds of places. Wyatt called them black-and-tans, rough-and-tumble taverns where Black and White were welcome to dine in equal squalor.

"Don't look much, but Ike's brother's a butcher, and Ike makes the best ham and cheese sandwich in the borough, that's for sure. Got cheese special from Wisconsin or that McCadam from Heuvelton. Won a medal at the Chicago World's Fair."

Nearby saloons put forth no better face, so I followed George into the dark room, curtained from the early-afternoon sun. Men—only men, Black, White, and shades between—hunched over their lunches, which were mostly of beer and whiskey. The men carried their occupations with them. The scent of soot, furnaces, horses, and the slaughterhouse mingled with the hard-edged sweat of heavy toil.

George ordered two ham and cheese sandwiches along with a couple of ales—a wise choice, water being the last thing to trust in such a place. We found a wobbly table and awaited our order while hard eyes took our measure.

"George, you were there laughing at Sammy's fundraiser. Why not perform?"

"Len wanted me to, had a row with the stage manager. Owner said they could do a Negro show or a White show, but didn't want no trouble with a mixed show, even in Manhattan. I've done mixed shows. Brought into the police play, *The Inspector*, back in ninety. I got $25 a week."

"Does it ever bother you, like last night, the guys going on, and you the only Negro in the room?"

"Maybe not the only one."

I cocked my head.

"I forget you're new. Lots of us think Charley Case is mixed. It gets under his skin, so to speak, so please don't say nothing. I like Charley."

"How can you tell?"

"Oh, little things. Blood will tell."

Our beer and food were deposited on our table with all the charm of a wagon dumping manure, and though the ale tasted like watered-down weak tea, the ham and cheese butty was a work of culinary art. How did this place, frankly one step away from an abattoir's outhouse, produce such perfection? Thinly cut slices of cured ham had been fried in a pan, their edges curled and browned. They were bathed in a light coat of bright white mayonnaise, layered with a slice of honest-to-God Emmentaler cheese all encased in fresh crusty sourdough bread. Obviously, Ike was a good chef who'd made bad career choices.

My teeth sank through tender sourdough. Had Ike just whipped up the mayonnaise? A kiss of lemon tweaked the tongue, balancing the pleasant musk of the Swiss, all framing the perfect char of the ham. We both devoured our first half as if it were our last meal. Then George gave me a look.

"Mr. Joshua, I'm working on a new act for my street performing, beyond singing. Give me your right hand."

"What?"

"Gypsy showed me palm reading, said people go nuts for it."

I complied with my right hand, even though I really preferred to pick up the remaining sandwich. George made a big show of examining first my palm, then the back of my hand, then palm again.

"Well, marriage lines are strong and unbroken." He pointed to two little lines under the side of my pinkie.

"Head line and heart line don't meet. Maybe conflict between what your head wants and what your heart needs."

"Does this codswallop work on the tourists?"

"Ha. Don't believe in all that séance or astral-plane nonsense, but why shouldn't hands tell something about a person? My doctor always gives the hands a peek. While they may not really tell me your future, I'll bet they reveal plenty about your past, maybe even things you don't know."

"Whadda you faeries up to?" The voice was behind me. "Playing handsies?" I had to twist and tilt my head back to take him all in. A big, hairy man with a head like a large block of wood. The man grabbed George and my hands and flung them apart, knocking my plate and food to the floor. I didn't think. A switch flipped. I saw red and was on my feet. Up in his face shouting. "Friggin' 'ell, mate."

"Out of my way, Miss Nancy."

He gave me a hard shove, forcing me to stumble back. My heel landed on my own ham sarmie, sliding on a coat of creamy mayonnaise. My leg flared out, nearly taking me down. Mean laughter burst throughout the room.

I was on him fast, a green lion eating the sun. My hands were on his chest and stomach, surprised by the little give in his torso, like leather stretched over steel. I used all my weight to push him and grunted, "You manky twonk."

The big man fell back a pace but was caught by a lanky, yet muscular, Black man. He'd entered a few minutes before, still wearing his butcher's smock. The lanky man kept fingering an object in his pocket. I positioned myself to punch the big man in the throat.

Out of nowhere, I heard George launch into the whistle part of his specialty number.

"Hey, sounds just like the whistling coon," a man in the back said.

"Dead ringer," agreed another.

"Me in the flesh, and we ain't no swish. Just practicing my palm reading act."

Then George threw back his head and let out a grand peal of laughter. Half the crowd grinned. The big man didn't. He stared at George, then called across the room.

"Hey Zapper, lookie in that piano for the sheet music."

The aforementioned Zapper went to a broken-down piano abandoned in a corner, its top cluttered with beer bottles and old *Police Gazettes*. After poking around in the piano bench for an interminable minute, Mr. Zapper strode double-time across the room waving the sheet music to "The Laughing Song." On it, a photograph featured George W. Johnson smiling broadly.

George kept on whistling clear and flutelike. Some of the men tapped their feet. Maybe George was on to something. Perhaps his songs could be a bridge into men's hearts. We could all laugh away the bitter anger of the world.

The big man roughly snatched the sheet music. He glared at the photo and then at us.

"Get. The fuck. Out."

George's expression soured once we got down the street.

"Got a death wish, son? Don't like White folks assuming we all trying to cut people, but some coons actually do have da' razor. I own a pistol but had to hock it. And if I'd pulled a gun, it would have been the OK Corral in there."

My heart was still racing, a part of me disappointed that the fight had been aborted.

"Sorry. He was so rude."

"Lots of people rude. You should try being a Black man. Can't be picking battles with all of them, especially if they're big, angry, and ready to carve their initials into you. You really think you could take those mugs? You some secret John L. Sullivan?"

"I lost control, I know."

"You were talking gibberish and acting the fool. You sure you're not Irish?"

"No, but a Yorkie's just as bad."

"Now we can't go back there for months. And don't be printing none of this kerfuffle in the newspaper. Don't need no more trouble."

George reached into his coat and pulled out a handkerchief, lovingly unfolded it to reveal the remaining half of his sandwich.

"Least got this last bit to savor."

It struck me that George had developed a special power. Not the super strength of Hercules, or the skillful courage of David fighting Goliath. His power allowed him to bend in the gale without breaking. Sometimes it made him invisible. The simple ability to go along and get along. A price was paid, the soul flayed atom by atom, and George accepted the deal. I owned the luxury of impulse, aggression, blunder, regret, redemption. He could only adapt and endure.

Chapter 9

"You are up to something. Where are you leading us this evening? You look like Peck's Bad Boy about to prank his father."

Wyatt held the door for me and winked. "*Au contraire mon frére*. Only trying to further a friend's education."

"Then *bon mon ami*, but you strike me too eager a *professeur*."

Wyatt tipped his hat. "*Je vous en prie*. I'm, indeed, dedicated to my studies."

"That is what makes me nervous."

We rounded the corner of my building, a blast of frigid late-February air buffeting our faces. Luckily, last week in a small shop near Broadway's Ladies' Mile, I discovered a proper covert coat: poacher's and ticket pockets, line stitching at the cuffs, in a dark green-brown. If one was ever out in the countryside, how was he supposed to ride a horse in a long Chesterfield? I harbored suspicion the shop had shipped the coat over from Cordings in Piccadilly, cut out the labels, and replaced them with their own.

In the last light of day, I spied our normal coach swapped out for an old-fashioned two-wheel stanhope pulled by a chestnut Gelderland horse.

"Aw mate, where is the Spider? This is really a one-man gig."

"Chief's got it, or George Thompson running errands. Wound up with the show buggy. We can both squeeze in fine. A hungry beggar can't write his own bill of fare."

The Gelderland high-stepped, and off we went like politicians on parade. Wyatt assumed a professorial tone.

"I know you're a reserved sort of gent, especially for such a young man, but you can't understand New York and its people without regarding the underbelly."

"Blazes, Wyatt, last few months that is all I do. I have had my fill of writing about plantation diddies, rube comics, cakewalks, and sentimental odes to Mum and Dad. That is my punishment. Why does Nowak hate me? He does not even know me."

"Doesn't have to. Hates the idea of you, of received wealth, received status. Me, it don't bother. My line's always been dirt poor. I'm probably doing better than any of them did. But what I heard is, Nowak's grandfather was a big shot in Poland—not royalty, but military, maybe even a general. Got mixed up in a revolt against the Russians. Didn't go so well, and the whole family had to hotfoot off to Paris, except they forgot to bring their money.

"Don't know the details, but Nowak's mother wound up a very young wife living in New York on Barren Island out in Dead Horse Bay. Close to hell as mere men could conjure. Thousands of putrid carcasses were piled onto barges. Horses mainly, but dogs, cats, pigs, and whatnot. Fat, blood, rotting flesh stewed into glue and grease, soap, fertilizer. Mountains of garbage too. Intolerable in winter, downright inhuman in summer. Even the Irish wouldn't live out there. The unholy stench of the furnaces, it marks you, makes you sick, and if you wander into town, people turn away. You reek of death."

"In that case, I am doomed!" I said it theatrically, but I really did feel trapped.

"Maybe you can get on his better side—he doesn't really have a good side."

"How would I manage that?"

"He acts all righteous, but he's got a weakness. Likes the art prints."

"It's hardly shocking to like art."

"I mean racy types. French cards, ones that look like innocent ladies, but hold them to the light and ooh-la-la. If you could get him something rare from London, who knows."

"Sure, I see myself writing to Margaret or my father, 'Hey, can you get me some filthy picture books?' "

"They don't have to be the real down-and-dirty stuff. Nowak likes the pretense of refinement. I believe they call it erotica." Wyatt hooked his thumbs under his suit lapels and pushed out his chest. "The filth you can read in a nice dinner jacket."

I shook my head. "God help me. So, now I am to be a Holywell Street smut peddler?"

"Worth considering. Anyways, let's get back to exploring the underbelly. Not talking variety houses and coon singers. I mean real bellies and breasts and legs and snatches. I've made a study of the female form. Should write a book: *The Infinite Variety of the Flower Red*.

"I mean, no matter how fond you are of your swinging manhood, you get right down to it, it's just a simple pump. Now a vagina, all the folds, the scent of interior life, the body cleaved, it's all . . . primal. Think that's why we dress them up in pink lace and cover them in perfume. They're too darn close to the jungle, to primordial soup. Come on, they create life in their bodies. Ever thought how weird and crazy that is? But I'm mesmerized. Bewitched. Every woman I see, I long to caress the lines of her flesh."

"Wyatt, really. You are a married man." I thought of Nowak's accusations.

"I love Becca with all my heart. I do. But society's got her thinking sex is a sin even with a husband. I swear, sometimes she catches herself having too much fun. The next day, she's on her knees praying for forgiveness."

"You are talking about the mother of your children."

“Yeah, some nights in the dark I put on goldbeater’s skin so she doesn’t mother no more children.”

I said nothing, wishing this line of conversation to end. We reached the southern end of Manhattan. Wyatt began to school me as if he were a learned scholar of the flesh trade. There existed a pecking order, as it were, to adventuresses, prostitutes, and whores.

On the very bottom, signboard girls—poor wretches who lived on the streets, servicing desperate men in back alleys and behind billboards. Close behind, the streetwalker, who at least had access to a fleabag hotel or apartment. The cribs, little more than horse stalls, were haunted by women too old, unhealthy, or ugly to go anywhere else. Such places were frequented by b’hoys, men demanding entertainment too rough or bestial for the better establishments.

The girl in a public house differed from her sister in the upscale parlor house in that her surroundings were shabby and that she received a lower rate of renumeration, which she made up for by increasing her workload. In these so-called dollar houses, a customer could actually drain his organ for as little as fifty cents.

The parlor girl, plying her trade at fancy brothels occupied the top end, unless a woman could make the rarefied leap to courtesan, a pampered mistress to the very wealthy. The best of the parlor houses were members only. It served to promote loyalty, catered to clients’ particular proclivities, and provided a mechanism to discharge members whose proclivities turned too twisted or dangerous. On the other hand, multiple partners, alternative entry points, or a mild bit of binding and whip play could all be accommodated, should the gentleman’s purse be sufficient.

Hovering around the professional wing of the oldest profession emerged charity girls, normal, fresh-faced girls angling for a new dress, or tickets to a top show they could ill afford, or just to snag some quick cash. They offered themselves as a man’s date for the evening with the implication of promised quid after the pro quo.

Wyatt declared one motivation for Becca being such a Goody Two-shoes as her need to distinguish herself from her younger sister, who felt no shame in providing such dates to supplement her income—even, occasionally, after she married. When Wyatt pointed out in his sister-in-law's defense that prostitution wasn't technically illegal, Becca served him nothing but cabbage for a week.

A thorough teacher, Wyatt insisted that I witness the skin game in all its manifestations. The signboard and streetwalkers distressed and depressed me. I could imagine no pleasure in their transactions. Even when such women smiled and beckoned us, an aura of weary detachment clung to them, nurses changing bedpans. What quality of mind allowed a man to achieve arousal, and what drop of contentment obtained in such consummation? Self-release was preferable to such an arid mockery of passion.

When we stopped for up-close examination, I felt a wave of shame. We were treating these unfortunate humans like insects pinned to cork. Wyatt secured the horse.

"Wyatt, did you forget how to tie a rope? What is that loopy mess?"

"Getaway hitch, a bank robber's knot. One pull and we're out of here. Like the bar where no one takes his hat off, in case they got to make a run for it."

After assurance from Wyatt that we were merely window-shopping tourists, we entered both the so-called cribs and a disheveled public house.

"You wouldn't trust these places anyhow. They could be panel houses. Some scoundrel hides behind a fake wall, waits till you're knee-deep in flagrante delicto, then springs out and nabs your watch, wallet, and maybe your pants, and flees."

I grew relieved when Wyatt piloted us back uptown. He intended one last stop at a club of which he was a member, saying I must see the high-class end of the spectrum. There was no arguing with him when he set to a course, and since he remained the closest I had to a real friend in America, I felt loath to upset an obviously good night for him by repeatedly whining, "Take me home."

Wyatt started winding up and down streets as if searching. "I believe we need to fortify ourselves before we continue."

"Is it not too late? I forgot my watch, but I assume we have passed into the a.m. by now."

"Ah, there we are, the sporting man's oasis. I give you the night lunch wagon."

More a night mirage. Two sailors in rough pea jackets, and a toff in a tuxedo with a feathered showgirl on his arm, stood clustered around a long wagon with a two-horse team. The incongruous assemblage seemed a piece with the wagon, which was not at all like the ubiquitous work wagons hauling all manner of goods and not-so-goods throughout the city.

Elaborate decorations covered the exterior, with Italianate illustrations of goddesses framed in elegant carved moldings. Crystal gas lamps lit up its side. More light poured out a window.

"Kinda hoping for Owl Night Lunch," said Wyatt. "He's got a grill, but this'll do."

Inside a compact rococo palace of gleaming white-and-gold, five-foot-tall statues held aloft crystal lights, first Christopher Columbus standing with hand on globe, the other curiously featuring a female flamenco dancer. The owner and young son served minced pies and coffee from behind a small, decorated counter. The pies, while cold, smelled fresh. We ate outside on a bench, and I surveyed our surroundings.

"Wyatt, a question."

"Go 'head, shoot."

"No offense, but I was led to believe New York was an incredibly filthy city. Travel books talk of piles of manure, food scraps, and the general muck of life; that dead animals rot on the curb for days, waiting for a knacker man to cart them off to be rendered. Yet as I examine here, and the lowlier haunts we visited, the streets are as clean as London."

"Kinda funny thing. If you'd showed up last year when Tammany Hall ran things, it was filthy, and always had been. But we just had a police corruption scandal so over-the-moon that even the Tammany machine couldn't hold back the storm. Voters ran them out, and put in Mayor Strong on a reform ticket. That's how we wound up with Teddy Roosevelt as police commissioner. TR's been putting a squeeze on some gambling and bawdy houses, but I guess it's better than crooked cops. I'm more riled at Representative John Raines and his drinking laws. He's aiming to mess up the party come April Fool's Day."

"Right . . . but what about the streets?"

"Getting there. See, Roosevelt wouldn't take the cleaning job. Too hopeless, not enough glory. Mayor Strong found this Waring fellow, called himself a sanitation engineer, dressed his men in white like they were surgeons."

"The men in the pit helmets?"

"Yup. When they first went into the rough spots, like Five Points, those boys needed police escorts. Folks didn't trust nobody from the government, they threw bricks at them. After a few weeks, when the tenants realized their streets were as spick-and-span as the rich areas, and people weren't getting sick from all the crap, they changed their tune."

"I'm afraid I have not paid attention to city politics."

"Enjoy the reform while you can. Those Tammany boys will buy their way back, mark my words."

We finished our snack, tipped the young server, and headed to Wyatt's club. He boasted that his club imitated a famous bordello, Kate Woods House of All Nations, whose fame rested on its stock of French, German, Asian, African, Irish, and of course, English girls. A sporting man might traverse the globe with his trouser sword, without leaving the borough. We pulled to a halt on Sixth Street near the top of the Tenderloin District, where bordellos were chasing the theaters, like Hammerstein's New Olympian, up into Longacre Square.

The madam greeted Wyatt warmly, and they chatted whilst flipping through a book of women's pictures. I drifted off to the piano player, just finishing a spirited "Oh, Dem Golden Slippers" before launching into an equally boisterous "Streets of Cairo." Listening to its snake-charmer melody, I automatically thought of Dr. Qabash and my unfulfilled promise to visit Baltimore. I slipped the player two bits on his promise to play Chopin, and he added there was a Franz Liszt number he'd been banging his head against for three months but thought it time to give it a go.

When I looked about for Wyatt, he was gone. I inquired, and the madam informed me he'd gone upstairs and that Per would show me the way. Per was a geologically-sized blond Swede, muscle stretching the cloth of his sack suit. He affected the stoic mien of a Buckingham Palace guard without the sense of humor. Per made sure I caught a glimpse of his brass-knuckle pistol contraption. I skipped any small talk.

We ascended an elegant, curving chestnut staircase. Per ushered me into a room that was painted a glowing lavender. Expecting Wyatt, I didn't see him. A hint of lilac greeted me, and the piano music filtered up through the wrought-iron heating grate, a bouncy "Oh! Susanna." I wondered if I'd wasted my money on the pianist.

Awkward and stranded I noticed nevertheless the warm glow of electric lamps even here in a house of ill repute when many a London estate was still illuminated by gas. A brass bed took up most of the space, with a small decoupage dressing table in one corner, on which sat a flagrantly yellow ceramic bowl and pitcher.

"Bonjour, darling."

I jumped with a start, banging my buttocks against a bedpost. The woman giggled as she emerged from behind a Chinese-lacquered dressing screen.

"*Mon cher, voulez faire l'amour*?"

A thousand French teachers winced. I asked, "*Tu es originaire d'où?*"

A blank stare then a rote, "*du bisous*?"

"A kind offer, I am sure, but madam let us dispense with this fiction. You are no more French than I am Swahili."

"Ooh, you talk like a book." She slid into a broad New York accent. "Your picnic, you paid for French."

"I assure you, I did no such thing."

"Well, your buddy Mr. Wyatt did."

"Damn him."

"Brighten up, sweetheart. I may not *be* French, but I *do* French. I'll take good care of Mr. Friendly and the twins as well. You'll find me very open-minded."

Passing over to the bed, the woman sat with a cheery sigh. I tried hard not to stare. She posed in a near state of undress. A V-neck bodice displayed—more than contained—her breasts. Elegant feet were exposed in Roman sandals, orange ribbons laced across her instep and climbed the ankles of her naked legs. Crowning her head was a turban: satin, a rainbow of crimson, royal blue, green, and yellow, a small silver aigrette in front. Her slightly slanted cat's eyes looked me up and down while she gave a low whistle.

"Aren't you the Prince Charming? Love the black, wavy hair. And clean-shaven too. None of those whiskers scratching up my nethers. If I can coax you into a bit of bird washing, I'd almost do you for free."

I blushed. I couldn't help it. "I must leave. There has been a mistake."

"No, no. You can't run off right away. They'll think I did something wrong. I won't get paid. You have to stay awhile. Besides, don't you fancy me?"

As she said this, her right hand tugged at the bodice so that her breasts popped free, and with her left fingers, she traced a pert nipple. She was only the third woman I beheld naked, and in spite of my intentions, a spark shot through my loins. I marveled at the variety of the bodies I'd touched with my eyes.

Maid Jenny was a big, healthy lass. She would laugh and threaten to smother me with her full bosom, her nipples wide and dark against pale skin. To the opposite, the Paris girl (It pained me to realize I'd never learned her name) hadn't wanted to reveal her chest whilst we made love. Her "bee stings," as she called them. I finally induced her with kisses down her neck and shoulder. Indeed, they were as much protruding nipple as bosom, but they fit her boyish frame, and I gave them rapt attention to prove their splendor.

I shook off my thoughts and returned to the matter at hand.

"It is not my place to fancy you or not. I have a love back in England whom I intend to marry someday."

"Serious business. You've done the deed, waxed the deal?"

"I should say not. My beloved is pure."

"Might be a Puritan, if you catch my drift. Is it wise to buy a carriage without taking it for a spin first?"

I considered her words. Under many watchful eyes, Margaret and I managed only kisses and furtive fondling, though these had been passionate. I believed also that the way a woman danced gave window to lovemaking, and Margaret danced with a ferocious intensity, barely allowing my lead.

"Anyway," she continued, "someday isn't today, and half the men who come here are already married. Hey, if you feel the need to marry, you should marry me."

"What? You—I—I do not even know you."

"That's the point. You should get to know me. I'd be a marvelous wife. I'm a huckleberry above a persimmon, I am. You can be sure I know how to take care of a man. I'd have you play-the-whale every night, and I've got five ways to do it. But see, I'm smart too. I read a lot, and not just *Black Beauty* like the other girls. Just finished William Dean Howell's *A Hazard of New Fortunes*. That title is a Shakespeare reference, you know."

"All right, I will call your bluff. If you are so well read, what are Howell's three essays? He said they went off like wet fireworks, but I found them quite insightful."

"Ha! I should slap you, but I'll play. 'Are We a Plutocracy?' 'The Nature of Freedom,' and let's see . . ."

"Enough, madam, I concede."

"No, you started. It's 'Who are Our Brethren.' Right?" At that, she smiled and performed a breast-swaying shimmy while she recited: "Fraternity is not natural but necessary for freedom and equality in a mass society.' You should read Howell's *An Imperative Duty*. Can't clue you in about it without ruining the surprise. Anyway, I'm from a big family, so I know how to mother, but if you want to wait on children, I've lots of experience with the womb veil and bicarbonate. And I can cook. I bought that brand-new *Boston Cooking-School Cook Book*, very scientific. Working through all of Fannie Farmer's recipes."

I laughed. "Please tell me that is not her name."

"What? Are you a schoolboy, snickering at a pun on derriere?"

"Excuse me, but in my country, 'fanny' doesn't refer to a lady's bum, rather it is her . . .'

"Ooh, you mean this."

She slowly parted her knees. I wasn't entirely surprised to find her yoni on view, the whole crown and feather. When the maid Jenny had seen my reaction to her crotchless pantalettes, she pushed me playfully and said, "Silly, 'ow do you think I'm to piss?"

Time slowed in the lavender room. I knew propriety man-dated retreat but felt rooted to the floor, felt the long privation since I last fully reveled in the flesh. The Paris woman had been a happenstance encounter on an aborted Grand Tour of the continent. I'd seen her at a sidewalk café: waif thin and large, round eyes that stared at me longingly. I quickly realized her true object of desire was my plate of coq au vin. When I bid her join me, she made no charade of pride but methodically devoured multiple courses—escargot, Roquefort cheese, duck à l'orange. Only one nourishment she refused: my course of frog legs, which she despised.

The stray had followed me back to my hotel garret. Whether out of gratitude, transactional obligation, or to completely fulfill all her hungers, she offered herself freely and fully in her own manner. The maid Jenny had gazed directly into my eyes and covered my mouth with deep kisses, our lovemaking easy, joyful, her thrust matching mine, two dancers on a spindle. Not so the Paris woman. She'd closed her eyes and arched her head back when I entered her. I set a rhythm, but her hand stroked her knot to her own time until at last her mouth formed a perfect *o* and I let myself go, both arriving at our destination but on two separate trains.

As to the Haymarket district houses of ill repute, I'd kept a wide berth, adopting a superior attitude about those who sank to use them. When the Paris woman slipped out in the middle of the night, I wondered if our rendezvous amounted to as much.

The woman in the lavender room cleared her throat. "Well, you just going to stand there? I showed you mine. Hey, you're not one of those Parkhurst fellows, come to reform wanton women? I warn you, if Per smells a reformer, he'll crack your head open."

I wanted nothing to do with the obviously capable Per. "Who is Parkhurst?"

"Oh, you're new here. He's that zealot with the American Purity Alliance. Went undercover with private detectives. Didn't trust the cops, said they were on the take, said the police raids were tipped, a form of official playfulness. He caused such a public stink they shut down Scotch Ann's Golden Rule Pleasure Club. Called it Satan's Circus. Mind you, not the nicest place; basement cribs with young cherry boys painted up, acting like young girls. I don't see why we should all get painted with the same brush."

"Madam, I—"

"Call me Lady L."

"The letter or E-l-l-e?"

"I started with Laelien, but the poor boys made such a hash of it that I picked something easy. The letter *L*."

"What is your real name?"

"What's real? I'm whoever I say I am. This is the land of the free. Now, we're not going to sit here playing whist. Come over here and do the agreeable."

As the words left her lips, she began to rub two fingers in a soft circle through the folds of her sex, the light catching on wet flesh through curls of raven hair, her bud of Venus glistening as she worked it to-and-fro.

"I can tell you want me. It's all over your face, and you're obviously tight against the seam. Let's see Adam's dagger. Bet it's a handsome one."

"Mada—"

"Lady L."

"Miss Lady, I—"

"No, just Lady L."

"Lady L, I am only here in my official role as a reporter, collecting intelligence for the news."

"An exposé, huh? Well, then you'd better expose yourself and get inside your story. Your friend promised an extra gold dollar if I let you come to fruition anywhere you wanted, and I'm not leaving money on the table."

No doubt I was fully aroused, hot in my clothes. Would it be so wrong to surrender to raw desire, to get that moment of life called the little death, to have her body engulf and surround me, to revel in our instinctual animal reality? My thoughts turned to Margaret, her sacrifice of extended virginity, her desires, her resentment of Jenny, her ignorance of the Paris woman. Those acts were preludes to Margaret. This smacked closer to betrayal.

"My mind is set. My conscience cannot allow it."

"Oh, hell then."

Lady L bounced to her feet and assumed a businesslike manner. "Better sound like a bit of bed work in here, or Per's going to bust in and I won't get my pay."

She grasped the bed frame, banged it lightly into the wall twice, and said loudly "*Ooh, mon cher*," then bent to adjust the laces on her sandals.

"Hold on. That is it?"

"What? Oh, you're embarrassed, aren't you?"

"Of course. At least allow me my self-respect."

I quickly took hold of the bed and started swaying it against the wall. Lady L bit the side of her hand to keep from laughing loudly. Her mostly naked frame shook with muffled merriment.

"Okay, my prince. Let's give them a show."

Lady L climbed upon the bed, making the springs stretch and squeak. "*Je veux plus*!"

We were both smiling now. I could hear the piano player finally playing Franz Liszt's Liebestraum No. 3, the *Dream of Love*. I sped up to match its rising climax. I whispered French to Lady L and she cried out, "*Plus vite, plus vite*!"

She stayed inches from my face, the full view of her loins as she leaped, her breasts almost striking me in the face as she landed. I became aware I could smell her—sea breeze, gin, enticement. I was painfully erect by now. The urge was unrelenting to turn charade into carnal enactment.

I closed my eyes and kept thrusting the bed in rhythm to the music, 1-2-3, 4-5-6, player not too fast, honoring the theme: "Love as long as you can. Someday at the grave, you will mourn."

Lady L reached full Jenny Lind voice, singing out "*oui*, *oui*, *oui*" over and over. As the music notes cascaded, her voice rose in pitch until she ended with a garbled "*Baisé!*" and fell down on the bed, crying with laughter.

A knock came at the door. Per's voice. "You okay in there?"

"Sublime," Lady L replied.

As I started to leave, Lady L leaned over the brass bed and kissed me on the lips. I didn't pull away.

"What's your name, Prince?"

"Joshua Banks."

"Joshua, you come see me, okay? Not here. I eat at Jimmy's, the all-night restaurant on Sixth Avenue, nearly every night around seven. You should get to know me."

"What is your real name?"

"You'll see it on the marriage license, baby."

I waited for Wyatt out by the stanhope gig, trying to clear my head and let the blood return to the rest of my body. Wyatt emerged and bounded down to me.

"Jumping Jehoshaphat, Josh. Know you were pent-up and all, that's why I brought you out tonight, but hell. I was in the anteroom with the gals when you started with the fireworks. The gals said Lady L is usually pretty quiet. When she went off, they were clutching their pearls like a bunch of church ladies. Now they all want a dance around the barrel with you."

June 1896

Dear Joshua,

Please forgive the tone of my last letter. My words were true, but upon reflection, they may have been delivered more gently. I find it difficult to confront my father for his hand in this, and I fear that I transferred my pique on to you. It's no help that Mother never challenges him unless he oversteps into household affairs. That may serve her. The kingdom of kitchen and hearth is too small for me. I refuse to be a Saint Theresa, foundress of nothing, sobbing after unattained adventures.

I do press Father in my way. No day goes by that I don't mention some woman of science. If I talk of Mary Somerville the astronomer once more, I think he may shout. He's almost ready to send me off to a dowdy lady's college to major in literature. I won't have it. I can read a book myself, thank you very much.

Dorothea Beale has founded St. Hilda's College in Oxford. There I could study chemistry and other sciences as I wish. Why a nation would let half its minds go to waste, concerned only with tea sandwiches and nappies, is a mystery to me. Father likes to quote Amiel: "Destiny has two ways of crushing us—by refusing our wishes and by granting them." I'm well acquainted with the former and am ready to take chances with the latter.

I want to be more than that bird in a cage, as they say. Nothing to do but preen and display plumage for the gratification of others. All I hear is "You're lucky, you're ever so lovely." Well, I'd like to be appreciated for something more than fleeting beauty. When I stand before St. Peter, what will his book say? "She made herself pleasant for men to gaze upon?" Beauty is often more burden than gift.

I should thank you for the Indian clubs. I've learned to lift and twirl them to great effect. Ted also showed me how to jump rope. Not like children, like a boxer. Mother and Father would pitch a fit if they saw me. I warn you, I'm getting strong. When you return, I shall match you blow-by-blow in sport or . . .?

I've put the Fens incident behind me and got back on the horse, as they say. I can't rely on coachmen my whole life. My only problem is my father's stablemen. They insist I ride sidesaddle. What sheer folly. No man chooses it. The curse of Venus makes us more suitable for the saddle, not less. Men don't want us to gallop, but we will.

Men continue to treat women as infants, and when we rebel, they dismiss us as hysterical. A so-called doctor diagnosed my friend Sarah as hysterical. I know her true illness. She'd gone clear past mere boredom to full ennui. And their cure? Her family bought her a Vigor's Horse-Action Saddle. You sit astride the contraption and adjust its vibrations to your liking. I sat on it for nary a minute, and went immediately flush and felt like a schoolgirl climbing a gym rope. Sarah rides the Vigor to full hysterical paroxysm nearly every day. I dare say she may never marry.

Sarah did say I should take some interest in your circumstances. Have you made acquaintance with any of your lodge mates? Met any interesting men, or women? I'd so like to meet Nellie Bly. You know, she traveled around the whole world in less than Jules Verne's eighty days. She also went undercover in an insane asylum to write an exposé. I can't believe she was able to do so. You must tell me what it's like for women in the States.

Do not misconstrue the infrequency of my letters for lack of interest; I don't care to blather on with nothing new to say.

I feel that I live the same day over and over. How many ways are there to say I miss you?

Awaiting,
Margaret

September 1896

My Dearest Margaret,

I have spent the last months collecting notes of interest so that I do not blather on, as you say.

I regret that I have not met the famous Nellie Bly. Mr. Hearst, to his credit, does hire some fine female writers. Due to my assignment to cover low amusements, I meet most of the popular performers but am unsure if any are well-known back home.

One of the chaps, a singer named Len Spencer, has a famous father, Platt Rogers Spencer. He is the fellow who created the fancy Spencerian handwriting style, all flowing loops and swirls. Afraid my writing looks the country farmer's next to that. Len is close with an older Negro gentleman named George Washington Johnson. He sings, whistles, and laughs on recordings. They are really quite popular. I will send you cylinders. If there is no machine in your house, take it to my brother John. He will be delighted to hear new selections. Be careful he does not make you listen to hours of marches and speeches.

George is a fine fellow. He has given me real insight into the conditions of his race. As you may have read in Robert Louis Stevenson's or Rudyard Kipling's accounts, no one would choose to be Negro in the land of the free and the home of the brave. Do not, however, believe Kipling's nonsense about Black blood "throwing back with annoying persistence any attempt at education or uplift." You will meet Negroes of all aptitude, from the muttonhead to the learned professor, with every stop in between. They are no more resistant to refinement than a Welshman.

George took me to the Church of St. Mark in Brooklyn. I

tell you, if only our local pastors could shake off their dreary formality and preach a sermon like the emotional stem-winders of the Rector Herskin, I would find myself in the pew more often. And the music! Neither our common liturgy, nor the Negro spirituals of the Jubilee groups. There needs to be a new term for it. What they have done is taken old hymns and say "Jesus, Lover of My Soul." (Its message of refuge and comfort from the tempest sets well with them). That music they bend and twist. Where once was plain singsong is now sparked with exaltation, shouts, calls, responses, and clapping. Parishioners wave arms and step in place in holy bliss. Even I swayed in high spirits, myself. What a refreshing difference from resigned participation at the local service in Wensleydale.

Shame the city is to condemn the building to make way for the East River Bridge to Manhattan. Here is the thing: I was the only White face in that beautiful Gothic church to witness before God that moving service. In practically all things, from the cradle to the graveyard, school, saloon, and house of worship, America is intent upon prohibiting the Negroes from mixing with Whites. They want to keep pushing until they push them God-knows-where so Whites need never interact or even think of them again.

Instead, Blacks in America have gone about making their own places, stores, restaurants, and even banks. There is still mixing in a few areas and institutions, but as the turn of the century approaches, I fear which way the turning will go.

You asked how women are treated. Nothing is too good for an American man's daughter. Girls mix with boys in many schools. Women are allowed in conversations they would be excluded from in Europe. They have a naturalness around men and seem mainly to have escaped what Oscar Wilde called:

"The subtle evasion and graceful mendacities of high life in Europe."

As to friendships, aside from Wyatt, I do not have much contact with the other men at the paper. Editor Nowak has made it so unwelcoming; I show up only to drop off stories. I have spent pleasant hours with a fellow Britisher in my building, Dr. Clifton Kameny, a doctor of psychology. He posted an advert for a fencing partner. Marvelous footwork; I have to be at the top of my game to best him. The Doctor maintains box seats at the opera and ballet, and has been kind enough to invite me on occasion. In the past I attempted to introduce Wyatt to *Tartuffe*, but he fidgeted through most acts and snored through the rest. Clifton is forever throwing parties. His is the only flat large enough for a baby grand piano. Have no fear about such parties, they are usually strictly stag.

By the by, please inform your friend Sarah that Dr. Kameny called hysteria a wastepaper basket of medicine where one throws otherwise unemployed symptoms. A young colleague of his, Sigmund Freud, wrote an entire book on hysteria, but Clifton thought it all poppycock. He did say this young Freud fellow is postulating promising theories about how we are inexorably shaped by our childhood slights and traumas. Lord help us. If true, I am doomed.

One last bit before I sign off. I hope you don't think it too cheeky or rude, but as you wrote we must be open to each other. I am sending you several rolls of the most wonderful new product. I encountered it when, of necessity, I used the water closet in Clifton's flat. Instead of catalog pages or newspaper by the loo was what is called toilet paper. A long roll of pleasant paper that you tear off at perforations and use to wipe your bum. I needed to go to a pharmacy in order to acquire a quantity. If you are wondering, a pharmacy is like our chemist, but with a what-not-shop crammed in. The chemist, a Mr. Baker, told me the rolls are really made by Scott's Paper Company, but they do not want their name associated with you-know-what. He so went on and on about the staggering accomplishment of "the deliberate punctuated weaking of paper." I had to fake a coughing fit to get away from him.

What a strange note to end on. Since you have banished poetry from my letters, I will simply say I love you. I have missed you every day of this long year and will miss you more each day of the next. If I can establish my writing and return under my own sail, it will be worth the wait.

All my love,
Joshua

Chapter 10

On Sunday, October 18, 1896, the cartoon character called the Yellow Kid took his two-toothed grin, black cat, yellow billboard smock, and carpet bag right out of Hogan's Alley at Pulitzer's *New York World* and led a marching band into a new home at McFadden's Row of Flats in the pages of Hearst's *New York Journal*. On posters advertising the grand switch, one of artist Archie Gunn's voluptuously bosomed showgirls with thigh-high skirts and stockings, led the Yellow Kid by a leash loose around his neck. It wasn't surprising when Hearst succeeded in luring RF Outcault to bring his wildly popular character to the *Journal*. Hearst treated Pulitzer's *World* as a talent agency.

Back in February, Hearst poached the *World*'s Sunday editor, Morrill Goddard. When Goddard expressed a reluctance to abandon the crack staff he'd painstakingly assembled, Hearst hired them all. Pulitzer convinced Goddard back for twenty-four hours, only to see Hearst up the offer. The full staff deserted, and not even the office feline remained. Editor after editor was purloined by Hearst. *The World*'s austere publisher, Solomon Solis Carvalho, left to become the *Journal*'s editor-in-chief.

Goddard proved to be a particular boon to me. Nowak continued to sabotage my work at the *Daily* with last-minute assignments, slashed word counts, and dropped bylines. But Goddard's Sunday paper maintained separate staffs, print, and distribution schedules. Nowak cut no ice with the higher status Goddard. The Sunday paper became a monstrous beast on occasion, reaching one hundred pages, ravenously chewing up content. At five cents to the daily's two cents, it was still a bargain. The main section resembled the *Daily*, except stuffed with all manner of stories. Dinosaurs, miracle cures, and extraterrestrials vied for space with short stories and excerpts from top writers. Lavish illustrations by Gunn and others ranged from ballet dancers and actresses to scantily clad chorus girls.

To get the Yellow Kid and beat Pulitzer, Hearst purchased custom-made, full-cover Hoe Company presses. These were put to full use in three color supplements: the *Sunday American Magazine*, the *Women's Home Journal*, and the *American Humorist*. Goddard's reporters were as tired as they were competitive, enabling me to place performer profiles, show reviews, and stories fed to me by Miss Moon on the outrages or accomplishments in the colored community.

Most contact with Miss Moon occurred by phone. If she visited the city, I would try to find her in the headquarters of various causes she worked for. I knew she would be in New York in the run-up to Valentine's Day. Black statesman Frederick Douglass chose the fourteenth of February for his birthday. The much-admired man passed on last February, and Miss Moon said the Bethel Literary & Historical Association in DC would be celebrating, and she would be in New York to establish Frederick Douglass Day as a national holiday of sorts. Born a slave, Douglass only guessed his birth date, so Bethel and others thought they might move the celebration to the thirteenth or eighteenth so as not to trample the tender feelings of those who might complain Negroes were stealing away Valentine's Day.

My letter to Margaret was perhaps not entirely forthright. A true account of my activities may have been inconvenient. I spent too many late nights with Wyatt, sometimes sure-footed, often catch stepping from one place of amusement to another.

"It's the job," Wyatt insisted whenever my remaining good sense checked its watch or cried out for sleep.

On the plus side, my ticket was stamped, now accepted by the singers, stompers, gin-slingers, and the whole motley as part of the entertainment fraternity. No longer a mark, I shared the space inside the tent. Instead of a hush, I heard all: the broken arm—blind drunk, staying with a friend—thrown out for messing with his wife's sister, the young ingenue's spa trip—*wink*—hasty abortion. I knew of Hearst cavorting with a sixteen-year-old dancer, Millicent Wilson, a girl briskly gone from the titillating show, *The Girl From Paris*, to the nearly obscene *The Telegraph Girl*. He could be seen prowling about town with Millicent, shadowed by her eighteen-year-old sister there to protect Miley from having to take her own "spa trip."

Whilst I was pulled into the belly of the show business beast, I noted George Johnson not hanging out with the other performers as much as before. I always made a point of discussing current events with George to get his take, but as the year went on, I saw less of him. When Len Spencer approached me at the theater to seek some press on a new act he represented, I took the opportunity to inquire.

"What is the deal with George? I heard he is diligently cranking out cylinders, but he is a no-show at night."

Len let out a long sigh. "Yeah, well, the short answer is, he's found himself another woman."

"That is good, no?"

Len seemed tipsy and slurred his words a bit. "You know how I feel about George. He's the sweetest man on God's green earth but has the worst taste in women. The year before you showed up, George lived with a German or Swiss woman; I don't even know her name. He claimed her as a common-law wife. In any case, this White woman was found dead in George's bed."

"Not good."

"Some busybody neighbor tells the cops that George and the German quarreled, so they arrested George on suspicion of murder."

"But how—"

"Is he not in prison? Yeah, what's the chance of a colored man beating a White gal murder rap." Len slapped his hands together and made a magician's disappearing flourish. "Poof, never even makes it to police court. The DA, the police, can't figure what killed her, she just up and died. No marks from a beating, no wounds. Maybe her heart blew out, maybe she pickled her liver to death. George said she chain-smoked and would get awful coughing jags."

"I am sure George did her no harm." In truth, Len was a more dangerous presence. While generally good-natured, he would use violence when provoked, and a small scar on the left of his chin was evidence of such. "What about this new woman?"

"She's 'bout thirty-five, and George is pushing fifty. Good-looking mulatto woman. Drifter, no family. I think she's a gold digger. Drinks gin like she's trying to build a reserve. When she's full, she yells and abuses poor George. I heard him beg her not to bring so much gin home in her apron."

"Why is he permitting such behavior?"

"Men get lonely. You should know." Len took out a silver flask and took a pull. "The worst thing is, I think George thinks he'll reform her. Treats her almost like a daughter. The other night she's got all this heavy makeup on, but I could see she had a black eye. George had been working all night with me at the theater. She'd been out with her young friends, hangs with a tough crowd. Wish he'd find himself a big sweet mama to take care of him so I don't have to worry after him."

"Len, if there is anything I can do to help, let me know."

"He'll be moving soon to 198 East Houston Street, and for sure, she'll follow him there. I'm stuck in the theater or the agency.

When you and Wyatt are galloping about, can you check in on him? Especially late in the night."

I also did not fully divulge to Margaret a comprehensive account of the goings-on at the Croisic. Wyatt lived a slice of the sporting life, but when everything is said and done, he did have a wife and children who served half anchor to a respectable life. For the bachelors at the Croisic, there were no such constraints. They worked only to afford their licentiousness. Their nights were spent in an endless pursuit of amusement and pleasure. Some pursuits were legal: saloon, dime museum, public bath house, and the dance halls where you paid for a lady's drink with hope of a dance and more. Most others were varying degrees of illicit: card games, horse betting, billiard parlors, brothels, and blood sports both animal and human.

They were men about town. The bachelors never went home as long as there was anything more interesting to see, or anywhere more inviting to go. They certainly harbored no interest in the endless purgatory of matrimony. To a man they were Jack Tanner, the main character in George Bernard Shaw's *Man and Superman*, where Tanner speaks of marriage as "apostasy, profanation of the sanctuary of my soul, a violation of my manhood, sale of my birthright, shameful surrender, ignominious capitulation, acceptance of defeat."

Except for when their beastly needs drove them to cry cyclops's tears into the columns of Venus at some whorehouse, they kept the company of men. This they did at all manner of clubs, from the volunteer fire brigades and political fraternities all the way up to the exclusive Knickerbocker Club. At the Knickerbocker, the right sort of fellow could lounge at all hours in well-appointed parlors, play on fancy billiard tables, sip fine wine or brandy, and indulge in high cuisine and expensive cigars. If one wished, one could find solitary comfort in any of the scores of leather-bound books lining the shelves, or more likely engage in the main draw of the club: the convivial ribbing of clubmen, the gross ribaldry, the flagrant gossip, and on occasion, the deep discussion of men, morals, and the stars in Heaven.

Of course, Dr. Clifton Kameny was a member. My neighbor at the Croisic even belonged for a time to the Zodiac Club, a circle so elite, so Pierpont Morgan, that only twelve members could be admitted at any one time. Clifton relinquished his seat so that a dear friend might join.

I stretched the truth, telling Margaret that Clifton's gatherings were uniformly stag. Whilst most of his parties were men only, high-society duties required that he host couples and unaccompanied women. So, I arrived at Clifton's séance unsurprised to see several women, including the medium herself. (Females supposedly contained greater predisposition to spiritual perfectibility.) One of the ladies dressed and moved as a man. While jarring at first, I recalled the similar behavior of the writer George Sand. This woman, who went by the name Sam, was witty, and within minutes, one took no notice of her comportment.

After refreshments, the medium emerged from a back room, cloaked in layers of oriental robes that revealed her long limbs and bare feet. A tortoise-shell comb tightly held back her strawberry-blonde hair.

Clifton pulled me aside. "You've expressed skepticism of spiritualism. I bid you not to share such thoughts with the other guests. And no names if you write this up."

He'd carefully selected guests, who were not aware of the debunker, watchmaker John Maskelyne, who skillfully replicated the Davenport brothers' cabinet of ghostly violins, or that the New York sisters Kate and Margaret Fox never contacted real spirits but were only facile with cheap stage tricks.

"Joshua, be so good as to give me your vow to keep an open mind, or at least a closed mouth."

"I fancy it the price of admission."

"Indeed, for the benefit of the others."

As we gathered around a table, the lights were switched off. Only a small, distant candle remained to save the room from total darkness. A stern warning issued that if we left our seats, broke the circle, or turned on the lights, the medium's decorporal essence might be trapped in the spirit world, leaving the poor woman an imbecile, or her essence might snap back so violently as to snuff out her life.

The medium implored her spirit guide to engage with us. Two of the women guests had recently lost infants to disease and sought to contact them. One wore an elaborate memento mori or mourning jewelry of fossilized driftwood with a cross woven with her departed daughter's hair. The medium gained contact with her spirit guide, a rough-hewn Spanish buccaneer. As he spoke through her, her voice became low, gruff, and accented. Dual pinpoints of light streaked around her head. The spirit claimed these as the souls of the children and assured the mothers their children were at peace beyond the grave. The mothers were each allowed to ask four yes-or-no questions. Being child spirits, they'd only recently learned to respond with knocks, one for yes and two for no. The mother's wasted inquiries disappointed me:

"Are you in any discomfort?"

"You know I love you?"

Chastened, I realized the mothers were in search of comfort, not intelligence of the afterlife. The children gave their distinctive raps, the mothers sobbed, and I was glad for the darkness.

Expectation was the séance had penetrated the spirit world as far as possible. Each of us relaxed our grips on our neighbors' hands when the table tilted, then levitated, then fell with a bang. After a collective gasp, and then confusion, we all fumbled to rejoin the circle of hands. The medium gave a guttural moan almost as if giving birth. A series of crackling noises sounded as the medium's moan became the Spanish buccaneer's raspy words.

"The children are not content! No. Their love is so strong they crave corporeal contact."

One mother shuddered and exclaimed, "I've been touched by a phantom hand!"

The mother on my right nearly yanked me off my chair as she cried out, "My Emily, my Emily!"

Next came a rustling and whoosh of air. On either side of the medium, a glowing death mask of an infant hovered in the air, features indistinct. Low, childlike whispers came from different parts of the room. I thought I heard "I love you" and "I miss you." Difficult to be certain. *Boom.* A flash blinded us all.

The medium chanted in her own voice in an accented language, neither Latin nor Greek (both which I studied), but some fairy tongue. At last, she said a brief prayer in English. Many at the table sighed in relief to see the lights switched on. The medium rose wearily to her feet and told us she must go lie down to regain her strength, as she had come close to a point of no return and was shaken to her core.

Days later when Clifton came knocking on my door with an invitation to the theater, I still brimmed with questions. He passed Wyatt in the hallway. I intended an evening in, as Wyatt headed to his gentleman's club and now preferred that I not accompany him to that particular establishment.

Wyatt told me, "You're a good friend, Josh, but a bad influence on the girls. We can't have them expecting a bravo performance every time. I go there to relax, not to do gymnastics."

I jumped at the opportunity to press Clifton on what I'd experienced at the séance. The chance to attend the legitimate theater was a pleasure in itself, and hocus-pocus articles did well with the *Sunday Journal*. As fit his station and social calendar, Clifton went about in a black-and-gold double brougham with coachmen on call, so the brisk November weather didn't concern. I put on my best bespoke Huntsman suit and left the covert coat on its hook.

Clifton provided me a bit of home. He'd resided in America for many years and even took on citizenship. Still the custom and manners of Suffolk clung to him, despite having been born and raised in Bury St. Edmunds and not leaving England until he came to the US for his psychiatry degree. There was no need to explain a turn of phrase or instruct him on—what appeared to be a grand mystery in America—the proper way to make a cup of tea.

Clifton's career choice had caused a bit of a tiff in his family. A Kameny boy could aspire to any occupation as long as it was solicitor, barrister, or judge. He claimed if you set off a bomb on Crown Street, you could take out generations of Kameny men as well as several ghosts haunting the Old Bailey. He further scandalized the family by moving to America, the only consolation for them being Clifton's firm commitment to bachelor life, so his errant tribe would die with its sole member.

As we stretched out in the coach, I could restrain myself no longer.

"You must tell me how she did it. I am sure you know."

"You didn't find the séance compelling?"

"It certainly was easy to be carried away in the moment, but I cannot accept the supernatural materialization of the two children."

"Isn't all religion supernatural? The faithful see an invisible hand at work in the affairs of men."

"That is different." It came out a little too forcefully, and I tried to calm myself.

"Is it? Don't some people claim to hear the actual voice of God, or experience visions? Do saints and angels float about us, protecting us from harm? At minimum, faith requires the belief that water can be made wine, that whole seas can be parted, and the dead can be brought to life."

"One can be devout and accept the realities of science. Religion tells us how to go about the world, not how the world goes about."

Clifton stroked his trim Vandyke. "So, I couldn't tempt you to a few hands of cards?" The brougham was modified to include a small fold-out game table.

"Not until you reveal the truth."

"Truth is a thief of delight. If I let you in, you must swear not to breathe a word, especially in the paper."

I placed my hand over my heart. "On my mother's grave."

"A noble oath. You see, my dear boy, the whole thing's an experiment. You know my psychiatric practice is primarily directed at men and women's sexuality, especially sexual identity. That's led me to a study of belief in general. How do the devout decide their belief is correct and superior to all others? How do we form the belief that one sex or race or nationality is inferior, and hold that belief even when confronted with clear evidence to the contrary?"

"Do not think me rude, but we will be at the theater soon. I don't want my mind on magic tricks during the entire performance."

Clifton took the deck of cards he'd been holding hopefully, and put them in his coat. "Very well. I handpicked the attendees of the séance. Different levels of education, religious adherence, class background. I liked you there in any case, but you being the son of a landed baron was a lucky accident. I wanted to see how open each person was to the experience—ah, but I see you are impatient for the raw mechanics.

"You noted, no doubt, the medium, Miss Taylor, was both long-limbed and barefooted. She and her assistant, the dapper Sam, received access to my room for several days. Two wires were strung under the table, one with a metal weight and one wooden. Miss Taylor is extremely flexible. She easily reached up with her bare toes and plucked those wires to produce the appropriate rapping."

"Sam was her confederate?"

"Not accomplice—assistant. It's hardly illicit."

"Most definitely chicanery." My neck was getting hot again.

"Come now. We're going to a play, no? You don't expect absolute truth on the stage. There's an element of illusion in most entertainment."

"I beg to differ, but go on. What of the phantom hands, the table levitation?"

"I assisted on the table. You recall Sam sat next to Miss Taylor, and I sat directly opposite. Pads were fitted under the table so the three of us could lift it with our knees. We only managed a couple of inches, but in the darkness . . . some guests swore it had hovered a foot in the air.

"I can see you're displeased with my playing a part in the deception, but it's my experiment. As to the phantom hands, all of us were holding hands around the circle, but of course, Sam and Miss Taylor had free use of one of their arms at any time. They each simply used a mechanical extending grabber to reach the woman's arms."

"And the pièce de résistance?"

"The materialized faces? Our medium's specialty. Quite simple, really. Miss Taylor donned several layers of robes. The outermost had thin whalebone slats embedded so she could flip the robe up like a screen. On the black fabric were the faces painted in oil of phosphorus. Sam does a remarkable job of throwing her voice in high falsetto to complete the effect."

"You knew the two mothers were going to ask about their departed children. Is that not a cruel trick?"

"Not at all. I didn't allow actual rag babies to run around. Both women's children died of sudden illnesses and were subject to speedy burials, mothers cheated of the opportunity to say goodbye to their loved ones. Each woman said they gained a good deal of peace from the encounter."

I didn't want to let Clifton off the hook so easily, yet I didn't have friendships to burn. In any case, we arrived at our destination. The Hoyt's Theater marque spelled out our evening's entertainment: *A Florida Enchantment*.

December 1896

My Dearest Margaret,

I am delighted to have received the Christmas card. You must have searched high and low to find such an elaborate folded design. Alas, I found nothing to match it, so am sending a note to wish you Happy Christmas and good tidings for the New Year.

The Yanks do a right cheery Christmas here in New York, though an octogenarian copyeditor told me his family did not really keep Christmas until we Brits gave them the Dickens, so to speak. There are a couple of odd traditions. At department stores like Macy's, long lines of children impatiently wait their turn to climb upon the lap of a man dressed in a Santa Claus costume and inform him of their consumptive wishes. That the children do not suspect this impostor, there being several Santas in town (a few not even managing a real beard), is beyond me.

The other tradition is much less self-serving, a charity called the Salvation Army. The leader, Booth, calls himself a general, and members wear ersatz military-dress uniforms. Around Christmas, members stand out-side with a large kettle, like the ones down at the London wharves, into which passersby drop donations for the poor. To attract attention, a member we saw in the Bowery rang a foot-long bell so loudly that I believe people were giving alms just to stop the noise. I overheard a crotchety old man grumble about saving another drunken bum, so I made a show of a large donation only to spite him.

I attended the queerest play with Clifton: *A Florida Enchantment.* After the horrible reviews, I doubt it will cross the pond, so I will not be spoiling it for you. I'm not sure I remember all precisely, but let me give you an idea of the bizarre plot.

An heiress, Lillian, travels to Florida accompanied by her mulatto maid, Jane. Lillian quarrels with her fiancé, Fred. She suspects, with some reason, he is unfaithful. Plain old melodrama? But wait.

Lillian purchases a mysterious box from Africa containing a vial labeled "A cure for women who suffer." The vial contains four magical seeds that change a person from one sex to the other.

To get revenge on Fred, she swallows a seed and instantly transforms into a man. Still dressed as female, she rushes around in a randy fever trying to seduce all the women. Since she is now Lawrence, a man, she must have a male valet not a maid, so she forces poor Jane to ingest a seed and become Jack. I should say here that Lillian was played by a woman who did a fine job in portraying the mannerisms of a man, making muscles and blowing cigar smoke into Fred's face. Jane was overplayed by a minstrel man I recognized, Dan Collyer, in blackface.

At some point Fred, in frustration, takes a seed and transforms into a woman and now attempts to seduce all the men. This confuses and angers the men, who end up chasing the former Fred off a pier to a watery death.

I may be alone on this, but I rather enjoyed it, as comic farce instead of drama. It was research for Clifton, since he deals with gender in his psychiatric practice. I must quote you a sampling of the reviews; they are deliciously vicious.

"The lowest depth to which the theatrical stage can be sunk by tasteless speculators."

"A few of the most indecent ideas that mortal man has ever tried to communicate to his fellow beings."

I thought the male reviewers were overly sensitive to Fred kissing the other men, but the *Times*'s Annie Russell dismissed the play as silly and vulgar: "Instead of avoiding causes of offense, it almost might be imagined that the author had sought them, so grossly and persistently did his characters disregard the ordinary proprieties of life."

I have only one other item to report. You may be shocked to learn that I attended a séance. Maybe not, as I understand Arthur Conan Doyle and our Queen have sought to reach out to the dead. I must ask you to wait until I return to relate the encounter.

I hope the time will pass quickly so I may see you again. I have much writing to complete before I leave here (mostly about New York, as I have only managed quick trips to Philadelphia and Boston), but if a human can go from conception to child in nine months, so may a book.

All my love,
Joshua

Chapter 11

With surprise and some measure of apprehension, I read the note the doorman handed to me. It was unlike Nowak to request my presence. Rather, he ignored me unless batting away my stories. I still couldn't fathom why my privileged background bothered Nowak but Hearst's didn't. The message, however, was clear: to come at once.

What could I have done wrong? I racked my brain on the coach ride over. As for the *Journal*, my postings were mainly poof pieces on singers, dancers, and comics. I sent to London several stories fed to me by Miss Moon, including the push for an anti-lynching law. I copied those to Nowak, shocked that he had printed a few.

Maybe they were more palatable since I endeavored to frame my articles on the plight of the Negro in America by focusing on people heroically working for justice. If anything, my approach to Nowak was cowardly. As I entered his office, I girded my loins and resolved to confront him directly.

"Sir, is this about the lynching articles? I insist that it's important the public be—"

"The what? No. You take me for a bigot?"

Nowak's face reddened. His menacing eyes impossibly became fiercer. "I'll have you know, I'm no such thing. I've not a word against the Sicilian or the Greek. They've as much right as the Polish to make America their home. And for sure, the Negroes, this is their home. I wish nothing but open doors for the Negro. It's a waste of national resources not to. Why, I've refused to attend another National League baseball game ever since 1887—and I adore baseball. I used to love to sit on the third baseline with my glove, snag a few foul balls. Listen, I attended that game where the Newark Bears sat out Fleet Walker and George Stovey, two of their best players, all so that race-baiter Cap Anson wouldn't get any black on him. Weren't asking to marry his daughters. Just play the damn game. Let those Negro boys rise or fall on their own credit. The Cuban Giants have been my favorite team ever since."

Baseball still a mystery to me, I pressed: "Then why am I here?"

"You've got a package, you royal dimwit. I know what it is, says 'Oliver' in full caps right on the box, but that old crank TJ Hanks in the mailroom threatened a federal offense if I opened it. Go on."

Nowak pulled me by the arm over to a large box on the floor, then stood peering over my shoulder like a boy who'd just discovered a misplaced Christmas present. The appellation "OLIVER" meant nothing to me. Nowak, meanwhile, shoved the hilt of a sword-shaped letter opener into my palm. Slicing open the box, I reached through the packing paper and lifted the machine into the air.

Nowak waved me to place it on the desk in front of his chair. The nickel-plated Oliver No. 1 was majestic: black keys, numbers and figures listed below the letters, and twin towers of steepled typebars.

Nowak grimaced. "Sheesh, they should've gotten you a Hammond No. 12. That's what the Chief is bringing in for the *Journal*. If it's a good enough typewriter for us, it's good enough for you."

"Is the Oliver special?"

"You even know how to type, Cub?"

In truth, my experience was limited to a few hours dotting about on an old Remington #2. "Of course I do."

"Yeah, yeah. Grab some paper over there. A carbon, too."

Nowak loaded the cartridge and set into typing. He seemed at peace, a snarling dog who'd been thrown his favorite toy.

"Ah, listen to that glorious sound, the literary piano."

"You appear quite at home."

"Damn right. I typed on an original Sholes and Glidden, sewing-machine treadle and all—a beast. I worked Caligraphs and Crandalls, but this one *is* special. Even an idiot like you must see it."

I studied the machine as Nowak clacked away, typebars rising and stabbing the paper, the legs of a mechanized spider spinning words. Nowak set out the same phrase over and over: "Now is the time for all good men to come to the aid of their party."

"I can read what you're typing. The cartridge is not blind."

"Exactly. Look, you can't leave the Oliver in your rooms. You have maids and building supers?"

"Yes?"

"It could go missing. Tell you what. There's a small storage room just down the hall. I'll set it up there. You and I will have a key."

I assented, mostly because I doubted I wanted to adapt to the Oliver. I enjoyed the touch of pen to paper.

"And Cub, don't let on you have sort of an office. You'll stir up the others, and you don't need any more detractors."

"Detractors? Is Mr. Hearst unhappy with me?"

"Kid, he hardly knows you're alive."

"Mr. Carvalho, then?"

"The grim Quixote? No. In fact, he wants you to start working up an in-depth article on same-sex perversion, to be published the day that pervert Oscar Wilde is released. Word is, the degenerate gets sprung this spring. Carvalho figures it'll come off more refined when reported by another Brit. He wants it all—history, men, women, and especially scandals. Talk to doctors, the whole kielbasa, don't censor or edit. We'll cut it down here."

An immediate and fierce *He is Irish not British, you dolt* came to mind, but I was too shocked at receiving an assignment from Nowak, even one forced upon him. Thinking it best not to draw attention to this breakthrough, I went back to the subject of the typewriter.

"I'm taken aback that the Old Man had lain out for a fancy Oliver. He is frugal in the extreme."

"I bet he is. This is an older demonstration model. They don't make them anymore. The No. 2 has a removable cartridge. He probably Jewed them down hard."

"Pardon, Mr. Nowak. Since you spoke earlier about your welcoming view of all our brethren, I should tell you many Jewish people find that expression extremely insulting."

"Insult those fiends? Impossible. The rabbinical cabal is an abomination that's brought universal misery and wretchedness across the globe. Money-stained fingers reaching everywhere. If not for the Jews, Poland would still be a state, unpartitioned."

"How are the Jews possibly responsible for the czar? Have not the Jews suffered along with the Poles? The papers say the Russians conduct pogroms on the Jews. Many have died."

"Phony news. Jews cause trouble wherever they go. Look at that Judas, Alfred Dreyfus, selling out France to the Germans. Degradation and Devil's Island is too good. He should hang."

I knew I should make my excuses and leave, but I couldn't. I hoped I wasn't turning red.

"Many French think him wrongly accused, all because he is a Jew. There is talk of evidence pointing to another officer," I said.

"Let France be French. Drop the scales from your eyes, Banks. You think the German Jews in England are loyal subjects? Rothschild may waggle himself a baronhood and sit in the House of Lords, but they're all internationalists. Are you aware of the botched Jameson Raid down in the South African Transvaal last year? Rothschild's puppet Cecil Rhodes tried to set off an uprising for diamonds and gold."

"You misstate Baron Rothschild's actions. His bank lends to all: Austria, Egypt, Russian, and indeed, the USA. My father dealt with Rothschild and claims him honest and forthright."

"Your father's bamboozled. We'll see what the British think after the Jews pull them into a war with the Boers. You'll cry out for jus sanguinis."

"I think you take a seed of truth then conflate it into a twisted forest. Falsity compounded by each degree of truth contained. For every wealthy Jew, hundreds barely find bread. For every Jew in a position of influence, a thousand Saxons. Remember, this paper, your own *Journal*, disputed Reverend Halderman's claim that the Jews own New York."

Nowak sighed and ran his hand through his hair. "I'm not saying the Chief is a stooge. He's a fighter on a lot of fronts. It's just, he's got lots of cash, high finance. He doesn't want to ruffle the Jews' feathers. Jews manipulate the common press. You have to look elsewhere for the real truth. Here, take these."

Nowak riffled through a cabinet and handed me two books: *The Jewish Cemetery in Prague* by Goedsche, and Osman Bey's *The Conquest of the World by the Jews*. I could feel the weight of misplaced hate in my hands. On my way out of the newsroom, I tossed the books in the wastepaper bin, a Parthian shot. I hoped Nowak would see them.

"It's certainly audacious." Clifton set the tea tray on his parlor table and paced around me. "It will be a delightful caper to pull off. Is she ebony?"

The question embarrassed me, but it was a reasonable inquiry. "No, tea with a touch of milk—no, too washed out—warmer, maybe lightly toasted bread?"

Wyatt, who'd been sitting quietly, shook his head. "Toasted bread? Really? You two've lost your minds. You won't get away with it."

"Hush Wyatt," Clifton said. "It's a Bal Poudré.

Wyatt stared at Clifton with palms up in a "what" gesture.

Clifton explained: "A masquerade party with a Louis XV Versailles theme, and German, Spanish, American, English of the period. The Bradley-Martins withheld the requirements until the last minute so every costumer, milliner, dressmaker, wigmaker and jeweler are besieged, and every old wardrobe will be ransacked."

"Doesn't that make you two's scheme more impossible?" said Wyatt. "The party's tomorrow, you know."

"No, Wyatt, because I have, as you say, an inside straight." Clifton made a hand gesture as if fanning cards. "I'm intimate with all the theater people in town. That includes all the costumers and makeup artists. They'll be able to lighten up Miss Moon as much as need be."

"You are sure no one will see through the ruse?" I said. "If Miss Moon is embarrassed, I believe she will never forgive me."

"Don't worry. She'll appear quite natural, even though natural isn't necessary." Clifton winked. "Women courtiers of that period often wore hideous layers of face paint."

"I am concerned, and will have to allay Miss Moon's fears to convince her. She has beautiful features, but her nose, her lips, are not overly but yet distinctly African."

"No fear, my boy. Leonardo's an absolute artist. He can thin out her nose and shape her lips. You'll see. He'll make her face a mask and then create what illusion is required. He did up that old hag Henry for a ball last year. You would've thought he was Don Juan."

Wyatt sighed and rubbed his forehead with his palm. "Why isn't Clifton going if this is such a grand to-do?"

"It's a couple's event. A fatal social faux pas to attend solo. My regular for such occasions, the Dowager Whitney, is away on safari, so I'm passing on my invitation to Joshua."

"Okey-dokey then," said Wyatt, "but Josh, why in blue blazes are you going, and why with Miss Moon?"

"It is a huge scoop," I said. "What a story, here and abroad. And my book is becoming more about class in America. This soiree will be historic. Others may write about it, but to be in the belly of the beast—"

"And Miss Moon?" Wyatt seemed to catch himself and added, "I mean, I like her and all, but you have to admit, it complicates everything."

"She is in town and the only woman I am familiar with in New York."

Wyatt let out a grunt. "Familiar? Ha. Lady L asks about you all the time. She'd jump at the chance to cut the rug at some fancy ball."

I couldn't restrain a slight blush at hearing Lady L mentioned. "It would do her a cruelty. No matter my explanations, she will interpret such a high-level invitation as some manner of courtship. On the other hand, given the prejudices and social constructs of our times, Miss Moon will be under no such illusions."

"That settles it." Clifton rubbed his hands together. "And I know precisely what costumes you'll wear. I saw them in a play two years ago, and they never throw out such elaborate costumes."

"What?" Wyatt and I asked in unison.

"King George III and Charlotte, Queen of the Americas."

I began to chuckle, and so did Clifton. Wyatt stared.

"Why are you two giggling like schoolgirls?"

Clifton regained his composure. "I must first emphasize that Queen Charlotte is much admired even if George is a mixed affair. Fifteen heirs issued, thirteen survived. Mozart dedicated Opus III in her honor. Well, she was German but descended from a branch of the Portuguese royal family. The Portuguese didn't just colonize the land in Africa, they colonized the women as well."

Wyatt looked perplexed. "Are you saying . . .? I don't believe it. I've never heard such a thing."

"We do not really advertise the fact, especially to the rabble," I said.

Clifton nodded. "Most paintings downplay it, but if you look at Allan Ramsay's coronation portrait, you can see she is positively of African linage."

He looked back at me. "Joshua, you must take the brougham. You cannot pull up in a hack for this affair. Also, you'll need Wyatt to drive."

"Why me? Wyatt said. "You've got a coachman."

"I may have need of him tomorrow, and Wyatt will be more useful should an extraction prove necessary. The ball begins at 11:00 p.m. You'll want to wait until after the lackeys have announced the guests and the characters they impersonate. Now get about your business. You must convince Miss Moon and get her to Leonardo at the theater tomorrow by seven at the latest."

It almost didn't happen. I attempted to explain the necessity for the ruse. First I needed to convince her it would be a refined affair, not at all like January's French Ball, which had made headlines for its open debauchery. Miss Moon was by turns intrigued, offended, obstinate, and enticed. She'd come to New York specifically to deliver me pictures of lynchings and other debasements, as well to fully brief me on anti-lynching bills and Mrs. Wells-Barnett's recent activities. She chastised me for attempting to force her into a ridiculous charade in order to carry out her duties.

I could see Miss Moon was torn. Part of her, a still-young woman, longed to cross the newly installed velvet ropes at the Waldorf into such a fabulous party. The other part feared the demeaning repercussions of revealment. She expressed deep suspicions of Leonardo's abilities.

"Clifton was insistent that Leonardo is a magician with makeup. You will be in wig and gloves, and a high-necked gown."

Despite all the assurances and promises of an enthralling

adventure, the proposal continued to lose ground until I stumbled accidentally on the proper lure.

"Miss Moon, are you afraid of the dances, *les moulinet*, the gallopade, the minuet?"

"Afraid? *Afraid?* Why should I be afraid of a dance? You think a formal dance is above me? That a two-step cakewalk is all my kind is capable of? I will take your gallop waltz and leave you panting. The minuet? I'll show you regular and Viennese, and three different mazurkas to boot. Take me to Leonardo at once. Afraid of a dance, *hmph*."

Steam rose from the nostrils of the horses in the cold November night. We approached the Waldorf-Astoria on the West Thirty-Third Street side, as guests were to use Manager Boldt's private entrance. Wyatt leaned down to the compartment.

"Got to be two hundred police surrounding this place. Pretty sure I saw Teddy Roosevelt himself."

Clifton's arrangements included a concierge of his acquaintance to signal us when the Hungarian Band reached its seventh selection, Maestro Koevessy's violin solo on "Légende" by Wieniawski. We would take our time making sure the introductions were complete. When the moment came, we entered without incident. In truth, our theater outfits were so majestic I thought they might have let us into Buckingham Palace. We moved through private rooms to the hotel proper and up to the second floor. There, preparing the guests, were hairdressers, costumers, and modesties in over a dozen rooms, including the Astor dining room.

As we descended to the ballroom on the first floor, we heard the Hungarian Band play Wagner's "Lohengrin." Along our way stood antique vases filled with a rainbow of roses and a massive mirror framed in American Beauty roses.

Crossing the threshold, our senses flooded. Ancient tapestries emblazoned with acts of royal chivalry draped all the way to the floor. An attack of roses of all colors had been launched against the tapestries and lay on the floor or clung in the folds. The Hungarian Band played hidden behind a bower, an arching explosion of long-stemmed roses.

Miss Moon whispered to me. "My God, there's another room."

We passed out of the salon, through corridors of woodland bowers, carried on waves of floral fragrance to a fantasy forest of green leaves and tiny incandescent lamps, into the main ballroom. Miss Moon couldn't help but gawk, then caught herself.

"This must be all a matter of course for you."

"Madam, not in Yorkshire."

I'd served my time at a myriad of obligatory fetes and masquerades, and once or twice found pleasure, especially when matched with an energetic dancer such as Margaret, but a Yorkie would have been taunted to tears for the dripping excess that met our eyes.

Fifteen huge mirrors were sunk like jewels into an immense wall of lowzet garlands, entwined demousa vine and a relentless display of mauve orchids. About the room, touches of blue silk gave birth to an issue of pink roses. A further rain of pink roses obscured the upper minstrel's gallery. Below, imported clematis overhung ivy-covered flirtation nooks.

The Bradley-Martins had embraced an inherited fortune and filigreed it with the marriage of their daughter to the Earl of Craven. Of course, the host chose to stride about as Louis XIV, the Sun King himself. The hostess matched this with the odd choice of Mary, Queen of Scots, uncharacteristically plump and busty for Mary Stuart, and flouting a necklace from the real Marie Antoinette. None of the fifty costumed Antoinettes prowling the party seemed to mind.

I, who'd been raised in wealth, was still gobsmacked at the naked display of it. John Jacob Astor appeared as Henry of Navarre, but his mother, one of the Antoinettes, was festooned with $250,000 worth of jewels. Oliver Belmont wore a suit of armor with gold inlay so heavy he moved like an anchor. The fictive Romeo and Juliet cavorted playfully with Joan of Arc. Empress Josephine engaged in rapt conversation with Sir Walter Raleigh. I was sure I was witnessing the greatest concentration of millionaires ever assembled on earth.

Back home, even Daisy Greville, the countess, became so ashamed after the infamous Bal Poudré at Warwick Castle, she converted to socialism, although she did not relinquish her champagne flute. I didn't foresee any socialist conversions imminent among the seven hundred or so guests.

Before general dancing could commence about midnight, it appeared necessary that no less than three quadrilles of honor clearly displayed the social order, starting with several couples containing both Martin and Astor. As I returned with Roman punch, I saw a George Washington breaking character to drill Miss Moon on her identity. I hurried to her side, spilling punch with each step.

"President Washington, delighted to finally meet you."

He turned his puzzled attention to me. "You're actually British, aren't you?"

"I should think the King of England would be."

He gave a forced laugh. "Yes, George the Third and Washington. We should meet on the dance floor for a rematch."

"They say you will return to your farm. If you do, you will be the greatest man in history."

He brightened at the reflected flattery. Miss Moon still looked pained.

"Now if you will excuse us, I have need of the Queen."

I handed Miss Moon her glass and took her free arm as we moved in a stately pace through the crowd. We quickly agreed it prudent to sit out the initial formation dances, the stars, the visits, and the like, that required frequent changes of partners. We would wait for the couple's dances.

When the time seemed opportune, Miss Moon kept playacting.

"My Lord, might we take the floor?"

The dancers were performing the long scarves and winding alley dances. Several couples formed a corridor holding aloft scarves to create a canopy of hues. At the end, a woman wound herself up with the scarf of her partner, who led her under the canopy of scarves, playing her out like a yo-yo at the end, then taking their place on the canopy line for the next couple. I noted, for the first time, that Miss Moon revealed a charming dimple when she smiled.

We danced well as a pair, but not so much as to draw stares, as a few flashy couples did. Miss Moon generously allowed my lead, while still adding her own improvisations to the glide mazurka's slides and little leaps. We spoke little and smiled much until a slow minuet, when Miss Moon's face turned serious.

"I haven't forgotten we've business to attend to."

"Come, my Queen, let us be gay. Did you know that in the court of Louis XIV, dancers of the minuet were expected, and encouraged, to kiss?"

"My Lord, the punch has gone to your head. Would you so easily breach your oath to me? I'm here as co-infiltrator, not beau. The lynchings continue, and yet they never see the front page of the *Journal*, *World,* or *Times*, if they receive any ink at all."

"I share your concern, but know there are those who feel that when something happens all the time, it ceases to be news. Besides, Hearst is obsessed with Cuba. He is intent on writing America into war with Spain. The drumbeat has gotten so shrill, New Jersey libraries have removed the *Journal* from their shelves. People have begun to dismiss us and the *World* as propaganda, calling us the Yellows, like the comic, *The Yellow Kid.*"

"The papers barely covered Plessy vs. Ferguson last May, before forgetting it completely."

"Surely that court decision will have little effect outside the Deep

South, and how long can Southerners continue to awkwardly walk backward?"

I could immediately tell I angered her.

"Your Highness should take care to be better informed. Separate but equal is a door to decades of inequality and second-class citizenship. If you can segregate a people, you can subjugate a people. It has deteriorated each hour, in Boston as well as in Atlanta, in Denver and Detroit as well as in Mobile."

Miss Moon made an increasingly convincing case as she cataloged the construction of Jim Crow across the nation. She explained how segregation of entertainments followed conveyances. New churches and private schools were set up to shield White children, especially White girls, from interaction with Negroes. Most insidious of all was the deliberate sorting of black bodies into concentrated areas, a reservation system parallel to White society. Different geography justifying different resources, conditions, and outcomes. State after state were rewriting their very constitutions to cement Jim Crow as foundational law.

Miss Moon only relented when a surprise volta dance made it impossible to both dance and talk. A few turns in, she allowed herself to take pleasure in the dance, and when I aided her sauté majeure, she leaped very high—no easy task in her long green-and-gold gown. I didn't mind in the least that the volta required the partners to pull intimately into one another, face-to-face. I'd read that Madam de Valentinois recited the psalms to allay her guilt whilst dancing the volta.

We were just finishing when Clifton's inside concierge waved us over and handed me a note.

> Upon further reflection, I deem it advisable that you leave before dinner in the Empire Room. You'd only be six to a table, and the opportunity of detection of our little charade is

too high. My man will see you off with a basket sampling of dinner.

Clifton

The concierge led us to Peacock Alley so we could walk the nearly thousand feet from the Astoria to exit the Waldorf, where Wyatt waited, already fortified by our dinner baskets. Before we could make a clean getaway, I witnessed a police officer attempting to take Stephen Crane into custody for public drunkenness. As I knew Crane from the paper, I ran to his aid. I think the officer relented only because of the hilarity of King George pleading the famous author's case. He allowed us to bundle Crane into a cab home.

Wyatt played the gallant and helped Queen Moon into the brougham, then placed the baskets inside.

"Wyatt, do you want some food?"

"Don't worry on me. Clifton's a real prince. He's had them smuggling food out to me all night. I'm about ready to explode from beef Jardin in béarnaise sauce, half a dozen plover eggs, and the most luscious French ice cream with cherry kirsch and candied chestnuts."

"Are you fit to drive? You look a sip shy of squiffy."

"Naw, didn't even finish my champagne. I'm on the Keeley cure, bichloride of gold. I got the initial four injections yesterday and have been dosing the liquid cordial every two hours."

Wyatt held out a medical-looking bottle, two-thirds drained. I took off the cap and smelled.

"My God, man, it reeks of a surgery. Wyatt, I briefly attended medical school, and all I detect is alcohol and bella-donna. Keep this up you will be seeing fairies."

"Becca saw the advertisements—thought it would be good for me."

"Deal with that later. Shooting gold into your veins, and downing this poison, cannot be healthy."

I poured out the remainder into the gutter. Wyatt seemed relieved. He guided the coach through Central Park while Miss Moon and I shared a very late dinner, or perhaps the city's most extravagant breakfast. As the coach meandered by the Reservoir, we feasted on caviar-stuffed oysters, turtle, foie gras, and suckling pig—only a hint of the twenty-eight dishes served back at the ball. Wyatt stopped the brougham near the Great Lawn so we could gaze on the seven-story Cleopatra's Needle as Miss Moon and I finished our Moët & Chandon.

Examining the hieroglyphs, I felt a pang of homesickness and a vague sense of guilt. Two years ago, I sat on the Victoria Embankment in London with Margaret, admiring this obelisk's twin from Egypt.

"I think it's time you drop me at my lodgings, King George," Miss Moon said. "I'll see this costume returned by evening today."

Our delicacies had been consumed in light-hearted gusto, but now Miss Moon's bright spirit seemed eclipsed by deep thought.

"What is it? I hope I have not made some error in decorum. I so wanted you to enjoy the evening."

I saw her swallow hard, and she fought back tears.

"It's just—for moments tonight—I didn't have to worry or fear moving a black body through the world. I met the gaze of others, who judged me solely on the grace of my dance, the height of my leap. I fear I may never know that feeling again."

Unedited Special Feature
JOSHUA BANKS

The New York Journal
May 19, 1897

OSCAR WILDE RELEASED

Today prisoner C33 walked out of Reading Gaol, a man free of physical confinement, but with his name still in the stocks. After two years of hard labor, perhaps he took solace in one of his own witticisms: “Every saint has a past, and every sinner has a future.”

Most readers have already formed a fixed opinion about Oscar Wilde, especially those who consider themselves pillars of moral authority. We should all take pains not to fall into the trap prisoner C33 warned of: “Morality is simply the attitude we adopt toward people we personally dislike.” I ask the reader to open their mind, if not their heart, to what the finest medical minds have to say on the sexual proclivities at the center of this scandal. First, for those who have been scaling the Himalayan mountains for the last several years, I will review the blazing meteor arc of Oscar Wilde.

Americans first became aware of Wilde through his successful lecture tour here in 1882. Some found aestheticism, its focus on beauty and pleasure, unmanly, but Wilde was known to acquit himself well in a school fight, and when in Leadville, he descended a mine shaft to drink whiskey and joke with the miners.

The decadent hedonism of the central character in the novel, *The Picture of Dorian Gray*, offended the tender public. Wilde toned down the more flagrant homoerotic aspects between editions, but does not Gray end the novel dissipated, then dead? While others object to the Biblical depictions in his play *Salomé*, who does not delight in the web of secrets played out in *Lady Windermere's Fan*, or the alternative persona adopted for town and country in *The Importance of Being Earnest*?

If not for Wilde's misguided entanglement with young Lord Alfred Douglas, Wilde would be celebrated, not pilloried. Unfortunately, as the playwright admitted, "I can resist everything except temptation."

The facts of his fall from grace were fully covered on these shores and were a grand cause célèbre in Britain: Lord Douglas's father—the Ninth Marquess of Queensberry's—oddly phrased and misspelled calling card left at Wilde's club "For Oscar Wilde, posing somdomite," Wilde's reckless overreaction suing the Marquess for criminal liable, Wilde flippantly playing to the courtroom crowd while digging his legal grave, the threat of tawdry testimony of lower-class male prostitutes, Wilde forced to withdraw his case and reimburse the Marquess.

All this is sufficient to wreck a man. When Wilde was arrested at the Cadogan Hotel on charges of sodomy and gross indecency (acts just shy of buggery), he was reported to be carrying a Beardsley illustrated *Yellow Book*. The odd periodical with its promotion of decadent excess reflecting on Wilde. Alas, this reporter has on strong authority that the story is false. It was, in fact, the yellow-bound *Aphrodite* by Pierre Louÿs, a racy bit of bestselling trash. It might be more appropriate if he'd been clutching Joris-Karl Huysmans's *Against Nature*, with its embrace of the irrational, rejection of accepted culture, and insistence that a true artist can replace mother nature by sheer artifice.

Clearly, the state was determined to see Wilde convicted and imprisoned. By the time he stood in the dock and defended, "The love that dare not speak its name"—the affection between an older man of intellect and a younger man full of joy, and the glamour of the life before him—Wilde's fate was already determined.

What can modern science tell us about the persistent occurrence of same-sex attraction in history? This reporter was fortunate to interview Dr. Clifton Kameny, renowned expert on sexual preference and identity. Recent scholarship questioned the traditional thought that engaging in a homosexual act was a choice that an otherwise normal heterosexual man might make for various reasons. We know of prison sex that occurs due to young men deprived of recourse to women, and the infamous rum, sodomy, and the lash of long sea voyages. That same individual who so indulged, upon return to female society, would revert to male-female relations.

Now some researchers like Havelock Ellis argue that homosexuality should not be considered a crime, but instead a congenital, involuntary physiological abnormality. Nature, not choice. Dr. Kameny is wary of this approach. While he supports the goal of decriminalizing sexual behavior, he is reluctant to have homosexual acts come to define identity.

"We're transforming the practice of sodomy into a kind of interior androgyny. The sodomite had been experiencing a temporary aberration. We risk turning the homosexual into a separate species. This might lead to increased opprobrium and discrimination."

Dr. Kameny agrees with Dr. Magnus Hirschfeld of Berlin on the universality of homosexuality. He breaks with his colleague on the theory that male homosexuals are by nature effeminate.

"Hirschfeld should know better since he, as I, have treated extremely masculine men in positions of command in the army."

If we look at sexual inversion in women, the reader is likely to imagine the lurid trial of Alice Mitchell. The public wanted to connect her murdering her female lover with Mitchell's attempt to pass permanently as a man. The idea that lesbian pathology leads to madness may comfort some people's prejudices, but one need only to note the number of spinsters living together in so-called Boston marriages, to refute that idea.

Dr. Kameny's hope is that society can develop an expansive view of the range of acceptable sexual identities. He envisions a future continuum of masculinity and femininity that exists within both genders without the need to hyper-categorize.

All this is too late to save Oscar Wilde. Only time will determine if he is hero or villain.

June 1897

Dear Joshua,

I hope my brief holiday cards and notes have kept me in your thoughts. Be assured your notes have been a comfort. I should have written a longer letter, but I've a wonderful excuse. Father relented and permitted me to attend St. Hilda's College. I didn't tell you in case I dropped out. I only just returned from first year. I can't express how transformative it is to challenge the mind with science, math, and astronomy. In return, I had to agree to appearances at the full social calendar. What a bore. But college is worth a slew of tedious parties.

Did you read what asses the boys at your alma mater made of themselves? Cambridge was to grant women equal degrees. You'd think we threatened to cut off their manhood. Undergrads hung up women in effigy. One example hung on the Trinity Street bookstore, a scholar in bloomers and striped socks riding a bicycle. Boys mutilated them. Shot fireworks at the windows of the women's colleges. Nearly rioted like fussy children until the vote was defeated. I know you cherish your school tie, but I shall make you burn them all.

Sorry you missed the Queen's Diamond Jubilee. Union Jacks hung everywhere. There were more flowers than you can imagine. The dear Queen was still in mourning black, but all else was so bright. The American Mark Twain—well received, by the way—said it was more an event for the camera than the pen. The grand procession had seventeen carriages, the royal family and representatives from all the Dominions. It's amazing, if not alarming, that this tiny isle rules over a quarter of the world's population. We're on every continent. The sun truly never sets on the Empire. Don't dare tell Father, but I think we may have overextended ourselves, like Rome, France, or Spain.

We encountered your father James at the Jubilee. He was feeling out of breath in all the tussle. My brother and I sat with him awhile. It arose in conversation on horses that you were a promising steeplechase rider. Your father said near championship level. He couldn't say why you gave it up.

Joshua, why didn't you tell me? Now that I'm riding again, you must show me how to jump. Not the stone walls mind you, but the course jumps.

I must tell you these almost two years have been so hard. I felt a forgetting curve, all the good events like a string of pearls bunched at the beginning. I fear that, reunited, we will only remember being separate. Does that make sense to you?

Well, no matter. You don't need to write back, for I shall see and embrace you in a few short months.

Impatiently,
Margaret

Chapter 12

As I stood on the curb waiting to be picked up, I paced back and forth in the stagnant July heat. Wyatt's wife, Becca, had summoned me to dinner after almost two years of hearing him alternately praise and complain about her. I fretted over what to bring. Wine? Knowing Wyatt's bouts with intemperance, I disposed of that idea. Pie? I knew a marvelous baker, and Americans were obsessed with pie. But what if Becca also baked pie, and mine was embarrassingly superior? I settled on a selection of Dutch cheeses, Beemster Classic, a young Gouda, and an odd hard cheese with cumin and cloves, the last forced on me by the cheesemonger, who called it Nail Cheese.

Wyatt evidently shared my anxiety, because he pulled up with a sour face and brusque manner. I mounted the aging Jenny Lind, once colored a shiny plum but now a weathered gray, its jaunty fringe faded and gap-toothed. I didn't say anything but stopped to wipe the dust from the bench seat.

"Not up to standards, Your Majesty?"

"Be fair, Wyatt. This nightingale is in decline."

"I don't want to stand out in my neighborhood in a fancy rig. I'd stick out like cuff links on a gravedigger. People would think I'd won a lottery and start asking for loans."

"I understand."

"Plus, if Becca sees that Spider, she'll want to know why I've never taken her out in it."

We weaved down toward the Lower East Side. Watching the

familiar muscular gait of a Cleveland Bay pulling our buggy triggered sentimental memories of childhood Yorkshire.

"I can't believe you're going to up and leave," said Wyatt.

"It is my home, Wyatt. My term's concluded. A new man replaces me in September. He will need your help."

"I'm not a whore."

"My God, you are mad at me for leaving. That is really so sweet."

"Shut the hell up."

"No, no, sincerely. Not sure how I was going to say this, but I will miss you severely. You must come visit. I can pay your fare."

"I'm not a charity case." Wyatt looked indignant.

"Of course not, but you must stay with us in the country. We have rooms in Mayfair as well."

"You really sound like a pompous toff."

"Picking up the lingo, eh? I suppose I did. The point is, I do not hold our friendship cheap."

"It's so unfair. As I get older, there are fewer and fewer people who I want to spend time with."

"We have several weeks. We will make the most of it."

Wyatt brightened. "Hey, let's share a toast of champagne on the way back to your hotel." Then he frowned. "There's no wine at dinner tonight."

Entering the Lower East Side, I realized I practically ignored this part of the city. The neighborhoods vibrated like a beehive turned inside out. In the quiet avenues uptown, most activity took place behind closed doors. Here, life played out on sidewalk and street. Wyatt was right about the absence of fancy coaches. Instead, all manner of conveyances vied for space: brick wagon and fruit truck, wheelbarrow and bicycle, pushcart and pram. Wyatt parked the rig in front of a kosher butchery and was immediately waved over by an orthodox man (beard, forelocks, black hat) sweating in layers of wool. The two shook hands warmly, then launched into a pidgin of English and Yiddish. I recognized Yiddish from vaudeville comics, but could not decipher a word of the brief conversation. Wyatt returned with a newspaper tucked under his arm, and waved me to follow.

Pushing through crowds on Orchard Street to Wyatt's building, I asked, "Who was that?"

"Asher Lustmann, the butcher. Good man. Gives me a discount. In return, I do odd jobs for him on Fridays, in case he needs to take a delivery or something while he keeps the Sabbath."

"What was he saying, the pointing and all?"

"His wife and daughter are in my apartment. Asher's hungry, wants me to send them home."

"I get you knowing French, but Yiddish?"

"Oh, it's in the air, you kind of pick it up. And Asher gives me these." He held the newspaper written in Yiddish with a masthead that read *Forvard*. "I can't quite get Hebrew, but Yiddish reminds me of Pennsylvania Dutch. These people sort of remind me of the Amish."

"What do you mean 'reminds' you?"

"I told you my sainted mother was from Inishmaan Island. Desolate place, I hear. Stone walls, fog, cliffs, sea. After a few years, New York overwhelmed her nerves, so she moved us to Lancaster, Pennsylvania. We lived among the Home Amish. They can be standoffish, but they recognized my mother as a plain and devout soul and accepted us. Nice place to grow up, but we had to come back to the city for work."

"Wyatt, you never mentioned your father."

"He could be raising a bowl in Ireland for all I know. All Mother would say is that a son is a grand improvement over a husband."

As I stumbled into the tenement from the sun-bleached pavement, my eyes were slow to adjust to the dimly lit interior. Having become so accustomed to electric lights in the States, I mentioned the scattered gaslights to Wyatt.

"Damn glad to have them. Plenty of tenements are still using kerosene lamps. We've a working sink in our kitchen, and a shared toilet and bath on each floor. God, I hate outhouses. Broil in the summer and freeze your ass off in the winter. If I'd moved us in to a place with outhouses, Becca would've left me for sure."

Wyatt gave a courtesy knock before leading me into his flat. We entered into a kitchen, past a large stove covered in cooking pots spewing heat like a captured sun. I smelled cabbage, pork. A large open window took up most of the wall, letting in the air from front parlor to kitchen.

Clustered around a table in the parlor were two women with two young children and an older girl. At first, I mistook both children as girls, then determined the younger as a boy still in pipe curls and a dress. Wyatt read my face, shook his head with a finger to his lips. All hands were rapidly assembling bunches of artificial flowers. Stacks of faux florals surrounded the room. Mrs. Lustmann and her daughter were obvious by their clothing and Eastern European features. Becca, in simple gingham dress with her hair up in a bonnet, rose to greet us.

"Sorry for the mess. The sweater, our buyer, comes to collect these arrangements tomorrow."

"Well, least I did not bring flowers," I said.

Wyatt chuckled mildly, but no one else joined in.

Becca assessed me much as a trapper deciding how best to gut and skin a deer.

"Wyatt tells me you're soon to head home."

"Yes, to England."

"You'll be replaced?" She forced her face into a semblance of a smile, but her eyes were unmerciful.

"Indeed."

"Shall the new man also cover the gaudy amusements at all hours?"

"I should hope not, madam. If they send a common bloke, I dare say he might get on better with my editor, Nowak."

"Right. You're a baron or something?"

"The younger son of a baron. My brother John shall be the only baron."

"Hardly seems fair, does it? I see you brought us a gift. You needn't, you know."

Becca took the box and mechanically removed the Beemster and Gouda, placing them on the small table in the kitchen. When she saw the spiced cheese, she smiled in spite of herself.

"Nagelkaas? Where on earth did you find Nagelkaas?"

"The monger said it was rare."

"I must take half to my mother. She will be beside herself."

At that precise moment, I nearly screamed like a frightened girl. A large gray squirrel had leaped from God-knows-where onto my shoulder and immediately nuzzled his damp snout into my ear. Everyone burst out laughing, even the stern-faced Mrs. Lustmann, so hard her wig shook. She was still chuckling as she and her daughter left.

"Judy," Wyatt yelled. "Put Mungo back on his chain."

Mungo bounded across the room and was scooped up by the girl. She nearly fell overreaching for the pet. I realized she wore leg braces.

"Sorry," Wyatt said. "Judy wanted a dog, but it's too cramped in here, and if it barked the neighbors would hate us. What's more, we can collect nuts in the park for free. Mungo sorts them by size."

"Mungo?"

"Named after Benjamin Franklin's squirrel. He wrote a eulogy for his."

I was grateful to have lightened the mood, and gathered some sympathy. Nevertheless, I'd nearly spent a penny in my trousers.

Dinner went pleasantly enough, but I sensed that I'd done some slight to Becca and she was not yet ready to forgive. She grew especially frosty when Wyatt rose to take me back to the Croisic.

"Don't be banging about when you get home." She turned her back on us and started clearing the table.

Back in the Jenny Lind, I turned to Wyatt. "Why did your wife treat me like I stole the silver?"

"She's mad at you for keeping me out late."

"It's only once or twice a week."

"Yeah, about that." Wyatt looked at me sheepishly. "I may have told her I was working with you when I went to the club or a boxing match or—"

"How many nights?"

"Hey, it's hot and cramped in that apartment. And my daughter sleeps on a Murphy bed in the parlor, so we need to be quiet."

"How many nights?"

"Pretty near all of them."

"Blimey, Wyatt. You prat. It's a wonder she didn't poison me tonight."

"I don't think so, with you leaving soon."

"Maybe you should take me directly to my rooms."

"Not a chance. Once you're gone, might hardly get out at all. Remember, you promised me a champagne."

"Think it was you who promised yourself a champagne."

"No matter. A deal's a deal."

Wyatt waited no farther than Gramercy Park before we stopped into the cozy confines of the Portman Hotel bar. A vintage shy of Bradley-Martin Ball standards, the champagne's chilled, toasty bubbles were a welcome balm to the heat that lingered on into the night. Looking relaxed for the first time all night, Wyatt ordered us both a Geo Sayer Three Star brandy to chase down the bubbles.

"Can't imagine what it'll be like once you're gone. Hear London's some pumpkins, but please tell me you're going to miss it here."

"First, I only get to London a few times a year. I keep telling you we are actually well-to-do sheepherders and farmers. I do admit, the estate houses are a bit luxe."

"Josh, you didn't answer the question."

"Yes, of course. Life here seems normal to me now. Soon I will walk upon England's green and pleasant land and find it strange for the first time."

"Yep. Had the same feeling coming back from out west. Any plans for your last days in the New World?"

"That is a problem. Nowak knocked me off track, for sure. Articles on showgirls and coon singers are not putting me in the pantheon of journalism. And my travelogue is turning into an American class system book that refuses to be written."

"Hey, you should write about the Stampeders, gold rush in the Yukon."

"Lordy, Wyatt, did you jump a round of brandy while I was in the loo? I am not crawling six hundred miles from a tent-and-shack town to watch desperate men try to coax virgin pay dirt from the permafrost."

"So, you've been reading about it too. Heard it's really ugly. There's part of the White Pass Trail they're calling Dead Horse Gulch. Littered with horse corpses."

"Wyatt, stop. It breaks my heart. Do these men not know how to load a horse? An Egyptian doctor told me Arabs unload their camels when they make a stop to give the beast equal rest. Have the miners' lust for gold deprived them of simple decency, or do they hold all life so cheap?"

"Okay, no gold rush. How about closer to home? You keep up with the East River murder?"

"What, an unlicensed stout German midwife, shady boyfriend,

and a dismembered muscled Turkish bath masseur? No, must have missed that one."

"Don't be so high society. People eat that stuff up. They stuck the Turk's head in plaster and threw it in the river."

"Aye, the rabble always love a gruesome murder. A headless torso washes ashore wrapped in a red-and-yellow oilcloth bound with twine. The shiny object distracts them from the real crime, why some are so rich and they are so poor."

"Oh, Baron Von Cares a Lot. Strange position for you."

"Maybe. At least my family makes things: On Montserrat, indigo and sugar; in England, wool, mutton, onions, and grain. I have issues with my brother John, but he works hard every day—office, market, fields. Some people give nothing, lay back in ease, yet each day they are wealthier."

"Josh, keep your eye on the ball. It's still a great story. The *Journal* prints the pattern of the oilcloth *in color*. Reporters find the store in Queens where the midwife bought it. Case solved. If not for the *Journal*, the arm of the law is palsied."

"Sorry. I agree with the *Times.* So help me, Wyatt, I often agree with the *Times*. I am appalled by such noisy detective work."

"But the *Journal*'s making a difference. It's the journalism of action."

"My dear Wyatt. In England we already tried this. It proved an ill fit. With all regard to William T. Sneed, there is no government by journalism. The press needs to expose, to reveal, but it is not their place to legislate."

"That's way too serious for your send-off. This bar is too cerebral. Need to move on to somewhere louder and wilder."

I yawned. "At least, I think, last call will save morning Joshua from evening Joshua."

Wyatt grinned like Carroll's impish cat.

The next establishment we entered displayed a definite step down in decorum: the floor unswept, and the pattern on the wallpaper so faded I couldn't tell if it displayed roses or lewd faces. As promised, the crowd was boisterous, except for a few gents searching for important messages in the bottoms of their glasses. I glanced at my watch. It was clearly after closing time, yet we only obtained our seats at the bar after two men, who had been sharing a bottle of questionable claret, rose and headed for the center stairs, one climbing, one descending.

"Going to hotel rooms." Wyatt said, close into my ear.

"This hardly rates as a public house. It cannot possibly be a hotel."

Wyatt had already turned to greet the bartender and order us two whiskeys. Just as the whiskey was served, another barkeep plunked two plates down in front of us, each with the saddest, most unsavory sandwich. The grayish bread encased desiccated cheese, and brown, spotted lettuce.

"Wyatt, what is this scam? We didn't order—"

The bartender abruptly grabbed the putrid sandwiches and put them on a tray with two beers, which a barkeep carried to a table. The vagabond sandwiches were plopped in front of two new patrons, who paid attention only to the beer.

"Mr. Wyatt, who your friend?" The bartender stood at my elbow. I took him as the owner, his eyes flitted about the room even as he spoke.

"This is my good friend who is soon to be fleeing back to London, His Lordship—"

"Please. I am Joshua Banks, at your service."

The bartender didn't introduce himself but looked to Wyatt. "I'm afraid he's going to pick up the Raines. Those sandwiches are already five days old." He gestured at the plates continuing their trek around the barroom. "If he's real hungry, I've got a big jar of pickled eggs that won't kill you."

I banged a slightly tipsy fist on the counter. "Could someone tell me what in bloody hell is going on? Those vile sandwiches, and how are you even open, and serving liquor?"

"He don't get around much, huh?" mumbled an old drunkard to Wyatt's left.

"Sorry, Wegie," Wyatt said to the bartender. "Joshua's more of an uptown fellow."

"Okay, I explain to him. Senator Raines and his buddy Roosevelt don't like our sort of place. They say we bad for society. They called my customers vagrants, tramps, bums. What does a senator from Finger Lakes know about city, and TR, he wants be mayor.

"So they pass this law last April Fool's Day, yeah, but not funny. Raise my liquor license three times as much. You got to be eighteen to drink. All kinds of restrictions. Close right stroke of midnight, no golden hour. Thank Lord Jesus I'm not two hundred feet close to school, or church, or I'd have to close and move. This my building. What am I supposed to do to make living?"

"The purity police were trying to break up the party," said Wyatt.

"Did it work? I mean, is this all illegal?" I asked.

"First weeks were real bad. Paper headline: 'RAINES MAKES A THIRST.' I thought I'd have to go back to Palermo. Then we see the hole, what you call . . ."

"Loophole." The old drunk was still listening.

"Yes, loophole. The fancy hotels with rich big shots, they can serve liquor whole week, all hours with meals. Working man, he's got just few hours after ten laboring. His one day off, no drink on Sunday. So, if *they* hotel, now *we* hotel. We put up walls in attic and basement. We got ten rooms, stay cheap. Need to serve food, so throw cloth over pool table and serve you a Raines sandwich."

The old drunk, who imagined himself an equal part of the conversation, pitched in. "Over at Iron Mike's place ain't even real food. Thing's cut out of rubber and painted."

I ignored the drunk and turned to Wyatt. “Assuredly, the police will not stand for such a farce.”

The three of them looked at me with mock seriousness, then broke into laughter.

Wyatt cleared his throat. “DA said a cracker isn’t a meal, but a sandwich is. The courts agreed and said we’re hotel guests.”

“So, you see.” Wegie smiled. “We better. Open all I want. No last call, even Sunday. If I didn’t sleep, I never close. Those tight collars, they shoot themselves in their own petard.”

It became clear that Wyatt intended I not just be aware of the existence of the myriad Raines hotels but that we attempt a census. I lost count of how many bars we researched, as I went from squiffy, to seriously overserved, to nearly crapulous before trying to slowly drink myself sober. At one point, I awoke in a sticky captain’s chair alone. When I inquired after my companion, a barmaid cracked that he was in one of their rooms interviewing a young lady about a possible position. Without a memory of what borough lay outside, I waited until the pair appeared, rumpled and sweaty.

“Come on, mate. If we do not leave soon, the sun will rise and vaporize us like vampires.”

The woman giggled and clung to Wyatt for support. “Hey, can’t you just fly away like bats?”

Wyatt eased her into a chair and ceased to pay her any attention. “We’ve got one more stop. Got it all set up. You need a souvenir to take back, something to remember us by.”

On the way toward Hudson Yards, after threatening several times to wrestle away the reins, Wyatt finally revealed his brilliant plan, namely that I should get an American tattoo. I assured him that, except for the scars acquired falling from horses in steeplechase, I'd no intention of branding my body.

It was the best argument my drink-addled brain advanced. Wyatt's brain had much more experience, and a higher tolerance, so he proved the better negotiator, working me down to a compromise. Wyatt would get a tattoo as well. Stepping from the dark into the operating-room brightness of the tattoo parlor forced me to squint—with walls bleached white, the ceiling an unexpected, brilliant sky blue.

Tattoo Nick was expecting us. As late as it was, we waited as he finished on a sailor. A girl in smudged party makeup watched her name appear on the sailor's forearm. Nick brought to mind the Greek fishermen observed during my truncated Grand Tour. He wore no glasses but periodically checked his work through a square magnifying glass mounted on a stand.

When finished, the couple stumbled off, arm in monogrammed arm. Nick methodically sorted the money into the cashbox, shook his head at the departing couple, and started to pontificate.

"Obviously, I don't think a tattoo's always the result of bad life choices. I don't regret any of my illustrated memories."

From his elbow to wrist marched a fantastical army of stars, planets, words, and animals, real and imagined, vibrant in reds, greens, yellows, blues and purple.

"But I always try to talk them out of names. Nice heart with an arrow, maybe initials. I perfected a way to turn letters into shapes if things go south. But no, those two were set on Abigail. Suggested Abby, but his girlie nixed it. He might as well buy that pan; he's already stuck with the handle."

Nick laughed at his bad pun, then shook Wyatt's and my hands. "Now, what you mugs seeking?"

Confronted with the actual event, I realized that, before agreeing, I should've insisted on a decision of what manner of tattoo. I considered backing out, but Wyatt pushed me farther into the room and gave an exaggerated shrug.

"Aw, you mugs ain't going to make me get out the book? Guys poke through the whole damn book, some of those designs pieces of art, and after thirty minutes, they wind up with a devil or a cross."

"No, not that. Joshua here is heading home to London, and he requires a souvenir of his American sojourn."

"Oh, so we've had a sojourn, huh?"

In the absence of new alcohol, my body turned to ridding itself of the poison. Clammy sweat broke out on my forehead, and my stomach soured.

"Thought maybe an American eagle," I said.

"An eagle?" Nick appeared truly offended. "Every skata county is lousy with eagles. Germany, Russia, even the Queen's got eagles. You'll have to do better than that. Ink don't just wash off, you know."

Wyatt took a long swig off a pocket flask I hadn't seen before. "What about the flag?"

"I am not plastering my arm with the bloody flag of a treasonous colony. That is too much. God save me if I am ever discovered branded with any flag than the Union Jack or the Cross of St. George."

"So, death to tyrants is out?" Wyatt was laughing at my anger. "It has to be uniquely American, or it ain't worth squat."

Nick waved us to stop. "If I may make a suggestion, gents, what's more iconic than Lady Liberty?"

"You are proposing the Statue of Liberty on my arm?"

"Not the whole statue, unless you want it shoulder to elbow. Two, three inches, it'd look stupid, no detail. This is poetry, least amount to conjure the image. You only need the torch. Since I know you're a fellow Mason, you can think of it as the Torch of Enlightenment, the Flaming Torch of Reason."

Wyatt rolled his eyes. "How do you two know that?"

"We just do," Nick and I said simultaneously.

"All that secret society crap."

"Not secret, just private," I said, and Nick nodded.

"Didn't think Greeks were Masons," Wyatt said.

Nick struck a mocking pose. "Why not? The Great Orient Lodge of Hellas—a labyrinth of irrational procedures. That's so very Greek."

"All right, my good man," I said. "A torch it is. You have a picture of the design?"

"Don't need one. Can do it from memory."

"Uhh . . ."

"That even makes *me* nervous," said Wyatt.

"No worry, I've seen it a million times. My uncle Philik helped build it."

"Are you fuffin' me about?" I shifted back and forth in the chair.

"On my honor. Everyone talks about Bartholdi, but he only designed the outside copper. That's only two pennies thick. He needed Eiffel to design the iron skeleton that holds the whole thing up. But there's your problem. Copper to iron, especially with all the water, corrodes right through. So, my uncle was on the crew installing asbestos insulation between the copper and iron. He died a few years ago—his lungs gave out on him—but he used to take me there all the time. He didn't like going into the torch if there was a crowd, said it wasn't safe. He claimed Bartholdi removed some supports from the arm to make it slimmer."

I started to fade, my resistance draining out of me. I removed my shirt. "I am in your hands, Sir."

Nick set to work, yet kept waxing nostalgic.

"Uncle Philik was good to family, but was a little light-fingered. Never hurt a fly. On the other hand, if it wasn't nailed down, well. He figured the plans and drawings would be valuable after Lady Liberty got finished, and there're multiple copies, right? No big deal if a page or two goes walking.

"Here's what I bet you don't know. America wasn't the first choice for the statue. Bartholdi wanted to erect a torch-bearing woman down the southern end of the Suez Canal. The money fell through, and they erected the Port Said Lighthouse instead. I love Lady Liberty, but she's never going to be a good lighthouse."

I broke in. "Why would the Arabs want the Roman goddess of liberty on the Suez?"

"That's just it. The drawing my uncle acquired wasn't 'Liberty Enlightening the World.' No. It was titled, 'Egypt Carrying the Light to Asia,' and it portrayed a veiled Egyptian peasant woman. Bartholdi reworked her into Libertas. Slapped that big Roman nose on her like on one of those Brutus coins. I always thought she looked a little too manly."

The torch materialized on my arm, high on my shoulder. "That's so a short-sleeved shirt would hide it," Nick explained. I began to relax. Nick's artistry with ink was impressive. Several shades of green and gold, and yellow and warm black, added depth and clarity. He took some liberty with Liberty, stylizing enough to make it his vision whilst clearly conjuring the original.

"See, the hand's important. She doesn't roughly clutch the torch like a pump handle. Her fingers encircle it gently, respectfully."

"Hey, Nick, where'd you get your fancy machine? Looks less painful." Wyatt was watching intently.

"You're lucky. It's really only been around five or so years. Sam O'Reilly let me have one of the first ones. You wouldn't want to be the first skin I tried it on, but now I can ink anything."

That's when I flinched. From out of nowhere, a tabby cat launched itself into my lap. The tattoo pen skittered and jabbed.

"Goddamn you, Apateon." Nick started to push the cat off me, but it hissed at him. Then it nuzzled into my lap.

"Wow, Josh. Really got the animal magnetism working tonight," said Wyatt.

"If Apateon wasn't such a good mouser, I'd booted him out years ago. He pretends to be my cat, but he loves everyone else."

Not a true ginger, the cat was butterscotch with vanilla markings. I scratched his little chin, and he began to knead bread with lethal claws on my leg. Apateon purred, and I persisted.

"Nick, sorry about the flinch. Is it ruined?"

"Well, I wouldn't made that line, but I'll blend it in, make it part of the design."

In a few minutes, he was done. I stood to admire, and to assess the error on my new addition. I smiled in the large, full-length mirror.

"I know, big mirror. You've no idea where some men and women get tattooed," Nick said. "I've closed the shades more than once. Right, you're next. Get in the chair."

Wyatt hesitated. "I'm not supposed to get the same thing, am I?"

"What's the matter?" Nick frowned. "Isn't it top-shelf? Come on. I want to get home."

"No, it's great . . . it's just . . . I don't know. Is it too chummy to have matching tattoos?"

"You know how many sailors are walking around with the same anchor on them? It don't mean they're dating."

It was the first time I saw Wyatt blush. Nick shook his head.

"Okay, tell you what. Instead of the torch, I give you the head and seven-spike crown. Very iconic."

"You'll make it look good?"

"Get in the chair. Lucky tattoo, seven spikes, seven wonders of the world, seven continents, Muslims have seven heavens, that crazy monk who wrote Revelations put in seven churches, seals, trumpets, bowls of Wrath. Number of God you know."

Wyatt nicked another shot from his flask. "I missed that sermon, but sounds good." He pulled his shirt over his head and pulled down the top of his union suit. "Make her fierce."

On our way back, the early birds of the city were waking. Scattered lights appeared in kitchens as laborers fortified themselves for ten to twelve hours of toil.

"Your wife is really going to hate me now."

"What'd you care? You'll never see her again."

"I really meant that about you visiting, Becca and all."

"We'll see."

"Wyatt?"

"Yeah."

"What is wrong with your daughter?"

Wyatt took a deep breath and let it out very slowly.

"Not really sure. We got back from Vermont, 1894, camping, swimming, trying to escape the heat of the city. She started crying about a terrible headache, pain in her left leg, then right. Next thing, she's almost paralyzed. Doctors said some virus had crept up her spine. She was flat on her back for two weeks. Thought she might die. Pulled through, but her legs are messed up."

"I saw the braces."

"She can get around the house with those, or crutches. When I take her to church or school, we have to put her in a wheelchair. Do you know how hard it is to move around New York in a damn wheelchair?" Wyatt's voice cracked.

I shook my head and let him talk.

"We got a high curb on our street, so I chopped out a little piece and put in a cement ramp. Wasn't hurting nobody. The goddamn landlord complains, the city rips out my ramp and puts back the curb. Asher Lustmann—remember the butcher?—he sees all this. Now, I don't really know him at that point; I'd just been in his shop once or twice. He goes to his rabbi, and the rabbi goes to the ward boss. They tell him the butcher needs a ramp to get the hand trucks in and out of the store. It wasn't two, three days and boom—the city puts the ramp in. The thing is, I know he's already got a ramp in the alley behind the store. Don't nobody ever tell me anything about greedy Jews. I love that man."

Chapter 13

I wasn't looking for Luther Halsey. We'd met once before at a ghastly American invention, the surprise party. Who thought mass deception jolly? A poor soul lured into a room. What do they expect? Tea? Gentle conversation? If they were lucky—a bit of snug? Instead, screaming friends pop out of corners like East End Street robbers. If you weren't carted off with heart failure, you were trapped for hours of forced merriment.

Luther (he didn't ask, but went immediately to first names) made an impression. As if an average man was kidnapped—muscles strangely inflated—forced to ingest vast quantities of caffeine, then launched back into the world, his speech was more of a sermon, since it always carried moral certainty.

I was standing in front of Clifton's apartment at the Croisic, searching after Clifton and hoping to squeeze in some spirited fencing before my long ocean voyage. And also to thank him for his repeated kindness to me.

"He's not there, you know." Luther watched me knocking on Clifton's door. "Off to the Dark Continent, safari. A last minute kind of thing."

"I hardly thought of Clifton as a big-game hunter."

"Oh, that snoot? 'Course not. They're only taking pictures."

"Sounds grand."

"Ridiculous!" Luther's pinched voice pitched even higher. "Humans are natural-born hunters. Eyes forward-facing like a predator. Minds attuned to the thrill of the hunt. We're refining ourselves out of all manhood. I've often laughed at the weaklings who thought themselves good because they had no claws."

"One should be careful about throwing your lot in with Nietzsche. His philosophy is only for the young and strong."

I'd intended that as a parting shot, but Luther pulled in closer and louder. "Then it suits you to a T. I don't mean to be disagreeable, but the constant feminization of our society will be our downfall. Will we cede all the virile qualities to evil men? Our gentlemen are becoming too gentle, and not enough men. If we don't keep the barbarian virtues, we won't be able to defend the civilized ones."

"What, be brutes? No room for strength and sensitivity, for conquest and cooperation?"

"Sure, you Brits have cooperated yourselves all over the globe."

That jibe meant little to a son of the empire.

"Be that as it may, I must be off. I hoped Clifton would join me for fencing. Have to scrounge a match at the club."

"Wait—you're looking for exercise?"

"Yes."

"I'm your man. Come to the YMCA with me. I'm an official. We have a full gym and basketball court."

"I did not understand anything you just said." I was shifting from one foot to the other, waiting for a chance to flee.

"Young Men's Christian Association. Basketball is a team game, nine on nine. Sorry, five on five now."

"Never heard of basket-ball."

"I'm not surprised, it's an American invention. Naismith dreamed it up a few years ago. Imagine a tennis court, wood floor, no net, peach basket hung high at each end. You got a round ball you pass, or bounce up and down, and dribble to move. The objective is to move past the opposing players and shoot the ball into the basket for a score."

"What then?"

"Someone climbs a ladder and gets the ball."

"Seems it would rather slow the game. Why not punch a hole in the bottom of the basket?"

"I didn't make the rules. It's great as is. Good exercise. Mostly colleges and YMCAs playing, but it's going to be huge."

"I have a fencing uniform, not clothes for basket-ball."

"It's one word, and they'll lend you all that at the Y."

I accepted that Luther wasn't about to let me wriggle off the hook. When we entered what Luther called "the Y," I actually became happy I stopped resisting. Airy and light, it contained a gym with full complement of weights, along with gymnastics horse, rings, and parallel bars.

Thankfully, I didn't have to engage in basketball. The court was already in use for another recently made-up game: volleyball, a sort of mutant badminton played with fingers. Luther said volleyball catered to older or less-fit members not ready for basketball. The young chaps absorbed in the game were not aware of this, as they jumped their height in the air and flung their bodies about the court so violently that several landed flat on the floor.

I wanted no part of that, so after begging clothes from an attendant, Luther and I worked out in the gym. My borrowed shirt, shorts, and jockstrap, the attendant assured, were freshly laundered with bleach, and the chemical odor confirmed the claim. The shorts were of a coarse, scratchy weave presumably to encourage members to provide their own uniform. After a thorough round at the heavy bag and punching bag, I mentioned to Luther that I smelled chlorine. I was surprised to find myself a mite giddy when he informed me the Y maintained an indoor swimming pool.

Luther was quick to pour cold water on that idea. "The pool's nice, but you really want to swim laps? You should be exhausted after the way you went after the heavy bag. Come with me to the Russian and Turkish baths. Be my guest. Won't take no."

Luther proved a man of his word, so I found myself wrapped only in a towel in the initial relaxation room at the banya. Luther hurried us impatiently to the second room, what he'd come for. In the corners, racks of stones stood over glowing charcoals. The dripping water produced a dense steam that reminded me of London fog.

"Hotter than the hinges of Hades in here," I said. Every inch of my flesh was sweating.

"You bet, probably over one-eighty. The steam's better than the Turkish bath. You can feel the toxins draining from your pores."

"I need to sit before I pass out. My brain is sweating."

For all his brusque manner, Luther wasn't a bad man. The same forces that fermented regressive impulses in him also inversely brought out shafts of enlightenment. Religious devotion drove him to the social gospel and a desire to improve the human condition even if he didn't always equally respect the humans he was improving. He talked of fighting corruption, alcoholism, crime, child labor, and improving water and food safety. Surprisingly, the man who had quoted Nietzsche also railed against the New Thought movement making ground in America. The concept that a man's circumstances reflect what is happening in his mind, and therefore, the poor should just think themselves out of the slums, or damn them for their lack of godly ambition.

He mostly promoted "Muscular Christianity," a familiar concept to me, having been force-fed the boy's novel *Tom Brown's School Days* and its promotion of fighting spirit mixed with Christian morality. And everyone in England knew of Reverend A.O. Jay using the boxing ring as a pulpit to minister to his "gentlemen barbarians." Some in England turned the concept to justify empire, arguing Britain and its people had more vigor than its colonies. George Washington and his fellows disputed that notion, and my father always insisted that one day India would do the same.

Luther expressed no tolerance for Calvinists, whose Augustine dualism of soul and body meant the body was base and shameful, and therefore, sport was frivolous. You couldn't be a soldier for his Christ without a strong arm.

"We didn't have to worry about this in the past when every man swung an axe or drove a plow. We've lost the frontier and become too civilized. The feminist sentiment's captured our schools and churches. Have you been to a service over here? A weekly Mother's Day with sugary sermons and weepy music. We need more hairy-chested ministers, not weak-kneed tea sippers lunching with old ladies. Shorter, pithier sermons, more this world and its struggles, and less of the next. Ditch plaintive hymns and sing of courage, bravery, and triumphant faith."

At this, Luther broke into a high-tenor rendition of "Onward Christian soldiers marching as to war . . ." He choked up a bit. "Now that's a hymn for a man. And could we please depict a more masculine Jesus? He cracked a whip and flipped the money lenders' tables, for Christ's sake. Don't draw him like a namby-pamby milksop."

I didn't tell Luther I had a soft spot for the gentle Jesus, washing a stranger's feet, beckoning the little children to come to him, the caring spirit expressed in the shortest sentence in the Bible: "Jesus wept." We left the steam room and plunged into an icy pool. Luther approvingly gauged it at fifty degrees. I remained unconvinced any of this ritual was healthy, but it surely reminded me that I was indeed alive.

Andy, a copy boy at the *Journal*, sat waiting for me in the lobby of the Croisic. "Mr. Nowak wants you right away."

He need not gone to the trouble. I had every intention to stop by the *Journal* before leaving for England. First, there was no way I'd let the Oliver typewriter stay in the lustful fingers of Josef Nowak. By now, I was smitten by the machine, occasionally typing nonsense just to watch the word ballet of its keys.

Second, there were three stories about race matters that Miss Moon had alerted me to. If Nowak balked, I'd try the *Sunday* or *Evening* editors. I kept my contact with Nowak to a minimum, but at this point, what harm could he do?

Every time I entered Nowak's office, I was struck with the feeling he existed as a planet with its own atmosphere. It was no different this time. Nowak said nothing for a full minute, studying me up and down like an Aurelian with a butterfly on a pin.

"Seems we're stuck with each other."

"Come again?"

"You're not going home—not yet."

My knees buckled. I couldn't process what I heard. I made a sound that only approached speech.

"Yeah, big surprise for me too. I was pleased as punch to see your ass on a boat out of here, but I got this wire." Nowak held the telegram like he had fished it out of the loo. "Listen, kid. Sir Covington says you have to stay for I don't know how long. Your replacement can't come. Guy's wife had a difficult pregnancy. Preemie. She's flat out in bed, and the baby's still at the hospital. No one else is available, so . . ."

"No, this cannot be. I am to wed."

"Funny, he actually mentioned that. It says here, 'Not wise to formalize the engagement until circumstances clarify.' Look, I don't know how you're bellyaching about a marriage when you're not even engaged. Now, if I were you, I'd count that a blessing. The marriage thing is tragically overrated. Take the big Chief, for example. He'd have to be running for president before he'd marry that chorus girl."

I made for a chair, but Nowak stopped me.

"No sitting. You don't sit in my office. I'm trying to figure out a way to get rid of you. Get back on the entertainment beat and out of my way. I've got no time for you. If you haven't noticed, we're up to our ears in news. Greece and Turkey stopped talking war, then we got all that East River murder ink and Eva Valesh's big interview with President McKinley. But mostly, we are wall-to-wall on Cuba, and that butcher General Weyler and his concentration camps. The *Journal's* got stringers all over the islands. If the Chief gets his way, we'll be covering a war with Spain any day now."

Nowak pointed rudely at the door. "That reminds me, don't be sticking your nose into the Cuba thing. That's American business, you second-rate royal. Don't let the door hit you on the way out."

Shattered. Numb. I didn't know what to think. "Until circumstances clarify?" What was I to make of that? The Old Man certainly couldn't be suggesting I take over my putative replacement's entire two-year term. Could he? It seemed next to impossible, which just meant possible.

What did the Old Man say to Margaret? What if he didn't say anything to her? I'd been ready for a mission to repair the bonds of affection, in the flesh. To now have to attempt that task at 3,008 nautical miles crushed my spirit. I resolved to write Margaret immediately, no matter how difficult. I searched my mind to concoct a balm of words.

As I sat in my room at my writing table, I was aware of another distinct feeling, one I didn't want to accept or admit, unwanted, but persistent. There was unfinished business; I was unfinished.

Part of me wanted to stay.

October 1897

My Dearest Margaret,

I do not think I have words to express what I am feeling sitting here in New York when I should be onboard ship heading to home and your arms. You barred me refuge in poetry, so I will talk plainly. I know not how much your father has shared with you, that the chap who was to replace me must stay in England to tend to a bed-ridden wife and sick newborn. It would be heartless to expect him to do otherwise.

Your father is adamant that the position not be left vacant, especially as America may be drifting into war with Spain. Most likely, a new candidate will apply, and I will be out of here in three or four months. Then I will be delighted to introduce you to horse jumping. Have John or Aubrey take you out on Nike so she can get used to you. She is the best steeplechase horse I have ever met.

Let us be candid. Can I really say no to your father when I am asking for his daughter's hand in marriage? My willingness to sacrifice in pursuit of duty can only elevate me in his eyes. Your mother has always been kind toward me. She realizes what the loss of my own mother has meant to me, while not imposing herself as a mother. It would be exceedingly strange for me to write her directly. Indeed, it might be disastrous. On the other hand, might you probe to see if she could nudge your father into quick action finding a new replacement for my position?

I promise to make this delay work for our common betterment. While my *Journal* editor has rejected my attempted editorials, I will push your father to let me publish on the editorial page, which should increase my public standing immensely. Exposure shall help me obtain a publisher for my book, whatever it may be.

By the way, I am proud of your studies at college. The Cambridge boys do not deserve you. I am certain you will excel. One of us should persevere to graduation. Just do not become too much a swot.

In the future, we will sit by the fire with our children by our sides, and they will laugh off our tale of minor troubles and delays.

Please send me encouraging words.

Love,
Joshua

Chapter 14

It was nearly the end of February 1898, and the only message I received from Margaret was a non-messaged Christmas card. The illustration was of a lone woman skating on a frozen pond. The postmark indicated she was home from college for the holidays. She must have received my letter. I expected a cross reply, but this wasn't good, and no Valentine card at all.

What an impossible situation! If I deserted my post and returned to England, the Old Man might see it as personal affront. He could withdraw support for the marriage. Would Margaret be willing to defy her family? She had never behaved as if wedded to luxury but had never lived in its absence either. What a start to matrimonial bliss, her striped of dowry and pension, and me, of course, fired, and likely blackballed from the other London newspapers.

My father, despite his disappointment, would never desert me. He'd find some dreary position for me. Unfortunately, Father wasn't aging well. What happens, then, when he shuffles off this mortal coil? John is married, and his family grows ever larger. Our familial ties remain tense, and my relationship to his wife—his issue—nonexistent. I doubt he would deign keep me on as a perpetual ward once he became a baron. Clearly, I would need to find my own way in the world.

If only I could get Margaret to see that the delay, the separation, was but a passing impediment. Not cancer, nor even a crippling wound, but maybe a bad cold, perhaps a fever. In any case, one day you wake and you've forgotten it completely.

The problem with this rationalization? I barely believed it myself. My absence continued to do serious damage to Margaret's and my love. "Absence makes the heart grow fonder" was fiction, a fairy tale. Fondness may linger in memory. Passion and ardor fade in time. Our story was going from flame to smolder. Were we to marry merely fond?

Then I must hope that a thousand kisses and ten thousand kindnesses return the full measure of Margaret's love for me.

Time did not improve my position with Nowak. He still blocked the majority of my articles, especially attempts at politics. Strangely enough, Nowak let post some lynching stories Miss Moon had fed me. If not for the ever-hungry *Sunday Journal*, I'd be hard-pressed to call myself a newspaperman. Normally assignments were puff pieces on celebrities. My most popular report was a throwaway on the insane American pastime of crashing two speeding locomotives. During the "Crash at Crush" in Texas, two boilers exploded, flinging earth and metal, maiming spectators, killing two. No, if I wanted any renown, I needed editorials. The *Journal* was not an option, so I'd have to look to London.

At least now there was a strong subject to cover. President McKinley had ordered the USS *Maine* from Key West to Havana Harbor, ostensibly to protect Americans on the island, though they appeared at little risk. The real reason, of course, was to protect wealthy business interests and thwart Spanish influence in Latin America. The gambit proved costly. The USS *Maine*, having been put in harm's way, exploded, instantly killing sailors, marines, and officers—over 250 in all.

Hearst and his paper couldn't content themselves with reporting the truth. Before the Naval Court of Inquiry finished its investigation, the *Journal* filled its front page, accusing Spain of mining the harbor.

More reckless, the *Journal* printed as fact rumors of a torpedo hole in the ship, a tale soon proven false.

When Congress passed a nonbinding resolution that Spain relinquish Cuba, and gave the president authority to take action if he determined it necessary, the front page screamed, "How Do You Like the *Journal's* War?" Congress hadn't declared war. The president hadn't requested a declaration; instead, McKinley reiterated he did not read "the Yellows."

Anything that might stoke the public passion for war, the *Journal* provided. A drive was formed for a *Maine* memorial. Papers offered rewards for information, real or imagined. A "War with Spain" card game was created.

I felt the *Journal* was partly responsible for the thread of events that led to the sunken ship in Havana Harbor. For several months the previous year, the paper elevated the story of an obscure, reportedly eighteen-year-old Evangelina Cosio y Cisneros into a national obsession. The girl had been thrown into the notoriously dissolute women's jail at Casa de Recogidos without so much as a trial.

The instigating act remained much debated. Spain insisted that Cisneros tried to lure Commander José Bérriz into a trap. Cisneros supporters claimed that the virginal "Cuban Joan of Arc" had rightfully defended her maidenhood from the unwanted sexual assault of Bérriz.

If Hearst had stopped at sensational stories and stunts, he'd have loitered in the ugly boxing ring of what now passed for American journalism. Instead, he jumped the ring and made himself and the *Journal* an unelected arm of American foreign policy.

I burned to say something, to warn this adolescent America to keep its foreign innocence a little longer.

Hearst funded adventurer Karl Decker to enter Cuba and break the beautiful Evangelina out of jail. Had it ended in blood and failure, war might have begun then. Through conspiracy and bribes, Decker somehow succeeded without firing a shot. The *Journal* proclaimed: "An American Newspaper Accomplishes at a Single Stroke What the Red Tape of Diplomacy Failed to Bring About in Several Months."

Evangelina, dressed in flowing bridal white, was paraded by Hearst through the streets of New York from the Waldorf to a rally at Madison Square Garden. The *Journal* declared the power to act with "rank illegality" if in its judgment (Hearst's judgment), things were going wrong, and the *Journal* could set them right. The spectacle sickened me. Whether or not it ruffled some feathers, I would have to speak out.

Through all this tumult, the new dawning year stumbled, frozen, into being. New Year's Eve celebrations were to be canceled due to approaching ice and snow. Hearst's influence and money made sure it went on anyway with a hundred thousand souls packed together in City Park and lower Manhattan to watch parades of floats backed with pulse-quickening patriotic music. Unending volleys of fireworks sent skyward to beat back the icy rain startled a team of horses that ran madly over several members of the seventy-first Regiment Band.

I determined to make use of my extended stay, considering trips to Chicago, Washington DC, and Cincinnati. I still needed to drop by Dr. Qabash in Baltimore. I thought it rude not to alert him, to just pop in, but had never found the time to make plans.

The only person happy about my turn of events was Wyatt. He admitted that Becca was not. After hearing the news, she didn't speak to him for three days. Not entirely in jest, I told him I didn't feel safe eating at his tenement any time soon. I made him promise on his mother's grave he would stay home at least three nights a week. Wyatt reluctantly gave his word, but not before dragging me out all night to see a Veriscope exhibition of the Corbett-Fitzsimmons fight.

"We got to go now, Josh," Wyatt insisted. "Who knows how much longer the film will be in New York. It's like a traveling circus."

Sitting at the Academy, with the lights dimmed and a very wide screen lit up, I was impressed by how real it looked. It was a leap from Edison's clumsy kinetoscope boxes, peeping into a viewer to watch a man sneeze or a horse run. The hubbub of common life on film.

Clifton usually dragged me off to witness any advance in film. *The Kiss* I saw projected on a screen. Twenty seconds of May Irwin from the *The Widow Jones* canoodling with John Rice. All in all, still flickering novelties. What I'd seen of the French Lumiére Brothers were snowball fights and scenes of nature. More innovative was *The Cabbage Fairy*, with a sprite picking real babies from a cabbage patch. Reportedly, the creator, Alice Guy Blaché, shot it on a Paris patio. If she was any indication, perhaps women would find a real inroad in this new medium. Fortunately for my national pride, I recently discovered that in my absence two Brighton lads, George Smith and James Williamson, had released a trick film with transparent ghosts.

Fine enough, but these attempts featured a minute or less of fleeting images. Wyatt and I now beheld over ninety minutes of the American champion "Gentleman" Jim Corbett, and the Cornish challenger Bob "Ruby Rob" Fitzsimmons trying to pummel each other into the mat. Fourteen three-minute rounds filmed, even the one-minute rests, with corner men energetically fanning the boxers. At our showing, a local boxing expert stood on hand to give a running commentary.

As a bonus, the event was a pugilistic spectacle with its own narrative arc. Boxing, a blood sport, remained illegal in many states, its status lowbrow. Lawmakers in Nevada rushed through a law allowing the fight to take place in Carson City on a sunny St. Patrick's Day with a film crew and a $15,000 purse at stake. The expert stated the peculiarities of the duel as if it were just now occurring before his eyes.

"In Corbett's corner stands the famous sheriff Wyatt Earp with four other hard men, all brandishing revolvers. They're mirrored by five similarly armed men in Fitz's corner. All determined to guarantee a fair fight. Western legend Bat Masterson is one of three timekeepers, and the famous old bare-knuckler, John L. Sullivan, is serving as master of ceremonies."

The more agile Corbett, ahead on points and delivering a lot of damage, knocked Fitz to the canvas in the sixth round. The expert went on, this time explaining in the past tense:

"When confusion led to a long count, the veteran referee George Silver feared the ring would erupt in smoke and gunfire. Fitz struggled to his feet, and a depleted Corbett continued to rain blows on the long-limbed 'Freckled Wonder.'"

Loyalties aside, I acknowledged Corbett as the more stylish fighter, his footwork impeccable, but he was having trouble landing solid hits on Fitz. Finally, in the fourteenth round, Corbett made an error, or maybe Fitz masterfully set it up, but Fitz landed a stone hammer of a punch into Corbett's solar plexus (Wyatt thought it his liver), pushing all the air out of Corbett, who crumpled to the canvas. By the time Corbett had caught his breath and rushed Fitz, it was too late. The fight was called, the British Fitzsimmons the new champion.

I felt a certain sense of shame and disloyalty, I'd been rooting for the American.

February was still cold when the rap of the bellhop came, accompanied by the business card of Len Spencer, requesting me to join him in a hansom cab outside. George was in trouble. By the time we arrived at Forty-First Street, all I knew was that Roskin Stuart, the woman living with George, had jumped—or was pushed or, in any case, fell—out their second-story window. Len and I leaped from the cab and sprinted to George, who sat on his front steps, whittling a stick.

"What the hell, George?" Len said.

"This?" George pointed the knife at the stick. "If the poplar branch is nice and green, you can slip the bark down and carve a nice whistle in there."

"No, damn it. Where's Stuart?"

"At the hospital, of course, after all that."

"Hoped she wasn't at the morgue."

"She'll be at hospital for at least twelve days."

"How are you even here?"

"I've got to accept a delivery from Sears for her. Bust cream and clouts. Now that we've got mail order, we can get the same things you White folks can."

"George, listen. How come the cops didn't lock you up?"

"Said charges were pending."

"Pardon me, Len," I said. "Is it not wise to obtain a barrister for George? In case Miss Stuart's condition degenerates?"

"Fellas, she's not Miss, she's my wife."

"Shake it George." Len snapped. "You didn't marry her now?"

"Common-law wife."

"Takes more than her popping in a few weeks at a time." Len started to pace. "What charge are they thinking about? It could be attempted murder, you know."

"They ain't going to charge me no such thing, because I didn't attempt anything. It's her own fault. If she hadn't been drinking gin and pitching a fit, she wouldn't've fallen nowhere."

"How's it that she's even alive?" Len asked. "I looked at the pavement that runs up to the front of the building. There isn't any blood."

"Grass yard on the Fortieth-Street side. We got a mess of rain this week, so it's spongy back there."

"I told you that gal was 'trouble with tits.' What if she says you did it? As much as she drinks, she may not even remember what happened."

"Oh, she'll be mad as a wet hen, but she won't press no charges. Not worried over that."

"Anyway, I brought Joshua along so we can set this right in the papers before the *Police Gazette* turns you into a crazed killer Negro. I can see them quoting your song: 'And he whistled when his wife was dead.' I wish you hadn't sung that part. We can't have that kind of bad press. Your gigs would wither to nothing."

Len continued to me, "Obviously, she was hanging out laundry, or cleaning the window, when she slipped."

George gave a small chuckle. "She never cleaned no window of mine in her life."

I sat down with George to work out what the public would read about Roskin's accident. The livelihoods of artists were so dependent on public image, and the public fickle. A musician is a sharecropper with two good suits. Without music jobs, George would be on the street. It was all he knew.

I considered everything I'd learned about the music business in America, or at least in New York. The whole thing operated one step away from criminal enterprise. Other industries promoted a veneer of stable autocracy, but entertainment reveled in cutthroat merit. Anybody could make it, and no one knew who would. Money alone could not buy the public's love. So, farm girls and street toughs could tap or punch their way to the top. A fantasy world both ugly and beautiful, a crazy fragmented mess. I wondered how long before a huge monopoly, oil or railroad, would buy up the whole music business.

Before I left to file the story for the final edition, I couldn't help but ask George one last thing.

"Given your fame for whistling, what reason do you have to carve one?"

George gave out his signature belly laugh. "Not for me, for Roskin. If I wasn't here when she fell; she might have lain on the ground all night. She couldn't get herself on her feet. In case she gets herself in trouble again, she can blow this here whistle."

March 1898

Joshua Clarke Banks,

You do try my patience. You may think I've waited long to write. Rest assured, I wrote you three letters before this one. Those were thrown into the fire. You wouldn't have liked them.

Why am I never consulted on matters that directly affect the course of my life? I'm repeatedly treated as a child, or an attachment, that must simply go where it is placed.

I fear you assume I or my mother have much sway on my father. He takes little counsel from men, and none from women. Mother never interferes with Father in matters of business. She says, "What if he took my advice and it turned out wrong? What then?" When I try to bring up your extension, Father only says, "We're interviewing candidates for the position," or "It'll all work out." Then he changes the subject to the next society ball. You'd think him a matronly socialite, the way he focuses on the social calendar.

Interviewing candidates? I can't believe there aren't hundreds of ambitious young men champing at the bit to go to America on assignment. How can it be so hard to pick one? You had no special qualifications for the post, and you were sent. You may have to stand up to Father at some point. He does not appreciate or respect conciliation.

Thank God I have my schoolwork or I'd gone mad. At first, I couldn't decide whether to concentrate on math or science. I've become obsessed with cosmology. You'll think me a full anorak. I'll talk to you of nothing but nebulae and red giants when you return.

I did ride Nike. I believe she misses you as well. I thought it quite strange that neither your brother John nor your father had the slightest idea of what you were about in America, or when you were scheduled to return. Don't you write each other at all? Even Aubrey complains your letters tell nothing.

If I were a man, I'd have already boarded a steamer, unaccompanied, and sailed to America to fetch you. I'm denied this course merely due to my sex. I've talked to my brother about escorting me to visit you, but I'd have to wait until he is off from university in January.

If you don't come home soon, you will drive me to take up bareback riding, or I shall have to borrow Sarah's Vigor machine.

Reluctantly waiting,

—M

May 1898
Editorial – London

AMERICA BLUNDERS

by Joshua Banks

Having seeded and nurtured the American continent into bloom, and after certain unpleasantness, it is clear that it was best for Britain to sever its familial ties to the American colonies. America and Americans were never to be appropriate partners in the great responsibility and burden we British bear in bringing enlightenment and order to the world.

Likewise, the United States is a country particularly unsuited for empire. Britain brings generations of established hierarchical order and unshakable tradition to its colonies. The United States is all about individual action and innovation. President Washington wisely advised his fellow citizens to resist the lure of foreign entanglements. Yet America has gleefully declared war on Spain.

It is in no way my intent to ignore Spain's heavy hand in quelling rebellion in Cuba. All civilized nations should condemn such excesses. But opprobrium does not license intercession. Even if we give full sway to the so-called Monroe Doctrine, it should only permit the United States from preventing new colonization activities in Latin America. Does America now contend that it exercises full domination over the entire Western Hemisphere? Surely it does not think it could question Britain's sovereignty over the Falklands?

What is to be said about the assistant secretary of the Navy, Theodore Roosevelt, ordering Admiral Dewey to attack the Spanish fleet in the Philippines? The Spaniards surrendered quickly, but will the insurgents embrace American masters any more than the fleeing Spanish?

There are deeper concerns as well. It is at least American constitutional intention that the franchise is extended to the Negro, although Southern states still employ insidious barriers to frustrate that intent. Also, if the suffragettes are to be believed, women will have the vote any day now. How is America to remain true to its ideals if it leaves its natural confines and plants itself around the world? If America does subdue the Philippines, will its inhabitants become American citizens? Will they vote in American elections?

America blundered into this affair with a naive enthusiasm for war that should concern all nations. Special attention should be paid to the manner in which newspapers, especially the so-called Yellow Press, beat the drums for war. Let us not forget the late claims of a torpedo in the USS *Maine*, now discredited.

When a paper declares that a journalism of action allows it, unelected by citizens, to send its own agents into a foreign country to break that country's laws, what remains of democracy? Might railroad bosses and oil barons raise armies to carry out foreign policy as they personally see fit?

This frantic hunger for combat is exemplified in the want-to-be cowboy, Teddy Roosevelt, who is expected to resign as assistant secretary of the Navy to seek a commission in the cavalry attacking Cuba. It is being suggested that all manhood is being forfeit by those men and boys who do not forthwith throw themselves into this misadventure. Even a major news publisher is being mocked as Willeboy and shamed for "sultanic languor and sybaritish luxury" instead of going personally to war. I fear such men may take their wealth and organize their own ill-thought military operations, putting at risk American soldiers and foreign policy. Who knows what interest such men have? I recall that one of the aforementioned publisher's own columnists said he could not take the publisher seriously, for he reminded one of a kindly child: thoroughly undisciplined, and possessed of a destructive tendency that might lead him to set fire to a house in order to see the engines play water on the flames.

As the USA heads down this questionable path of conquest and empire, its press must stand as objective presenters of truth and dogged questioners of policy and power, not cheerleaders of destruction.

Chapter 15

I spent the first seven months of my extension disappointed but in good spirits. Carousing the city with Wyatt, backstage passes to the shows (and what's not shown), a never-ending parade of youthful muscle and blood. Filling journals and pitching stories now felt more normal than returning home. After two and a half years, I was a common face at every opening night, variety show, two-bit music hall, and exhibition. The show people embraced me for my generally enthusiastic reviews and discretion. Unlike others on the entertainment beat, I didn't spill ink on their peccadilloes. The drunken no-show, the stage-door Johnny or Jane—or, in one case, both—noisily helping the artist "rehearse his lines"— none of it left my pen.

There lies the reason Len Spencer chose me when the Stuart woman fell from George's window. While he didn't expect me to lie, he expected fairness and avoidance of the sensational. On a positive note, no charges were brought against George. Not only did Roskin forgo a complaint, she was living with George again. The reporter on the police blotter did tell me that Roskin promised: "I'll get hunk with him when I get out"—whatever that meant. Neither Len nor I thought the situation healthy. No matter the merits of magnesium chloride and water each on their own, the two caused mischief together.

Clifton returned, and often offered his second seat at the opera, symphony, and ballet. He retained his British reserve, listening more than talking, sparing his advice. I thought of him as much of a kindly uncle as a friend. Luther continued his mission to counterbalance such feminizing high culture by dragging me to the gym at the YMCA. If only to repair an excess of late nights and libations, I joined the Y. Luther managed so far as to get me to fumble about with a basketball. I played him one-on-one the few times when no one was around to witness the travesty.

For a man, a young man, on the cusp of marriage, these final laps in the pool of independent bachelorhood were a guilty pleasure. For the first time in my life, since the moment I'd boarded the steamer, all parental supervision was stripped from my life. The *Journal*, and indeed, Nowak, cared not of my comings and goings as long as deadlines were met. I might rise early at five with the chirping birds or sleep until the chimes at noon. Whiskey and frog legs were a conceivable breakfast, as was a dinner of milk and eggs. When the cold ice blew, I could sensibly don my covert, or bear the weather with no one to fuss to or question me. I missed Margaret dearly and was ready to start a civilized life, but I wanted to stack up some adventure first.

Of such mind, as I was about to head out on a pleasant May evening, I sat in the lobby, waiting for Wyatt to arrive in the Spider. There was a young girl singer, Ada Jones, and we were keen on catching her act. She performed comic songs while colored slides projected on-screen down at Huber's Palace Museum, a place that also featured freak shows, dancing monkeys, and an armless pianist who played the keys with his toes. Wyatt entered, casting quick glances about the room, studying faces.

"Come now, Wyatt. Are you already three miles down the road?"

"What? No. Sober as a corpse."

"Corpses are embalmed, you know."

"Josh, not the time for clever repartee. Change of plans. A note—definitely from the *Journal*—got the code. No signature, though."

"We going to a different show? Or . . . did we get a real story? A shooting, a labor riot, a—"

"No, Josh. Just says to take you to North Brooklyn, Greenpoint, and drop you at an address."

"A bit overly dramatic. Oh God, it isn't one of those hideous surprise parties. I never told anyone my birthdate."

"Stop, you got to take this serious. It don't smell right. Why aren't they meeting you at the office? Why all the way cross town? It doesn't even say what the place is. If I were you, I'd pack a firearm."

"Sorry, Wyatt. Left the Lee-Metford by the hearth back home."

"Here, take this." Wyatt made sure no one was looking at us. Leaning close, he passed a small Colt rimfire derringer covered in filigreed gold.

"Fancy."

"Yeah, it's a Cuno Helfricht engrave. Helped a pawn broker out of a jam with some toughs, so he gave it to me. You only get one shot, so if you get in trouble, take out the lead guy. And don't bump the thing. It's all ready to go."

"You are making me nervous, but I am sure there is a simple, non-nefarious explanation. Probably some theater cast party or celebrity shindig they want me to cover."

"I'm instructed not to follow you in."

"Keeping the hoi polloi at bay. Must be elite."

Wyatt reddened. I held up my palm.

"In any case, I have your little one-eyed protector to watch over me. If you are still concerned when you drop me off, park around the corner. My mother gave me a bobby whistle the first time we went to London in case I got lost. I've carried it ever since. If there's any trouble, you will hear it, loud as a siren."

The address was on Manhattan Avenue between Nassau and Greenpoint. As we approached, Wyatt gave me the lay of the land. In the last few years, the whole neighborhood had taken on a Polski smak, a flavor of Poland. The first Polish church, St. Stanislaus Kostka, was already built, but not finished, on Driggs Avenue with plans to double its size. From butchers, bakers, and barbers to undertakers—all recent Polish immigrants—the neighborhood was fast becoming the largest Polish enclave outside of Chicago. Polish hands could find work at the Haverman Sugar Plant and the American Hemp Rope manufacturing company.

"Hell," Wyatt said. "We deliver the *Journal* here, but most read their own weekly, the *Zgoda*."

"Please, Wyatt, you do not also read Polish?"

"Read it? That's like a whole other alphabet. Nah, but I can understand some of it if they talk slow."

Walking into the address, a restaurant with a Polish name, I was confused to be ushered back to see Nowak, and only Nowak, sitting in a circular corner booth. He was sending off a pink-cheeked waiter as I approached. He didn't bother to stand.

"Ah, Banks. So glad you could make it. Please, sit. I didn't want to order your food until I was sure you were here. Good food like this, well, you don't want to let it wait. Here, here, sit."

Nowak handed me a plate with bread and salt. Unsure what to say, I said nothing. Nowak said nothing but started eating the meal already at his place. Having grown up around livestock, I recognized pig's liver with sautéed onions. There was also a large, steaming bowl of tomato soup. Nowak paused from his meal to dab at his lips with a folded cloth napkin.

"I need to get back to the paper, and I need to speak to you, so excuse me for starting my dinner early. I assume you know nothing of the delicacies of Poland, except maybe pierogi. A whole cuisine, reduced to pierogi. So, I've ordered for you.

"I've gotten you tea. I'm not sure you're up for the boza." He gestured at a milky drink that looked fermented. "Tonight, I favor simple fare. But for you, Królewskie Jadlo."

"Thank you." This was all wrong. What was Nowak up to? A Judas kiss? It felt like the cheerful hospitality of the hangman administering the prisoner's last meal. I nibbled on a piece of bread—warm, crusty. All the while, Nowak ate and studied me. He dabbed his lips again.

"Let me ask you a question. You fancy yourself a good writer?"

Did the situation call for false modesty or blind confidence? I cut the difference.

"I do not claim to be Henry James or Twain, but I acquit myself professionally."

"Really. You tell me you intend to become a journalist? This isn't a rich-boy frolic?"

"Journalism, yes. I have no fallback."

"That's a shame, Banks. You're lazy, you just want it handed to you. You're not a complete hack. The Wilde story and some of the lynching pieces were pretty good, but you haven't studied the craft. A carpenter needs to know the difference between an eight-penny and a ten-penny nail, and when to use them. You call yourself a writer and don't know an asyndeton from an antimetabole."

Uncertain whether Nowak wanted a response, and before I could offer him one, my meal was set before me.

The waiter made an elaborate gesture of uncovering the dish. "*Smacznego*, sir." The waiter bowed slightly and withdrew.

"Well, go ahead. Taste it." Nowak sounded like someone feeding a pet or a child. "The beef roulade is zrazy wolowe zawijane. The house filling is a smear of mustard, bacon, pickles and onion, a drizzle of cream sauce with mushroom. See? Sublime."

It recalled a similar Bavarian rolled beef dish but with a more complex mix of flavors, each one divine.

"Now you must try the mizeria. The cucumbers are cut thin enough to see through, and the sour cream is livened with chives and dill. The cook uses a little too much sugar and lemon juice for my taste, but *eh, co nie*."

The mizeria was, indeed, creamy and refreshing, but my mind was racing with questions. Why was Nowak acting like a grand auntie? Was he toying with me?

"Listen, Banks. Tradition, it's so important. You know, you are what you eat. Okay, so we assimilate—to a degree. My mother, she adopted the ketchup, but we must also keep the polskosé. I tell you, the mother comes from the homeland and brings its traditions. She cooks as in the Old Country, and the family is nourished in its heritage. But the daughters are lazy and make no effort to learn. One day, the mother is gone, and the daughter cooks the American way, which makes dogs tuck their tails between their legs and hide. And we have pork chops, and ham and eggs, over and over until the husband and sons are indifferent to everything. The Polish soul within them starves and dies."

I could take it no longer. "Why are you telling me all this? Why am I here?"

"You've done a very foolish thing."

"Pardon?"

"Young men do impetuous acts, but lines were crossed."

I felt a cold sweat break out on my forehead.

"You see, Banks, loyalty is a tradition, a bond. When you wrote that editorial, when you criticized this country, your host, and you repeated the mocking of the Chief, your employer, you broke those bonds. You were disloyal."

"Did Mr. Hearst say—"

"Shut up, Banks. I'm the one talking. Mr. Hearst doesn't have time to read the London papers, but I and others do. We can't let this go. It's bad precedent. Breeds subversion, disrespect, mutiny. I wasn't sure what to do about you. Took months. Then our man in London gets a tip to check out your family down in Montserrat. Nothing fleshed out, rumors. What with the war and all, we've got reporters and stringers all over the Caribbean, even a fellow Brit. It only took a couple of days for my guys to turn up all this."

He raised a large manila file folder from the seat beside him. Nowak did not throw it on the table. He laid it as gingerly as if it were a bomb.

"White mischief. Think they call it in the islands. Seems great-grandfather Nathan Noah Banks's tastes ran toward the exotic. Poor Martha Wellington Banks, so hard to keep up appearances. Oh boy, what a scandal. Good thing so far away from the British Isles, huh?"

I stared into Nowak's hawk eyes, which now burned with fire.

"I do not have a bloody idea what you are going on about." I knew it wise to control myself, but the words came out hard and mean.

"Drop the act, Shakespeare. I've got all the family secrets right here." He gently patted the file. "Birth records, mortuary descriptions, a hand-tinted copy of a painting of your grandfather, Philip Hamish Banks."

It bothered me that he tossed my ancestors' names, full names, as a cat sports with a mouse before the kill. Of equal irritation was his mention of a painting of Grandfather Philip. Unlike my other relatives, whose elegant portraits lined the halls of our Yorkshire riding estate, Philip was notable for his absence. He died on Montserrat at a rather young age, never having time to sit for a portrait, or so we were always told.

"After Philip's unfortunate demise, Mary Alice stayed on at Montserrat. She was a good thirteen years older than Philip and heading toward spinsterhood when she was imported from England to wed Philip and clean up the bloodline. Your father, James Andrew, the grand baron who fled the island in his youth, only visited her once. Broke her heart, it did."

"You cannot possibly know what my grandmother thought." It

came out as a shout. A muscular doorman poked his head around the wall to look at us, but Nowak smiled and waved him away.

"That's just it, Banks. I do know. When Mary Alice died in 1872, two years before you were born, your family had her remains shipped back to Aysgarth for burial. Your father arranged for a local agent on Montserrat to liquidate what remained of the indigo plantation and all belongings. He wanted only proceeds returned. Everything was sold, including Mary Alice's personal letters, and better still, her diary. A local historian bought the lot, stuck it in his barn until my men bought it. Makes for riveting reading."

I tried to collect myself. "I hardly think the frequency of my father's visits to his mother a major scandal. Also, he did not flee the island. He was sent back to receive a proper education."

"*Ojejku*!" Nowak shook his head with a long blink of his eyes.

"I. Don't. Speak. Polish." I could barely control myself.

"I. know," Nowak mocked, and sat back and steepled his hands. "You really don't have a clue, do you? Ha, so I'll be the one to hang dogs on you. Martha Wellington Banks isn't your great-grandmother. Nathan coupled with a Montserrat Negress, Philip Hamish Banks, their mulatto bastard. If you go by the painting, kind of light-skinned, so they tried to pass him off as legitimate, but you can see it—the hair, the nose.

"Nathan thought he could breed the stain out of the family. That's why he imported the Whitest woman he could find, Mary Alice Trent, to marry Philip. Your father, James, the quadroon, did the same by marrying Elizabeth Opal Mildenhall. You, Joshua Clarke Banks, are a mere octoroon, one-eighth Negro. A couple of more generations, and I guess you're out of the woods. The stain is washed clean. But around here, one drop of black is black, and I reckon it would ruin your father, and you, and the rest of your family if it got out."

Paggered, incapable of speech, I started shaking. The derringer lay puny against my leg. My mast snapped and impaled my hull; I started taking on water, sinking.

"Take a sip of tea, boy. You look pale. Don't you dare chuck any of that fine Polish food."

By now, I'd sunk to the bottom of the sea, the pressure of the ocean on my chest.

"What—what are you going to do?"

"See, that's where you're lucky."

"Eh, I do not suppose you will show any kindness."

"Kindness? My kindness is legendary. Listen, a lot of editors, with a juicy story like this, would put it in the papers before a heartbeat. That's exactly what the London tipster wanted, I'll bet. To disgrace you before you ever make it back home. Well, that's not my circus, and you're not my monkey. I just want your highfalutin, unqualified ass out of my newsroom. I can't send you home before we get your replacement. Hearst doesn't want anything to screw up the deal with our correspondent on the London rag."

I felt the pressure increase. Cold darkness surrounded me.

"Wouldn't you know, Fate will have her way. Our reporter in Denver eats a can of poison beef, and bang, he's dead. Why the hell he's eating canned beef when he's living in Cow Town—well, he always seemed kind of goofy."

Nowak paused, leaned back, and stretched out his arms. "So, here's the deal. You agree to request the Denver position until time comes to steamer yourself across the pond."

"If I do not?"

"I'll print every salacious detail, damn the consequences."

"Why not just order me to Denver?"

"Technically, I can't. Only the Chief can. You got to request it. Right now, only me and my guy in the Caribbean know all the dirt. We haven't even shared anything with the London tipster; we only said we're still poking around. I already typed the letter on the Oliver." He handed me the paper. "You sign right now, and I'll approve it. Want you gone by the end of the week."

I surfaced enough to hold the pen and sign my name, then felt myself being pulled farther out to sea.

"Cheer up, Banks. Be an adventure. Don't let that food go to waste. I got the cook to make you some faworki, angel wings, for dessert. He didn't want to, after Lent and Easter. Bad luck. And I ordered you a brandy. You look like you need one. Oh, and you best leave the Oliver typewriter with me for safe keeping. There's a Remington waiting for you in Denver."

Nowak stood, rubbed his hands like he'd finished digging a grave, then strolled out the back of the restaurant. I sat there, fixed, buried at sea, and waited on the brandy, then sent a waiter down the street (with my police whistle as confirmation) to tell Wyatt to go on alone. I'd find a cab and didn't want conversation.

What would I tell him? Or anyone? The familiar pain flared in my left arm. I'd resisted taking any more of the mummy powder Dr. Qabash had left with me, but not tonight.

PART II

Manifest Destiny

Chapter 16

"Josh! Don't know if you're a dupe or a damn lickspittle!"

Wyatt was actually calming down. Moments before, he'd shown an impressive command of Anglo-Saxon curse words, oaths, and all manner of human and animal body parts and functions. He still prowled around my parlor like a trapped animal.

"Denver, swamp me. Swapping New York, world at our feet, for Denver?" Wyatt was pacing, agitated, running his fingers back through his hair.

"I do not see why this has to concern you," I said.

"'Cause I have to tail after you."

"New York, yes, but not Denver," I said but was flooded with a wave of relief that Wyatt might accompany me.

"No. What's that you call your publisher? Oh yeah, the Old Man. Well, he and your actual old man, together with not-so-old man Hearst, think it'd be best if I tagged along on your frolic to Cow Town."

"I am not a child," I said.

"Well, maybe not to you, but . . ."

"If it pains you so to leave, you could decline the offer."

"I can't."

"Why? You think I need you?" I was getting miffed, despite not wanting to change his mind.

"Not so much anymore. It's just, the money's too rich to turn down."

"Thank you for your warm personal loyalty, Mr. Brown."

"Aw shit, you don't know. I've got a good game in this town. I've been out west. I've seen the elephant, and I don't need a second look. This is causing all kinds of family problems."

"I see. Becca's not happy with you abandoning her."

"Worse."

I arched an eyebrow.

"She wants to come along, kids and all."

"Could you go back and forth every few months? Likely a year at most."

"She wants to rent a house, more room for the kids. I'm telling you I don't want to get stuck in Denver."

"Come now. The Wild West, adventure, the frontier."

Wyatt shook his head. "Haven't you heard? Frontier is done, over and gone. The government said it nice and official. We won the 'west' part, but we lost the 'wild' part."

"Wyatt, I hardly think—"

"I hear Denver's gone chinless," Wyatt said. "Women have taken over, and now it's all church clothes, parlor manners, and watch your language, all that 'moderation.' You couldn't get St. Louis? Old St. Lou is a wide-open town."

As Wyatt continued to lament the death of his New York sporting life, I gave a secret sigh of relief. I might not wish to tell him outright, but I still did *need* Wyatt. More than that I *wanted* him along. I never had a true chum, not the kind I read about in my youth: storybook friends sharing rumbly-tumbly adventures, always helping each other out of jams.

Boarding school relationships were primarily transactional. I gave myself permission to believe I had something more with Wyatt. There existed none of the competitive urge that so bedeviled my interactions with my brother John. Wyatt and I truly wished each other well and took no hidden delight when the other stumbled. Not so with my companions back in England, schadenfreude being the one German word the British knew well.

I also let myself believe that Wyatt owed nothing to my father nor Margaret's father, and Mr. Hearst surely had plenty of duties for Wyatt in New York. Who knew? Maybe he even asked to go.

There is no third warning bell on an American train, nor second or first. A hearty "All aboard," and the train is fast away, passengers be damned. On the other hand, you may rest assured your luggage will actually accompany you for thousands of miles, faithfully jumping railroad lines, whereas British railway companies managed to lose your baggage on a trip from London to Bath. We were taking the New York Central because it left from Grand Central Station and, with a change of track in Galion, Ohio, continued on as far as St. Louis, Missouri, where a change of line finished the journey to Denver.

No sooner had I settled in with my still-reluctant companion when we were accosted by an endless parade of boys—train butches—hawking all manner of trifles: lollipops, popcorn, newspapers, peanuts, and oddly, ivory ornaments. Even more annoying were the salesmen peddling insurance and patent medicines. Wyatt nearly fell prey to a fellow selling Clark Stanley's genuine snake oil liniment. The fellow claimed Mr. Stanley as the Rattlesnake King, although I pointed out to Wyatt that the concoction was manufactured in Rhode Island. Mr. Stanley appeared surely confident in his product. The label claimed relief from everything but nagging wives and taxes—frostbites, chilblains, bruises, rheumatism, neuralgia, sciatica, lumbago, contracted cords, sprains, swellings, and more. Curiously, it claimed to be useful with curing toothaches and sore throats, and at the same time, it warned it was only for external use. Thankfully, the conductor who was checking tickets saved us. After dodging that bullet, Wyatt told me of witnessing a one-legged man on a train attempting to sell a poem bemoaning his misery.

I determined to turn my banishment from New York into an opportunity. Heading west renewed my plan to compile a travelogue of the type that had been so popular in Britain in recent years: the sophisticated Englishman insightfully skewering unruly America. Even if the Yanks might think the frontier was dead, it remained alive in the European imagination. No account of the USA was worth a tinker's dam without portraits of the awful majesty of the untamed West.

My British reserve having faded, I resolved to talk to as many passengers as possible and get some feel for the lives of citizens outside the New York crucible. Wyatt provided a fine accomplice in this task. He shared that peculiar American quirk of being able to start a deep conversation with complete strangers.

Hungry, we made our way to the Pullman dining carriage. Wyatt's mood improved when he learned we had a sleeping car, as he called it. Wyatt thought it unlikely that Mr. Hearst had 'sprung' for such a luxury and 'figured' my paper must have 'chipped in.' I instead saw my father's hand in this, always helping me to fall gently.

The Black porters, and all the porters were Black, had changed out of their dark-blue outfits and labeled caps they had worn loading the luggage and now wore smart white jackets for dinner service.

Waiting for a table, I became confused hearing passengers referring to different waiters as George, or just boy. One porter, a dark, distinguished-looking older man, graying at the temples, approached to tell us there might be a short wait. I took the opportunity to ask, "My good man, what is your name? Surely you are not all George."

"No sir, that'd be Mr. Pullman, rest his soul, but I'll answer to it just the same."

"But what is your name?"

"Ralphie, sir." He finished every utterance with a polite smile.

"Strikes one a tad familiar to address a man of your age with a boy's name. Feels like you would have to call me Joshie just to even it out."

"Oh, I'm sure I wouldn't do that, sir. I'll be back to fetch you in a few minutes." Ralphie gave a courteous little nod of his head and went off to attend to a table that was about to finish eating.

"You're not getting him to break character, you know," said the man waiting in front of us.

"Pardon?" I said.

"Pullman works these poor devils to death for low wages, makes 'em buy their food and uniforms, but it's still the best job any darkie's gonna find. Sure as hell beats picking cotton. These boys are working for tips, so they'll take a lot of guff."

"I see," I replied. So, finally, I found a true servant class in America. Many European travelers complained bitterly about the surly arrogance of American waiters. One Frenchman explained these waiters were rude because they only served at the table incidentally while waiting to become president of the United States. Footmen, cooks—no matter. The White servant in America sincerely believed he'd retained the option to become the master. These colored porters knew they had the same options as most English servants: labor in the fields, or become a convict. Truthfully, most Negroes didn't even have the recent wretched opportunity to sweat blood in a factory.

I'd witnessed men like Ralphie in the manor houses of England, especially those with a large staff. My father preferred a lean staff. Where he might have called a boy servant by his Christian name, he used Mr. and Mrs. with the older help. Father so respected our butler that everyone was instructed to call him Mr. Crenshaw, despite some guests grumbling at the indignity. I do not believe I ever heard his given name.

"Gents." The man in front of us began talking again. "May I make a proposal? A table for four has opened up. They'll be reluctant to seat only you two, and they'll wait for a deuce before seating just me. I suggest we dine together."

Wyatt piped up. "Don't see why not." Laying the groundwork of revealing my African quandary would have to wait. A crowded dining room might not be the proper forum, in any case.

"Where're my manners? The name's Ben Lewis, sometimes Big Ben, like that big old clock tower of yours."

I almost corrected him that Big Ben, technically, was the nickname of the largest of the five bells in the clock tower, or St. Stephen's Tower if you like, but even I realized I'd sound like a pompous arse.

"Heading up to Albany for a big union meeting," he continued. "I'm glad for the company."

Wyatt and I made our introductions. Mr. Lewis's plan worked. We were seated and ordered quickly.

Mr. Lewis was one of those people whose life engine runs so hot, one suspects they have an extra furnace. His speech and manner indicated he'd managed to embrace education whilst spurning any accompanying refinement. Though his nearly black hair and mustache were trimmed like a Wall Street banker, his deportment suggested a middle-weight, bare-knuckle brawler dressed up for a funeral.

Ready for spirited conversation, it quickly appeared we had stumbled into a lecture. Finding me not only foreign, but also a newspaper man, Lewis deemed it his solemn duty I get the 'skinny' on the Struggle. Though evangelistic on the righteous cause of labor, his scarred knuckles suggested pugilist more than prophet.

"That Georgie may be afraid to speak ill of the newly departed," Lewis gestured toward the porter. "But I'm under no such compunction. I don't give a fig if Pullman raised half of Chicago out of a swamp. He was a feudal lord and a murderer."

I choked down a wholly inappropriate laugh, since he was telling *me*, a man whose family tree was rooted in feudal lording and quite possibly fertilized with a murder or two.

"He didn't have to pull the trigger himself with the strikers. He had the government in his pocket. Local police weren't having no trouble till the Feds sent the cavalry and soldiers' bayonets stirring everybody up, Feds pretending it was about protecting the mail. Do you kill folks over a late letter? On the Fourth of July, no less!"

Lewis banged his fist on the fine linen tablecloth as the crystal chandeliers clinked, and we diligently worked our way through a second bottle of French claret.

"The papers reported a mob, a riot," I said.

"Those weren't no union boys. Maybe a few, but you can only push a man so far. What, a few hotheads burned up some railroad property. Does that grant the right to kill dozens?"

Lewis was not looking for a discussion, only an audience, so Wyatt and I merely shook our heads.

"Damn right. Whoever actually set those fires probably already skedaddled before the shooting started." Lewis took a healthy mouthful of wine. "The owners are playing with fire. You get it down so there's only two classes, the filthy rich and ragged poor. That's two dangerous classes."

Thankfully, Wyatt refrained from any of his "Your Lordship" quips, or anything else that might have starkly revealed my upper-class status. I even backed off on the crispness of my acquired Oxford accent to more of a neutral Cambridge one. My family had just barely entered the royalty, and I merely stood in the doorway, but my family was wealthier than many an earl or duke, and my father would never let me truly fall into the lower classes. I could be embarrassingly pitiful, but not a pauper.

It was becoming achingly clear to me that I'd never much considered the British class system. It had always been the natural order of things, be it holy or mean. Who would be the baker if not the baker's sons? Who would work the fields but the children of farmers? Just as the progeny of the barrister would find their place in Court or

Commons, the maid's offspring would inhabit laundry and kitchen. If England's growing industrialization threatened to crack the class foundation, the structure still stood, for now.

America, however, aspired to be different—a society without classes, or at least the ability to rise and fall from one station to the other. Was the American experiment starting to prove that its early social and economic mobility was an aberration, achieved only by accident or forcible intervention? Perhaps it was the nature of society that a few inevitably reveled in excess as the many struggled in need.

Mr. Lewis fell behind the pace of the dinner and appeared to be concentrating on the liquid course. We soldiered on to the third bottle of claret with Lewis as our chief gunner.

Lewis took a significant sip and continued. "And the courts are in the companies' pockets, too. Companies keep merging, taking over monopolies and trusts, and pretty soon, instead of working for the one big shot in your hometown, you're working for a collection of big shots clear cross the country. They don't have to worry about running into workers at the park, in church, or at the county fair, so they got no shame squeezing the working man. But do the powers that be go after the monopolies?"

"I gather they don't," I said, just wanting to hear my own voice. Wyatt appeared caught up in Lewis's enthusiasm.

"McKinley's got no stomach for trust-busting. No, they take that Anti-Trust Act and the Interstate Commerce Clause and go after the unions. If we so much as talk about a strike, we're a restraint of trade. Put our man Debs in jail. Take away a man's freedom of speech in the name of free labor and freedom to contract. I call it wage slavery. We're not their property, just a business cost, so they don't care if we starve or die. Companies trying to take all the skill out of jobs, cut it all up into simple tasks so they can bring in unskilled obedient men, call it scientific management."

My attention drifted to a porter that was meticulously folding napkins and arranging table settings as if expecting the Queen. Another porter inquired if there was a problem with Mr. Lewis's steak and asked if we would be enjoying a cheese course before dessert. Lewis took the clue and set about devouring his steak. Neither Wyatt nor I jumped in to pick up the conversation, afraid we might distract Lewis from the accomplishment of his task. The apple cobbler from the next table smelled tauntingly delicious, so we sat in quiet, each man to his own thoughts.

My mind kept dwelling on Ralphie and the other Black porters. They needed to navigate the strong currents of both race and class. I wondered if my newly discovered smidgen of Blackness negated my class advantage, and might my father, with his larger dollop, be ruined in his social standing if Nowak revealed our hidden ancestor? Such knowledge actually changed nothing, yet everything would change.

Miss Moon recently enlightened me about the constant incidents of rape of slave women, by masters and others (along with the rare secret love match), to the extent that nearly every African American was commingled with European blood. Should that then elevate their status, their class? Not to the White citizen, who claimed their race superior to all, but also so fragile it is completely tainted by the slightest admixture of the other.

Ralphie and the porters had raised themselves out of fieldwork. Were they a new class? Did the enslaved plantation have the luxury of internal segregation? Had those toiling in the sun and rain resented the slaves working in the relative comfort of the main house? Now nominally free, would colored people create new class distinctions based solely on education, wealth, and merit, or would they create races within races? Already the Creole of New Orleans with their opera and French lessons looked down noses at their darker cousins. Perhaps they would mirror the White majority's attempt to cull its ranks of undesirables, classing some as brutes. I often heard gentlemen and ladies on the East Coast refer to the Scotch Irish populating the mountains of Appalachia as practically subhuman, calling them waste people, mudsills, and White trash.

Without the hundreds of years of tradition enforcing the British class model, Americans were confused as to what justified status. College professor or cowboy, self-made robber-baron or iron-muscled laborer? Who was more noble, high-society maven or gritty factory girl?

Lewis, once returned to his task, engulfed his slab of beef so quickly that I thought to look under the table but checked the impulse. The cobbler, with its confederation of tart apple and crumbly crust, was finally served to great enjoyment. Truly hesitant to spoil the cheerful mood, my aristocratic pedigree did not permit silence on one point.

"Mr. Lewis," I said, trying to keep a tone of irritation out of my voice. "Earlier you equated Mr. Pullman being a rank murderer to being also like a feudal lord. Whatever did you mean?"

Wyatt must have grown tired of remaining passive, because he interjected with a mouthful of apples and crumbs that threatened to escape with his words. "The town . . . He built a town for the workers, named it Pullman."

Lewis leaned forcefully toward the table, preparing to bellow, caught sight of a passing young lady, and lowered his voice to a harsh whisper. "He didn't build it for the workers. That town was a money-making proposition. Pullman said so himself. He turned a profit off his laborers. Even when the Depression hit, and he cut wages and laid off men, he never cut the rent."

"Sounds like a cruel landlord, not a feudal king," I said.

"Hey, I'm not taking potshots at King Arthur, but in our country, in this day and age, you can't expect to treat a grown man like a little child. Pullman owned and ran the whole town, no government. He posted rules of behavior, what entertainments were appropriate.

There wasn't but one saloon in the whole town 'cept the one in the fancy hotel, for visitors. We didn't fight wars to be free of kings and the church just to let corporations be our masters."

Wyatt chimed in. "You know, Pullman died so afraid of workers taking revenge on his body that he made sure the casket was encased in steel and concrete. You got to earn that kind of hatred."

I searched my bowl but could find no more cobbler. Lewis asked us to stay for whiskey and cigars, but I begged off, claiming a headache. In truth, Lewis exhausted me.

Before I could fully retreat to the sanctity of the sleeping carriage, Lewis pulled me in close and, in a confidential tone, said, "Write this in your paper. I'm afraid there's serious trouble coming. There was blood on the streets of Haymarket, and there'll be more blood till we get treated with human dignity, eight hours for work, eight hours for sleep, and eight hours for what we will. We want more, and we're gonna get it."

I detached myself and headed back to my carriage, a bit of reading and, I hoped, a sound sleep. Lewis had made a point—even if I wished to ignore it and cling to the world of my childhood. In France, Germany, even Mother Russia, those at the bottom were growing restless of supporting those at the top. Britain had known labor violence; there were fourteen killed in the Peterloo Massacre, but that was nearly eight decades ago. Had we English learned? Perhaps violence was not essential to change society. Less than ten years ago, the London dockers had struck and got their tanner without a shot fired, and with Cardinal Manning actually mediating.

I might have said such to Lewis, but I wasn't really confident in the future. Instead I stood staring out the window, watching the dark landscape rush by a mile a minute. Everything seemed different now. Change moved too fast, especially in America. Americans rushed to trains, rushed through meals, rushed to embrace every new technology, and soon, it appeared, they might rush toward empire.

The new was good by its very newness, and history was bunk. I, too, kept rushing forward, or was I only falling?

Chapter 17

The persistent presence of Black porters served as a constant reminder of what I was running from, and the absence of certainty of what I was running to. I watched a tall, deep-ebony porter make up the bed, careful not to tuck the pillow under his chin as he slipped on the pillowcase. I tried to imagine what earthly connection might I have with his authentic experience of life as a Negro, just because I shared one-eighth common ancestry.

"Blood will tell." Tell what? That lips may be thin or full, noses narrow or flat? Was blood a red magic elixir embedded with ghosts? If I could take a transfusion of a quart of the ebony porter's blood, would I feel the sting of a single lash of the master's whip? Might it impart to me a map of struggle and perseverance? No. It was only blood, oil in the machine.

I needed to work all this out, march it around the field, and get a look at it, but who could I trust? It was past time for me to drop off a letter to Margaret at the next station, to explain why I up and left New York, running nearly a continent farther away from home, her, and marriage. Much as I loved and respected Margaret, I didn't know how to share this secret with her. We simply escaped any discussion of our views of other races, such matters inconsequential to our romance. I knew her to be my intellectual equal, or better, but education guaranteed no sure shield against her reacting in revulsion or disdain. Bigotry of late had taken to parading about dressed as science, with learned professors confidently pontificating on the inherent hierarchy of the races, curiously with the White man, no matter his education, abilities, or intellect, always atop all members of all other races.

Did Margaret have a right to know? Our children would carry only one-sixteenth of the mark, a stain so faint as to be invisible, and their children at one thirty-second. In livestock you would consider it to be bred out. In any case, for now, I chose not to burden her with knowledge that she would, in turn, need to keep from her mother and father, and indeed, our own issue.

I decided not to confront my father immediately, despite my belief he must already know. Burdening Aubrey, throwing her world completely out of orbit, struck me as selfish and unnecessary. She would tell John everything. He'd always been sweet to her. She even took his side when John "stole" Nike at the steeplechase championship, citing firstborn prerogative.

I knew only one person to unburden myself to: Wyatt. There is never a good time to tell a friend you are not the person you have presented yourself to be. Not the normal bit of dodge we all use, touch of makeup on a blemish, a youthful indiscretion mercifully forgotten, but no, a full false identity, a mask. Wyatt deserved to know why he was being dragged away from his beloved New York. The longer I waited to reveal the truth, the more he might resent it. A subterfuge kept too long would turn to deceit, and eventually, to betrayal. Several times I started the matter with Wyatt, only to be muted by the sudden appearance of a conductor, passenger, or porter. When the possibility arose of an excursion from the train, I determined to seize the opportunity.

Like too much in my life, I'd not really been involved in the planning of the train route of the journey to Denver. Truth be told, I held only the sketchiest impression of where all the states were located. Cities like Indianapolis, St. Louis, and Buffalo were more of a mystery than New Delhi or Istanbul. So, it was a pleasant surprise to learn that our train was scheduled to pass a hair's breadth from Niagara Falls.

Wyatt did not understand my giddy enthusiasm. "It's a goddamn tourist trap," he insisted.

I tried to explain to him that an Englishman would be thought daft if he passed up a chance to see one of the Great Wonders of the World. My father, not the most patient man, had queued for most of an hour and paid a fee to witness Frederic Edwin Church's magnificent painting of the Falls, back when the image had toured England; a solo exhibit. Unlike the Niagara paintings of Sargent, Twachtman, Vanderlyn, and many others that framed the Falls in the landscape surrounding it, or the strange bird's-eye view by John Bachman, Church thrust the viewer out on the rim of Horseshoe Falls, engulfed in the power of nature. My father had brought opera glasses so as to study every inch of the nearly eight-foot painting.

"Well, I've been there, and Church left out all the hullabaloo crap," Wyatt warned.

When I discovered that on American trains, unlike the British, one may simply walk off, enjoy the day, then resume one's travels, I insisted on going and pressed Wyatt to accompany me. Approaching Niagara, I saw, and heard, what Wyatt was all up about. The area edging the Falls was a barker's carnival of tacky amusements of no apparent design. Indian bazaars shared the scene with Chinese pagodas, camera obscura rubbing shoulders with dancing pavilions. Church and his kin had also mercifully erased the electrical power plants and hotels that tarted up the view like the chip shops and arcades on Brighton Beach.

"You think this is boorish," said Wyatt. "They've got a sideshow with a pig that counts, and Jo-Jo the Dog-Faced Boy."

"Oh my lord, not the poor Russian lad? With hair all over his face? I thought he was in London."

"Nah. PT Barnum bought him. He's either here or touring the States."

"Poor boy. They make him bark and carry on, you know. Not right."

"It keeps him in bread and sausages, I guess. Hell, we're all barking for someone."

I had no reply to that and instead regarded the Falls. Despite the ragbag going on around us, the thundering tons of water raging over the brink of the Falls were majestic. Standing close to the edge, bellowing mist wetting my face, pushing away the smell of hot dogs, the roar drowning out the cries of carnies and children, civilization and its self-absorbed constraints melted away. Perhaps a God in Heaven cared deeply for humans, but His creation certainly did not. Nature might crush you in an instant, not out of spite but sheer indifference. Status, power, race, even piety meant nothing to these rushing waters. My head and heart roiled with concern—Margaret, Nowak, success, or failure—but the Falls held no answers.

I did sense that the carnival hubbub at the rim didn't lend itself to serious revelation, so I urged that we take the guided tour to the Cave of the Winds. Among the handful of tourists in our group, two were conspicuous. Frenchmen were lugging an elaborate film camera and tripod. From Goat Island, we all descended carefully down the circuitous spray-soaked staircase. I grew grateful for the flimsy rented mac, though my trouser legs and squeaking shoes were sodden. After fumbling while awkwardly attempting to get the hood up over my bowler, I gave up and tucked my hat under the coat. By the time we reached Aeolus Cave, Wyatt and another man followed my lead with their headwear. The ladies probably thanked Providence for hatpins, as one fellow watched remorsefully as his straw boater hat sailed out to be devoured by the hungry waters.

Finally, our small tour group stood contemplating the cascading waters from behind Bridal Falls. I maneuvered Wyatt away from the others, the roar of the Falls hopefully masking our discussions. The novelty of the film crew assured that we were ignored.

"Wyatt, I must say—"

"Yeah, I know, that's a shit ton of water."

"Well, yes, but no. What I mean to say is . . ." I wished I'd rehearsed a speech. The words withered in my mind.

"Out with it, man."

We were both leaning in to hear, our heads nearly touching. "You deserve to know the reason I needed to leave New York."

"Needed? Thought you asked to leave," Wyatt said. "For that damn book you keep talking about writing."

"That's not it. Nowak made me."

Wyatt shot me a puzzled look.

"More accurately, he gave me a choice of running back home or going to Denver."

"Stop dancing around."

I wasn't dancing, but I felt like Blondin crossing over the turbulent Falls on a slippery tightrope, afraid of a misstep. "Nowak wanted me gone. He discovered a family secret. He threatened a scandal."

"Come on, Your Lordship. How bad could it be? Spill."

"Back on Montserrat . . . my great-grandmother, she . . . she was a Negress." I needed to force the words out like an exorcism.

Wyatt jerked away as if punched. He then stared at me like we'd just met. He waited, a moment that felt interminable, studying my face to see if I was making a bad joke. Surely my family's dirty secret must rather be larceny or murder.

Then Wyatt leaned in so I could hear him over the relentless torrent paces away. His face was set, his voice low and hard. "You selfish son of a bitch."

My tightrope shuddered, and I slipped into the abyss. "What?"

"You heard me."

"But I thought you had the right to—"

"No. No. No. Not for me, for yourself. I never, never needed to know any of this."

"But the truth," I said.

"I'd preferred a lie. And what, pray tell, am I supposed to do with this information?"

"I really haven't thought it all through. My mind has been a jumble. I need someone to help me sort it out."

Wyatt's face went from anger to disgust. "You know, I've shared a cup with you. I've slept in the same room. Here I think I'm rubbing elbows with a high-tone lord when I'm actually slumming with a nigger."

"Wyatt, please. That word."

"I can see now why that word bothers you and your mulatto dad."

"Not mulatto. I believe the unfortunate term is quadroon."

"Shut the hell up." Wyatt's face was wet from the mist, but I thought he might be weeping. The Falls seemed to howl now.

"I am still the same man," I said.

"Are you? You led me on all along."

"Wyatt, I assure you I had not a clue about this until Nowak showed me the report."

"Come off it."

"That's the reason I need to keep Nowak from going public. I am quite certain my brother and sister do not know. My dear mother had no reason to suspect. Jesus, Mary, and Joseph, I cannot even be sure my father is aware. He was sent to England at a young age, and his father was reputed to be relatively fair-skinned."

Wyatt was about to curse, or perhaps strike me, but the tour guide scuttled us out of the cave, past the constant deluge, and up the dreary steps to the top. Wyatt went ahead of me and did not look back. Soon we were again milling through the scrum of crowds and concessions. After a while, Wyatt's demeanor calmed from angry to sullen.

"You will not tell anybody, will you?" I asked.

"Who would I tell? Hearst? He'd kick your barely-Black ass back to merry ole England. There ain't no Negroes on the newspaper. What good would you be to anybody then?"

I realized I'd not considered Wyatt's feelings, only my own need to confess. I set myself to gently warming the very cold shoulder of my sole close friend in America.

It would be several hours before dinner and, knowing Wyatt possessed a serious sweet tooth, I suggested we get a treat. Wyatt, if not enthusiastically, nodded his head in agreement. Weaving past the fried meat stalls reeking of grease, and the souvenir Indian bead stand, we found the precise ticket, an ice cream vendor. Wyatt claimed the last two spots on a nearby bench, and I went to order. I returned with two tulip-shaped, footed vases, each brimming with two scoops of vanilla ice cream, a generous coating of cherry sauce, topped with an upturned dollop of whipped cream and a nestled maraschino cherry, along with two long-handled spoons.

"Oh my, come to Papa." Wyatt, like a growling dog distracted by a squirrel, was too taken by desire to maintain his glower. "What's this?" he asked.

"The special. The vendor kept mentioning Stoddart Drug Store down in Buffalo. He referred to it as a sundae, for some reason. There were peanuts as well, but I thought it a step too far."

"This is perfect," said Wyatt, already mining a deep hole in the cold mound of white and red.

I took a taste. "Agnes Marshall, this is good."

"Is that some odd British swear word?" Wyatt mumbled with the spoon in his mouth.

"No. She was the so-called Queen of Ices back home. A fine-looking woman, at least by her picture. Our cook used her recipe book to make cream ice on my birthdays."

Wyatt had dispatched nearly half of the treat. "Was it as good as this?"

"I hate to admit it, no. There are a few things you Yanks get right. Americans are more willing to look at an honored tradition and say to themselves, hey, let's pour cherry sauce on that thing."

"Josh?" Wyatt's spoon rattled in the glass.

"Yes?"

"Can't we just ignore this whole blood thing?"

"I don't know. I don't think so."

"One-eighth don't amount to much. Damn hard spotting any African about you. I mean, you could be one-eighth woman and I wouldn't fuck you."

"Ouch. I do not know whether to be offended or relieved."

"You know what I'm saying."

"Yes, I do. I'm still trying to figure this out myself. I could certainly use some help."

We sat quietly, finishing our sundaes. I nervously waited for a sign whether I'd lost Wyatt or not. Was I destined to lose everyone?

"You gonna eat that cherry?" Wyatt asked, licking his lips.

I handed him my glass and watched happily as Wyatt fished out the cherry with the long-handled spoon and ate it without a thought.

The train trip returned to its daily and nightly rhythms. We passed through Cleveland, changed tracks in Galion, Ohio, and on through Indianapolis and St. Louis. At the rail hub in Moberly, Missouri, Wyatt insisted on visiting an establishment called the Sycamore, a bawdy house whose ladies had gained much renown among the train personnel Wyatt had chatted with. He was told they might have a

New Orleans ham kick, where pantsless women attempted to kick a suspended ham while men leered at the contestants. I begged off, claiming a migraine. Wyatt did not protest. I believe he wanted some time apart. Whilst outwardly Wyatt had, indeed, chosen to just ignore the blood thing, underneath, I sensed a germ of tension that now infected our friendship.

I stood with others at the train yard, watching a railroad bull go from carriage to carriage, checking for tramps. Three hobos had apparently saw him coming, for they bolted from a freight container, their sacks bobbing on their backs, the rail cop shouting curses, waving his billy club.

There it was again. The issue of class in this classless society. We all wore badges of status: our manner of speaking, the words we used and those we did not, the carriage of the body as we walked or even sat, how we held a pencil or fork. The colonists had been proud of the superiority of their rustic ways over the fussy mannerisms of the decrepit Old World. Nonetheless, humans are bent on order and rank, and the Americans did not reinvent human nature. I wished for some way to help the hobos, but I would not be their hero today.

I had saved Margaret's life once. The massive sire horse had towered over her on his hind legs, his huge hooves heading menacingly toward her skull. I'd been lucky, they said, when shielding her, to have only suffered several cracked ribs and a lacerated forearm.

The truth, I now saw, was that it's easier to be a hero than a good man. Back then, I'd had no time to think, to reason the pros and cons, to search for excuses. I must have appeared the proper white knight in the Fens that morning, wounded, framed by an opportune sun lighting up the spring dew like jewels clinging to the fields. How much disappointment had I caused Margaret since that fantastical introduction?

The last long remnant of Kansas and into Colorado was bleak and arid. Where the rolling hills, the maple, oak, and sycamores of New

England provided a comforting familiarity, this vista was foreign and unforgiving. Confronted with such barren vastness, Americans could scarcely tell you the miles to your next destination but measured distance in hours, or days, away.

June 1898

Dearest Margaret,

Settling into my situation in Denver. I have not received a reply from you to my Niagara post and thought I might have heard from you by now. I will not repeat justifications for my move west, since there is no more that I can say at this time, and I know you find repetition a bore. I take no ill will from present silence, only that you wish my speedy return, when we can chat away to our heart's content. In the meantime, I plan to correspond with you as if you were at my elbow.

I am staying at the grandest hotel in town, the Brown Palace. I have my own suite with maid service, bath and loo, hot and cold running water—spring water supplied by its own artesian well 750 feet below the ground floor. I'm not sure what I think of this luxury. I see my father's hand in this as the previous holder of my position roomed with a family in town. I took a right ribbing from Wyatt, who called me His Majesty of the Palace. He, by the way, is set up in a quite adequate flat strategically near the City Park, as his wife and children shall be joining him, presumably before Christmas. In fact, his wife has entreated to come west immediately to escape the summer heat of New York. While some of the West is desert, Denver is quite elevated (the Mile High City, they say). It gets hot, but not as stifling as New York City.

I gave serious consideration to rejecting my posh surroundings and acquiring more modest lodgings, but Wyatt insisted that, first, it would show me a blessed fool (the word he used was more colorful), and second, I would come off as an ungrateful, petulant schoolboy. He also pointed out that the Brown Palace was ideal for meeting contacts and businessmen, and carrying on reporting for the *Journal*. I have taken to referring to it as the Brown hotel, or just the Brown, but I am afraid that paints me as either ignorant or as an affectation.

There are images of griffins emblazoned throughout the hotel, no doubt a reference to the Rocky Mountains, which loom like Titan waves, first dark and then snowcapped, forever approaching the city. The griffins remind me instead of childhood English fairy stories, hearth, home, and of course, you. How marvelous it would be if you were here, sharing a brocade loveseat in this beautiful atrium lobby that soars nine stories up to a stained-glass roof. They even do an English afternoon tea service. Mother, however, would not have approved, as they do not do it correctly. Your wit and knowledge would be a delightful curative for what passes as conversation among the merchants, financiers, and speculators who regularly fill the lobby.

The businessmen talk of business and nothing else. You know my sincere wish to succeed at my own endeavors and to provide for a family, but the American men have determined that the meaning of life, at least for their sex, is the single-minded pursuit of money. I recall the composer Offenbach's impression of Yanks, "As a child, 'dollar' was the first word he heard; as a youth, it was his first love; as a man, it will be his only passion."

Americans are always rushing and jostling one another, seeking opportunity and advantage. Indeed, funerals must be conducted at a trot, the unfortunate, and now superfluous, to be disposed of quickly so that the moving may return to commerce. When finally retired home in the evenings, they sit in rocking chairs so they can keep busy, even at rest.

Most men of business do not see painting nor play, nor the inside of a church unless their mother or wife drags them forcefully. At dinner parties, care must be given not to seat two men together of similar occupations, lest they ignore all others to endlessly talk shop.

Perhaps I am envious of the men's industriousness. I am not striving to build a railroad through a mountain, or disgorge coal from the maw of the earth, or balance room upon room, attempting to scrape the sky. Truly, Offenbach himself was in need of funds when he toured here and was pinching a thousand dollars a performance, so he was not above filthy lucre.

I know you have become active in women's issues, so I must tell you something. The women have been able to vote in state elections here since 1893. Maybe I can bring some of this enlightened notion back to England. I tell you, the women in Denver go their own way much of the time, with all manner of clubs, lectures, meetings, and social causes.

I look eagerly for your reply. I know I try your patience, but please lend me this gift of time. I promise to repay you with eternity.

All of my love,
Joshua

August 1898

Dear Joshua,

Sorry for the delay in my reply. I stayed at college past the semester. A group of us were organizing for suffrage. I must do my part. So, the Niagara and Denver letters only recently came to hand. I wish I could engage you more in correspondence. I really do. It's not in my nature. I need to look into your kind eyes. I need to feel the warmth of your hand on my arm. I need to hear the steady cadence of your voice and breathe in the unique scent of you.

Joshua, really, it is nearly three years! Wasn't that the original plan? I remember. No more than three years. Lingering on in New York, I understood. I should very much like to see that city myself one day. Now Denver? This excursion should not take months. See what you must and make your way home.

I've encountered your brother John at recent events. I don't understand your resentment toward him. He speaks nothing but well of you. John said you had twice the head for numbers than he. He implied that it would be reasonable for you to take over the estate books once your father is no longer able. Honestly, Joshua, I don't mean to doubt you. Writing is such a speculative career. My cousin Adie has her poems printed by a small press. First-rate. Of course, she is married and doesn't expect her poems to sustain her.

One last thing. You know I'm not eager to participate in the social calendar. My family's station means I'm obligated to do so. Should certain gossip reach you, I want to explain. My father insists that, at these social gatherings, eligible young bachelors be allowed to dance and converse with me. I realize this might pain you, but we're not formally engaged. Father is a man of business. He believes you're either on the market or off.

Please don't let it trouble you. Most of these suitors are egotistical, strutting gamecocks or bored party boys. In any case, there can't be many more firstborn viscounts, earls, and marquees to trot out in front of me. I did accept riding instructions from Lord Abel Merryman. He agreed to introduce me to rudimentary jumping as well. Lord Merryman started me on bareback. He said I should get a visceral feel for the naked power of the animal. I must admit I found it altogether thrilling. I took his offer only to gain experience so that I may ride with you when you return. I trust that will be soon.

Hurry home,
Margaret

Chapter 18

My father said living in the shadow of a volcano was unremarkable if one had grown up in its ever-presence. Likewise, the Rocky Mountains became the grand backdrop to a long-running opera—once impressive but now barely noticed by the actors. The Brown persisted as the palace to its steady flow of visitors but held no more surprises for me. I knew each set of railings contained ten panels. Two wrought-iron panels had been installed upside-down. If asked, the management insisted this was done on purpose so as not to assume that men were capable of reaching the perfection of God. One error being sufficient for the purpose, the second may have reflected the plethora of nearby saloons.

Days were a repetitious dance: gather information, write up stories, send them off to London or the *Journal*. Nowak seldom printed my pieces except routine cattle or mining reports. Both were boring, and the information received of questionable veracity. My father always warned of investing in mining: "A mine is a hole in the ground with a liar at the top."

Cattlemen proved not much more trustworthy when it came to business. They may have been kind to their families and willing to help a neighbor in a snowstorm or fire, but when it came to commerce, sharp dealing abounded.

Father had still not written (apparently "letting the boy stand on his own two feet"), but clearly, he kept tabs on me through the Old Man. I wrote regularly to Aubrey but remained vague, since she was close to John and told him everything.

Evenings were spent mostly keeping my own company and keeping my diary of the day's events. I made little headway turning notes into a class exposé or travelogue. I couldn't help but doubt my ability to accomplish the task. That distant morning on the steamer leaving Southampton, it all appeared within grasp. Years in now, success was a phantom, still present but too bored to actively taunt anymore. Ben Lewis, the Pullman porters, the sporting bachelors, George Johnson, the White coon singers, and all the others I met in New York weren't at all what I'd expected when I came to America. Naively, I'd pictured Ben Franklin, Lewis and Clark, and Kit Carson, New England town hall meetings and mid-prairie barn raisings. A scent of that remained, mingled with a musk much more complicated. Time and human nature weathered the myth of America. Class mattered, gender mattered, ethnicity mattered, and in ways both blatant and sublimated, race mattered. Uncomfortably, I faced the decision of what mattered to me.

Like many polite Americans, I too wanted to postpone confronting difficult issues. Problem being that plenty of other people—mostly ones filled to bursting with anger or fear, or ignorance or conspiracies—were ready and acting on their emotions, and the direction they surged toward was dark and unforgiving, even if they saw only sparkling mirages of nostalgia and heritage. Those forces gave no sympathy for someone in my predicament.

What to do about the trickle of Black blood invading my English body? Proclaim it? That hadn't gone well with Wyatt. How well with the rest of the world? Could I really ignore it as one might an albino in the family tree, a quirk not needing mention?

Did I really think Nowak would keep his precious little scandal all locked up? One cantankerous morning Nowak might throw my family and me into the public fire just to see what lovely flames would consume us.

I reluctantly came over to the opinions of Miss Moon—that

resolution of the Negro issue wasn't just slow and halting, but that the situation was deteriorating. New forms of servitude were replacing the old, and Blacks in America were facing decades of discrimination, marginalization, proscription, and outright violence. I'd been naively hopeful when I arrived on these shores. I pictured an America awakened from its Civil War nightmare, chastened, resolved to make things right. For a moment, twenty-two Negroes had been seated in Congress, including two in the Senate, from Mississippi, of all places. Now only one congressman remained, the ironically named George H. White, history already being rewritten, painting Negro leadership as corrupt and buffoonish, a blight on a branch of the dear Old South to be pruned away. Meanwhile, at least a hundred Black men, or even boys, were killed by White mobs every year. Miss Moon made sure I heard every occurrence and urged me to write their stories.

I did what I could—in part. I confess, in order to please Miss Moon. The American papers, especially Mr. Hearst, were filling their pages with the Spanish-American War. The public showed little regard for stories about one more dead Negro "brute" who most likely was guilty of something.

I had better luck getting London to print a small article on poor Frazier Baker. The very fact that he, a Black man, was postmaster, supervising a post office, and therefore, White workers, so incensed the noble White folk of Lake City, South Carolina, that they were compelled in predawn to set fire to the post office, incidentally also Postmaster Baker's home. That, however, wasn't enough for the good Christians of Lake City. As his family fled the burning building, the mob shot and killed Postmaster Baker and his two-year-old daughter, Julia.

That not only tragic but heinous act on February 22, 1898, had angered me even then as just a foreign bystander. Now, after Nowak's revelation that I'd skin in the game, it both baffled and enraged me. What instinctual fury inflamed these mobs who, after all, were only people—your uncle, brother, the man at the grocery, the farmer up the lane—what turned ordinary folk into half-mad chickens pecking the blood spot.

Hence, when Miss Moon telegraphed me news of the November riot in Wilmington, North Carolina, I felt shattered to the core. She put me in contact with several eyewitnesses. I didn't bother to submit my article to New York; if Nowak did not kill it, Hearst might. I sent it, marked URGENT, to London, boldly suggesting headlines. I prayed the Old Man would print it.

VILE BUTCHERY IN AMERICA

Day of Terror—White Coup d'état

by Joshua Banks

White-painted church steeples may pierce the sky in Wilmington, North Carolina, but it was unholy terror that gripped the town on November 10, 1889. A mob of more than four hundred—not spontaneous, but carefully planned—rose up and massacred Negroes and burned the local Black-run newspaper, *The Daily Record.* The Southern press has downplayed the death toll at eleven, but sources from the town claim that closer to sixty were gunned down, with many bodies thrown in the nearby Cape Fear River. The stench of rot turned up further victims in the surrounding forests and swamps, where many sought to flee the carnage.

Tensions had been building since the elections of 1894 as self-avowed White supremacists bristled under what they proclaimed was the unnatural state of Negro rule. To the contrary, ousted Mayor Silas P. Wright and the defeated governor are both White men. The predominately White

Fusion party was made up of White Populists and Black Republicans.

Determined to claw back power, Democrats formed Red Shirt militias to intimidate Negro citizens and prevent voting in the recent November 8th election. The Democratic Party's campaign had but one slogan, from the mountains to the sea. . . "Nigger, Nigger, Nigger."

Supremacist rallies were held, and their leader, Colonel Alfred Moore Waddell, stated proudly in a public speech, "We will never surrender to a ragged raffle of Negroes, even if we have to choke the Cape Fear River with carcasses." This reporter's contacts say that, indeed, the river ran red with blood.

Taking back statewide control in the November 8th election did not placate the White supremacists' raging fever since Wilmington, which was nearly two-thirds Black before the massacre, remained in the hands of the Fusion party.

Readers should be warned that the perpetrators, who have installed themselves in power, with Colonel Waddell as mayor, along with their supporters, are already at work creating a false history of the grisly events, attempting to turn a long-planned massacre and coup into a story of reluctant and heroic rescue. It will not be a surprise to see monuments erected.

Trustworthy sources confirm the actual facts. Mayor Wright, the board of aldermen, the police chief, and all Negro office holders did not voluntarily resign, suddenly convinced of their own ineffectiveness. They were run out of office, and out of town, at the barrel of a gun, and in fear of death. This was the first coup d'état on American soil. A naked act of White terror.

There was no "race riot" instigated by pistol-wielding

Negroes, though slanderous illustrations portraying such fantasies have already appeared. For several months, any Negro seeking to purchase a weapon for self-defense has been denied that right. Even out-of-state orders to New Jersey have been referred back to the local office, who will not sell a gun to a Negro. By contrast, each person in the White mob brandished pistol, shotgun, rifle, and in one case, that instrument of mass indiscriminate death: a new Gatling gun.

In addition to those summarily murdered, over two thousand colored merchants, tradesmen, and their families were driven out of Wilmington—now no longer a majority-Negro city.

Another issue must be directly confronted even by the most delicate of our readers. That is, the supposed justification purporting that these heinous acts were necessary to defend White womanhood from the danger of the Black brute. This fear of sexual mixing is both a canard and is at the very root of the matter.

Readers may have heard of an incendiary article in the *Daily Record* that debased White womanhood by suggesting that many of the reported assaults and rapes were more likely the result of consensual, amorous interest of White ladies toward Negro men. It also called out White men for their dalliances with Negro women, both consensual and not. While the satirical tone of editor Alexander Manly's piece was unfortunate, his main points were valid and were written in direct response to an earlier provocation. They can only be understood in context.

Well-known suffragist, Rebecca Felton, gave a speech, widely reported, accusing the Negro man's libidinous machinations as the greatest danger to White farm women. She went further, stating, "If it needs lynching to protect woman's dearest possession from ravening human beasts, then I say lynch, a thousand a week if necessary."

Mr. Manly was able to escape the lynch mob in Wilmington (with the help of a password supplied by a White friend). So fair of complexion is Manly, that he was offered a rifle by Whites guarding the outskirts of town, in case he might encounter the fleeing Black editor. *The Daily Record*, however, was perfumed with kerosene and burned to the ground.

What does this say for the future of the Negro in America? I have heard some say that slavery was not the original sin of America, but rather an evil inheritance from the Old World, burned away with a great Civil War. But what of this Jim Crow? Conceived by America and dedicated to the proposition that the Negro shall never be the equal of the White. A class of inferior Americans forever. Booker T. Washington promised if African Americans learned a trade, worked hard, and strived to supply their White neighbors with useful services and goods, then the Negro would rise and thrive. By all accounts, the Negro citizens of Wilmington were a model of such behavior. Through sacrifice and toil, Negroes had built businesses: restaurants, barbershops, tailor and chemist shops. Blacks were bootmakers, plumbers, watchmakers, stevedores, wheelwrights, as well as real-estate agents and architects. Not only were they civil servants, but they protected both White and Black citizens as police and firemen.

All for naught. No commission of inquiry will be formed. No congressional action will be taken.

I sent a copy to Miss Moon in New York City, where she currently lodged. I admired her dedication to her cause, which now, however remotely, I determined my cause as well. Clearly, Wyatt wasn't to be my sounding board or confidant on my racial quandary. I convinced myself I should confess all to Miss Moon.

I often tried to break through her rigid formality. I entreated her to call me Joshua and told her I'd be honored if she allowed me to address her as Eva. She gently informed me such intimacy was, perhaps, not quite appropriate but thanked me for my warm offers of friendship. I must have written and destroyed three or four letters in which I poured out all I knew of my African heritage. Why should I think she possessed magical answers to questions I fumbled to fully form? Would she think more or less of me? Or might she see me as an insulting twit, complaining of a sudden attack of African infection?

I had no real reason to believe she would want to help me, less reason to believe she had it in her power to help me. Only hope.

Chapter 19

Wyatt was giddy on the curb outside his apartment. He acted like a first-time father, not a man greeting his fourth child. A little over a year ago, in New York, he acted demonstrably somber about the burden of his second daughter. When his kids had been confined to a Lower East Side tenement or the street in front, Wyatt's fatherly instincts had extended no further than a pat on the head and occasional piggyback rides. In Denver his children developed into coconspirators in each of his hairy-chested explorations of Western nature.

We'd all made it through a brutal winter. The sky dumped snow every day, starting on November 27, 1898, into February. At least fifteen feet by April, and nearly double that before spring. Over a hundred people killed by avalanches and the cold were forced to wait for earthly graves and eternal slumber.

My carefully planned New Year's reunion with Margaret in New York canceled, my train ticket useless. Margaret's brother, her only available escort, had been forced back to university. Forty-foot drifts pushed aside by seven locomotives with a rotary plow were immediately replaced by fifty-foot drifts. Men and trains were carried into icy rivers. Most of the country was held in an arctic blast that saw the East Coast getting thirty inches of snow in one day.

Now—here—under a broad, blue, June morning sky, Wyatt bounded about the white-laced pram like a man who'd won the lottery without buying a ticket. He rocked the carriage back and forth, springs squeaking, as he waited for Becca to ready the other children for church.

"Who's my best boy?" Wyatt cooed between inserting first the right and then the left fist of his infant son into his mouth.

"What is this surprise you mentioned?" I asked.

"We named the boy."

"Jolly good, but hardly a surprise."

"After you . . . sort of."

"And Becca agreed?"

"Well, she named the girls. Now she insisted on Moses for the baby. I wasn't gonna let Moses be his first name."

"Well," I said. "Joshua Moses, very biblical."

Wyatt shook his head. "Not Joshua. Your middle name, Clarke, but without the *e* on the end. I like it, sounds kinda Western."

"But how? I never use that name in public."

"Ha. It was on your luggage when you got off the boat in New York."

"I am honored, Wyatt. In fact, I'm right chuffed t' bits."

Wyatt grinned at my laps into Yorkie.

"Listen Wyatt, are you sure about using my name, considering what we talked about in Niagara?"

Wyatt stiffed. "I'm not considering anything."

"Becca does not know?"

"She sees what I see, and I don't see any evidence of anything to consider."

"Wyatt, you cannot ignore—"

"I'm gonna leave it right there." He held up his palm.

Judy, the oldest of the two daughters, came at a half-shuffling run (her left leg was still hamstringed from polio) to fawn over the baby, cutting off my rebuttal. Becca soon followed, two young ones in tow.

"Will you be coming to the baptism, Joshua?" she asked, smiling.

"Love to attend, but I have a story deadline in less than an hour. I regret to say no."

Wyatt shook his head at my obvious falsehood.

The truth was embarrassing. Admitting it would be hurtful. Though I myself harbored no animus toward Roman Catholics, my mother's family contained a deep, unexamined streak of anti-papist fervor. Mother made it clear to us that she'd rather see us in Hell than in a Catholic church. Her mother, my dear Gran, on her deathbed, went so far as to make my siblings and me swear an oath to avoid any contact with Catholicism.

I construed the oath rather liberally. Colleges, schools, and such didn't count. Great works of classical music featuring the Mass were primarily artistic and cultural in nature, and were required knowledge for the educated man. Cathedrals might reasonably be entered, if one was sightseeing in Florence or Paris, as long as no service was being performed. All that was certainly fine, but a baptism with a Mass certainly leaped over the line. My secret discrimination didn't fit comfortably, but Gran had been exceedingly kind to me at the most awkward times of my youth, and I didn't want to envision her spinning in her grave.

I helped the children into a cab with their proud parents and paid the fee as a baptismal gift. Once sure they were out of sight, I crossed over to the park adjacent to Wyatt's flat.

I needed to take stock. Thoughts tumbled, and I struggled to put them in proper order. My failure, or rather inability, to focus on long-term plans meant time itself would soon snatch that duty from my hands and take me where it willed. It was probably only months before I'd be forced to return to England. The Old Man had already, a bit too graciously, extended my assignment in the US past the normal two or three years. Associates back home at the paper recently clued me in that a newly minted wunderkind, as well as a seasoned workhorse, were both hell-for-leather to take over my position.

Coming around a hedge in the park—what?

"Damn!" I leaped out of the way, but my trailing right hand rapped soundly on the end of a handlebar. The boy biker, obviously attempting a land speed record, did not slow down. Instead, he redoubled his efforts and wheeled out of the park.

My leap might have been balletic had the landing been uneventful. Sadly, it was not. The ball of my foot touched down at an inconvenient angle on a patch of green-gray moss fully saturated with morning dew, divot peeling off, my legs flung to opposite compass points. My trousers, designed for more refined movements, rebelled at such athleticism and ripped open in a manner, and with a loudness, I previously assumed reserved for circus clowns. All to say the resulting circumstance completely negated my initial relief that I managed to remain on my feet.

A grizzled old groundskeeper, the single witness, snorted and laughed for maybe the second time in his life. I wished him dead. Not knowing what to do, I took off my suit jacket and hung it around my waist like a backward Masonic apron. Retreating to a bench, I sat down, disgusted.

What if John, or my father, or Margaret were able to see me at this moment? They would shake their heads, saying, "Ah well, he did try now, didn't he." I just wanted to stand on my own two feet, make my own way, and instead here I was, sitting on a damp bench with my ass falling out my trousers, not sure how to get back to my room with any dignity at all. It was too much to hope that at least one aspect of my life could happen to go well.

I worried my relationship with Margaret continued on a downward spiral. While I tried to engage her in my letters, Margaret's missives were mainly store-bought cards, Christmas, Easter, with the merest note, like a child's obligatory acknowledgment to an auntie or uncle.

My heart sank last February when I realized she wasn't bothering to send a card for Valentine's Day. By March I realized there was nothing more pitiful than a grown man moping about a missing Valentine. I probably didn't help by sending a cartoon Valentine featuring a cat that was far too glib about love conquering time and distance. The truth is, time and distance will beat the life out of love. With due respect to the poets, love is not an ocean, nor the sun, nor a pyramid. It's a human experience; it must be constantly fortified or it fades. Too long from our lover's gaze, too many touches unmade, and the lovers awake, the spell broken.

My hand started to ache, to swell. The handlebar had included a bell lever, which opened a slit across my knuckles. I let the blood wash the wound, then pressed it against my trouser leg to stanch the bleeding. Leaving in haste that morning, I'd forgotten a handkerchief. The pants were ruined, in any case. I was lucky the world still perceived me as a White man. I could only imagine the reaction that a semi-naked bleeding Negro, risible and menacing, would have caused.

The Blackness issue was never far from mind. I'd not made much headway in enlisting Miss Moon as confidant. I'd teased out little personal information: her favorite sweet, saltwater taffy; she was an early riser, despite her surname; she was afraid of spiders but defiantly killed them on her own; roses smelled like death to her—pink and white carnations were better, thank you very much. Even so, she invariably turned our phone call or correspondence back to feeding me stories to write on the plight of her race in America.

Lynchings continued without pause. Ida Wells, now Wells-Barnett, and representative George H. White, pushed mightily to get President McKinley's help in pushing a federal anti-lynching bill through Congress. "Why a federal crime?" I'd asked Miss Moon.

"We can't trust local authorities. They stand by and say nothing while our men are pulled out of jail and hung from lampposts."

A close reading of the newspapers suggested President McKinley was more interested in Southern redemption and unity than spending political capital on preventing lynching. High promise existed at McKinley's inauguration; he swore the oath on a Bible from the bishop of the Black AME Church, and kissed the Bible to seal his oath. Lately, in the war with Spain, the President's reluctance to allow Black troops to participate effectively doomed them to second-class citizenship.

Eventually, Black lieutenants were allowed to rise to colonel and lead Black troops, and three Black regiments of Buffalo Soldiers fought in the battle of San Juan Hill. Upstart Theodore Roosevelt praised the bravery of these "smoked marines." I sent all the stories to London and New York despite Nowak's pledge I would not take one line of type away from his New York boys or the stringers down in Cuba.

Miss Moon had reluctantly provided me some valuable insight, gained under my guise of writing an article for London on the role of skin color in the lives of African Americans. She first hesitated, not wanting to air dirty laundry, but as I promised, there would be no release of the article in America. She wanted me to get accurate information, an easy promise to make since I never intended to write the article; I only wanted to know.

Miss Moon imparted painful experiences from both ends of the spectrum, she describing herself as being a neither here nor there mid-cocoa. Her father, who was fair, found solid work as a domestic and handyman in fine houses in Georgia. Her mother, ebony as burned wood, was unwelcome in these same houses, and even more insulting, in many elite light-skinned-Negro houses as well.

"What about a person of African descent who was, let us say, as light as me?" I inquired.

"They might decide to just pass," she said. "Remember Mr. Plessy, of the Supreme Court case?"

"Of course."

"Mr. Plessy had to inform the conductor he was Black. That's one of the reasons they picked him for the test case. It wasn't a problem when everyone thought he was White. Why suddenly a problem once he claimed to be Black? So yes, they might have to get their hair straightened, or some ladies might need to wear a wig, but several will pass. You see, Mr. Banks, so many slaves were raped by lash or circumstance that we often wear the features of our captors on our faces. The bulk of us can't pass even with that, so we must fight for our rightful place."

"I am curious about the role of the light-skinned within the community of the colored."

"Haven't you noticed? There are exceptions, of course, but many of our elite leaders are light-skinned. Their White sponsors favor them, it's true, but we people of color acquiesce too easily to their superiority. I've heard Black men who are darker than I state they only find women a shade or two lighter than me beautiful enough to marry."

"I find it impossible to believe that any man with functioning eyes would find you anything but beautiful."

"Now Mr. Banks, really, you're such a flirt. My point is, we—my people, my race—have deeply drunk the poison of racism. It has infected our souls."

Pain snapped me out of my thoughts back to my present condition. My hand was now throbbing with each pulse of my heart, but the bleeding had ceased. I wasn't eager to rise and begin the long, humiliating walk back to the Brown hotel, or to a cab if I could find one. Feeling defeated, I slouched and tilted my head back to gaze at the vast blueness of Denver sky. Four diminutive swallows dove and bobbed, bedeviling a large raven and driving it from their nests.

"In bit of a pickle, huh, feller?"

Startled, I almost leaped to my feet but, self-conscious, caught myself. The old groundskeeper had come up behind the bench, a battered pair of hedge clippers dangling in hand. He looked like a bantam boxer gone to seed but still dangerous in a corner. “Didn’t mean to pop up on you. You ’bout jumped out of your pants, or what’s left of ’em.”

“Have I not provided enough amusement today?”

“You did put on a hell of a song and dance back there, but I ain’t here to mock.”

“What then?”

“To throw you a bone, son. If you’ll take it.” His mouth turned up into something between a grin and a smirk.

I tried to tap down my anger. “I suppose I would have laughed if it were not me.”

“Sonny, the Sphinx would have chuckled at that show.”

“What now?” I asked.

“If you look over there, see my toolshed?” He pointed a calloused finger at a clapboard structure not much bigger than a Beefeater’s guardhouse. I nodded.

“You go ’head in there, you’ll see a drawer. There’s an old pair of gray cavalry pants in there. They don’t fit me anymore, but they’d be ’bout right for a young’un like you. Ain’t stylish no more, but they’d get you home.”

“A drowning man should not complain about the weave of his lifeline,” I said.

“There you go.”

I felt ashamed of my earlier anger. A surprising wave of emotion flushed my skin. “You are too kind, sir. How can I repay you?” As soon as the words left my mouth, I regretted the tone. I hoped he didn’t think I was cheapening his act of kindness by offering petty payment.

“Help the stranger,” he said. “It’s what we’re called to do, though it’s so much easier to be a selfish jackass.”

"Thank you," I said.

"And son, you don't need to be bringing those pants back. There comes a time when you got to let things go."

Chapter 20

Time is the ultimate enemy. Nothing, and no one, can resist. Time was killing my ambitions, my plans, all in the most casual manner. Seconds, minutes, months, years, repeat. People think time flies most swiftly with excitement, with fun or danger, but time also rushes by with routine, the mundane.

Of the travelogue-turned-social-commentary (the key to making my name back in England), I had scarce notes and scattered pages leading nowhere. My Pepys daily diary was recorded accurately, if not always faithfully, yet it was difficult to turn it into a popular book. Most of my journalistic output, which I originally hoped would provide some clever stories, were repetitive reports. I felt trapped inside a dream, writing the same article again and again, my actions the never-ending mirror reflections in a sideshow fun house. This new day promised the same.

My correspondent assignment in the States approached inevitable termination. Margaret grew increasingly distant but also more insistent that I return home, formalize our engagement, and accept whatever position her family, or mine, charitably offered. I was softly failing again.

Needing to clear my head and think, I left my room at the Brown and headed down to where the building came to a point like the prow of a great ship. This innovation, I was told, mandated when Mr. Brown's founding vision of diagonal streets sailed into the city fathers' regimented north/south grid at Broadway. The Brown pointed the way to my destination, Trinity Methodist Church. During my confinement in Denver, Trinity often served as a restorative, not so much house of worship, but temple of music. A dominating pipe organ covered the entire altar wall with a choir of pipes, with an organist fond of scattering Bach (JS and CPE) among the basic hymns. I considered my sporadic attendance at least a partial rebuttal to Minna Mitts' inquisition of my faith.

I stood admiring the Gothic elegance of Trinity with its Castle Rock rhyolite soaring up to the steeple. The organist called the church a volcano for God since rhyolite birthed from clouds of magma, pumice ash, glass, and rock falling to earth at Castle Rock near Boulder, Colorado. My attention, however, turned to an unexpected figure approaching, a man in black with a preacher's collar, exiting not the chapel but rather the gambling hall that neighbored it. He wasn't the local vicar. Instead, he was clearly a Chinaman.

As he closed distance between us, I took his measure. He was lanky, thin, shy of six feet, but tall, I thought, for a Chinaman. A wide-brimmed friar's hat sat upon coal-black hair cut short and neat. His eyes were not slits as in nursery books, more sideways teardrops, but the hooded lids and almost absence of eyebrows gave his round face a distinctly oriental cast. His skin was pale but not quite ghostly; I'd known several ruddy Irishmen who were less White than he. All I knew of Chinamen were children's fables, Dickens, Defoe, none-too-kind portrayals of wicked, violent opium zombies or conniving, sophisticated Mandarins stroking long mustaches with femininely long fingernails.

Did I really expect him to be yellow? Is anyone really yellow? Certainly, out here in the West, there were Chinese laborers turned bronze and golden brown from the sun, as were some of our old Yorkshire field hands on my father's estate. What of me now, the octoroon? My father, the quadroon? What of skin? Would the mighty Empire crumble if Britons were suddenly wrapped in ocher, and the conquered turned alabaster white? If the perception of color washed from our eyes so that all now appeared ashen gray, what new differences might arise to define and divide us?

The incongruity must have left a puzzled look on my face. He read my expression and said, "You expecting a coolie hat and slippers?"

"I . . . Pardon?" I managed.

"Oh, English. You know, not all Chinese clean laundry. I, for instance, clean men's souls. We're all Johnnies to you, Chinese, Korean, even Japanese, all the same. Even in China, we are not one."

"You don't have to be rude, I meant no offense," I said. "You do stand out, like—"

"Like a Chinese preacher?" He smiled.

I relaxed a little. "Joshua Banks, Sir. I apologize, but my professors at Cambridge left the impression that all Chinamen were Buddhist."

"Or Confucian, or both, or like me, Christian. Allow me, sir. I am Chen Ning Yang. Not 'Chinaman.' I am Chinese American. I'm not here to make money and go home. This *is* home. I've been a citizen since 1880, beat exclusion by two years. Shaved off queue and put on American clothes."

"But, may I ask, why a preacher?"

"Am I a Heathen?"

"Now wait, I did not make any such claim."

"No, no, it is the title of essay by Wong Chin Foo, the great Chinese American preacher. He was in all the White newspapers. He spoke and wrote so beautifully in English and Chinese. You English playing Chinese whispers. Millions have no problem speaking Chinese. English is hard, but soon, I will speak like him. He ran Chinese papers in New York and Chicago. You must have heard of him."

"Afraid not. Just recently arrived." I felt a twinge of shame for understating the length of my stay in the country, and a pang of embarrassment that all I knew of the Chinese were railroads, opium dens, and the miserable unfortunates of London's Limehouse slums. "Do tell me."

Chen went on. Wong Chin Foo emerged an interesting fellow. Well educated at Louisburg College, he debated "Chinese-must-go" orators, successfully arguing for Chinese Americanization. He introduced newspaper readers to chop suey but lost the battle against the Chinese Exclusion Act, which not only renewed in 1892, but now required Chinese to register and be photographed.

Chen's charming exuberance was contagious, and I was enjoying a conversation for the first time in months. Trinity and the play of the pipes would have to wait.

"Let me tell you a secret." Chen leaned in. "There are weak forces and strong forces. Politically, we are weak. We cannot elect our own. Your courts say we are not White or Black, and the Mongolian cannot be citizens. I've never met a Mongolian myself, but the point is, we can be Christian. Religion is a strong force. You cannot convince White America to treat Chinese fairly just because it's humane and Declaration of Independence says, 'All men are created equal.' No, but you say to the devout American that we are all creatures of God Almighty, all creatures of his love, maybe then the White heart softens a bit. White man says the Golden Rule is, 'Do unto others as you would have them do unto you.' The Confucian Silver Rule says, 'Do not do unto others as you would not have them do unto you.' You make the spiritual connection, and maybe they see us not as subhuman invaders to be hated and feared, but as fellow believers, a brother in Christ."

"I see the strategy, but do you really believe in Jesus as Christ?" I asked.

"Do you?"

I hesitated too long in answering, which made Chen's steady smile widen. The easiest response, to flippantly and indignantly insist yes, felt wrong. For some reason, Chen's sincere honesty inspired me to reciprocate with truth. What, though, was the truth—my truth? The Banks family met their spiritual and, it must be said, reputational, obligations by regular attendance at our local place of worship, as expected of good Anglican families. While my father could quote chapter and verse with ease, he was more likely to quote Shakespeare. Father always concerned himself with the appearance of propriety and respectability, and the avoidance of any action, or lack of action, that might bring even the smallest blemish of scandal or disrepute on the Banks name. He never showed any great religious fervor and regarded with suspicion those who did. Mother, always the devout one, had insisted we say our evening prayers, observe Lent, and so on.

"I suppose I am a man of faith and a man of doubts," I finally replied. "I am not sure your plan to reach men's hearts will be effective. Self-confessed 'good Christians' have caused their share of great evil in the world six days of the week, then prayed in the pews on Sunday. I fear the ugly impulses of race superiority will not yield so easily. I doubt the White man will give you a seat at his table anytime soon."

"We don't need a seat at his table right now," Chen said. "You know, the wonderful Mark Twain said we Chinese are quiet, peaceable, and industrious as the day is long. You let us have a workshop, and we build our own seat and table. If we can only do laundry and sell suey, then we do it. We build our wealth as a people, generation by generation."

"Until one day there will be a Chinaman as president," I said facetiously. I was happy Chen did not take offense, only corrected my usage to Chinese American.

"Probably not for long time," he continued. "Irish, Italian, and Polish will all want to go first."

"Maybe even a White woman in that line?" I asked.

"They must get the vote first, I think."

"That's not happening anytime soon, so your people may have a shot."

"You laugh, but everything is possible in this country. China is an old man, this country is still a child, still changing. There's still time for the nation to become what it proclaims itself to be."

"One can only hope, my friend."

As I wished Chen well on his quixotic quest, the bellboy from the Brown ran up, saying there was a special delivery message from London for me marked urgent. London meant the Old Man. While I continually sent articles and messages to London, I rarely received any. Nervous, I made my way back to the main desk to discover my fate.

When you are in the midst of an extended losing streak, if you draw a wild card, you are naturally surprised, and in fair measure, suspicious. *Why?* you think. Is this just a ruse to keep me in the game, increase my bet, only so luck can wreak havoc on me all the more on the next flip? On the other hand, who would fold with a wild card without one more draw? These thoughts flooded my mind as I scanned the instructions from London. If the Denver assignment had become the purgatory Nowak desired, the letter offered, if not a complete escape to Heaven, at least a reprieve back on earth.

While Hearst's American readers delighted in every modern advancement of American enterprise, the English responded with a yawn or derision. The Old Man himself deduced that the British were very keen on the more exotic topography and manners of the US West. If the rebellious colonies managed to best their civilized betters, must it be precisely because we Brits were too long civilized? Americans' noble British blood had been set free in a primitive Eden and returned to full primitive flower, the sterile cultivar gone to hearty rootstock. What good was it, then, to hear of great buildings and high culture? As the Old Man put it, "That's what the British public wants to read, by God. Show us the wild river, not the bridge; the canyon, not the cannery."

Therefore, he'd made arrangements for guides to take Wyatt and me on a proper adventure to Yellowstone and environs, and write about awesome nature. I felt a tad miffed that the trip was a spur-of-the-moment arrangement between my future father-in-law, the Old Man, and shall we say, my detractor, Nowak, without any concern for my humble input. I realized with a flash of envy that Nowak appeared better at warming up the Old Man than I did, and I worried that Nowak might have booby-trapped the entire endeavor.

Whatever the Old Man's motivation, an adventure might be a welcome diversion and kick start to my ambition to make a name with the British reading public. I resolved to avoid the dual extremes of British tourists I'd witnessed since ensconcing in the West and would not try to "cowboy" myself. My old English bowler hat was fine. Reasonable outdoor gear was available for gentlemen with chaps only if absolutely necessary. I'd also heard horror stories of insufferable tweedy Englishmen pontificating on the superiority of the British way. I set myself open to adapt, but I wasn't a complete babe in the woods. My father, being fond of the hunt, trained us for the outdoors, the tent, the campfire. I looked forward to the smell of horses and the simple pleasure of a day's ride fulfilled.

Several days of travel separated Denver from the rendezvous point with guides who would take us to the Grand Teton and on to Yellowstone. That allowed them sufficient time to gather horses and supplies. Wyatt and I, in contrast, were required to leave almost immediately. I didn't know the Old Man to be so impulsive, but as with my departure from England, the whole enterprise appeared guided by sudden whim.

The hasty nature of our departure antagonized Wyatt to no end. He remained reluctant about the entire adventure and made his displeasure plain with a revolving display of petulant silence, random cursing, and threats to up and quit. The former man-about-town apparently now settled into the day-to-day life of Denver, eschewing the saloons and bordellos for potluck dinners and school plays. I knew, however, an additional factor to Wyatt's reticence other than the comforting pull of hearth and home, and the excitement of his new son.

Going out on the range reminded Wyatt of his time in the army. I grew up enduring the droning adventures of distant uncles expounding on their exploits in this or that imperial war, as if it were all great sport. Wyatt said next to nothing about his experience. Except for the cavalry spurs and belt buckle he occasionally wore, there were no outward signs of his military service.

No outward signs, yes, but Wyatt carried a mark deep inside. One late night in a bar back in New York, he'd let slip that he'd seen bad things—wrong, evil things—costumed as glory. Wyatt found no sport in combat, only gore and the press of advantage. He who killed the most with the least regard or regret reaped the reward. I tried to convince him our excursion promised more of a walk in the mountains, as he often enjoyed with his family, but I think he found my obvious eagerness annoying.

A resigned but moody Wyatt sat waiting in the lobby of the Brown Palace to meet me and head over to catch the train to Cheyenne. We were nearly to the door when the bell captain ran up, shouting.

"Mr. Banks, Mr. Banks. You've got a letter." The rotund man panted as he fished it from a sack. "You're very lucky to get this before you go on your trip. This mail was rerouted because of construction. Normally take three more days to get here, for sure."

I recognized Margaret's handwriting on the envelope. I stuffed it into my pocket to read at first opportunity.

"Come on," said Wyatt wearily. "We'll be late for the train."

The cities of the West grew out of feral towns that were ushered into being as camps of necessity set up to plunder ore, timber, and fur, or as way stations to wilder lands. Towns grew like God's favored, pulsing with the hot blood of the ambitious, only to be forsaken and abandoned, dusty shutters clanging, rusty windmills gone to rack and ruin, all reclaimed by the relentless wild. The towns that survived, that moved from mere obligatory associations of men to real communities of multigenerational family bonds, were joined in a geographical wrestling match to determine which would grow, thrive, and dominate, and which would not.

Cheyenne, Wyoming, on the fabled Intercontinental Railroad, was predicted to win that match with a Denver considered "too dead to bury." But the city fathers of Denver did not let it happen. They raised the funds and tied their city into the surrounding train lines, including the Intercontinental. By the time Wyatt and I rode the line from Denver to Cheyenne, it was clear the Mile High City ruled as the metropolis of the Rocky Mountain West, and Cheyenne was a lesser squire.

As we neared Cheyenne for our transfer, I pulled out Margaret's letter and began to read.

September 1899

Dear Joshua,

I have tried to hold my tongue, I really have. I have tried to give you the time you thought needed for your foray. No more. I cannot. Do you hate me? Why else would you stay another year away from me? Four years, and not a single trip home.

Heaven knows I've considered giving up on men entirely. What a bore this endless parade of suitors has become. Your continued absence just encourages them. They contend you must have lost interest or found another love in America. What else would explain your actions? What can I say to dispute such claims when I'm starting to believe the same?

Father has told me that Lord Abel Merryman inquired about taking my hand in marriage. Lord Merryman added that, should I be amenable to his offer, he would make sure a small observatory dome be erected on his estate so that I could continue my heavenly studies.

Abel is a fine man, a generous man, but you are my love, my hero of the Fens. You must come home to me. Now. Mother is still so charmed by you. She would have me wait in the wings for you until I was old and barren. Father told me to pause a few days. If I still felt the same then to send this, call it what it is, an ultimatum.

Joshua, I love you. I have since that dusty day in East Anglia when you gave your all for me. I long for you, but I need to be longed for in return. Here it is. If I do not hear back by return post that you are making arrangements to set sail back to England, to my arms, I will consider our romance at its end. I can't remain stranded in amber.

Also, I don't know if your brother John wired you. He says it's not really serious, even made Aubrey promise not to worry you about it, but your father had taken ill recently. He was confined to bed for a time but is back at work. Thought you should know. He will be so happy to see you again, as will I.

Come home to me.

Love,
Margaret

Chapter 21

The air was knocked out of me. In truth, if I'd put myself in Margaret's position, I might have anticipated this development. Despite her interest in having a career or some serious involvement in science, Margaret also desired children. She saw no reason to be denied both. She told me her plan to have children while young so she might still be vital when her grandchildren arrived. Her own grandmother had been a withered hulk, and Margaret would have none of that.

Puzzled by Old Man Covington's involvement in all this, I ascribed some ill intent in the Old Man's contradictory advising Margaret to send the ultimatum and at the same time conveniently hastening me out of Denver before her letter would arrive. I needed to be careful with how I proceeded and what I alleged, as the Old Man was still my boss and putative future father-in-law. Margaret adored and admired her father, so it was best not to make any commentary but only state facts.

I ran to the Western Union Station the moment the doors opened at the platform in Cheyenne. Our train ran late, so there was barely time for a short message before catching the next train. I dictated the following telegraph:

> Your father sending me to Yellowstone STOP Out of communication STOP Need time STOP More soon STOP Love you STOP

Running back to the platform, I already regretted not paying for the "I" before "Love you." The clerk had talked me out of extra words. "Love you" seemed too cheeky to hold the appropriate emotion.

We changed trains to a big ten-wheeler for the Overland Route west to Green River. Wyatt and I were scheduled to meet one of our guides at the station, or as the locals said, "depot," as though they'd just popped off the boat from France. As we stood in a light drizzle, a solid block of a man with the build of a short rugby captain approached us.

"Hello, I'm Manuel Vallarta. You're Misters Banks and Brown?"

We nodded, and he motioned us to follow him. He spoke with a pronounced Mexican accent I recognized from my time in Denver. Wyatt, apparently facile with all languages, replied in Spanish, which appeared to please Manuel immensely.

Manuel (we agreed quickly that an atmosphere of formality wasn't conducive for interactions in the wilderness) had arranged for us to accompany a river barge of tie hacks (men supplying wood ties for the still-expanding rail lines) up the Green River to their base of operation. There to rendezvous with Ohanze, our Indian guide, who would bring horses and supplies.

My mind brimmed full of questions to ask Manuel—about Mexico, but more so of Mexicans in America. But why should he be a spokesman for the myriad experiences of his people any more than I of Britons, I who had never set foot in Wales, or a good half of London, for that matter? I wondered if among the Latin people, there were many who resented the imposition of Spanish culture, who wanted to reclaim their indigenous ways of life cleansed of foreign mingling. At any rate, my curiosity would have to wait, as Manuel left with Wyatt to purchase food, and I watched the bargemen load keg after keg of beer onto the boat, the men running back and forth to the strangely Moorish building that housed the brewery.

An odd addition to the cargo intrigued me, two French rapiers carried gingerly by a boatman.

"Pardon me," I asked. "Are we expecting the Three Musketeers?"

The man thought a moment, then laughed. "No, only two. Actually, the foreman up there wanted a set of fencing swords. This is as close as we came. Damn things is dangerous as hell. They can grind the edge dull and cover the tip up the lumber camp."

The boatman wandered the deck, searching for a place to stash the deadly weapons. Finally, along the stern, he slid each into tubes usually reserved for fishing poles.

The large barge was a rather tatty homemade affair, part keelboat, part platform ark, with a makeshift steam engine cannibalized from a more respectable steamboat. Two other men who were hitching a ride assured me the barge was a fine rivercraft, as it possessed a shallow draw and would not run aground even while heavily loaded. They were miners of trona, a mineral processed into soda ash for making glass, and were in search of new sites. It dawned on me that the majority of people came west intent to pluck their fortune off the land. They held no doubts it was theirs to pluck. Hard labor was required, and these were not lazy men, but there was an element of opportunistic theft to it all. The land of the many, profiting only a few.

All aboard and finally underway, we watched the town recede from view. I wanted to ask Manuel some clever questions about Incas and Aztecs, but after some sampling of beer, all I managed was, "Manuel, how did you wind up here?"

"Same as you, took the boat." He did not smile.

"Yes . . . I mean no. Why?"

"To make a living." Manuel looked away from me to two large elk grazing by the river.

"You have not always been a guide?"

"No."

I waited. Nothing. The barge rocked among choppy rapids. "Before?" I asked.

"Oh, cattle. In Mexico. Here too."

"Why stop?"

Manuel scratched his ribs. "No jobs. 1886, the Great Die Up."

"Come again?"

"Blizzards, droughts, competition from Midwestern cattle. No money. I thought you might know. Lots of Brits and Scots in the cattle market."

"Ha," said Wyatt, eavesdropping. "Irish landlords."

"I did not know," I said. "My family raised sheep, not cattle." I probed, "Why not go back home to Mexico?"

"This is Mexico, this is home," said Manuel, his voice rising in agitation.

"Was, you mean," said Wyatt flatly.

"Gentlemen, could someone please enlighten me? I don't follow," I said, bracing myself as the boat fidgeted in the rapids.

Manuel made a sweeping gesture with his arm. "My grandfather, forced to go to Juarez. That wasn't our home. Our family lived all around here, Alta California, Nuevo Mexico, generations."

"Manuel, maybe you should mention the war?" Wyatt asked. "Border's a little south now."

"Border, ha," Manuel huffed. "No border. The border is a mirage, an incomplete conquest."

"I don't mean to get in a tiff with you, Manuel," Wyatt said. "Seeing that we're traveling companions. May have been imaginary before, but it's a pretty hard border now."

"Humph. Rain comes down hard, the Rio Grande shifts for miles." Manuel's eyes had narrowed.

Wyatt, trying to snatch civility from the jaws of contention, said in a smiling tone, "Well, friend, you'll just have to get used to being American."

I, meanwhile, frantically frisked my bag for the flask of brandy I'd stashed away. Finally in hand, I offered it to Manuel and turned the conversation to moose, elk, and the weather. As the boat and our conversation maneuvered into calmer waters, I realized I'd asked the wrong question.

That question carried the same rebuke, whether brutally naked, or perfumed and dressed up in ruffled silk. "What brings you to these parts?" might as well be, "What are you doing here?" or outright, "You don't belong here." The question was selective. All my time on these shores, even with my acquired Oxford accent, I was only asked it once, and that more invitation than interrogation. If my hidden African blood knotted my hair or shaded my skin, I would have encountered the question in offhand comments, casual stares, and outright accusations. Thoughtlessly, I'd challenged Manuel's right to be an American, doubly galling coming from the mouth of a tourist.

The river journey, at first welcome, turned mundane as the barge showed incapable of any real speed. One day we stopped altogether, as we were flagged down by several men standing on the bank of the river. The barge pulled up to a makeshift dock that looked thrown there overnight. After conversing with the shoremen, a boatmate came back to us on the barge and demanded a dollar from Wyatt and me.

"What for? I thought we already paid our fee," I said.

The boatmate shook his head. "The heavy storms created a sandbar round the bend. We're gonna need mules to help pull us through. Gonna cost us five bucks, and Cap said you gotta pitch in."

"Sounds a bit dear, no?" I said.

"Well, 'less you want to strap on a harness, that's the fare. Come on. Everyone has to get off the boat and walk around to the next dock."

After some delay and some damage to the craft, the mule team finally pulled the barge through a soup of water, mud, and sand. The Captain informed us repairs must be made, and wrestled another dollar out of our purse. At least it provided an excuse for a cookout on the riverside.

Our trip continued, and I reminded myself to treat Manuel not as a curiosity or servant, but as a companion. A man of few words, he liked to play cards and was delighted to find Wyatt fluent in poker as well as Spanish. I'd picked up popular games back at the bachelor hotel, but I remembered the warning that had accompanied my instruction. "If you're in a card game, and you look around the table and cannot spot the sucker, you're the sucker."

Manuel wisely refrained from taking too much money off the miners and hacks, but harbored no compunction against ridding Wyatt and me of our funds. I heard it said a genuine gambler is an example of courage, energy, and enterprise misdirected. Mostly, I thought of a quote from Heywood Brown: "The urge to gamble is so universal, and its practice so pleasurable, that I assume it must be evil." Wyatt and I soon learned to keep the stakes very low. Still, Manuel or Wyatt would relieve me of all my pocket money, return it so as to keep the game going, then wipe me out again. Our boredom was such that the cycle repeated enough that my skills sharpened to not require constant mercies.

We considered it a gift when Cap announced the need to stop at an old settlement house that included a working well pump to refresh our drinking water supplies. I longed to step off the barge and unknit the kinks in my legs.

The boat navigated a rocky, clefted bend that leveled into a pocket valley. It was immediately apparent that no one lived in the only visible structure, which had once been a house. The main king beam had cracked close to the middle well on its way to total collapse. Only the odd pane or two of glass remained in any window. A sturdy tarp would, at this stage, provide preferable shelter.

Gliding toward the remains of a dock, the barge lurched into reverse, sending poker chips skittering across the deck and causing a few of us to have to check ourselves from falling.

"What in Sam Hill?" Wyatt muttered as he scrambled around the deck, trying to reassemble his winnings.

Turning to the shore, the problem was obvious. In the tall, fallow grass, between dock and water pump, crouched a large mountain lion.

Ears folded back, the lion swayed in its crouch, signaling an imminent charge. Cap had realized the cat could easily clear the leap into the barge if we didn't abort our landing so roughly. The carnage the wild cat might inflict before his inevitable dispatch provided a circumstance to be avoided at all costs.

The grass obscured most of the beast. It didn't care about stealth, however. It showed its teeth and let out a long cry of warning.

Wyatt went to Cap. "Not to brag, but I was classed a sharp shooter in the cavalry. I could shoot—"

"Don't you dare," said Cap. "That shot would echo like a dinner bell for every outlaw, bandito, and casual thief for fifty miles."

"What? Is Butch Cassidy supposed to pop up in the middle of nowhere?" said Wyatt. "I heard he's got his hands full of Pinkertons, including that hired killer Tom Horn, after robbing the Overland Flyer."

"Dealing with Butch would be a polite exchange next to the cold-blooded bunch who hunt this river. The boatmen may be half horse and half alligator, but we can't beat them. They'll scout us out. It's obvious we've spent up our cash, but we're loaded with enough beer and supplies to make us more than worth killing. They'd set up an ambush—nowhere for us to run. We either go up the river or down."

Wyatt glanced over to Manuel. "You're the cowboy. How 'bout you lasso him?"

"Nah, not 'less he comes out of that deep grass, and if he did, he's going to accelerate a lot faster than a bull."

"Everyone settle down. I make the rules here." Cap pushed us aside and headed for the hatch. "I think we still have an Indian pump full of Max's stink-bomb grizzly bear spray. That'll drive off a charging rhino or the Devil himself."

Cap went below while the boatmen grumbled. They'd not seen Max nor his fabled spray in years, and one well-placed shot from a rifle might not be so bad. They really wanted to finish this trip and tap those beer kegs. We could hear Cap banging around below deck. Meanwhile, the cat kept watch in the grass, and the current inched us unawares toward the dock.

I believe the cat and I realized the proximity of the barge to the dock at the same instant. We both responded on instinct. The cat coiled, cocking its muscles, then charged for the boat. In defense I pulled a rapier from its tube and leaped from boat, to pier, to ground, trying to block the cat's path.

I have no way of knowing what mountain lions of yore encountered from pillaging conquistadors or French trappers, and whether such genetic memory could be passed through genes, but I was sure this particular lion had never experienced a man running straight at it, waving a silver stick shimmering in the sun. The cat abruptly stalled its attack and took up a defensive position a few feet in front of me.

I switched from en garde to octave position to protect a rush at my legs, hoping my reflexes were quick enough to raise my blade if the big cat leaped at me. My rare fencing victories against John always came from constant aggressive offense, so when the cat's body rippled with agitation, I moved in to affect a slashing saber attack. I couldn't afford a fencing lunge that might leave me fully exposed to fang and claw.

Then time stopped. The rough hemp of a lasso encircled my chest, the rapier jolted from my grip. The air smelled of rotten eggs and chemical esters that brought tears to my eyes. I saw Cap right beside me, furiously pumping the Indian sprayer, and the mountain lion scampering away in absolute terror from the onslaught of Max's infamous grizzly bear spray. Last, I heard Cap yelling at me, "You stupid son of a bitch, you stupid son of a bitch!"

After Manuel untied me, the water storage filled, and Cap's face returned to its normal color, I tried to explain my actions. Cap wasn't having any of it.

"Never. Get off. The boat. Billy was on the helm, you could have told him. There was time."

"I did not—"

"I don't want to hear it. That mountain lion was a mother just protecting her cubs. If you'd taken time to look, you would have seen cubs by the front porch of the house. If by some miracle you didn't get mauled and actually killed the mother, we would have to kill the cubs before they starved to death."

"I hadn't thought about it."

"That's obvious. I may cart up supplies to miners and loggers, but that don't mean I'm crazy 'bout what they do. I love these wild lands. I love that, out here, a man ain't any more than the snake that might bite him, or the rocks that might slide down on his head. My mother used to say that God may love you, and God may have made nature, but nature doesn't care about you one tiny bit. It's hard to believe the east of the country was once just as wild as here. If we don't watch out, all these lands will be as chockablock as central Boston."

I peered off in the distance. "You really think that's possible? This nation is vast."

"The path becomes a road, the road becomes a rail, the rail a station, the station a town, the town a city. People pour into Denver, St. Louis, all one-time outposts."

Cap surveyed the landscape, scraggle pine trees framing multicolored rock hoodoos. "This boat's all I got to make a living. It's hard to think I'm helping to destroy this land. What did John Muir say? 'Any fool can destroy trees. They can't run away.' "

"Should I know of Muir?"

"He's a writer like yourself. I must've read his forest piece in *The Atlantic* thirty times or more. There isn't much reading material on the boat."

Cap pointed his finger upward and recited, "'The axe and saw are insanely busy, chips flying thick as snowflakes, and every summer, thousands of acres of priceless forest with their underbrush, soil, springs, climate, scenery and religion are vanishing in clouds of smoke.'"

"You think his words will be heeded," I said.

"Words? Can't rely on just words. You got to act. Remember what St. James said about faith without works, without action? No, Muir's an activist. He pushed Yosemite into a National Park. He's working hard to safeguard more. Even then the moneymen try to ruin it all. You'll see it in Yellowstone. Thomas Cook and the lot will turn that place into Coney Island if you let them."

Our arrival at the lumber camp was greeted with indifference, but the beer received great fanfare. The lumber company truly *had* spared every expense in erecting the temporary minimum necessary: dormitory, mess hall, office, sawmill. Not bothered by paint, everything languished a weathered gray. Abandonment would outpace rot. The effect was dreary and stifling. The tie hacks like the miners led peripatetic lives not with God the prime mover, but wealth.

The center of their universe was its substance, quality, and especially quantity; their happiness was not from virtue but from wealth torn from the earth.

In places like this, one felt keenly the unnatural absence of women and their modifying effect. Men endlessly cycled through work, eat, sleep, swear, gamble, and occasionally fight. Without women, imbruted. There was no attempt at culture and little regard for hygiene. Without the discipline, code of conduct, and common purpose of the military, or the elaborate social hierarchy and codes of the city, life was stripped to its essentials. I mused that a camp should at least be required to hire a fiddler to enliven the atmosphere. I, however, had no intention to offer my services in that regard.

We were relieved when Manuel informed us that we would grab a quick meal, then a wagon would take us to meet Ohanze. We sat to a hearty meal of game, and potatoes, and surprisingly, fresh vegetables seasoned with fresh herbs. We then discovered that the chef maintained a substantial garden behind the mess hall. The lumber company reluctantly agreed to this extravagance after a wave of illness-halted work, the cause traced back to lead in canned vegetables.

The sight and scent of the garden invoked a wave of nostalgia and homesickness—not for Yorkshire, but for our secondary farmland in the Fens near Ramsey and Warboys. My father was one of the original landowners who bought Appold's Pump at the Great Exhibition of 1851. The powerful steam pump drained Whittlesey Mere, the lowest lake in lowland Britain, leaving fields of fertile, rich peat. I felt most at home in the onion and grain fields. My brother and father rarely went there, cursing the black clouds of fen-blow during the spring plow. It became my little fiefdom and the place I first set eyes on the lovely Miss Margaret Bryce Covington, the daughter of a neighboring landlord.

I despaired having to think about the ultimatum in her last letter;

my brief return telegram was merely a delay, not a response. Still, I hoped to salvage this American experiment, to publish a riveting Yellowstone adventure to great acclaim, or at worst, modest success. A flimsy belief, but belief was all I had.

I witnessed not a single book at the lumber camp other than a dusty Bible. Before we left, I offered my shopworn copy of Rudyard Kipling's *The Jungle Book* to the chef in gratitude for the splendid meal. Its themes of wolf-pack justice and the natural order of the jungle seemed appropriate to the setting. He hugged me like a long-lost brother, declaring "Food for the soul, food for the soul," and he sent us on our way with a care package of fresh vegetables: peppers, onions, and herbs. I felt a pang of guilt knowing a copy of Twain's *The Adventures of Huckleberry Finn* still hid deep in my bag.

Chapter 22

A sour little man drove us out past Pinedale. The only words he uttered were to settle payment. Manuel told us we were at the old rendezvous site, where hundreds of fur trappers and mountain men used to gather annually in the twenties and thirties.

In the clearing stood an Indian in standard ranch wear, blue jean trousers, checkered shirt, leather vest, and cowboy boots. He was a touch shorter than me, though his posture made him appear taller. I found it difficult to gauge an Indian's age after thirty, but he'd clearly seen his share of days. Surrounded by only four horses and a pack mule, he nonetheless appeared to be the general of an army.

The Indian nodded almost imperceptibly at Manuel, who returned the code, his subtle body language indicating the Indian in charge. He studied Wyatt and me up and down as a Yorkshire horse broker examines a new stallion. I considered the possibility that the man spoke no English. For a moment, I entertained embarrassing thoughts of sign language. I was about to ask Wyatt if his language mastery extended to tribal tongues when the Indian broke off his stare and doffed his hat.

"Greetings, gentlemen. Allow me to introduce myself. I'm your guide, Ohanzee Kohana. You may call me Ohanzee. It's not a name too hard for you to get your lips around."

His precise diction threw me aback. Preconditioned by dime-store novels or nursery books, I expected a certain pidgin English, stereotypical "Me no wampum," not professorial speech. I suppressed the urge to comment. I'd already made trouble for myself by asking the wrong questions.

"Delighted to make your acquaintance," I overcompensated.

"Ah, you must be the Englishman, Mr. Banks," said Ohanzee.

"Please call me Joshua."

"I will." He regarded Wyatt. "So, that makes you—"

"Plain ol' Wyatt will do just dandy."

"Fine then. Wyatt, I must respectfully ask you to remove your cavalry spurs. I personally trained these horses. You'll find them bridle-wise, and quite responsive, without resorting to barbaric practices."

Wyatt glanced over at me and shrugged, but sat down to comply.

Ohanzee continued, "These are three magnificent creatures. I expect them to be treated with respect. Remember, what a horse does under compulsion, he does blindly, his performance no more beautiful than a dancer taught by whip and worry. The true majesty of men is in the graceful handling of horses. Joshua, you will ride Makȟá. I know you Englishmen are fixed on thoroughbreds. Wyatt, you'll be on Marengo." Ohanzee pointed to a beautiful gray that pranced at the mention of his name.

"Hold on a second," I said. "Marengo? Like Napoleon's horse?"

"Yes, so?" Ohanzee said. "Actually, he is more of a Morgan." Ohanzee glared at me. "I suppose you'd prefer I'd named him Copenhagen, after Wellington?"

"No . . . just . . ." I didn't know what to say, not wanting to poison the well before I'd even lowered the pail. "I saw Marengo's skeleton at the Royal United Services Institution," I finally managed.

"That's kinda gory, don't you think?" Wyatt scrunched his face.

"Rather on the small side for an Arabian," I offered.

"On such small horses, empires have risen." Ohanzee patted his mount, a stunning gold buckskin quarter horse. He combed his fingers through the horse's black mane and said, "And this, gentlemen, is Napoleon."

"You do know he finally lost that empire thing?" said Wyatt. "I learned that much history."

"The English got lucky." Ohanzee was baiting me now. "Napoleon had ten times the military mind of Wellington. And a civil code in your name is much more impressive than a boot."

I felt the heat and knew I was getting red around the ears. My fingernails uncomfortably clenched into my palms. Who did he think he was, slandering Wellington? I was ready to give him a right Yorkie bashing.

"You British take yourselves too seriously," Ohanzee said.

"I will let the past stand on its own," I said. At this point, I hardly cared if I offended him, so I asked, "But do tell, why so erudite?"

Ohanzee did not look offended but rather amused. He stroked his chin and said, "Oh, erudite, I like that word. My teacher at Carlisle used that one a lot."

"The fancy Indian school?" Wyatt asked.

"I wouldn't say fancy," Ohanzee replied. "That being said, marginally better than res schools. They beat me for not answering to 'Jack' or 'John,' or whatever White man's name they tried to brand me with."

"I was sent to boarding school," I said.

"You went willingly to revere and celebrate glorious Britannia. I was ripped from my family, my tribe, to scrub clean the heart of my being."

"You sure got a vocabulary out of it," said Wyatt.

"I loved grammar class," Ohanzee said, already mounting his horse. "They wanted to erase us, kill the Indian to save the man. Instead they just gave us another tool, like the horse and the rifle before. Tribes had no common language before. I wonder if we'd received English one hundred years earlier, things might be different." Ohanzee started turning toward the trail. "Good talk. Saddle up, we're burning daylight."

The next few days were magical, freed from the prison Denver had become. I still needed to formulate a full and proper response to Margaret. She deserved as much, but my spirit rebounded, finally engaged in the sort of travel readers in England might care to read about. Even without the head-start fame of Dickens, Kipling, Wilde, or Tchaikovsky, lesser lights such as James Muirhead proved able to catch the fancy of the British public. The trick to captivating the reader? Emphasize the primitive beauty of the American landscape and the most curious behaviors of its inhabitants.

We didn't want for scenic beauty. Every turn of the head presented a fully composed picture: streams glistering silver light, upthrusted peaks framed by evergreen, imposing moose and elk etched against the skyline. But not all lovely. Picking our way through fields of sagebrush grew tedious and drew a tirade from the usually taciturn Manuel. He called it diablo weed. Would be farmers spent months clearing, digging, or burning it out, only to see it reborn phoenixlike from its ridiculously deep roots. Demonic or not, it protected the wildness of the place by chasing off discouraged settlers who failed to tame the land.

The Teton Mountains, I found particularly affecting. Slender pine battalions attempted to march up the face of the mountains, nearly all wind-thrown or held back to foothills. Gray rock gravel completed the ascent to craggy spires. Alabastrine snow gilded the peaks as if painted by divine hand. One cycled through usual tropes: imposing, majestic, awe-inspiring, before leaving language altogether to bask in pure feeling, a moment of recognition. Despite all artifice of man, the natural world would be the one lasting reality, every man soon a ghost.

The French appellation, "the Tetons," confounded me. The towering peaks looked nothing like breasts, or at least, not any you wished to encounter. Perhaps these particular Frenchmen were without fair company for far too long. Ohanzee remarked dryly that it's good the French had not named the Grand Canyon.

As our band of four navigated the trail and spent time in camp, a cordial, if not convivial, atmosphere emerged. Ohanzee and Manuel noted approvingly that I did my share of camp duties; I'd always helped John Smalls, our gillie, on hunting and fishing expeditions. Ohanzee admitted general disdain for British "high toners" who did nothing but grumble, insisting on English saddles and refusing to eat with the cow servants.

While Wyatt wore mostly recommissioned gear from his stint in the western army, I was wary of looking like the clown in a cowboy costume. Instead, I imagine I appeared a lost country squire. Manuel explained to me that at such high elevation—we were at around eight thousand feet—the sun would burn skin very quickly. He insisted that I trade my short-brimmed bowler for one of his broad-rimed vaqueros. Oscar Wilde praised the practicality of Western wear, the wide-brimmed hat, cloak, high boots: "They wore only what was comfortable, and therefore, beautiful."

I grew especially fond of evenings at camp. Manuel proved a resourceful cook, substituting small game, squirrel, and such for the traditional pork in his mother's recipes of rice and beans, enlivened with vegetables from the lumber camp. Luckily, my father brought a taste for spicy food from his childhood in Montserrat over to Yorkshire, and that mother's family, after serving in India, had instituted a tradition of monthly red curry or vindaloo, since Manuel bombarded his dishes with an arsenal of dried chilis. Wyatt, not so prepared, complained bitterly, eyes watering, that Manuel was trying to kill him.

Riding Makhá reminded me of how much I missed Nike. I enjoyed brushing out Makhá after the day's ride and sneaking him treats Ohanzee had forbidden. Still, he wasn't Nike.

Horace Annesley Vachell said, "Around the campfire, all men are equal," and so in that forum, discussion flowed freely, if at times intensely, between Ohanzee and me. Wyatt would add a story or two about his adventures back east, but on his Western experiences, he remained strangely mute. Manuel, in his manner, said little, but did serenade us on occasion with a mouth organ. When I mentioned that the Mexican tunes he called norteños reminded me of German polkas, he nodded.

"Yes. My uncles played with the Germans. Waltz, mazurka, polka, all volksmusik."

"Germans?" I asked.

"Oh yes, and Swiss and Polish. They all came, built a church and a brewery, usually brewery first."

The first and only joke I heard from Manuel. Ohanzee, on the other hand, was regularly snarky, sometimes to our amusement, often not, and occasionally cruel. When Manuel bemoaned the loss of far-ranging longhorn cattle drives because of competition from Midwestern beef, Ohanzee dismissed the Texas longhorn cattle as tougher than buffalo hoof, and called it "eight pounds of hamburger on eight hundred pounds of bone and horn." After Wyatt made an unguarded slip of the tongue, Ohanzee started to refer to him as "the Irish one," or just Irish.

Exasperated, Wyatt exclaimed, "Aw come on, is it that obvious?"

"Like a leprechaun," Ohanzee needled.

Ohanzee didn't let me forget my status as tourist. My time in Denver meant nothing to him. "City of women," he called it. Clearly, some of my countrymen had proven to be poor ambassadors for the English way.

"East Coast dudes are annoying, but you British take the

cake, and not just all the habitual bitching that everything isn't tea sandwiches and clotted cream," Ohanzee said. Manuel quietly stood and left the campfire. I assumed he'd heard this rant before. "You people come here like we're some sideshow at an exotic carnival, blundering right through sacred ceremonies for profane curiosity. You see everything through your European eyes, understanding nothing." Ohanzee paused to drain the last of his coffee. "Worse yet are the searchers."

"Do not think I follow," I said, trying hard not to take any of this personally.

"I'm your guide through these wild lands. One of the best. Not a shaman. I'm not here to guide you on some spiritual journey. There'll be no sweat lodges, no quest, no crying for a vision. Just because you've read of power animals, you don't get to pick one."

"Hey, Ohanzee, what's *your* power animal?" Wyatt chimed in with a slightly mocking tone.

"An eagle, of course. Isn't that obvious?"

"Thought maybe mule," Wyatt said. "Can I please have a power animal, please, please?" Wyatt said it like a child asking for a balloon.

Ohanzee almost cracked a smile. "No, Irish, you cannot. You already have shamrocks and fairies." Wyatt's hearty laughter helped discharge the tension.

"But seriously, Ohanzee, if we tourists are such a burden, why do this at all?" I asked.

"What else am I to do? You know what the White man wants, even the so-called Friends of the Indian? To break up the tribal lands into tiny, individual allotments, weaken us, and then sell off the majority to White settlers. They call us Socialists; they seek to disperse the hive and deal with the bee."

Wyatt and I exchanged glances but remained silent.

"I can't stand the reservation. It bores and saddens me. It's hollow.

I know what it is to be a true Lakota brave. This guide work is as close to the old ways I can find. By shepherding the White man, I get to remain free on the land."

The fire crackled. We watched the orange, yellow, and blue flames wrestle around the wood. Three men hunched around a fire. It could have been hundreds of years earlier, but it wasn't.

"I considered Wild Westing with Buffalo Bill. I've no issue with Cody. He treats the Indians well, but that's all stories for White children. I took the White man's language, I learned his history, but he didn't wash away the Indian. I'm Lakota Sioux now and forever."

The conversation stalled. Wyatt got up, stretched, and said, "Well then, Tóksa akhé," and walked off toward the latrine.

I didn't tell Ohanzee my thoughts but sat still with the last flames warming my face and the night breeze cooling my back, maybe afraid my words would wound or anger him. Maybe afraid of being wrong, that I truly was a tourist, just another empty vessel spilling air and calling it wisdom.

I wanted to ask him why it would not be preferable in the long run to adapt, start their own towns and villages side by side with White people, and assimilate into Yankee America. I suspected what he might throw back at me with his knowledge of history: "Rome invaded you Brits. Why aren't you happy Romans? The Normans ruled England for hundreds of years. Have you become French?"

Of course, history is always more complicated than that. The Romans were mostly indifferent, and the Normans, in fact, left Britain a far different isle than when the conquest began, ancient fibers woven into the British cloth. Mostly, I surmised, Ohanzee feared that the Indian—the stories, songs, glories, and agonies—would all be subsumed, and in time, disappear, not even as a star in some new sky but a comet erased in a sun.

Over and over, I noted how Americans loved their Indian-named lakes and towns, their YMCA sports teams, along with legends of

Pocahontas and Sacajawea, but had little use for actual Indians. It was lovely as part of American mythic history, but it must remain in history, as inconvenient as Lancelot and King Arthur riding into present-day London and demanding to rule. As Americans now itched for empire abroad, many failed to see that the whole enterprise, from the Mayflower on, was always colonization and empire.

For all the blood, hate, and terror of the Black man's time in the United States, the solution to his problem was achingly simple, if seemingly unobtainable. After all that injustice, the Negro asked only one thing, to be accepted and treated equally as any other citizen. It could be done, never logically impossible. If the majority resisted, or refused to do so, it was merely sheer spite and bigotry.

The Sioux and the tribes desired an outcome so much more elusive and irreconcilable. The Indians were fighting for a place in time, a way of being, the past, the tribal mind struggling to grasp the unthinking mendacity of commerce. The businessmen in New York and Denver, the farmers in the Midwest, the waves of eager immigrants constantly disgorged from steamships, all of them were racing inexorably toward the future, and the future, be it ugly and rapacious or glorious and noble, always wins. This adolescent nation cared not about the past, only the now, and the now to come. The ever-new world. America had no answer to its Indian problem. The Indians only had dreams. America, the new empire, would ignore the Indians when it could, suppress them when interest conflicted, and obliterate them if it must.

Chapter 23

After leaving the Tetons, Ohanzee became very cagey, promising strange magic coming. Wyatt warned, "Anytime he starts that ornery Injun act, watch out. He enjoys making us the fool." I didn't feel entirely unprepared, having skimmed John Colter's account of Yellowstone. When whispery notes of disturbance rose to watery symphony, I knew we'd approached the lower Falls near Lookout Point.

The waterfall marked the transition from steadfast hard rock of the upper mountain to the soft rock of the lower carved canyon. Here and there, resolute strata of canyon mineral refused to yield to water, creating standing hoodoo sentinels.

Traveling farther into Yellowstone, I remained confidently prepared for any surprise—until the pale spitting mud. What to make of this sight, what to compare it with? In the more liquid area, white clam chowder, overcooked and boiling. In the dry, a heart beating, pushing up tendrils of molten mud thrown skyward, the Devil coughing up sputum. My feelings were as mixed as my metaphors. Spectacular, but unsettlingly otherworldly, its smell an imagined hell of rotten eggs and sulfur.

The first explosive burst of water from a geyser might have totally delighted me, had I not been forced to deal with the terror it instilled in Makȟá. Most horses like what they know and love what they expect, and a geyser is none of that. So, Makȟá pranced, skittish and jumpy, as we moved on to the hot springs.

Ohanzee warned of the dangers. Not just once, but repeatedly, annoyingly. Makȟá twitched, nervous as we approached a hot spring. It shimmered a bright, brilliant blue. Ohanzee instructed us earlier that the springs were colored not only by the minerals within, but also by their heat, brown, green, red, and blue, and deep blue so very, very hot. Ohanzee had warned us, not just once.

Mesmerized, I craved to peer all the way to its bottomless depth. Transfixed, I edged closer to the thermal pool.

A horse expends an almost unnatural degree of force on the small area of its hoof. The crust of soil and dust surrounding the pool gave way under the pressure. Below the crust, pyretic water, boiling almost for lack of oxygen, embraced Makhá's forelock. It found flesh and cooked it instantly.

The horse wrenched free and tested its blistered limb, stumbled, then collapsed to the ground, breathing quick and hard, his brown eye wildly searching for a new understanding of pain. I tried to roll free but was rather tossed like a contorted rag doll, landing roughly on knees and elbows, close enough to the rim of the spring to feel waves of heat. I imagined the rim giving way, the hellish sulfur water, the final punishment for my sins, my foolish, arrogant, meaningless life. Terrified, I scrambled to my feet. Blood mixed with dust to color my pants and shirt a dark ocher—more stunned than damaged.

By now Wyatt, Manuel, and Ohanzee had dismounted and approached the doomed and suffering animal. I wished for Ohanzee to excoriate me with vile curses. It would be best if he punched me in the face. I ached for confession, punishment, and possible redemption. It would not come, not from Ohanzee. He, along with the crippled horse, bore whatever pain, anger, or sorrow in eerie silence. He examined the hideously burned leg. Then he rubbed Makȟá gently on the head and softly sang in the horse's ear what sounded like a lullaby in Sioux. When he was done, he went to his horse and returned with a Winchester 1873 rifle.

Ohanzee held the gun out to me. "You know how to use this, right, wašicu?"

"Yes." It came out as a shaky whisper.

"Don't mess up. Don't let him see the rifle. You'll pay for the horse. We'll get a replacement tomorrow."

In the days that followed, an invisible membrane separated me from my companions. Ohanzee kept professional but only spoke to me when necessary. He left the campfire after eating, and only returned to it after I retired to my tent. Conversely, he and Wyatt began having long, late-night, hushed discussions in a collision of English and Sioux. Now Wyatt revealed his fluency. This added to my frustration, as I could not understand what they said, or, of course, if it might be about me. Manuel unemotionally thought of horses as tools and, as a working vaquero, had seen many come and go. Still, he looked down on a fool who would meaninglessly waste a valuable asset.

Wyatt tried to maintain a business-as-usual attitude, but I feared he was beginning to agree with my brother John's assessment that I'd forever swing between paralyzing self-doubt and impulsive overcompensation. My left side had taken the brunt of my fall, and I ached for the relief of the sling. But I feared it would appear a play for pity, so I gritted through it and resumed the treatment of mummy powder and stretching.

I studied and admired the confident competence of Ohanzee, my opposite, his knowledge and acceptance of his beliefs and actions in the face of all that might oppose him and his people. Perhaps he had little choice. If I should fall, my family would reluctantly pick me up, brush me off, and place me in a safe, unimportant office counting boxes and filling out redundant lists, pinch-punch, neither a credit nor debit to the Banks's account.

I redoubled my efforts to be useful as we made our way back to Green River for the train back to Denver. I brushed burrs out of the horses and helped with the cooking. Ohanzee noticed, I think, but said nothing. I took special care of my replacement horse, Onida. She was a muscular Arabian with a blackish bay coat. Onida's eyes radiated intelligence, and I recalled what the old strapper at our estate always said about female horses being smarter, and therefore, more dangerous. Maybe I was trying to make amends for my treatment of Makȟá, maybe I just needed a friend; but I felt myself becoming connected to Onida in a way I only experienced with my beloved Nike back home.

We all agreed to avoid retracing our route to Yellowstone. Instead we would head southeast through the Shoshone Indian Reservation in Wind River. Ohanzee's daughter and new granddaughter were living there. I agreed readily to the detour, looking for anything that might raise my favor in the group. Manuel went ahead to a telegraph station to arrange a meeting place for father and daughter. The reservation was vast, and we would only cross one corner of it on our way back to catch the train to Cheyenne.

Since my relations with Ohanzee were still tender, I asked Wyatt if he knew how a Sioux would be living with the Shoshone tribe. When I said I thought the Sioux were far away, Wyatt's mood immediately soured, and he stared at the ground for an uncomfortable moment.

"Pine Ridge. Sioux are at Pine Ridge. And she's not with the Shoshone. Ohanzee told me her husband's Arapaho. Arapaho pulled the short straw, never got their own res. Lived with the Sioux, an alliance, families knew each other, probably how his daughter Kimimela met her husband, but the Sioux kinda treated the Arapaho like poor cousins. So, they came out to Wind River. They're mountain

Indians really, not plains, and since Uncle Sam's not eager to carve out any more land, they're stuck with the Shoshone."

At Wind River we made our way toward the main lodge house and the outbuildings that ornamented it like rays from the sun. Kimimela and her baby—we didn't know her name—were coming into view in the distance on a borrowed buckwagon with a two-horse team. Wyatt noted that the Arapaho son-in-law smartly stayed at home. I surmised that Ohanzee and he were not the best of chums.

Across this bucolic vision slashed a bright flurry of motion from another direction. A federal agent pealed crosswise through the dust. That wouldn't have been remarkable, except that he approached on two wheels. Ohanzee and Wyatt looked confused at this whining contraption. I, for once, felt secure in knowledge. A motorcycle. John, my brother, having been pushed relentlessly to respectable adulthood, grasped for lost childlike pleasure by early attachment to every shiny new man toy. My father, solicitous of my brother and always looking for a leg up on his competitors, had investigated obtaining a motorcycle in the months before I sailed to America.

Father and John acquired a motorized bike from Germany to test on the estate. Despite their delight in the technology, the experiment failed. The most fleabag horse would still ride when given a simple ration of oats. The bike needed to be started by preheating a fuel tube with an alcohol torch. After a week of trying to start the thing in blowing rains, my father sent the cycle back and stuck with horses.

The German machine, though, had been a grand pride of Teutonic imagination, elegantly expressed in deep enameled black-and-gold trim, gleaming chrome handlebars, and rumbling fire and pistons. The federal agent's ride appeared simple and cruder, matte black, bike pedals, and motor. A low mechanical whine replaced the expected chug of an engine. The agent, bundled up in goggles, a hat, and a face scarf, appeared intent in his own world as his trajectory took him right past the buckboard driven by Kimimela. As they exchanged ground, the motorcycle emitted a flame and—*Bang! Bang! Bang!*

Even at a distance it startled us, sudden and loud. Marengo bolted, with Wyatt hopelessly pulling at the reins. Onida reared, nearly dismounting me, then settled. Napoleon, conceivably trusting the calm of his rider, circled quickly, then stamped the ground. Looking down, I saw the buckboard, out of control, and two panicked horses, careening. I heard Ohanzee involuntarily command, "No! Stop!" His words floated off with the wind.

Chapter 24

What does a horse actually think? Do thoughts become pictures, images, hieroglyphs drenched in meaning? How does he make a decision? Does he weigh the pros and cons, or does instinct dictate action? The shattering report of the backfire going off beside thc buckboard must have filled the horses' minds with a flood of stimuli. In horse-speak pictures: "Bad," it said. "Fear, death," it said. "Run."

Ohanzee and Napoleon shot off toward the road that wound lazily down around the fences, stream, and rock outcroppings to where his daughter and granddaughter screamed in terror. *No good*, I thought. *Too far.*

The horse team left the road and were fleeing over uneven ground, buckboard shifting one way and then the other, nearly tipping. I took off directly in the trajectory of where the wagon most likely would wind up. Ohanzee saw and understood immediately, changing course to follow me.

There were several obstacles to be jumped. It was a challenging course on a reasonable steeplechase horse. I didn't know if Onida was inclined to jump at all. She might pull up short, or even slam horse and rider into a rock wall. There was no time for reflection. Any minute, the buckboard was on course to topple over and crush Kimimela and her tiny daughter.

Fate granted a favor. The first test the big Arabian faced was a simple split-rail fence. Using every skill I'd committed to memory of muscle and mind, I tried to communicate with Onida. The horse cleared the low fence, but too closely. I told myself some horses leap only as high as needed, unsure if even I believed it.

I scanned possible routes to intersect with the flailing wagon, a quick hope to eliminate certain disaster: uneven foreground, interfering tree branches. Ohanzee and Napoleon cleared the fence and closed ground. For an instant, I thought Ohanzee might try to overtake me (Napoleon being the faster horse), but Ohanzee sensed my deliberate movements and allowed me to lead.

The creek did not look so wide, but the far bank fell off a good four feet. Some would think jumping downhill was easier. More like a death trap. Coming at full speed, as we were, I'd seen the horse's front legs buckle, the horse tumbling, or even if the horse remained upright, the awkward landing might throw the rider. As I moved my body in preparation for the leap, I could see Ohanzee mimic my movements. He moved slightly down the creek bank, wisely reducing the chance that if one of us fell, they would take out the other rider.

When things go wrong in steeplechase, when you make a false start, you feel it immediately. Your point of balance shifts unwanted; what should be taut goes slack, or what should be flexible becomes stiff. Even the air rushing by feels wrong. When right, a magic fluidity occurs. Thought centered not in human mind, not in horse mind, but between—one being. My mind had now cleared, my body memory rushed back, my legs moved girth-to-barrel-to-flank by feel—an asymmetrical, balanced dance of leg and hip and hand to the rhythm of the horse's music. I'd danced that perfect melody upon my dear Nike so many times. Now, only one partner filled my mind: Onida.

I leaned fully back and Onida found the landing in soft grass on the opposite bank, and continued on at a gallop. Ohanzee cleared and hung by my side like a shadow. My necessary confidence began to edge into cockiness when . . . *thwack!* A blur of yellow-and-black feathers erupted into my face—a lark flushed from its nest. I crumpled backward, nearly dismounted. But Onida and I had achieved oneness.

She was feeding off that feeling, and the sense of purposeful motion, and she wasn't ready to sever that connection. Feeling rider trust from back to flank, she shifted the center of gravity, righting me into position again, hardly breaking stride.

We approached the final obstacle, which, from afar, appeared reasonable, but now revealed itself on the limit of ability of both horse and rider. Over six feet tall, the barrier was a mishmash of stone wall, natural outcrop, and stacked brush. A twinge of fear gripped me. I couldn't accurately gauge the depth as the wall sloped away on the other side. In seconds, I needed to choose our launch point. If I picked the wrong spot, we faced a hard tumble, or much worse. Ohanzee would have no time to correct behind us and would collide with us while Kimimela and her precious infant would be flung to their peril.

The haunted memory of that long-ago steeplechase pried its way into my consciousness, forcing the image of the failed jump, the suffering horse, both hind legs ravaged and torn. My eyes blurred with tears. I waited for the pain in my arm to return tenfold. No, no. I didn't have the luxury of doubt and fear anymore. Dr. Qabash had told me Allah created horses from the Southerly wind to fly without wings and conquer without swords. For Onida to conquer, I had to let go of my bitter cargo, my shame, my haven, my excuse.

I couldn't let Onida sense my fear in any way. A rider who has lost nerve can send almost imperceptible signals to his mount. If the horse loses nerve too, all is lost. I'd witnessed big, strong jumpers run headlong into barriers with great violence, never even attempting to leap or swerve. I didn't have license to fail here, not again, not for me, for Onida, Ohanzee, Napoleon, Kimimela, and child.

At the last critical moment, I felt the world slow. Time lengthened. I was suddenly aware of the fringy heads of meadow grass peeking up behind the wall in all but one spot. My legs danced, Onida shifted, coiled, and jumped. Time continued to hover as we soared over sand and stone. I could sense Onida's trailing foot and pastern scraping gravel, but just barely. I saw a safe landing point and a clear path to the buckboard. I also glimpsed Napoleon pull up short and turn.

The buckboard horses were tiring but heading straight for rougher terrain, ditches, and stumps. It now occurred to me that I began this rescue with no plan other than clearing the first fence. As I came nearer the runaway wagon, the woman was no longer screaming but crouched, clinging and covering her child, praying, I hoped, to whatever Indian god might transform a scarcely royal lad from Yorkshire into a melding of Lancelot and Kit Carson. I searched my memory for any scrap of experience, any notion of what to do next, hoping to strike the Aristotelian valor between cowardice and recklessness.

If Ohanzee had made the jump, the two of us might have approached from both sides and calmed the horses. Unfortunately, the reins had fallen, been trampled, and torn clear away. Surely, I could not do it alone. A memory of one of Wyatt's dime Westerns flashed: rugged cowboy, most likely an outsider, leaps off his horse. Grabbing for the riggings, he almost falls to the dust to be trampled to death—but no, his strapping body rises up astride the horses as he saves the day. All I could envision was being slammed between two crazy horses and falling broken to the ground.

Then another memory, longer ago, a training game my father's groom made us repeat and repeat: riding at full speed, reaching over and plucking a short flag from a bucket on a pole. No other memory emerged. I came dangerously aside the bouncing wagon. Unfortunately, the only approach was on my left side. I needed Kimimela to hold the child out to me like a flag on a pole. She was still using her body to shield the child. I yelled for her to hold out the baby. She stared at me but did not move.

I'd asked Wyatt to teach me some basic Sioux, but I was a poor student. I didn't have the words for "girl," "child," or "baby."

"Wee-Yan . . . Wa-Buluska," I shouted, reaching out my hand. At best, I'd shouted something like "woman bug," but Kimimela's face changed and then set in determination, not fear. She slid over on the floor of the buckboard and raised her child, not over, but straight up.

Knowing I would need momentum for the grab, I first fell back, then came up close at full speed, plucking the child like the training flag, turning a quick circle, depositing the girl atop a tall stump, then again pursuing the wagon. The buckboard's wheel struck a stump, let out a sickening crack, and splintered but did not shatter.

Again, I got up even and stared into Kimimela's eyes. Still no plan, only desperation. I didn't have the skill or strength to lift her gently and place her behind me as some distressed damsel in Arthurian legend. This was real life—clumsy, haphazard, and deadly.

"Hee!" I commanded. "Hee!" *Come*, was the best I could think of. I hadn't learned "jump." I motioned she should leap not at me, but to reach for the horn of my Western saddle and whatever other tack she might cling to. I would grab whatever clothing or flesh presented itself, feminine modesty be damned.

It was not dashing nor pretty. It was, in fact, ugly and painful. While Kimimela's left hand reached the saddle, her right thrashed about and punched my throat, cutting off my air for an instant. I got hold of her upper thigh, but the wagon bucked, and her right boot wedged in the bench seat, pulling her out of my hand.

The wagon glanced Onida, who veered off sharply. I saw Kimimela's foot bend unnaturally before slipping from the captured boot. The buckboard sped another couple of yards, then struck a stump, this time shattering the wheel. Wood and metal lurched over like a great anchor and pulled the two horses to the ground.

Kimimela was trying to get down even before we came to a complete stop. I restrained her with both hands. In her shock and concern for her child, she didn't fully realize the extent of her injury. Her ankle was broken, lacerated. Her foot dangled, useless, blood soaking through cloth. I felt a pang of revulsion, the same sensitivity that had scuttled my medical career before it even launched. I swallowed hard. *Do not look away*.

She fought to get free. I had no Sioux words left to placate her determination to run to her daughter. By the grace of whatever god had jurisdiction at the reservation, Ohanzee rode up, cradling his granddaughter for the first time. Kimimela smiled at her father and child, then fainted.

Wyatt, Ohanzee, and I stood crowded into the small anteroom of a shack set up as an impromptu operating room. The bone on Kimimela's ankle had pierced skin. She had lost blood, my pant leg stained scarlet in evidence. I moved gingerly, silently cursing the horn on my western saddle. A wizened medicine man attended, thankfully aided by a muscular young brave. They set the bone and stopped the bleeding. Unfortunately, the ancient healer lacked medical supplies, and the nearest Bureau of Indian Affairs office was miles away. Miners passing us earlier told Manuel of a group of federal troops, who were quite close, bringing provisions to Yellowstone. Manuel had already ridden off to see if they could help. I had snatched my bottle of mummy powder, then thinking better of it, kept it in my pocket.

Wyatt broke the silence. "She'll be fine. Old guy's set a lot of bones."

"The wound was very dirty," Ohanzee said.

"Army always carries antiseptic," said Wyatt. "Manuel's a fast rider."

It struck me how easy and natural their interaction had become. How did they fall into friendship? So self-absorbed in my own misery and penitence after the Yellowstone incident, I discounted the hours Wyatt and Ohanzee spent together on the trail and around the fire. A surge of jealousy and bitterness for my isolation turned at once to shame for such petty selfishness ruining what I had done. I'd experienced an exorcism today. I truly did something on my own, and for someone else. Only now I wanted a pathetic celebration; I still desired validation from people like Ohanzee, my father, and my brother.

"Don't you have something you want to tell Joshua?" Wyatt asked Ohanzee.

"I won't be escorting you to the train."

"I see," I said.

"I need to care for my daughter and granddaughter until I can take them home to their village. I trust that's acceptable?"

"What else, Ohanzee," Wyatt injected.

Ohanzee looked at Wyatt, then back to me. "Manuel will make sure you get to a station to catch the train back to Cheyenne."

"You're one stubborn cuss," Wyatt said, shaking his head. "Come on—"

The door banged open wide, interrupting Wyatt and nearly smacking me in the face. Manuel charged in.

"A medic was traveling with the soldiers. He insisted on coming along with the medicine," Manuel said.

A large man in uniform entered, his skin a deep brown, and with him, a wiry young soldier much lighter in color, but also obviously a Negro, carrying a pack and a portmanteau.

The first man spoke. "Corporal Morris of the Twenty-Fifth Regiment at your service. Manuel tells me you have a young lady with a bad wound that needs to be sanitized and dressed."

Ohanzee shot across the room and shook Corporal Morris's hand.

"Private First-Class Gray will be assisting," Corporal Morris said. "He's an absolute craftsman with stitches, practically grew up a tailor. Little ladies shouldn't have ugly scars on their legs."

The soldiers hurried on to the bedside. Manuel excused himself to tend the horses.

Wyatt started, "Now, Ohanzee—"

Ohanzee held up his weathered hand and cut him off. "It's premature." The room fell silent while thoughts boiled inside the three of us.

My concern for Kimimela weighed on my mind first, but fleetingly. The unexpected arrival of Buffalo Soldiers renewed my internal struggle to come to terms with the African blood flowing in my veins. Ever since retreating out west, I tried to take the revelations of that day with Nowak and mostly go on as if any Blackness simply did not exist—just as Americans went about their current business, as if over two hundred years of the blood, toil, tears, and degradation of slavery never really happened. Or at minimum, any debt had been written completely off by the war.

If only the mass of Whites had truly ignored the Negro, or simply lumped the race in with the Sicilians and Irish and Slavs. What I witnessed in America amounted to the fashioning of new chains, more insidious and resistant to escape. Blacks were to be free but not free. The normal process of advancement impeded or blocked at every turn: education, business, social, political.

There was the obvious terror of the lynch mobs that my dear Miss Moon so nobly fought, but those acts were so morally evil, so biblically abominable that one might actually end them. But it had become uncomfortably clear to me that the greater lasting evil resided in the subtle bigotry of exclusion and the underlying justification of racial superiority. If the Civil War marked a first step in wiping clean the original sin of slavery, then the American people were hard at work, creating a new sin to take its place.

Yet ask the average American what he thought of the treatment of the Negro, and the impression was that he generally did not think of it at all. He certainly endeavored to shape his society that he should not be troubled by the plight of the Black race.

It's hard to tell the passage of time in such a situation. No clock chimed. No watch ticked. In any case, an accumulation of hours passed before Corporal Morris emerged, his military composure preventing an all-out smile, but he was visibly pleased.

"Mrs. Kimimela is awake and having some fine army cake and drinking some fine army tea." The tension of the room broke. "We drained and cleaned the wound with phenol, and Private Gray did his finest work to date. She'll be a little weak for a while. Ohanzee?"

"Yes?"

"Once the wound heals, you get your best medicine man to pull those stitches out. The old man in there knows his stuff, but his eyesight is none too good. We don't want to mess up Private Gray's masterpiece."

"Of course. I understand," said Ohanzee.

Pulling the bottle of mummy powder from my pocket, I offered it to the Corporal. I would not need it anymore.

The Corporal suppressed a laugh. "You go sell that to a dime museum. We're men of science, not hokum. I hate to be rude, but we're behind schedule." With that, the Corporal and a beaming Private Gray shook our hands and were gone.

"And now?" Wyatt prodded Ohanzee.

"I would have saved them," Ohanzee said.

"No," said Wyatt. "Joshua cleared the wall, and you didn't."

"If Napoleon were two years younger, we'd have been back and safe before Joshua cleared the first fence."

"But it didn't happen two years ago. Josh is the hero today," said Wyatt.

"You knew he was a hotshot rider, didn't you?" Ohanzee asked.

"Josh might have mentioned it once."

"You two are aware I am still in the room," I said.

Ohanzee stared me down. "You're not yet part of this discussion."

Wyatt put his hand on Ohanzee's forearm. "You're an honorable man. Tell him, or someday you'll regret it."

Ohanzee swelled up like the full tiger version of a tomcat, stopped, then let out a deflating sigh. "Joshua, thank you. You didn't hesitate."

"I had to do what I could," I said.

"Yes, today, you did," said Ohanzee. "What will you do tomorrow?"

If that last was meant to anger or offend me, it didn't. It was a good question. "I don't know how to answer that," I said.

"Hey, hey, you're supposed to be thanking him, not giving him the third degree," Wyatt said.

Sunlight and the smell of sage flooded through the open door as Manuel rushed in to tell us the horses and gear were ready. We needed to leave to meet the train.

"You forgot the name," said Wyatt, grinning.

"Not forgot, Irish, just declined. That's between you and me."

"Aw, you been calling Josh a knucklehead rich kid. Let him hear his new nom de plume," said Wyatt.

Ohanzee gave me a stern stare but could not maintain it, and the look in his eyes warmed. "Tasunka Okinya," he said in a stage whisper.

"Please tell me that is a good thing," I said.

"Hot damn, Joshua, 'Soaring Horse,' " Wyatt said excitedly. "You should stick that in your smug brother's face. He may get the estate, but does he have a nifty Indian name? No."

"It's just a nickname," Ohanzee said dismissively. "No ceremony, no dance, you're not honorary Lakota. Let's be clear. You saved two Lakota today. My gratitude is sincere. I'll be forever in your debt, but your people, the White people, drain away our lives every day. You and Irish, and your goodwill, you're like the few soldiers who did not fire at Wounded Knee. That is not enough to save us."

"For whatever it's worth, I am still honored."

"Good, and you still have to pay for the horse."

Manuel ushered Wyatt and me outside, complaining, "All these years, how come I don't get an Indian name?"

Chapter 25

I returned to Denver, surprised to discover that, while I had changed, Denver had not. The Brown Palace still buzzed with busy businessmen, and trains kept injecting the city, and the West, with load after load of Eastern greenhorns: the hopeful, the hopeless, and the last hope. What they embraced as their future, I felt already slipping into my past. Having shed my old skin, I resented being forced to wear it again, especially once I considered the metaphor. I didn't wish to see myself buffeted about, my life mapped by others, be that Nowak, my father, brother, or even dear sweet Margaret. I needed to make a change. It needed to happen now.

It appeared a good omen, then, when a telegram arrived, marked from Nowak himself. Normally, he never directly communicated with me, instead going through copyboys to make a point of my status.

Western Union

Come at once NYC STOP Geo. Johnson murder trial STOP Will talk only to you STOP Train tickets at will call STOP Paper's idea not mine STOP Do not settle in STOP Trial over in Dec END

Although it amounted to being forced back to New York, that choice was already my own. I corralled one of the paperboys whom I employed to run errands, and gave him a note to deliver to Wyatt. Jolly-good news for him, I thought, to return to his grand life in New York.

I filed my last story for relay to London, an odd footnote to the Civil War era. Thirty years had passed from the end of that struggle, but John Brown, the man who'd led the ill-fated 1859 raid on the armory and arsenal in Harper's Ferry in an attempt to start a slave revolt, remained a controversial figure. Celebrated in the "Battle Hymn of the Republic," and the only White man universally respected by Blacks, the South portrayed him as an unhinged lunatic and fanatic.

Therefore, when the remains of Lewis Sheridan Leary were unearthed, along with seven more of Brown's raiders who'd been killed at Harper's Ferry, it was kept secret. Supporters wanted the remains properly reinterred next to the grave of John Brown on the Brown family farm in North Elba, New York. All was supposed to be secret to avoid possible interference or outright violence. It was supposed to be, but on August 30, 1899, around three thousand mourners were on hand to show their respects as a single coffin, draped in an American flag and containing the bones of the eight raiders, was lowered into a grave next to John Brown. Reports stated they were buried as heroes in a dignified and emotional ceremony. Clearly, the ghosts of the Civil War still haunted this land.

On the eve of our departure, my concern grew. Wyatt neither showed to help close shop or acknowledge my note. I buttonholed the paperboy, who assured me he'd put the note directly in Wyatt's hand.

So, I sighed with relief when the front desk alerted me of a message from Wyatt. The note simply asked me to meet him right away at the park near his flat. I placed my packed luggage with the bell captain in preparation for the trip to the train station in the morning, walked out, waved down a cab, and headed for the park.

"Well, you look the proper Western gent," I said.

Wyatt sat on the park bench decked out in local kit, remnants of steer replacing cotton and wool, bull-heeled high boots, the new leather creaking as he shifted. He appeared not costumed, but converted.

"Sit with me, Josh." The weary stone-and-oak bench, its weathered memorial plaque unreadable, faced a pleasant grassy common, presently dotted with strolling couples and groups of families. Wyatt wore a serious mien, so I took my place beside him quietly.

Like an old married couple, we sat without talking, not out of rancor or distance, but of ease. We let the cool autumn breeze compete with the warm October sun, breathing in the aroma of browning chokecherry and box elder trees.

Wyatt began to fidget with the upturned brim of a new dark-pecan Western telescope hat, the kind favored by riverboat card sharps, not bull riders. Instead of the common leather and stud circling the crown, the band was a dance of bright turquoise, green, red, and white Indian beads. Having whiled away my share of time in a few haberdasheries, I noted he had gone all in on a 10X, full-beaver design. Definitely not the curio-rabbit-and-wool souvenir to pull out at parlor parties back home while waxing poetic of nights on the range. This hat was a commitment.

"I've been thinking," Wyatt said.

"A dangerous game, even for the more experienced."

"I'm staying."

I studied his face.

"I'm serious, Josh. I'm not going back east."

"What about Becca? She will miss home, surely?"

"Home?" Wyatt shook his head. "She hated the tenements, the smells, the crush, all of it. I've got five rooms now, and in a year or two, I could afford a small cottage."

"I did not realize she was so unhappy in New York," I said.

"I did," Wyatt said. "Not so much unhappy as angry, really angry. Isolated. Cooped up with the kids most of the day doing piecework, or dodging streetcars and carriages. Now my kids have gone natural, running the meadows and plunging into streams like wild Comanche. And Becca has flowered. She's joined women's clubs, she's planting a vegetable garden with the kids, and . . ." He hesitated.

"And?" I asked.

"She's warmed to convivial society, rumbusticating, a bit of the jiggery-pokery. Oh, she ain't never going to compete with those tenderloin French gals, but the suffragettes have convinced her that godly women have the same right to pleasure as any man, and she's taken it to heart. You know, the other night she lay waiting for me in bed all bathed, made up like we were going to a ball. Well, you didn't need to send me a printed invite, we—"

"Stop," I interrupted. "That is an excess of information, leading me to imagine far more than I wish to."

"You did ask." Wyatt winked. "Anyhow, it's all settled. I turned in my resignation letter to Mr. Hearst. Got a new position with the Pinkerton office in Denver."

"You have no experience as a detective."

"That might be, but the chief, James McParland, happens to originally hail from County Armagh, so he took pity on a fellow traveler. Sides, all you need is a sturdy back, a dead eye with a gun, and some common sense. Got all that in spades."

He proudly handed me his freshly minted agency card. I turned it over in my hand, expecting to see the peering all-seeing eye of their advertisements, or at least the implied threat of their slogan, "We Never Sleep." Instead, it merely certified him a Pinkerton with all apparent right to act with extrajudicial impunity, and with his name proclaiming reclaimed heritage while still retaining a whiff of Western myth: WYATT PATRICK MCSWAIN.

I shook my head. "The Pinkertons have cracked quite a few Irish miners' skulls, you know, Mr. Brown—or should I now say, Mr. McSwain. Even back in England we heard about the poor murdered women of the Molly Maguires. If my father treated his workers the way the mine owners do, I believe he would burst into flames trying to enter the chapel door."

"McParland didn't kill that woman. He almost quit over it."

"Perhaps," I said, "but he was a spy, and if a man makes a career out of deceit, what will he not do?"

I didn't know if I was expressing real concern for Wyatt, or because the possible loss of Wyatt felt like a limb was being slowly amputated from my body.

"Pinkertons are not like the storybook Western gentlemen of old Dave Cook's Rocky Mountain Detective Agency," I said. "I shared a few drinks with one of the Pinkerton men, Charlie Siringo, and he told me about McParland's hired gun, Tom Horn. They let him run rogue and kill about seventeen people, assassinated two ranchers, Tisdale and Orley. When he got to be too much trouble, they just sent him off to Wyoming, free as a bird."

"Don't worry. I'm not going to be fighting any miners, only rustlers and such. A stock detective. Denver's such a cow capital the Colorado Stock Growers Association will keep me busy looking after their interests."

I burned to fully confront Wyatt, accuse him of ungratefully abandoning Mr. Hearst (really me); turning his back on his career (really mine); and making a hasty, disruptive mistake he would soon regret (the regret and disruption all mine). I tried to force a smile, then settled for stoicism.

"You were always right helpful to me, Wyatt," I said.

"That I was, but I've a feeling that where you're headed, I won't be of much use anymore."

I considered his words. A tactful man, a thoughtful friend, would have accepted Wyatt's statement as the end of it, full stop: Jolly good to have known you, give my love to the missus. I did not. I knew there was more driving Wyatt's decision than fresh air and wide-open spaces. His features carried a look of weighty determination, not the hopeful promise of the pilgrim but the resigned burden of the penitent.

"Wyatt." I put my hand on his shoulder in an act of brotherly intimacy, not caring if it were appropriate or appreciated. "I understand Becca and the children wanting to stay, but you? You were such a man of New York. I have to accept your decision, but don't leave me to always wonder about your true motives."

I could sense Wyatt auditioning one or another platitude, evasion, reasonable falsehood, and outright perjury until, finally tiring of the pursuit, he gave up and told the truth.

"I have to make amends."

"For?"

"The killing, Joshua. The Indians. All the killing."

Wyatt stared out as he talked, as if he were watching his past play out before him. He'd fallen into the army young, hungry for a bit of action, already a sharpshooter, and risen quickly to the Seventh Cavalry. He felt no ill will toward the Indians. As a child playing, he happily donned war paint and feathers, whooping and waving a pretend tomahawk. If some called them red savages, well, the Whites were just as savage in pursuing their empire. He saw in the natives a nobility only available to people who were as one with the natural world. A whole race of Robinson Crusoes.

A great shock, then, when he arrived west to see the lowly state to which a once-proud race had now been reduced. Herded onto ever-shrinking wasteland, enduring crippling drought, the precious buffalo all but gone, the Indians lived on handouts of tainted food rations. Deprived of the hunt, men who were forced into idleness took refuge in the bottle. Or they accepted the most menial jobs the White man could not get a Mexican to do. My ignorance of it all was obvious, so Wyatt painted it out for me to see.

Out of Indian despair came a desire to reclaim a glorious past.

Out of that desire rose a prophet, called Wovoka, an Elijah promising rain and much more. The dead ancestors would come back to life, bringing massive herds of buffalo, and the source of all troubles, the White man, would be swallowed by the earth for his sins.

Why did so many tribes make pilgrimages to Paiute Wovoka and leave as believers, spreading his message? Maybe the Indians finally knew they were beat. Custer may have died at Little Big Horn, but the White man's war machine only grew mightier. The Indians needed an act of God, any God, and if the Christian God could send a Messiah, they would not say no.

Wyatt explained that many refused to believe the red Christ stirring up trouble was Indian at all. General Nelson A. Miles, who harbored presidential ambitions, expressed a popular theory that the culprit "impersonating the Messiah" was a full-blooded White.

Miles publicly stated, "I cannot say positively, but it is my belief that the Mormons are the prime movers in all of this."

A Cheyenne named Porcupine told General Rugers that he witnessed Mormons dancing with Indians. Porcupine also claimed to have seen the new Christ with wounds on hands, feet, and side. The Mormons denied any role, but the story was widely repeated, some drawing connection between the Ghost Shirt and LDS endowment robes. Certainly, the Mormons baptized over a thousand natives, eager to bring the rebellious lost tribe of the Bible, the Lamanites, back into the fold, and perhaps over time fade their red skin back to White.

Indian ritual and Christian biblical teachings fused in Wovoka's spirit world vision, and as a solar eclipse blotted the sun, the Wakan Tanka, the Great Mysterious Spirit, delivered divine instructions. To fulfill the prophecy, God needed the Indian nations, his new chosen ones, to dance, an old round dance, but as more White settlers grew more fearful, the dance took on a more foreboding name: the Ghost Dance. When the 7th Cavalry were dispatched to Pine Ridge

Reservation in South Dakota to tamp down any possible uprising, Wyatt confronted the Lakota Sioux and the Ghost Dance firsthand.

Wovoka may have preached a Ghost Dance married to nonviolence and passive cooperation with Whites, but the version Kicking Bear brought back to the Lakota left such niceties at the altar. The Lakota were wedded to resistance, their attitude militaristic. They would follow the required sacramental ritual of the dance, but if the earth needed a little help in swallowing up the White plague, they would be ready.

And on they danced. Wyatt had witnessed it all. A large circle of men, and strangely, also women, joining hands, sidestepping leftward, chasing the path of the sun, singing, chanting, not stopping to eat or drink. Falling into trances, receiving visions, crossing into the spirit realm where the dead were dancing too, and like the living, preparing for war. They fell into hypnotic swoons, collapsing with fatigue. Upon rising again, the dancers would tell visions of mountains belching forth mud to bury the White race and the return of the old Indian ways. Just as menacing as the dance itself were the Ghost Shirts, adorned with powerful symbols, the thunderbird, the stars, the moon, empowered with the magic to stop the White man's bullets.

I envisioned the mad religious frenzy of the ancient St. Vitus dance or Whirling Dervish, but Wyatt said it reminded him of the Kentucky revival dancing he'd seen at a camp meeting, where the faithful cried, shouted, and gestured wildly while their heads filled with visions and prophesies.

As Wyatt's voice seethed with anger, it was clear what bothered him the most. The whole mess might have all burned itself out and passed like a fever, if the army and the government had let it. They did not. Malice, ambition, and incompetence did their own dance. The Ceska Maza, the Indian police, in a rash gesture, turned an arrest of Sitting Bull (who, not long ago, had been signing autographs in Wild Bill's show) into a shootout, six police dead, eight Indians dead, including Sitting Bull. Then Big Foot's people were escorted to Wounded Knee Creek.

Wyatt shuddered, reliving it all. "We were giving the women cigarettes. Friar Craft was there. I thought it was calming down, but we couldn't find their guns. One guy just wouldn't move—like he was deaf or something. There was pushing, fighting, and some trigger-happy fool shot a gun. Then the Devil took over. We kept shooting for hours like we were trying to empty a river of bullets, sometimes hitting our own, and no Ghost Shirt stopped us, especially not the Hotchkiss guns.

"I think if it was just the men, they are warriors . . . men of war, but no, we didn't stop. We killed the young boys. Wouldn't they soon be warriors? Again, we didn't stop. We killed the women. They were fertile mothers of more warrior boys who would too soon be warrior men. Then the little girls, future vessels for future warriors. And we couldn't stop until even the babies were killed. After all, wouldn't they seek to avenge all this killing?"

"You were a soldier, Wyatt."

"How much evil will that excuse?" Wyatt's voice rose in anger. "There's no honor in obeying madness. Only a few refused. What if all of us rank-and-file had refused the orders? A handful of officers couldn't have rained down such horrors. The Devil depends on good men to follow the orders of poisonous leaders."

"I understand, but what can you do about all that now? You have your own responsibilities, a wife, your family, your community."

"I aim to help in some way."

"That's the problem, Wyatt. I am no expert on Indian affairs, but I think it is entirely clear they do not want your help, and especially not your pity, and I do not believe they care about your guilt. They simply want you to leave. Their true desire is that history wipe away all trace of the invasion of Europeans so they awaken one day to our absence, as if arising after a long infection."

"That godly power isn't mine. The dice has been thrown, and the money has already changed hands. The strong take, and the weak struggle. The aggressor tribes pushed the peaceful tribes into pueblos and hanging on cliffs for safety. Now the White man has come in like Noah's flood, but there's no ark and no promise. Some of that flood of folks ain't going to be the best of us, hungry, desperate, selfish, or just plain bad. There's going to be some history made that we can't be proud of."

"So, what the bloody hell do you think you can do?"

Wyatt laughed a sad, uncomfortable laugh. "That's the thing. Don't rightly know. I really don't. But I sure as hell ain't going to do anything about it back east. No, I need to be out here, where the opportunity may arise. I figure if the Indian has at least one more citizen around who wishes him well, who isn't trying to cheat him or push him off his land, that's a help right there. If Pinkerton has a dust-up with some tribe, better they send me than some fool who thinks 'the only good Injun is a dead Injun.' And maybe I come up with something better on down the road."

We paused. The breeze blew. The sun shone. The couples strolled. Wyatt's boots creaked.

"Wonder whose bench this was?"

"Pardon?" I said.

"The memorial plaque. I can't read the name anymore."

"Time and tide, and all that."

"Guess so. It must've meant something to somebody at the time, don't you think? A fair piece of trouble and expense."

"I suppose."

"I mean, you're lucky to get that much thought, even if you're eventually bound to fade and be forgotten."

"Dust to dust. Still, by gum, a grand bench it is," I said in my best Yorkshire accent.

"Aye, 'tis indeed."

PART III

The Trial

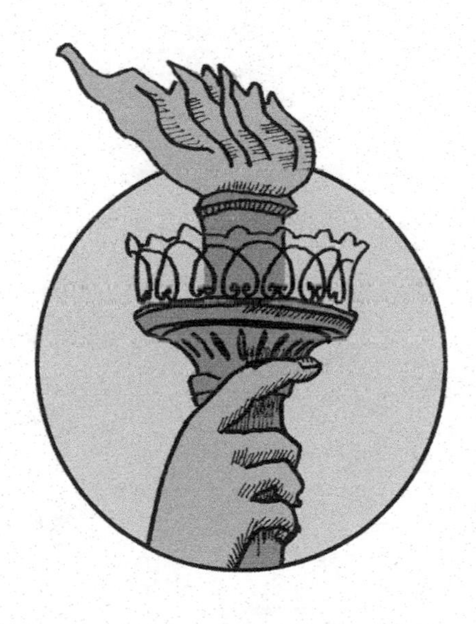

October 1899
Dear Margaret,

Happy news, I think. I'm writing from a train heading to Baltimore, then on to New York City. See, the terrible distance between us shall be halved soon. I hope this lightens your heart. I am called back east to cover a murder trial, my first high-profile assignment. Truth be told, my editor would have assigned the story to anyone but me, if not for the inconvenient fact that I'm a friend of the accused, and evidently, he will speak only to me. I do not wish you to think me callow to my acquaintance's predicament, but I shall take this reporting opportunity gladly. Our recent missives being unfortunately brief, I realize I did not inform you that my close associate and friend, Wyatt Brown, and his family decided that Denver is their proper home, so I travel alone.

My train was greatly delayed in Kansas City due to mechanical troubles. It turned out to be a boon of sorts. A conductor pointed me to a music hall where I might pass the time as I waited for the replacement engine to take us on our way. The hall rested on the seedy side, but I heard the most ingenious and curious music. A young African American lad, Scott Hayden, played the piano in what he called ragtime. The name fits. It is, indeed, raggedy music. Since you play Mendelssohn and Schubert so beautifully, I think you will appreciate a more thorough description.

Imagine playing a standard John Philip Sousa march, left hand keeping the underlying two-step oompa-oompa beat, but instead of your right hand pinning the melody securely to each beat, the melody shatters and skitters in constant syncopation all around the beat.

Master Hayden played his own compositions, including a corker called "Sunflower Slow Drag," but the crowd erupted for the tune "The Maple Leaf Rag," written by his mentor, Scott Joplin. I was told this song is all the rage, not just in KC, but back east as well. I will try to locate the sheet music and send you a copy.

It seems ragtime is almost as much a technique as a type of composition. Young Hayden was able to take several standard popular songs and two classical pieces yelled out by the crowd, and rag them also. I left truly impressed with the intelligence and creativity necessary for such innovation. It puts the lie to the idea that Negroes lag behind in intellectual development and mental prowess.

I raise this subject because we never had occasion to discuss our opinions of the darker races. Knowing you as a kind Christian woman, I imagine you see all people as God's creation. I worry that perhaps your contact with darker races may be limited to one or two disheveled, mumbling servants. If you have been so influenced, I implore you to reconsider. We British would not deign to be judged by a few drunken, unschooled, cockney ruffians. I assure you that given equal upbringing, education, and opportunity, these colored folks can match any Caucasian.

I do not mean to lecture, but I have important issues to discuss with you. We must be honest with each other. Surely we must, even though it is often easier to hide the truth.

This is not to ignore your ultimatum. I understand your frustration, but there is more at play than you know. My encounters out West, and indeed, all through this country, have given me new clarity. I know I must soon make crucial decisions that will determine the arc of my life. I have not yet

formed the right words to tell you all that I need to, but I will soon.

Always in my heart,
Joshua

Chapter 26

I tipped a porter to mail my letter to Margaret at next opportunity, but I remained conflicted about the content. There was no doubt I'd committed to revealing my family's ancestry to her, regardless of the consequences. She deserved as much, and any of my future actions would be bewildering without that knowledge. Everything else, however, remained completely up in the air, more so than any time before.

I chose to interpret Nowak's decision to route my train through Baltimore not as happenstance but a divine sign to fulfill my long-delayed promise to check in on my old cabinmate, Dr. Abdel Qabash. I wired ahead to meet at Lexington Market, not far from the Doctor's Greene Street office and residence. I treated myself to a short cab ride from the station to Lexington Market in order to save my legs since the Doctor mentioned in the telegram his intention to show me around town.

Even on a normal Friday morning, a holiday atmosphere buzzed through the crowds, teeming the stalls that spilled out from the awnings on the long, low-peaked building. Additional stalls echoed on opposite sides of the street, hawking all manner of goods, from apples and yams, to oils and salted ham.

Entering the building, I saw an immediate temptation of shortbread cookies covered in fudge. I shared such temptation, apparently, with a street urchin, about nine or ten years old, in a torn jacket and tattered wool cap. He pretended to retrieve a weathered ball, then reached up, snatched a handful of cookies, and ran off. The merchant cursed him by name and threatened to call the police. Seeing the young rascal needed nourishment far more than reform school, I settled the boy's account, putting some money on deposit for his next few raids.

Not wanting to keep the Doctor waiting, my attention turned to locating Faidley's Seafood, our rendezvous point. The Doctor sat on a stool at the oyster bar, which was odd since I believed Arabs were not permitted to eat shellfish. I quickly reminded myself that Egyptians didn't consider themselves Arab. I also reminded myself that in the four years since meeting Dr. Qabash, I expended no effort whatsoever to educate myself about the tenets of Islam, much less dietary restrictions. Thus, best to assume nothing.

"Welcome, my friend." Dr. Qabash shook my hand warmly. "I propose a bit of sustenance before we walk to the harbor." He signaled the shucker for two dozen oysters, then turned to me. "I presume you eat oysters, don't you? They're all the rage here."

"I adore oysters, and Chesapeake Bay ones are renowned, but I know many, like my brother John, who are repulsed by their texture, especially raw." I seized the opening to slake my curiosity. "To be honest, Doctor, I thought you would not."

"Ah, we all presume too much of those we don't know. Opinion is simple, truth complex. You're thinking of the Shi'ite, La'fari who only eat finfish. I'm Sunni, and though the Hanafi may prohibit it, I follow the Maliki school of jurisprudence. We aren't so severe as to exclude the delights Allah provides."

"Wise," I said.

"You know, Banks, in your Old Testament, I believe Leviticus and Deuteronomy say that shellfish are detestable, unclean, an abomination. It's you who should abstain."

"Doctor, in my experience, Christians are quite good at picking and choosing which abominations to condemn according to their existing preferences."

"True of all men," he said.

The oysters were set in front of us, bodies glistening in half shells. Dr. Qabash squirted his with lemon wrapped in cheesecloth following Baltimore tradition. The locals thought the acid helped disinfect any problem oysters, but in the Doctors's medical opinion, he highly doubted its efficacy. He did, however, savor the taste, though he wasn't so keen on the horseradish paste some locals smeared over the mollusk. We sat there and, like the Walrus and the Carpenter, made short work of the delicacies, filling our mouths with the taste of the sea.

"I love this market," Dr. Qabash said out of the blue. "When I first arrived in Baltimore, I felt completely unmoored. You were right, you know. The Americans, they saw me as African."

"Well, you are technically African."

"No, I mean as a Negro."

"You say that like a curse."

"I've no hatred for Negroes. I'm one of few doctors in the city who treats them, but neither you nor these Negroes are Egyptian. We're the fountain of civilization. We built great cities of knowledge and art when you Brits were living in huts. We created religion. Saved Aristotle for you. As the activist Mustafa Kamil said, 'If I had not been an Egyptian, I would have wished to become one.' Of course, you cannot really become an Egyptian, but four years here, and I'm an American."

There were other hungry customers waiting. In courtesy we yielded our seats. The Doctor insisted on stopping by the stall of AD Konstant & Son for sweets. He must have been a frequent customer, for the merchant greeted him with bright chatter as we waited in line. The candymaker appeared to specialize in a flat taffy embedded with an array of various nuts: cashew, pecan, Brazil, coconut, and peanut. Also on offer was pull taffy in peppermint, chocolate, vanilla, and molasses. The aroma of sugar and nuts reawakened my appetite.

The Doctor leaned over and whispered. "Watch out for the taffy.

Very chewy. You can lose a tooth in that stuff. We'll stick to what they call brittle. It's harder and crunchy. Martin says they sell mostly the peanut, but the black walnut brittle makes my heart sing."

Still looking for an opportunity to discuss my race dilemma with the Doctor, it didn't seem the right time. I tried to steer the conversation back.

"Do you really feel American? I mean, is this home?"

"When I'm in this market, it feels like home, it reminds me of home. You know there are foolish people who want to tear down Lexington Market and build a new one, just because it's a hundred years old. We have markets for millennium in Egypt. Americans haven't learned to honor their past."

"Some say our two countries are imprisoned by history."

"Nonsense. History determines fate."

"Doctor, you cannot believe that. In the fable you once told, didn't the prince escape all three of his fates?"

"You know, to tell the truth, I always thought the prince too lucky in that story. I'm sure the crocodile would have devoured him."

We finally placed our order and watched the clerk retrieve a large sheet of black walnut brittle and proceeded to break it into small pieces with a shiny miniature hammer. The pieces were wrapped in wax paper and placed in a paper bag. My mouth began to water; it was an effort to get my mind back on track.

"What I'm asking, Doctor, is have you become an American? Do you belong?"

Dr. Qabash considered a moment. "I won't lie. It was extremely hard at first. I started wearing this." He pointed to his hat, a tall fez, the color of dried blood. "Surprisingly, by standing out, it helped me fit in. It explained me to them. I still get asked why I don't wear a turban, as if I'm a Sikh or Sufi. And, of course, the beard. Less face, less questions." The Doctor gave a slightly bitter chuckle. "Come, Banks. We can eat our treat as we walk to the harbor."

He handed me the bag of brittle, then steered us down the street toward the law school, to something he wanted me to see. Around the corner of the school lay a church and compact graveyard. We stood before a white stone monument to Edgar Allan Poe. The Doctor patted the marker and said, "You know him, yes? He's something of a local hero."

"Of course. I assure you, Poe is famous all over the world. I've read a great deal of his work."

"Hmm. I didn't know of him until I moved here. The poetry is only competent. He's no Ibn al-Farid, or even Ahmed Shawqi, but the stories, they touched me. I especially liked 'The Masque of the Red Death.' "

"Sure. A prince throws a luxurious masquerade ball while peasants die of the plague. I think I attended that. They called it the Bradley-Martin Ball."

The Doctor ignored my reference.

"You see, the allegories are stronger than in his poems. The many-colored rooms—green, orange, white, violet—running east to west, from birth to death, to the seventh room, black with red windows and the ebony clock that strikes the hour. Each person's hour."

"Yes, and despite the prince's power, his fortress, his guards, and his wealth, death comes costumed like a plague victim and takes the prince."

"And all the partygoers." The Doctor clapped his hands in delight. "I think it's truer than the prince and his three fates. The more we try to resist our future, the faster it finds us. You can sail oceans, scale mountains, but you can't escape. You carry your fate with you. It's in your blood and bones."

"What if a person does not know their true blood and bones?" I asked. "What if a person is an orphan, or had amnesia?"

"God knows their path. Remember, one can forget their past, but one cannot forget their future."

"If that is a riddle, Doctor, I have no idea what it means."

"It means you ask interesting but slightly silly questions. Did you know that Poe, this great writer, died a pauper buried in an unmarked grave back over there?" He pointed. "Only later did people appreciate his art and honor him."

We both considered the portrait carved into stone. The stone already starting to weather.

"Looks a bit glum," I said. "Maybe upset they got his birthday wrong."

"Some of my patients don't believe it's even Poe in this grave."

"Come again?"

"See the hospital over there? That's only a couple of years old, but the medical school's been around for over seventy years. Students and instructors got a bad reputation paying for corpses, and this cemetery is most convenient. If you had more time, I could get us into Davidge Hall. A feat of architecture, two circular operating amphitheaters, one on top of another. But there are also little dissecting cubbyholes and secret stairways, exits to avoid angry mobs."

"I find that a tad grotesque," I said.

"What? When you go into surgery, you want your body the first one the surgeon has seen? It's better they butcher the dead than the living."

I explained to the Doctor that my queasiness around cadavers prevented me from pursuing a medical career.

"Don't feel bad," he said. "Schools lose several students every year encountering the dissection requirements. Some don't make it through the door. The smell alone stops them."

"I am happy to skip Davidge. But while we're talking medicine, I want to return this. Maybe it can help someone else." I handed him what was left of the mummy powder.

Dr. Qabash nodded knowingly. "You know that 'like cures like' idea—Paracelsus was a quack. It was always a placebo, perception creating reality."

"Yes."

"Courage, faith, even love are all perception, but still powerful."

We paid our last respects to Poe or, at the very least, his monument, and made our way toward the inner harbor. As we walked the breeze shifted, and I breathed in a comforting scent. "Is there a bakery nearby?"

"No, that's cinnamon. McCormick spice company, up on Baltimore Street. The first time I smelled it made me smile too. I buy cumin there to make fūl. A farmer in the market gets me fresh fava beans. I have to make it myself. Baltimoreans have no concept of the dish. I need it to taste like Egypt."

We arrived at the inner harbor, the pleasant aroma of cinnamon pushed aside by a thousand competing odors, and our ears were assaulted with sound. Gas motors coughed, horse teams clattered over cobblestones pulling creaking wagons, longshoremen shouted as they loaded or unloaded cargo. The many canneries that earned Baltimore the nickname "the nation's pantry" laid claim to much of the waterfront. Not a scene for an evening's promenade. A serious place of commerce. No one noticed the decaying slave pen where, a mere thirty-six years ago, men, women, and children were stored like chickens waiting to be shipped to auction in New Orleans. The Doctor and I sat on a wall and watched the hubbub.

The Doctor surveyed the panorama. "Americans, always so busy."

I pushed to get the conversation directed to my quandary. "Will you go back?"

"To Egypt?" Dr. Qabash paused an inordinately long time, as if scenarios were playing out in his mind. At last he said, "I don't know. I don't think so. In Egypt I fixed soldiers in order for them to fight again. Here I help a man return to work to feed his family. I've delivered babies who run and play. America has already changed me, as it has you."

"Me? Not really."

"I wish you could hear yourself. The man I met on that steamer sounded like an actor in a play. Just shy of 'hip-hip and cheerio, governor.' Minutes ago, at Konstant you complained about the line, not the queue."

"Changed a word. People here haven't a clue what a queue is."

"Not just words, Banks, your accent. You don't notice it because it happened gradually, but back in England, they'll think you're turning Yank." He put up a hand to cut me off. "Don't be defensive. It means you adapted to your surroundings. I, too, adapted. You ask if I'd go back to Egypt. I believe I've become too American to go back. The man you met on the ship does not exist anymore. Now then, let's have a go at that black walnut brittle. You don't think I'm going to let you walk off with it?"

I selected a few pieces of candy from the paper bag and handed the rest over to the Doctor. When I bit down on the confection, I could hear the crunch inside my head. "It's like eating a sheet of ice."

"I know. Isn't it wonderful?"

"The flavor is first-rate, but you said the taffy would pull a tooth. This might break one. I know my father's bridgework would not survive the brittle."

"Part of the appeal. One must earn the pleasure." The Doctor smiled.

I decided to take his good humor to get to the main reason I sought him out. "Doctor, I am faced with a quandary, and I should appreciate your wisdom on the matter."

He straightened. "Of course, but why me? I'm no oracle."

"No, but I don't know many men of your age and experience to whom I might reveal this matter. Our talks on the ship, I found you very thoughtful, and . . . I do not wish you to take this the wrong way—the fact that we are not extremely close makes it easier."

"The truth, yes. Easier to tell a stranger on a ship your darkest secrets than expose such thoughts to a brother or spouse. I told you on the steamer my estrangement from my daughter, and you said not to be so arrogant and proud. I finally sent her a letter. We're trying. I'll do what I can for you."

I felt a slight tremor in my hands but pushed on. "I fear I have not done a good job explaining my dilemma to others, so I will try to be clear. My editor, a man named Nowak, who, for whatever reason, took an immediate dislike to me even before we met, discovered that my grandfather was mulatto, a product of his father's dalliances with a Negress on the Island of Montserrat."

I searched for any reaction in Dr. Qabash's face. I found none. "Go on," was all he said.

"Nowak wanted me to go right back to England but did not have the authority. It would have been a complete failure on my part. A compromise banished me to the hinterlands out west. But now I am called back to New York and have run out of time. I do not trust Nowak. He needs me to cover a murder trial, but once that is over, he will have no reason to restrain himself."

"You haven't told your intended bride?"

"No, not Margaret, nor my family."

"Your delay may be seen as deceit. What do you intend to do?"

"I see only two options. I could leave for England immediately after the trial and hope Nowak loses interest in tormenting my family or me. I would carry my Black heritage as a secret scar, never revealing my true self to Margaret or my children, generations burying the stain."

"Or?" Abdel asked.

"Or I could own my blood with honor. I have no idea if Margaret or her family would accept or reject me. I cannot fathom how much pain the revelation would cause my brother, and especially my sister. Aubrey might be made a social outcast, perhaps unmarriageable."

"My friend, I've moved among the British both in Egypt and London. In matters of race, they're at best paternal, and at worst, well, you will be shunned. In both business and personal, in ways both flagrant and subtle."

Nervous sweat tingled on my skin. "I do not want to live a lie, but I do not know if I am prepared to live with the truth. In any case, Nowak may not allow me a choice."

A funeral carriage with a meager procession clip-clopped close by. It felt rude to continue to converse, so he and I respectfully kept silent as black-clad mourners passed. Once the procession reached a distance, the Doctor mumbled a short prayer then turned to me.

"You know, sometimes we concentrate so hard on the problem we block our mind from seeing the solution, like the Gordian Knot. If you keep thinking about how to untie the puzzle, you never think to cut it."

"You really are not an oracle," I said. "Not even Alexander the Great can just cleave my puzzle in two."

"No? You used to like the fables I told you on the ship. I have one for you now. Wish it Egyptian, but alas, I'm told it's from China. It illustrates that one can construct the question, so that one's mind is prevented from seeing all the possible answers. Shall I proceed?"

I sought hard truths, not fairy tales, but I'd learned that when someone sincerely offered help or wisdom, it would be foolish and self-defeating to rebuff them. The image of the Denver groundskeeper who'd saved my dignity while letting go of his past, and pants, came briefly to mind. And, after all, I came here because I thought Dr. Qabash to be the most open, generous, and earnest man I'd ever met.

"How can I say no? Spin your tale."

"So, there's a poor farmer who's forced by drought to take a large loan from a rich merchant who's old and ugly. The merchant loves his money, but above all, he cares for his high reputation in town. The next harvest, the old merchant demands payment of the loan and interest, but now the farmer is beset by locusts and cannot pay what he owes.

"The farmer, as they always do in these tales, has a young and beautiful daughter, not only lovely, but quick-witted and observant. The merchant decides having such a prize would further raise his prestige in town. He knows the girl and her father would normally never consent to marriage, so he makes a proposition to entice the farmer.

"The merchant will put two identically shaped stones, one black, one white, in a small cloth bag. The lovely girl will reach in the bag and remove one stone. If she selects black, then she will consent to marry the old, ugly merchant, and the debt will be considered paid in full. If she picks the white stone, she does not have to marry him, the debt is canceled. Refuse the wager, the full debt is due.

"The farmer is desperate, and the girl believes fate will protect her, so they agree to the deal. The next day, they meet the merchant on the black-and-white-pebbled pathway in front of the temple. The priest and a crowd have gathered to witness the gamble. The merchant kneels down and quickly snatches two stones and dumps them into the bag. To her horror, the sharp-eyed girl sees that the merchant selected two black stones, but only she was close enough to observe the cheat.

"Now, what is she to do? What are her options? She can take a stone knowing it will be black, and accept a hideous husband, knowing at least she saved her father from bankruptcy. Not good. Or she could expose the merchant's dishonesty to the assembled crowd. She would escape the awful marriage, but the angry merchant would take their farm, and they would be homeless beggars. That's no better. I ask you, Banks, what should she do?"

"Marry him and hope he dies soon?"

"Ah, there's the problem. You've accepted that there are only two options. I did say the girl possessed a clever mind. She put her hand in the cloth bag and selected what she knew to be a black stone, but as she withdrew her hand, she pretended to tremble nervously and dropped the stone. It disappeared among the white and black pebbles.

"The girl then spoke clearly so the crowd could hear. 'Sorry for my clumsiness, but the priest has only to look in the bag at the remaining stone to determine which color I selected.' The merchant, who cared so deeply for his reputation, could do nothing but hand over the bag and watch the priest produce the black stone. The girl did not marry the ugly old merchant, and the farmer kept his land."

He put his hands together as if closing a book.

"I think I have the point, but not my solution yet," I said. "I will approach it again with an open mind. Do you care if I go directly back to the train station? It's getting late."

"Not at all. Banks, you're sure about the Negro thing? I must say, it's very hard to see it in you."

"Yes, the evidence was quite persuasive."

"Well, I've two bits of practical advice."

"Not another fable."

"No fables. All men look pretty much the same with beards."

"I guess."

"More seriously, my mother gave me the wisest advice I ever received. She told me, 'Abdel, if you ever lose your way and don't know what to do, imagine yourself, your best self, five, ten years in the future. Ask him. He will know what to do.' "

Chapter 27

As I stepped off the train in New York, it hit me. Hard. I caught myself turning around to locate Wyatt, almost calling out to my phantom limb. He made, I knew, the right decision for him, for Becca, and certainly for his children. Living in New York, they spent most of their days assembling artificial flowers in a cramped tenement. Had they stayed, the children would've been sent out to labor.

If lucky they might be cash boys or girls, running sales slips, money, and purchases from department store inspectors to and from customers. Or they might wind up in the cotton mills, girls spinning and boy doffers changing bobbins. The millowners valued quick children with nimble fingers over their clumsy, arthritic fathers, and is it not a blessing to deny a child any time to spend in idleness or tempting amusements? Working six days a week, twelve hours a day, left little time for anything but sustenance and sleep. Riskier jobs included breaker boy, hanging dangerously over a black river of coal speeding by on conveyor belts, pounding coal to separate out any impurities—face blackened, lungs choked with coal dust.

While I understood Wyatt's decision, I still was selfish enough to allow myself to feel abandoned. I previously arranged by wire for Clifton Kameny to give me a ride, and my mood lifted upon seeing him waiting outside the station.

After a hearty handshake, I glanced about for his brougham cab, the one that always reminded me of Miss Moon, champagne, Cleopatra's Needle, and the ball. Miss Moon had recently informed me that the Bradley-Martins were forced to flee to England to escape a massive new tax law resulting from the backlash to their bacchanalia ball. No brougham. Instead, Clifton led me to a horseless carriage, a sleek two-seater with a back rumble seat and dual headlamps.

"What is this then?" I asked.

"Wave of the future, my friend. American Electric Mail Phaeton Automobile."

"You are driving yourself these days?"

"Don't act so surprised, it's quite fun, fifteen miles per hour. Also bought a Dos-à-Dos model with an enclosed cab and top driver."

We climbed aboard and glided off.

"My, it's quiet."

"Indeed. I have to sound the hooter at crossroads so people don't walk in front of me."

I nodded. "Back in England, a pedestrian—poor woman—Bridget Driscoll—struck and killed by a motor car back in '96."

"I'm afraid the car's tasted blood here as well. An unlucky September thirteen for the ironically named Mr. Bliss. Right at Central Park West and Seventy-Fourth Street. Bliss apparently helping a lady off the trolley when an electric cab ran him over, crushed his skull. Dead the next morn."

"Electric cabs in New York?"

"Quite a few. At least a hundred, I'd say."

"The driver charged?"

"Manslaughter, yes, but they found it to be an accident and dropped the charge."

"Clifton, you really expect people to give up horses, truly magnificent creatures, for a soulless hunk of steel?"

"Once an aspiring businessman figures out how to mass-produce automobiles, the price will drop, and they will sell like proverbial hotcakes."

"I saw a couple of petrol cars out west. Smoke, noise, a menace. I would favor a horse any day."

"Don't worry. Those infernal combustion machines will never last. You can break an arm from a crank backfire. And don't start with the steamers. Who in their right mind would drive around with the necessity of a fire aboard? No, in ten years the electric car will dominate."

I'm not sure why, but Clifton's total embrace of the motorcar, or more specifically, his cavalier dismissal of four thousand years of human-equine cooperation, irked me.

"A horse is unlikely to run out of power and leave you stranded on some back-country road."

"Please, Joshua, don't take it personally. This auto isn't evil or good. It's a vehicle, a tool. I know you've spoken of your affection for your horse Nike, and I'm sure she lives in comfort. But you must know many horses aren't so fortunate. You see them every day, underfed, overburdened, and beaten. Had they agency in the matter, I wonder how many would submit to noble servitude.

"In any case, there are forty-two batteries under us with a four-to-five-hour discharge rate. This ammeter on the dash tells the mileage capacity left. We won't be left stranded."

I sat in silence for the rest of the way to Madison Square, almost wishing for the masking rumble of a petrol engine. I never thought myself a protector of tradition, and still too young for nostalgia. Just everything seemed to be changing at once, like a drowsy clock that barely kept time, awoke, and sprang hours ahead. I'd also sent another telegram but received no reply from Margaret. I feared I was losing her. A time of disruption and big decisions, for this country and me.

Walking into the Croisic felt a bit like going home, until it struck me.

"Clifton. My flat?"

"What do you think? Your room was rented before you made it to the train."

I hung my head. "Sorry. The Croisic, the Brown Palace, all taken care of for me by my father. He must have missed my abrupt return to New York. I would have thought either Margaret or the Old Man would have told him. Clifton, I just need short-term lodging. Nowak has made it clear I will only be here until the end of George Johnson's trial."

"The Croisic is full occupancy. What's not rented, Marquis Logerot is renovating."

"Disappointing. Is there a nearby hotel you would recommend?"

"Nonsense, my boy. I have a large suite with a spare bedroom. The bell cap is already bringing your luggage to my apartment."

"That is too kind, but I cannot impose—"

"Stop, Joshua. I want to help. Let me. No one makes it entirely on their own. Mind you, it's not permanent—two, three months, just enough time to discover where things stand."

Clifton was right. I was so obsessed about making my own way, about not being a creature of my brother's charity, or beholden to Sir Covington, that I was reluctant to ask for, or accept, help freely given. "All right, thank you."

I felt comfortable standing in the familiar confines of Clifton's parlor, then realized that while coming here, both for functions and personal visits, I'd only ventured into the parlor and water closet. As I began to relax from my long travels, Clifton, for the first time, appeared apprehensive.

"Well then, I must show you the shrine."

"The shrine?"

"Your temporary room."

Bewildered, I followed down the hall and watched Clifton fumble with an engraved silver key and haltingly open the door.

"Oh Lord," I heard myself exclaim involuntarily. A faint scent of sandalwood greeted me. Light streamed in through an oversized window fitted with a stained-glass panel ablaze in a geometric tangle of red and gold triangles. Stepping inside, my image reflected from three walls, where tall mirrors substituted for paintings. At the remaining wall stood a bed with carved ionic columns as posts. The ceiling was gratefully free of mirrors, containing only the painted stars of the constellation Orion.

All of this wasn't even the room's most dramatic feature. Facing the bed was a Greco-Roman sculpture replica I recognized from Florence.

Hercules wrestling Diomedes. Imposing Hercules, holding the King of Thrace, son of war god Aries, humiliatingly upside-down. Both men were naked. Diomedes' final gambit was to grip Hercules' penis.

"The cause of much tittering among tour groups when I saw it in Florence," I said.

"It has that effect on some of my guests as well. I don't think the artist de' Rossi ever explained it. I'm not sure what Diomedes would have been about with that move."

We stood a moment, breathing sandalwood, watching our reflections.

"Anyway, there's a small ensuite you can access behind that mirror. Sink, toilet, and compact shower. Now I suppose I should fix some coffee and explain all this."

"Shall we retire to your parlor?"

"No, Joshua, a kitchen table is the best place to serve secrets."

My chair, well-crafted, still wobbled slightly as Clifton set out preparations for coffee. It dawned on me that Clifton was fond of elaborate ritual: the séance, the boudoir, and now the simple act of coffee making. Clifton inserted grounds and water into a ceramic vessel shaped like a steam train with a smokestack, metal chassis, and wheels. Its powder-blue enamel, illustrated with flowers and floating butterflies, disguised its threat of exploding like a tabletop hand grenade.

"The Toselli is a trifle, but I find it a pleasant diversion. Look, Joshua, I know you recognized the shrine isn't designed for female ardor. I trust your discretion and want to aid you in your moment of need, so my confession is forced. Let me be clear, I'm no Uranian, a female psyche trapped in a male body. I assure you, every fiber of my soul is at comfort with my masculinity. But Emily Dickinson was right. The heart wants what it wants, or else it does not care. My heart delights in the male form. I desire Adonis, not Aphrodite."

"What about the dowager? You two are always about together."

"Lady Whitney and I perform a service for each other. We both need to put on a show of normality. My research into sexual identity would be derided as self-serving if my proclivities were revealed. Lady Whitney doesn't want her family to pressure her to remarry. Her lavender cape hides my indiscretions, and my beard disguises her indifference."

"Dowager Whitney is a Sappho?"

"Not at all. She doesn't desire the touch of a woman. She wishes sexual congress with no one. Apparently, Mr. Whitney proved a massive disappointment in coitus profundus. She arrived virginal to her wedding night expecting a showstopper. Instead, Mr. Whitney barely parted curtains before discharging his seed."

"Poor woman."

"Evidently Mr. Whitney didn't improve much with practice. She thought the whole enterprise ridiculous, and she especially detested the messy consummation of Mr. Whitney's feeble bed work."

Clifton lit the small spirit flame burner under the cafetière-locomotive.

"She endured her wifely duties enough to produce heirs, but once her husband died, she vowed to never submit to bestial pursuits again."

I felt the need to defend the animal passions. "She need not submit but engage. Would she dismiss the singular pleasure that only women may derive from the act of love? I have witnessed it and believe it is more encompassing than a man's."

"I agree. I offered to set her up with a thoroughly expert young man, a two-way artist. I guaranteed he was cunningly capable of all techniques needed to make even a frozen tundra erupt in blossoms of flowers."

"And?"

"She hadn't one jot of interest. Made me promise never to mention it again."

"Clifton, we have been together often before I left for Denver. Why did I have no inclination of your . . . alignment?"

The Toselli whistled and puffed steam.

"You mean, don't you, why didn't I accost you? Force myself on you? I'm not a wild animal trying to mount every available male. Same-sex attraction doesn't turn us into a raging incubus unable to exercise any restraint. Really, I'm more careful and discerning than most men." He paused. "Besides, you're not really my type."

"I feel surprisingly hurt, and relieved by that statement."

"Tu-tut. I should be attracted to refined gentlemen like yourself. No, I go for burly philistines. There's nothing more stimulating to my libido than the sight of a chiseled working man, bare-chested, chopping wood, steam rising off his body on a fall morn."

The locomotive lurched forward from the shifted weight of water, which triggered a metal lid to snuff out the flame.

"When did you suspect—"

"Not suspect—knew, always. I also knew it wasn't advantageous to reveal. It's why I came to America. Eventually, I would act on my Paphian desires. But not in Wales. My family's in Swansea. My hometown may birth a poet someday, but for now the place is very buttoned-up. I love my family, and I didn't want to be the source of scandal and shame, so when I turned eighteen, I persuaded Papa that it was best if I completed my psychiatry studies in the US. After I got to New York, I switched my middle and last names from Kameny Grove to Grove Kameny to ensure my activities would not reach home. All the barristers, solicitors, and judges back home are Grove, not Kameny."

Now cooled, the boiler of the coffee maker created a vacuum, sucking filtered coffee back to fill the boiler. Clifton filled two demitasse cups from a bibcock at the front of the train.

I considered making my own confession to Clifton, exposing my African blood, but to what purpose? Clearly, he'd dealt with prejudice by hiding in plain sight.

"Then you had no choice?" The coffee was hot. Grains coated my tongue.

"What did Seneca say? 'Fate either leads you or drags you'? As you could see, Hercules is a favorite of mine. Still young and unsure of his path, two spirits in the form of beautiful women appeared to Hercules. I don't recall the exact Greek translation, but let's call them Softness and Virtue. The first offered a life of pleasure, the second a life of toil, but also glory.

"I imagine, one day, men like me will have to stand up and proclaim ourselves, to demand not only our equal right to exist, but our equal value. But I chose Softness. It's been the right choice for me. A friend says I should move to Berlin, that there's a thriving scene where men like me live and love openly, but I don't trust the Germans. I fear a crackdown."

Clifton sat back and looked straight at me. "We're good then, Joshua? You'll stay?"

"Yes, of course, but if you need your room, I could try to stay with Luther."

"Luther Halsey? You've not heard."

"What?"

"Quite dead. Heart attack. Playing handball in Brooklyn against local champion James Dunne."

"He fell dead on the court?"

"No, they always die after they stop. Dunne had run him hard. Luther, you know, suspected my goings-on."

"It cannot hurt to tell you now. Luther warned me to avoid you, but not why. He saw himself as a pursuer of virtue."

"There you are. You could say his pursuit of fitness was his downfall, but I have nothing against the man. He only knew what was in his own head."

"Do not judge him too harshly," I said. "While we wish that they become more enlightened, the world still has need of such men of action."

Clifton didn't respond directly, but he rose. "I suggest we dine early today. You'll need your sleep. Your friend Len Spencer was around yesterday. A reporter tipped him you were returning. He'll be by in the morning to take you to the prison to see that George Johnson chap."

Chapter 28

Len was prompt. Morning mist clung to my coat as I pulled myself into the coach. He'd sprung for a brougham instead of his two-wheeled rig to better fill me in on the way to the jail.

Len shouted to the driver, "Take the fastest route to Centre and Franklin. Don't spare the oats." He sat back. "We're lucky to get in at all. Usually only lawyers do. I had to pull some mighty strings."

"I should think. In England there would not be a chance. Colonel du Cane did not permit a peek inside. Hard labor, hard fare, and a hard bed—that was always his motto."

"Please tell me you've brought your press credentials."

"Of course." I casually checked my pocket, glad I picked the right suit.

"I'm coming in with you as your photographer." Len pointed to a camera under the seat. "Need some sympathetic press for George. Can't have the papers painting him as a wide-eyed ruthless Negro. It would ruin him."

"There is greater jeopardy than his career," I said. "George is fortunate she was clearly a mulatto. Had she passed for White, down South, he would have been lynched already."

"George will have a first-rate defense, don't you worry. I have nothing against lawyer Brown, at least he pled George not guilty at the inquest in October, but he didn't do much to counter the yarn spun by officers McManus and Boyle. And those nosy neighbors made it sound like they had a nine-round brawl every night. Now George has a top-shelf attorney, Emanuel M. Friend. He won a lot of big-time cases."

"How in the world can George afford him?"

"You don't realize how many people like George. Columbia Records put the word out across the country and pulled in a legal fund of one thousand bucks. Then Victor Emerson—he's the superintendent of recordings; you met him, I think—called all the talent together and told us, 'Well, boys, we ought to all chip in, because there is no telling when some of us might be in the same fix.' Even the newer men came through, a hundred dollars that night and another two thousand in pledges."

"Impressive, but still just a Negro's word. The jury will assume guilt."

Len shook his head. "Attorney Friend's got some young guy who's supposed to be a whiz at picking juries. And Rollin Wooster—he's one of Columbia's lawyers working behind the scenes—told me they already recruited twenty-one good Christian men of high standing to testify they've known George Johnson to be nothing but affable and good-natured in all circumstances."

"Len, you know I have to ask you . . . you are one of George's closest friends. I hate to bring up the death of the German woman, but you know the prosecution will. A man loses two wives, he starts to look more than unlucky. Do you think he killed Roskin?"

"No. I mean . . . I don't think he would." Len looked away and rubbed his muscular hands. Len was a powerful man, the kind who could cause harm but chose not to. "Who knows what anyone is capable of? Push the right buttons, or the wrong buttons on the wrong day, and the machine catches a gear."

"You think George caught a gear?"

"She certainly tried to push him there. Roskin was a mean drunk, and she was drunk a lot."

"But—"

"Wait a minute, Joshua. I'd rather you not write nothing than do a hatchet job. But think. Roskin wasn't a fragile flower. She'd slapped and punched George before, and she'd come home beaten-up from fights at the clubs. She wouldn't have just cowered against a man built like George. She would've fought back hard. I saw George before they took him. Not a scratch on him, or his face, his hands. Find the murderer, and I bet Roskin drew some blood."

"Then who?"

"She ran with a tough crowd. George was her sugar daddy. She had other boyfriends. My guess is, she crossed some muscle down in the tenderloin, someone you don't want to cross. Coroner's jury said she died of cerebral hemorrhage, but the grand jury claimed she was repeatedly beaten and kicked—on the head, breast, belly, sides, and other parts. Sounds to me like they're sending a message. Wouldn't be surprised if it was more than one man, maybe a woman too."

I wanted to believe George innocent. I also liked him. The most agitated I ever saw him was outside the black-and-tan bar after my rashness almost got us into a scuffle. Even then, his impenetrable cloak of good nature never slipped.

That's what I saw from my vantage in the White world. Did that cloak wearily slip when he entered his Black world? Did fifty-three years of suppressed anger finally discharge, gone to ground on a provoking conductor?

"What's any of us capable of?" Len injected.

My mind flew back to that wretched steeplechase, my mount already destroyed, my brother John complaining he should have won but Nike was too dumb and disobedient to his commands. Not only did he steal my victory, he also wasted his thief of Nike. I kept punching John so hard, still swinging as the stable men pulled me off. One later confided his relief that no hammer nor tongs lay within my reach, or he feared I might have crushed John's skull.

I formally apologized, and John formally forgave me, because that's what our father demanded, but I wonder if either of us changed our hearts.

The cab turned from Elm Street to Franklin to Centre. The Halls of Justice possessed an entire city square. The fact that the public universally referred to it as the Tombs was no accident or exaggeration. The architect John Haviland modeled the building after an ancient Egyptian mausoleum. Its Egyptian Revival columns intended to invoke the cursed entrance to a menacing sepulcher. Continued drizzle and fog added an appropriate air of doom about the place.

As we approached the portico of the entrance, the building gave the illusion of being only one story. I knew, however, that the structure continued down hundreds of feet into the bowels of the earth. The weathered guard who let us in wore an unsettling smile, his hat at a rakish tilt.

"Youse two follow me."

Our guide led us down into a courtyard, a patch of sky above hemmed in by walls. Something was missing.

"Guard?"

"Eddie."

I smiled, long over resisting the quick informality of Americans.

"Okay, Eddie. I expected the gallows to be here, supposedly in sight of the Bridge of Sighs that connects the men's and women's prisons."

"You're 'bout ten years too late. Handsome Harry's last one hung. Killed a cop. I walked him out here myself. December 5, 1889. I walked them all out. They used to call me Eddie Fetch 'em. We never kept the gallows out all the time. Took it apart after and stowed it. Last month, the warden ordered us to drag it out and chop it into firewood. All the cons are thunderbolt jockeys now."

"Beg your pardon?"

"You been under a rock, Joshua? Electric chair," Len said.

Eddie smiled at me devilishly. "You got a little English accent. Are they still hanging criminals over there?"

"Why, yes. The Bloody Code has been reformed, but for murder and treason, men and women still hang."

"Just fried our first woman this March. Well, not here, ain't got no chair. We's technically more jail than prison. The chairs are out in Alburn, Dannemora, and Sparkie down at Sing-Sing."

I stared blankly.

"You must not read your own paper," Len said. "All a mite grisly. Martha Place, housekeeper, married a widower. Martha didn't like the way the seventeen-year-old stepdaughter minded her. Like any of them do. But Martha's not going to let it go. She throws phenol acid in the girl's face, then finishes her off by strangling her."

"Suffocating her," Eddie corrected.

"Right," Len continued. "Then cold as ice, Martha dismisses the maid, with a bonus for arranging to have her luggage taken to the train station. When her husband, William, enters for his evening repast, Martha runs at him, waving an axe. Before he passed out, the husband ran and screamed so the neighbors came with a cop. They found Martha huddled by a broken gas pipe. It near blew the house up."

"Sorry," I said. "I have been out west, and I usually skip the police blotter."

Eddie cut back in. "See, it was a real big deal. No woman's been executed since they botched that Roxalana Druse hanging back in '87. One of the reasons they switched to the electric chair." Eddie stopped and stretched. "I been at this a long time. You hang a fellow right, their weight snaps their neck at the end of the rope, and it's over pretty quick. You mess up and the neck doesn't break, that's real bad. Seen guys take half an hour to strangle to death, struggling, eyes bulging, face turning colors. You don't want to see that.

"Druse? Even grimmer. She's just a tiny wisp of a woman. And they wasn't using a regular trapdoor fall. It was a suspension hanging. A weighted rope falls and Yanks the body in the air. Druse was so light she floated up like a high-wire girl at the circus. Took over twenty minutes for her to die. Since then, the governors or courts figure a way to reprieve any condemned women."

"Until Governor Roosevelt," Len said. "He refused clemency, called it mawkish sentimentality. TR barred the *Journal* and others from covering the execution, didn't want 'hideous sensationalism.' He only let in the *Associated Press* and Kate Swan, one of those stunt reporters. You know, the one who bought illegal opium and leaped out a rescue boat off Coney Island."

I considered the callousness of how we dispose of the condemned. "Eddie, you actually think electrocution is more humane?"

We'd resumed traversing the courtyard and entered a building. Eddie stopped again, then scratched his head.

"Never seen an electrocution, but I gots uncles, cousins, and nephews all through the system. My family's been in prison for generations." He gave a guttural laugh at a joke he must have repeated a thousand times. "My cousin down in Sing-Sing claims the Place electrocution went off without a hitch, but it ain't always so clean. Uncle Buck called the first one in Alburn an ungodly horror. Strong men, observers, got sick at what they saw. My uncle's been through dozens of hangings, told me it gave him nightmares. He couldn't use a toaster for weeks."

"I hesitate to ask, but what happened?"

"Young guy, William Kemmler, kills his wife with a hatchet. No doubt about it, he would have hung. Governor Hill authorized the chair in 1888, so they slap something together at Alburn prison and Kemmler pulls the lucky straw. The way Uncle Buck told it, the guards liked Kemmler. He was polite, if a little vain. Only thing he got upset about is when they started shaving his head for the electrodes.

He didn't want to look like no ogre. So, the barber took off the parts needed and left the Hyperion curl on Kemmler's forehead."

Eddie motioned for us to follow him down a hall to a set of stairs. He kept talking as we went.

"They hook the guy up, electrodes on the head and one on the lower spine. Kemmler tells them to take their time, do it right. Everyone's nervous 'cause it's the first one. The switch flipped. Hit him with maybe seven hundred volts for 'bout seventeen seconds, then turned it off. Kemmler is charred but he ain't dead. He's out but they see him breathing. Mind you, Edison's men electrocuted a 1,200 pound horse to death when he was trying to scare us off Tesla's AC, but these engineers can't even put down a man.

"Uncle Buck said the operators were yelling to turn it back on, but they can't. The generator's got to reset. Finally, they hit him the second time, 'cept jacked to over a thousand volts, and left it going two minutes. Jesus, Mary and Joseph, the man's head is smoking, and the electrode burned a hole right through his spine. My uncle said they waited for hours for the body to cool so's they could move him.

"Some guards complained they'd quit before going through that again. It smelled like a charnel house. Took days to air it out. That electric gadget inventor, George Westinghouse, condemned it as scientific butchery, said they would have done better with an axe."

We descended the four tiers of cells from the minor violators down to major crimes.

Eddie pointed to the lower floors. "We're full up right now, so your man Johnson's down in old murders' row. The cells are actually pretty nice down there."

"It is so damp and musty in here," I said. "Is that on account of the rain?"

"Nope, it's always damp here. Built on the damn Collect Pond. The building started to crack and sink from the start. Masons in here all the time fixing leaks. Part of the charm." He pointed at a fresh fissure, out of which a steady trickle of water ran.

I heard George before I saw him. The whistled melody of "Dixie" echoed off the stone walls. Eddie snickered.

"Inmate Johnson's been entertaining us for an hour each day. He takes requests. That's got to be from guard Mitchell. He's from down Alabama, still fightin' the lost cause. Always tell Mitchell what Lincoln said, when the North won, we reclaimed that song as one of the spoils. It's funny. My pop, God rest his soul, worked in the Pennsylvania system, one of those Quaker prisons. Complete silence. Wouldn't let them talk, much less sing or whistle. Prisoners supposed to reflect on their sins. Solitary confinement day and night. Drove them mad, Pops said. It'd be unconstitutional now."

"Reflection wouldn't work on me," Len said. "I can't get past an hour without talking to myself."

Eddied nodded. "We're all scientific now. All that Zebulon Brockway stuff, time off for good behavior, vocational training. We mostly just hold folks for trial here, but we still classify prisoners. Okay, here you go."

We entered murders' row, the air noticeably warmer and much drier due to two potbelly stoves glowing at each end of a long hall. We couldn't see into the cells, only the barred doors cut into solid, stuccoed walls facing each other. George sat on a small wooden bench in front of one of the cells, now whistling "The Blue and the Gray." A brawny blond guard was helping himself to a cup of water from the spigot of a sizable metal tankard atop a simple chestnut table. I assumed the blond to be Mitchell. His smile evaporated when he spied Eddie.

"What's all this?" It came out like a grunt as Mitchell stabbed his thumb in our direction.

"These press boys got permission to chat with inmate Johnson."

"Press? Down here? Ain't regular."

"You want to knock it around with the warden?"

"Nah, got two demerits already, I ain't makin' no waves. 'Sides, George here's been doing all my requests today. He's a good ol' boy."

Len snapped a quick picture of George to prove he and his camera were not deadwood. The flash exposed the true dinginess of our surroundings. I felt better when it faded. Eddie signed a clipboard, and withdrew after telling us to sign out at the main entrance once we finished.

"I sure am happy to see familiar faces," George said. "Only guest I've had is Attorney Friend."

"What's he saying?" Len asked.

"He thinks it's coming along. Had questions about the shooting and all. Case they bring it up in court."

I stiffened with a start. "What shooting? You told me she was beaten."

"Mr. Joshua, this was back in the summer. Roskin went and got my pistol out of pawn. She was drunk and angry and got a little crazy. She shot off a round but only grazed my ankle. I wrestled the pistol out of her hands. Had to run out in the street, and she was still trying to hit me. 'Course one of the neighbors reported it to the police. General nuisance and disorderly conduct. Got us deposed from 234 West Forty-First Street. Thought we were through, but she showed back a few weeks later."

"George, that sounds terrible for your case," I said.

"Attorney Friend thinks he can turn it around to show that, with all that provocation, I ran out rather than pistol-whip her."

"That's why he makes the big bucks." Len winked.

"Hey, Mr. Joshua," George said. "Before I forget. When you go back home, I want you to find me a fancy British lawyer."

"A barrister?"

"Yeah. I met a British sailor in here, and he tells me a fat Englishman named Bert Sheppard is doing my songs and selling all over the world instead of me. It's not fair."

"Getting harder every day to make a buck in the music game," Len said. "It's been three years since I did 'A Hot Time in the Old Town Tonight.' All they want me to record is coon songs and readings from the Bible. I want to sing ballads like Jose."

"Know what you mean. Why can't I record 'The Blue and the Gray,' or one of those new rags?" George said.

"Yeah, George, they should've let me sing 'Hello! Ma Baby' instead of the new man Arthur Collins, though I have to admit, he did a fine version. He introduces it as a coon number, but I don't see it. There's no darkie stuff in the lyrics, and he doesn't sound all that coony to me."

"Len, I told you what you oughta do. You should team with that illustrated song girl Ada Jones. It'll give you a whole new audience. She does comic sketches too."

As I grew increasingly frustrated over Len and George's lackadaisical attitude, Mitchell inched toward us.

"I thought you're supposed to be reporters, not singers."

Len shrugged. "Working man's got to take whatever jobs he can get."

"Guess that's right." Mitchell furrowed his brow and pointed his finger at Len. "What's wrong with coon songs?"

"Nothing at all, done many myself. So, you enjoy a good coon singer? What say I put you on the guest list down at Mack's this Friday. Got a girl?"

"Agnes."

"I'll put you and Miss Agnes down for a nice table."

"Much obliged. Agnes is always bitching we don't go nowhere."

"No trouble at all. Never know when you'll need a friendly face on the inside. Speaking of which, a couple of musician friends of mine are on the first tier, a bit of fisticuffs in a bar. Think we could go up and see them? I'll take a picture of you. There's better light at the top."

"Well, seeing you did me a turn, I guess it be copacetic. George can stay out of the cell, but I'd have to handcuff one arm to the bars on his door."

"Don't bother me none," George said.

With George secured, Len and the guard withdrew. If we kept our voices low, I could tell George what I really wanted to say. Before I could start, I felt a sudden brush against my ankle. I did not budge. I'd become inure to surprise entrances of pets.

"Don't worry, Mr. Joshua. That's just Old Nig. Prison keeper Connelly brought him in as a kitten to catch rats. He's a love sponge."

At my feet, a formidable black cat curled on the white diamond tile of the faded black and-white-patterned floor.

"It never stops."

"What?"

"The name of the cat."

"Aw, Mr. Joshua, it don't mean nothing. Lots of folks call their black dogs and cats Nig."

"Why not Blackie, or Cole, or Midnight?"

"You can't let every little thing get to you. What's it matter to you, anyhow?"

I crowded beside George on the bench and lowered my voice enough to prevent being overheard.

"It just so happens that my grandfather was mulatto."

"Knew it!" George slapped his knee, saw me shush him, caught himself, and whispered, "White people, they're not looking for it, so they're not going to notice. I saw it." George tapped his finger beside his eye.

"I cannot imagine how. Everyone else I have confided in found it hard to see. Curly hair, dark eyes, yes, but more likely a Roman invader of England than Negro blood."

"Oh, you are no doubt the Whitest Black man I ever did see, but there's blood. I thought I saw it the first night, the benefit for Sammy. Later, when I read your palm in the black-and-tan saloon, I knew for sure."

"Afraid I do not follow at all."

George stuck out his non-handcuffed hand, palm down. "Look at my hand."

"Not sure what I am looking for."

"Hush." George flipped his hand palm up. "See any difference?"

Ah, it is much lighter, almost white."

"Exactly. You study your average White man, and the color wraps around back and palm all the same. Yours isn't so extreme a difference, but it's there."

I turned my hands over and back, over and back. Certainly subtle. If I worked as a laborer in sunbaked fields, it could be written off as tanned and unexposed skin.

"George, you know my secret. I trust you will not disclose it."

"Disclose? Damn no. I don't need no more Black friends. How they going to help me out of this mess? Don't know what you got planned, but you got to promise you won't tell no one else 'til after the trial. Right now, I need you to stay royal. That's how you can help. And when you write about me all nice, it wouldn't hurt for you to put that baron stuff in your byline. Folks eat that up."

I wanted to challenge George's approach, acquiescence, and accommodation, but I didn't. I finished interviewing him about the case, then left when Len returned. How could I blame George? A Black man in a White man's jail. In a few days, he would be in a White man's court. A White press might sway a probably White jury.

No wonder he didn't choose this time to stand and fight for equal treatment, equal rights.

It might be a logical course for him, but Miss Moon convinced me it amounted to a course of defeat and degradation for the race as a whole. White America hadn't even offered Blacks a period of apprentice citizenship culminating as full Americans. Booker T. Washington's dream was an illusion. The South lost the war but won the peace. They were reimposing their segregationist policies not only in the old antebellum, but in the whole of White society.

The forward progress of Reconstruction had stopped. The grand opportunity lost. Sooner or later, new Black leaders, along with well-meaning Whites, would have to demand not just fair treatment, but equal treatment for Blacks, by any means necessary. There would be prayers for sure, but also blood.

Chapter 29

George's indefatigable optimism allowed him to sit on murder's row and not hear the ticking of the executioner's clock. I faced only the risk of failure and scandal, yet the weight of time pressed hard on me.

The situation with Nowak was unsustainable. Obviously, he didn't want me back in New York. Nowak was forced to retrieve me by Arthur Brisbane, the editor who made the *Evening Journal* profitable by taking it lowbrow. The trouble being, Brisbane showed signs of cooling on the story. What looked sensational—famous coon singer ruthlessly murders White wife—was now becoming just another tragic mulatto case.

At the *Journal*, Nowak said as little as possible. "Get the job done. Then we'll settle this." He actually closed his office door in my face.

Heading back to Denver would be going backward. In any case, a new reporter already volunteered and headed west as my replacement. We probably passed trains. I considered pleading my case directly with Hearst, only to find him gone since November for the Grand Tour, with Millicent and her parents in tow. Unlike my interrupted trip, Hearst was taking a six-month holiday through Europe and Egypt.

I suppose he needed the break after the Newsies summer strike and the lingering disappointment of not being governor. He thought money and the *Journal* would pave his way to the red-brick executive mansion in Albany, but the political bosses strangely wanted Teddy Roosevelt. TR had charged San Juan Hill as a hero. Hearst had fumbled with a refitted fruit steamboat, taken twenty-nine stranded Spanish sailors as prisoners to turn over to a reluctant American Navy, before limping home to a suite of private rooms at the Waldorf. Hearst may have helped cause the war, but he was no hero. If he wanted any hope of beating the equally ambitious Roosevelt to the White House, he'd better, at minimum, make an honest woman out of Millicent.

With Hearst so far away, Nowak would have free rein. In six months, any trouble with Sir Covington could be papered over. I would face this on my own.

One positive: Miss Moon now resided year-round in New York. I checked the papers for events or functions she might attend. I guessed right on two occasions and took note the solace I felt seeing her again face-to-face. With Wyatt gone, she became the one constant from my first days in America.

I wondered what she thought of me. Perhaps I was only a useful channel for publicizing her causes? I understood that possibility but hoped our relationship extended beyond transactional. As much as she labored for equal status, my perceived position as a White man created a static field, a barrier to overcome.

How different might it be if she knew of my African ancestry. I needed to accept the possibility it might not matter at all. My commitment to unmasking my history to Miss Moon remained unabated. I also knew it was inherently unfair to her. What magical response did I expect: a secret handshake, a sub-rosa manual?

As much as I burned to tell her, the telephone proved inadequate for such delicate conversation. Without recourse to study her eyes and gauge the shifts of her body, a silence or a sigh could be easily misinterpreted. Unfortunately, our encounters back in New York were less than private. Even if no one was right at our elbow, I couldn't risk a loud reaction from Miss Moon with others in the room. My own course of action remained murky. I didn't want options taken from me.

Miss Moon impressed and intrigued me even more now than four years ago when we first met. Her face and carriage were matured; still exuberant but serious, the last remnants of childlike innocence replaced by knowing determination. If I'd become more than an interested spectator in the present plight and possible future of Blacks in America, she was already a fully tested warrior beginning to think strategically.

"The focus on Congressman White's anti-lynching bill—I think it's misdirected."

"How so?" I asked. "The lynchings continue. You read of Sam Hose in Georgia? He was tortured and lynched after killing a White man in self-defense. They say his heart, liver, and bones were sold as souvenirs. Or in Alexandria, Virginia, a Black man was forcibly removed from jail by a lynch posse and hung from a city lamppost. The authorities stood witness but did nothing to stop it."

Miss Moon's face flushed. "But it's like wives seeking the law to say our husbands may not beat and rape us with impunity. That's well and good, but why did they think they possessed such impunity in the first place? The law could eliminate every tree and lamppost and every strand of rope, but if White people still view us as inferior brutes to be managed and feared, there will be no end to the innovations of degradation they will imagine upon us."

"Are you still opposed to Booker's incremental approach? He appears to be making inroads in the South."

"Oh, they embrace him because he offers a safe alternative. They may one day invite him to sip tea in the White House, although I wonder if they'll throw away the cup. Unfortunately, he's accepting a position of eternal second-class citizenship, a caste of untouchables, whether wealthy or poor. And I fear he will fight our new voices to retain his power."

"I was not aware of any infighting."

"John Hope and WEB Dubois have tried to keep disagreement

civil, but I've met new leaders like Monroe Trotter in Boston. They've had enough of asking for crumbs instead of insisting on bread. Frankly, they're tired of asking at all. There's a feeling if we don't act forcefully, the North will be as bad as the South. Then the only course left to us will be riot and fire."

"Surely no one wants that."

"I don't say I want violence, but if society wants tranquility without justice, if those in power will not hear our voices, then violence is the only language left."

Staring at Miss Moon, I finally admitted to myself my fascination with her wasn't entirely chaste. I admired her dedication to a just cause, but I also desired her. I suppose I had from that first day in Atlanta. Every time the thought came to mind in the past, I quickly pushed it away, an imp of the perverse, but there it was. Her penetrating gaze beguiled me. I couldn't help but study the curve of her bosom and hips, and I longed to place my lips on the nape of her neck exposed by her upturned hair.

I reminded myself not to mention any of these feelings when the opportunity opened to confess my Blackness. It could all sound like a fetish. The maid Jenny with her flaming red hair told me of her problem with suitors. "You never can tell if they're only after a strawberry bush. They got a kink for it and don't give a tinker's dam about me as a person. Any red-headed gash will do."

How magnified might that be with Miss Moon? *Oh, he is looking for a brown body to decorate his trophy room.* She might think I did not see her for the incredible wholeness of her being, but a mere titillation, an object of otherness.

I said my goodbyes and left Miss Moon before a reckless phrase or gesture telegraphed my feelings. On leaving, reflection forced me to admit something else. I not only desired her, I envied her. She knew to her very fiber who she was and her purpose in life. It glowed in her like holy fire. It billowed her spirit and illuminated meaning in her words. Even if society wouldn't let her be truly comfortable in her skin, she would refuse to lighten it to Whiteness even if she possessed the magical power to do so. Neither would she wield such a power to gray all humanity to a single hue. She chose to stand proud, to persist, and fight the good fight.

With mixed feelings, I approached the next item in my efforts to put my affairs in order before the end of George's trial and whatever fate I then faced. It regarded a stack of notes sent to my attention at the *Journal*. All were from Lady L. The notes fervently implored me to meet her at a delicatessen where she'd recently found employment.

Lady L frightened me in an odd way. Not that I felt abiding love as I did for Margaret, or the flush of romantic desire inspired by Miss Moon. No, Lady L aroused the "It," hunger without thought. The full force of the conscious mind had been required to overrule my loins that first encounter in the bordello. Her quirky aspects only increased her allure. At least there wouldn't be a bed in the deli—at least, I didn't think so.

I found my way to Ludlow Street on the Lower East Side and entered into the narrow confines of Iceland Brother's Deli. Lady L stood behind the cash register, decked out in a crisp white uniform. Stripped of exotic clothing and sensuous makeup, she struck me more as a fresh-faced tomboy. This effect was accentuated by the shortness of her hair. I'd seen nothing like it on a modern woman. The sides and back fell no more than halfway down her neck, curled in slightly, with bangs cut straight across her forehead. She reminded me of a raven Joan of Arc.

I could not recall the last time I received such a happy-to-see-you smile, and it lifted my spirits. Her shift break delayed, I ordered a pastrami sandwich to justify a table. While familiar with corned beef from a German deli I frequented when first in the city, pastrami was béarnaise to hollandaise sauce. The pastrami had been hot smoked for some time, the taste amplified by all manner of spices. Maybe ginger, cinnamon, cloves, allspice, coriander. Certainly, peppercorn and garlic. I sat blissful and surveyed my surroundings between bites.

Grill and counter claimed most of the floor space. Small, round café tables hugged the wall, and customers sat on the ubiquitous bent wood Vienna chairs that had recently invaded the city from the Thonet Company of Austria. I expected mostly Jewish clientele, but fine sandwichery proved an ecumenical pursuit. Also, prices were cheap and the portions generous. Bespectacled salesclerks at one table, laborers at another, and a vested banker in the back. My eyes paused on a solo patron with his back to me.

An instinctive echo quickened my pulse. He moved like trouble, with a weight lifter's neck, leg pumping, burning off excess energy. His Pant leg rose enough to see an ankle. The bone handle of a gambler's dagger protruded from his boot. More worrisome, his head kept turning toward the cashier station. When he got up to pay his bill, I focused attention on him. Instead of handing Lady L his money, he dangled it from his hand, forcing her to reach over the counter. At the last moment, he snatched it away.

"Hey doll, I seen you before at the club. It's me, Rand."

Lady L wrinkled her face like she was smelling bad fish. "Sorry. I don't know you."

"Oh, you know me all right." He performed the line. "Why don't you show me to the bathroom? You'll get the check and a big tip."

Lady L swung her left palm to slap him, but he ducked like a boxer and grabbed her arm and twisted it.

"You're going to have to work extra hard to make up for that, bitch."

I considered a run at him. If I tackled him at the knees, I might take him down, maybe get to the knife before he did. I would've tried it a year or two ago. I now realized he was too quick and too strong. He would see me coming and pin or cut me. What then, just sit? There was a limit to what one person could do when confronted with powerful evil.

Drop the black pebble.

I wasn't alone. With the other customers, there were seven of us, plus two countermen. I stood and faced the other diners away from Rand.

"Gentlemen, gentlemen all. May I take a moment of your time?"

Everyone turned my way. I loosened my diction. It felt—American.

"I came here four years ago, eager to discover the soul of America. I've seen its great cities, both north and south, and the vast magnificence of the Western territories."

My appeal to pride was effective, my audience rapt. Rand looked around confused, but he let go of Lady L's arm, allowing her to retreat to the grill.

"But other countries have grand cities and plains. What makes America so special? I'll tell you. All your ancestors came from all over the world for a better life. Not just the same life, mind you, a better one.

"I love my home country, but it's hard to imagine a bootblack thinking he or his children will ever be gentlemen. But you there, laboring with sweat and brawn. Someday your issue may be titans of industry."

"Here, here!" the man in the business suit exclaimed.

"Now I'm sure we've all engaged in activities we wouldn't want our dear mothers to know about."

"You got that right, brother," one of the clerks shouted. Rand was still standing flat-footed and dumbfounded.

"But our past should not impede our future improvement. Each of us witnessed the incident at the register. I don't know how low her estate, or dire her circumstances, have been, but here she is trying to make an honest living, serving us with grace and good humor. Now I ask you all to stand here with me. Stand for the principles that make this country great. What this man, this interloper, has attempted to do in tearing down this woman is not just rude, it's un-American."

Rand finally caught the direction of the wind. "What the hell you think you're up to?"

By then the three laborers were beside me. Seeing the tide change, the two salesclerks moved behind us. The businessman, having removed his suit coat, strode forward as well. I doubted his fighting prowess, but his two hundred pounds might be useful.

"You stupid shits better sit back down. You don't know who you're dealing with," said Rand.

"With whom," I corrected him.

"Okay, you ass, you got it coming."

Rand reached for his boot when the countermen broke through beside us.

"Stop right there." The first man brandished a twelve-inch butcher knife in one hand and a meat cleaver in the other. The second man nestled a marble rolling pin. He spoke like an owner or manager.

"You're out of here. Persona non grata."

"What? You're gonna kick me out for that magdalen?" He puffed himself up like a peacock. "I'm Rand. This is my place. I come here all the time."

"Check the lease. It's my place, and we don't need your business no more. You're on the list now."

"Listen, Buster, I don't have to take this." The threat had returned to his voice.

"Yes, you do. Now you listen. Ever since we opened, the cops on duty, we never take their money. Coffee, sandwich, all on the house. They all love us. And Rand, I do know who you are. Any funny business and you'll be dancing with the billy clubs."

Rand peered at each of us. “Your place is shit anyway.” Deflated, he shambled out the door.

I thought there might be some sort of celebration, slapping backs, shaking hands. Instead the men quietly filed back to their seats to finish their meals. They realized Rand was still out there, and other Rands as well. This wasn’t a war to be won but a battle to be fought day by day, year after year.

“Nice speech.” Lady L joined me at my table. “You believe all that red, white, and blue stuff you were preaching?”

“About half. It’s aspirational.” I couldn’t help thinking that Ohanze would have complaints about the “we all came here” part.

“So, you’re a lefty,” I said.

“The sinister hand. Mom tried to beat it out of me, but yeah.”

“That slap, probably not a good idea.”

“I’d had it up to here with guys this week.”

Now sitting close, I noticed the great makeup job that nearly concealed a black eye.

“Who gave you the present? Per?”

“No, but he didn’t do anything about it either. I mean, I can take a playful spank here and there, you know. Even had a regular used his pizzle like a little whip, but nobody gets to hurt or punch me. Under the old owner, that john wouldn’t have walked straight for a week. Come to find out the new owner knew the guy played rough, actually paid extra for the privilege. No one let me in on it. First, he’s calling me all sorts of names I don’t like. I’m thinking, you kiss your mother with those lips? Then we’re in the middle of a poke through the whiskers, and he suddenly starts to choke me.”

“What the devil?”

“Claimed I’m supposed to like it. Well, I smacked him upside his head and rolled off the bed. He’s up screaming that I broke his willy.

Runs over and punches me in the face. Pined me down on the floor and buggered me, broken willy be damned."

"I'm so sorry. Are you all right?"

"No. I'm not close to all right. I always felt like I was in control—I don't feel that no more. Others heard I'd quit and tried to recruit me at McGurk's dance hall. You know, the place where they drug sailors with chloral hydrate. But I heard their bouncer, Eat-Em-Up Jack McManus, is all handsy. Six of their girls committed suicide there, they were so miserable. You know what that creep McGurk does? Renames the place Suicide Hall to cash in on the notoriety.

"Anyway, I'm not going back to it, but it's real hard for a girl to make an honest living. I looked at domestic work. Only two to five dollars a week. Paper box plant wasn't much better, maybe six or seven dollars, if you keep your numbers up."

I took her hand. "Leocadia, I think I have an idea for you."

She cocked her head. "Hey how'd you—Oh yeah, my name tag. Manny insisted I use my real name. Who gives a daughter a handle like that?"

"It is a saint's name, from *Lives of the Saints*. She remained steadfast in her faith even when imprisoned."

"If you say so. Just call me L. So, what's your big idea? You finally going to marry me?" She fluttered her eyes.

I blushed. It always got me.

"Down at the newspaper and in offices all over town, they're hiring scores of women to type. Business is starting to boom, and offices are drowning in clerical and paperwork."

"They'll just hire a man. Always do."

"That's just it, L. Typing is new. You're not competing with men. The businesses like hiring women typists. They show up, take orders, and the boss can pay them half as much as a man. Still, ten to twenty dollars a week."

L eyed me warily. “I can’t afford to buy a typewriter. How am I going to learn?”

“I can get you a Hammond No. 12 from down at the paper. It may have a broken key, but it will serve. They give lessons at the YWCA.”

“What happens when they ask me where I used to work?”

“If you can type sixty words a minute, they won’t care where you came from. If need be, list me as a reference, and I’ll say you were an assistant.”

L sat back and flashed a bright splendid grin. “I always liked you.” She fished a cigarette from her pocket, and before lighting it, used her thumbnail to press a little sign of the cross into the paper.

“I don’t think that’s going to help. Those things will kill you.”

She laughed. “I’ll stop smoking soon as we sign the marriage license. See, Joshua Banks, now you got to save my life.”

Chapter 30

The final sands were slipping through the hourglass. George's trial would start in two days, December 20, 1899. With his blessing and indeed his insistence, I stood in a law office waiting to meet George's accomplished trial lawyer, Emanuel Friend. Word came that Friend, engaged in trial preparation for this and other cases, shifted my meeting to junior counsel Edward Hymes. The law clerk sensed my disappointment, assuring me that while only twenty-eight, and six years into his career, Mr. Hymes was sharp as a new razor. I nodded and hoped that I might be described in a similar fashion someday.

The clerk led me to a seat in Mr. Hymes's modern office while Hymes finished outside with their investigator. Everything in the office whispered quiet confidence and efficiency, from the klismos chairs to a trophy won at an international chess competition. It wasn't surprising, then, when Hymes entered looking a lawyer straight from central casting, his handshake quick and firm.

"Mr. Johnson thinks the world of you, Mr. Banks. Will we get some positive press?"

"Within the bounds of truth, yes."

"We can't ask for more. We only want to avoid the scandalous libel of the other scribes. Misstatements of the cause of death as poisoning or strangulation. Makes the defendant look complicit."

"I understand. Until I met with George, I thought the woman had been found in his bed, not out on the front room couch."

"Precisely. Their whole case is smoke, and we're going to blow it away."

"How can you be so confident?" I asked. "I'm gravely worried for George. The presence of a Negro in court accused of murder in this country almost ensures conviction. Many Negroes who faced less evidence than George lie in prison or the grave."

Hymes held his index finger in the air. "That's the very trap we hope District Attorney Cowan falls into, that all the case requires is to place the defendant in the apartment with the fatally injured Miss Stuart, and his job is done. Well, you shall see. We will object to every question and statement the DA makes. We will object to the color of his suit and shoes. If he posits that the sun came up that morning, we will make him prove that fact.

"The DA's office is so preoccupied with high-profile cases they've no time for this matter. The Roland Molineux trial alone is heading for three months and a price tag of two hundred thousand, the most ever spent, before they're done. I don't think they have much manpower or man-hours for the death of a mulatto drifter with no family to push the case."

"Mr. Hymes, I'm quite familiar with Roland, that smirking, handlebar-mustachioed ass. My good friend Dr. Kamany belongs to the Knickerbocker Athletic Club. They all believe Roland killed Henry Barnet with tainted medicine so he could take back that fickle Blanche Cheesborough and marry her. It would be a bad romance plot if not for poor Henry."

"But that's not the present case," said Hymes. "He's accused of poisoning Katharine Adams, the elderly aunt of the club director, Henry Cornish."

"Yes. I was told Roland went round at it with Cornish," I said. "He wanted the director out. Thought him too common. Roland liked to flaunt his wealth and his family's connections with the Republican

Party. Roland thinks himself the elite athlete, always preening. Well, Cornish made a fool of Roland and made him forfeit his membership. It's the talk of the club. Clearly, Roland tried to get revenge on Cornish by sending him headache medicine laced with cyanide. Only luck, good and bad, that Cornish escaped and his aunt did not."

"It may be clear to the layman, but that's not how the law works." Hymes stroked his chin. "Yes, he has motive, Barnet stealing the affections of Miss Cheesborough, and Cornish socially embarrassing him. He's the knowledge and ability, the family fortune is in the chemical dye business. Cyanide of mercury is used to blend dry colors. Molineux is trained in chemistry as well."

"Then it is settled. He's guilty," I said.

"No. You have left out one step. You've not proved Molineux mailed the poison to Cornish or Barnet. It's just such a gap in proof that the DA is making in your friend's case."

"I hope you're not saying Roland may go free. He is a smug scoundrel."

"The DA has handwriting experts tying Roland to the notes. I expect he'll be convicted. Now, as to your other point. Those unfortunates you mentioned in jail, or the grave, most had no counsel. Those who did had to settle on the incompetent, alcoholic, or down-and-out pettifoggers who take such cases. Some call for establishing a state defense bar, but others cry socialism."

"Money buys justice?"

"Sir, money buys many things. Money buys expertise that helps birth justice. My investigator just gave me information on the possible veniremen so that we may build the right jury."

"Build?" I knew Hymes was only trying to help George, but the thought of such manipulation upset me.

"Everyone says you're to be trusted, Mr. Banks, so I'm inclined to answer your question, but first I insist you give your word as a gentleman you'll keep such tactical knowledge out of the papers. We can't have the public see the sausage-making."

"You have my word."

"You see, the real practice of law is unwritten tactics and strategy, especially in defense. To paraphrase my colleague Andrew Hirschl, 'the skillful conduct of a trial may be compared to the jujitsu system of wrestling, which enables the inferior man with less weight, less strength, and less endurance, to win because he knows better how to apply the weight and strength he does possess.' We'll start with a very thorough voir dire to select the jury. Expect it to take the entire first day."

"How can that be? I sat in the Old Bailey—for a moment, I considered being a barrister. I scarcely remember a case where the first twelve veniremen were not selected."

"Yes, but Britain restricts jurors to men of significant real property. Only one-third of Englishmen may serve. More importantly, every juror will be some variation of Anglican property owner. New York requires some modicum of property, real or personal, but that still allows a cacophony of biases on the jury. It's our job to eliminate the negative biases and build affinity."

"Are you a secret swami who can peer into men's souls?"

"I can examine them, question their prejudices for and against my client."

"Justices at the Old Bailey shall never acquiesce to such badgering of jurors. Don't you fear you will embarrass or insult a venireman who ultimately serves?"

"That's why you use challenges for cause first so you can back them with preliminary challenges. Those don't require any reason."

"You speak of human nature like a science." My voice rose unintentionally.

"Mr. Banks, it is both art and science. The art of it is to read what isn't said. How a man folds his coat or moves among the other jurors. Does he shrink back or shake hands? Where's his gaze? I've seen Mr. Friend tell a small joke to opposing counsel to see which jurors smile or grimace."

"And the science?"

"In its infancy, mind you. We need more data, and a way to coordinate and store it all. To slice the individual into the several identities that influence his opinions and habits: age, education, economic status, race, of course; religion, politics, labor rights. In Mr. Johnson's case, we want to eliminate anyone with scruples against the theater and performers."

"There are such people?"

"Indeed, and we must watch for fraternal societies, masons and such. Whereas in most cases peremptory challenges would remove anyone in a temperance league, they might be sympathetic toward this defendant given Miss Stuart's reputation for violent drunkenness."

I stared at Hymes. "I would be excluded?"

Hymes smiled. "No offense, but without a doubt. What possible affinity could a man of your nobility and lineage have with the squalid world of the Negro?"

Hymes absentmindedly started leafing through papers on his desk. "I suppose if the evidence were more damning, we could try to hang the jury. There's a skilled lawyer I know, Francis Willman, who claims he can engineer a hung jury with one carefully chosen unreasonable man. Even better, jumble the box with smart and stupid, young and old, rich and poor, laborer and businessman, Jew, Irish, the lot, with the supposition that they will never agree on any verdict."

"Do you think George will have to testify? Will White jurors believe his words over the police?"

"First, not every White man has good relations with the police.

Second, we already made sure Officer Boyle will not be called to testify. He seems to have a problem with uppity Negroes. I've observed Officer McManus in court. I believe he will give an achingly dry, yet accurate, account.

"Everything will be done not to put Mr. Johnson on the stand. DA Cowan's overworked, but he's no fool. He'd take the opportunity to bring up every tiff the defendant ever had with the deceased. No good in that. Anyway, would they believe Mr. Johnson? Hard to say. If you ask a Southern venireman if he would convict a White man for killing a Negro, he'd outright admit he wouldn't. If you ask, he'll tell you that Jews, Catholics, and Negroes are not worthy of being believed. Here in New York, people are cagier. They don't think themselves racists or bigots, but they'd move to Alaska before they'd let their daughters marry a Negro. Fine with a colored employee, but put him in charge, they bristle. You have to ask subtle questions, on the order of, 'Do you think there will be a Negro Supreme Court Justice in the next hundred years?' "

I knew I didn't have the right, but I felt personally affronted by that question. "How would you answer, Mr. Hymes?"

He checked his watch and opened his office door. "I don't know. Never considered it as a reality. It only matters how *they* answer the question. Don't think about the race issue that much. It really doesn't affect me. Mr. Johnson is my first colored client. Not that I don't care. My family fought for the Union in the war, but if the Negro is to attain anything close to equal status, not just tolerance, they're going to have to carry the water themselves. No one's going to hand it to them."

Attorney Hymes proved true to his word. The voir dire dragged on through the entire first day of the trial, the last juror not set until the following morning. Remarkably, the jury included Martin Dodson, a respected real-estate broker, who happened also to be a Black man. As I joined the hundred or so spectators crowded into the Criminal Court Building, I spotted Len Spencer filing in with Samuel Moore, the man whose father had owned George and his father as slaves on a plantation near Harpers Ferry, Virginia.

"Mr. Moore, pardon me," I said. "Could I get a few words for the paper?"

Moore put out his hand to push me away. "Forget it. You newsboys trying to make it out that the folks helping George are only in it for the money he makes them. Well, I'm giving up a week of business to be here."

Len came to my aid. "Samuel, that's Joshua. He's friendly. It's that smart-ass from the *Herald* we're avoiding."

Moore still looked at me skeptically. "If you say so, Len. George trusts you with his life." Moore turned back to me. "Be quick, fella. I don't want to miss nothing."

I probed him as to his childhood relationship with slave George and why he would come such a distance these many years later.

"Attorney Wooster tells me he's got twenty men of good standing as character witnesses but thinks it'd be helpful to show George was always a kind soul, all the way back as a kid. Why, he was the best buddy a boy could hope for. If I was climbing the maple tree or jumping flips into the swimming hole, he'd be right there with me."

"But, excuse me—did he not have to?"

"Bullshit, son. All he had to do was be my valet. We had a bond. I'd known if he was putting it on. I couldn't go to my Jesus if I turned my back on him now."

Moore turned away and hurried inside with Len. I followed and took my place with the other press. Surveying the room, I saw many familiar faces: Charley Case, Jose, other performers and stage hands, the recording engineer, and surprisingly, guard Mitchell from the Tombs in his street clothes. The sea of White faces was punctuated with Blacks of various status. I didn't know most of them, but I recognized the Reverend with a few parishioners from George's church, and Ike the bartender from the black-and-tan we were run out of. It was impossible to read minds, but it felt as if everyone wished George well. Roskin Stuart appeared to be an orphan here.

DA Cowan rose and painted a dark picture. Johnson and his common-law wife, Stuart, were heard arguing at 2:00 a.m. the morning of October 12th. Stuart taunted and called Johnson names, accused him of killing his first wife. The defendant had said he would kill her if she kept it up. Later that morning when the police were called, Stuart was found on the couch of the apartment, severely injured, and later died in the hospital.

Hymes nearly interrupted Cowan. "Your Honor, we move for dismissal."

The judge peered over half-moon reading glasses. "Aren't we jumping the gun?"

"No, Your Honor. The proposed case is completely circumstantial. His evidence, if proved, and his witnesses, if believed, will still not connect the defendant with a crime."

Judge Newburger clearly looked unimpressed. "I assure you, counselor, there are many on death row as a result of circumstantial evidence. Murder victims have a bad habit of not testifying in their cases, and most murderers don't leap upon the stage like John Wilkes Booth declaring their guilt. Motion denied."

Lawyer Friend rose. "May it please the court, may we have the material witnesses excluded from the courtroom unless they are testifying so they are not tainted or restrained in any way?"

"That's a reasonable request, granted. Mr. Cowan, who is your first witness?"

"Mrs. Lena Small, an upstairs neighbor."

"Bailiff, lead the other witnesses outside."

Mrs. Small, while actually large, was mousy and shifted nervously on the stand. She testified that she often heard arguments from the basement apartment, not fighting, but angry words. A similar row occurred around 2:00 a.m. that October 12th morning. One exchange was particularly damning.

DA: Now, tell us just what you heard?

Mrs. Small: I heard her making the remark, "You killed your first wife, but you'll never kill me." Then he said, "If you call me," mentioning a certain name, "I will kill you."

DA: What was the name?

Mrs. Small: A Black son of a bitch.

I kept writing my newspaper story as it unfolded, with no idea of the outcome. The piece would have to be ready for the evening run of the presses. It became clear in my mind this would be my last story for the *Journal*.

The effect of Mrs. Small's statement was blunted on cross-examination, as she was quickly forced to admit she heard no disturbance that would account for Stuart's injuries. Things took a strange turn when Mrs. Small left and her husband Herbert sat in the witness chair.

Over the objection of the DA, the defense began to probe Stuart's drinking habits. Mr. Small, a tad too confidently, pronounced her a habitual drunkard and a fiend for gin. After DA Cowan broke in to question how Mr. Small could be so sure, Herbert at first tried to say both that he saw her drink gin in her rooms (Suspiciously, not only at 262 West, but in her earlier apartment as well), while simultaneously denying ever being in those rooms, until finally having to come clean. I wondered what he might have said if Mrs. Small was glaring at him instead of sitting blissfully outside.

Mr. Small: Was I in her rooms?

DA: Yes?

Mr. Small: I have been in her rooms.

DA: Were you in her rooms on occasions when you saw her drink gin?

Mr. Small: Yes sir, many times. I have seen her drink gin in her rooms, possibly ten or twelve times.

DA: Were you familiar with her?

Mr. Small: No, Sir. I never have been familiar with her any more than to speak to her.

DA: How did you come to go into her rooms? Were they social visits?

Mr. Small: No sir, not that. There was nothing concerned between her and me. She was simply a neighbor.

DA: Tell us how you came to go into the rooms.

Mr. Small: I went in socially because she invited me—

Hymes jumped to his feet. "I object to that. It is an effort to impeach his own witness."

The judge waved him away. "I will allow it."

Mr. Small: I went in simply because I wanted to see her. It was a liberty that she permitted, and it was something that I felt I wanted to accept.

The judge acknowledged the jury foreman, who asked a question from the jury. "To your knowledge, was Mrs. Stuart in the habit of having company at night, at any and all hours, with persons other than her husband?"

Mr. Small: Only people that wanted to drink gin. Anybody was acceptable, if they had some gin with them. Anybody, gentleman or lady, if they had the price of ten cents worth of gin, they were acceptable."

The sun outside burned through the morning clouds and shone through the windows, lighting the side of George's face. His features were neither the theater mask of tragedy nor comedy, but instead expressionless, calm. It couldn't be lost on him that Mr. Small's tortured admission helped muddy the waters in George's favor. Any number of people, friend or stranger, man or woman, might have cavorted and combated with Stuart that early morning. Still, to put up with Roskin's behavior for so long, George obviously harbored deep affection for her. It must not be easy to have the woman you loved portrayed as a reckless gin whore.

The following testimony of Officer McManus was fair, as Hymes predicted, delivered in a gruff, just-the-facts manner. The defendant had approached the officer on the street in the early afternoon, reporting a woman in distress in his apartment. When he entered the tidy apartment, McManus found a woman lying unconscious but alive on the sofa, a trace of blood oozing from her mouth, her jaw and eyes bruised. An intriguing detail noted a small wound in her upper lip, under her nose, and appeared to have been made by the stab of a hatpin.

Officer McManus related George's statements: Stuart came home about half past two stinking of gin, then he went to bed in a separate room and left her to herself. He found her passed out on the floor in the morning and lifted her onto the sofa. This was not the first time he had found her passed out.

Another neighbor, Hattie Thomas, confirmed the lip wound "looked as if it had been done with a hatpin." George had approached Mrs. Thomas first, when Stuart did not wake up, and her breathing became labored. He asked Thomas to come see Stuart. Expecting to find her "drunk as usual," Thomas instead became concerned, telling George, "That woman is dying." At that point, George went searching for a policeman.

Thomas said one more thing, an odd addition, something no one revealed until then. She mentioned hearing Roskin Stuart singing, to herself or others she did not know, at 6:30 a.m. on October 12th.

A prosecution mistake produced the wrong witness to testify about admitting Stuart to Bellevue Hospital. After testily admonishing the

DA to personally telephone the hospital and retrieve the right witness, Judge Newburger put the court in recess until after lunch.

On a bench outside, I scribbled copy for the story. Although concerned about George's future, I confess my mind focused on my own fate. The whole journey to America, all the occurrences, all the people, had been one long trial. The verdict was imminent, a life of meaning on my own terms, or a sentence of beck and heel, I my own judge and jury, my ruling becoming clear to me. Things would be lost, precious things, and things would be gained, but my decision was finally made.

First, though, George. We filed back into court and watched Dr. William W. Beveridge, admitting doctor at Bellevue, take the oath. DA Cowan was very keen for the Doctor to attest that Stuart's injuries, allegedly administered by Johnson, had been the direct cause of death. Dr. Beveridge proved an elusive accomplice. He stated that Stuart had arrived at the hospital bruised and with a cut on her lip, but the factor that made her condition serious, life threatening, was pulmonary edema. Prodded to explain the term to the layman, the Doctor described it as when the lungs fill with fluid. "Water lung," some called it. One of the symptoms is the sputum tinged with blood that Officer McManus had noted.

On both direct and cross-examination, the Doctor stressed that pulmonary edema was a terminal symptom, which could be the result of any number of causes—violent blows, yes, but also heart disease, illnesses associated with alcoholism, or from toxins, and even one's own aspirated vomit.

Finally, DA Cowan asked outright, "Can you please say what caused her death?"

The Doctor's gaze went from juror to juror. "Well, it would be impossible to say the exact cause producing her death. It's like saying a man died of a stopped heart. That doesn't tell you he was dragged underwater, or hit by a train. The woman's lungs stopped exchanging air. At that point, she died. More I cannot say."

Hymes jumped to his feet again, almost shouting, "Your Honor, we move for acquittal. The prosecution has failed to make a case. They haven't shown that Mr. Johnson inflicted the observed injuries on Miss Stuart, or in fact, whether the injuries occurred before or after any overheard argument. She may have fallen down, or left the apartment and returned alone or with an invited person. Regardless of how she obtained her injuries, the DA has not established them as the cause of death. And why would Mr. Johnson involve the police, who might potentially save Miss Stuart, allowing her to testify against him?"

Judge Newburger grunted at the DA's bungled case. He expressed a desire to continue, but turned a withering glare at the DA. "Does the District Attorney desire to be heard?"

DA Cowan replied sheepishly. He did not look directly at the judge. "I will say very frankly, Your Honor, that a conviction cannot be sustained in this case, and I think Mr. Hymes has substantially stated the grounds for acquittal."

"What does the District Attorney desire to do?"

The courtroom became silent. The DA looked at the judge sheepishly.

"I ask that the court recommend acquittal."

A shocked murmur coursed through the spectators but was quelled by a fierce look and call for order by the judge.

"In other words, I understand that the District Attorney abandons the case?"

"Yes, Sir."

"If that is so, that disposes of your motion, Mr. Hymes."

Hymes pressed, "I would wish to have a judicial disposition of it."

The judge sat up straight. "The District Attorney having abandoned the case, I do not think there is any action left but to direct an acquittal. Without passing merits on the case, or passing on the manner in which it has been handled . . ." Here he paused and glared at the DA. "I simply say to you gentlemen of the jury, you are directed to acquit."

At the pronouncement of the verdict, a verbal explosion of approval and relief echoed in the courtroom. Men and women rushed forward to embrace George. Judge Newburger practically broke his gavel suppressing the ovation. The bailiff was ordered to quickly clear the courtroom.

When George emerged into the outer lobby, a few White women pressed kisses on his cheek and forehead. A crowd of White men, including Len Spencer and Samuel Moore, jostled about him, hugging him and shaking his hand. As he descended the courthouse steps, his eyes squinting in mirth, he began to whistle, "I Don't Care If I Never Come Back."

Before being carried forward by the push of the crowd, I heard Rollin Wooster, the Columbia Records lawyer who had gathered the twenty-one now-unneeded character witnesses, giving an interview to the *Sun* reporter.

"Johnson's what you would call a good coon. He's too good-natured to ever have killed that woman. We're going to take him to a hotel tonight, or to Mr. Emerson's home, and give him a good dinner, sitting right down at the same table with him. I was glad I was first to shake hands with him after he was discharged."

That was the deal George had struck. The path of least resistance. I knew in my soul it could not be my path.

I stepped out of the courthouse threshold and shielded my eyes with my hand. Then I saw her. Standing at the bottom of the courthouse steps, brilliantly lit in the sun.

Margaret.

Chapter 31

Margaret's eyes scanned the mob outside the courthouse. It granted me a moment to drink her in. As much as she felt beauty a burden, she couldn't escape it. The passage from nineteen to twenty-three only served to sharpen and define the elegance of her features. If she meant to keep a low profile, she prepared in error. Her brilliant white calling suit was decorated on its cuffs, hem, and wide lapels with swirls of crystal beads that shimmered in the sunlight. A cobalt-blue riding top hat was accented by a rain of English ringlets that framed her face.

Once our eyes locked, she rushed to me with the fluid grace of a dancer. "Why am I not already in your arms?"

I realized I was frozen still as a statue.

"My darling—sorry—I'm in a bit of shock." My mind flooded with questions. "Why didn't you telegraph? Has your brother escorted you? How on earth did you find me here?"

"So many questions. Let's see. Your telegraph said you'd be back in New York, so I looked you up at the Croisic. Your friend Clifton said you'd be at this court. My brother didn't accompany me to America. I came alone. All rather last minute."

"But the Old Man—your father—he'd never allow that."

"It wasn't his choice, though he did precipitate it."

"I fail to understand."

Margaret hesitated a moment like she was preparing a rehearsed statement. "He's been playing at sabotage, Joshua. He hired and sent you here. He planned to keep you in America until he could marry me off to a real duke or earl. He never intended to consent to our marriage, but was too afraid of your family's power, of the repercussions should he outright reject you as his son-in-law. He couldn't be blamed if you just stayed away. I've come to end this charade and bring back my soon-husband."

"But your father?"

"He'll either take you or lose me, and for all his faults, he truly loves me. An estrangement would break his heart."

"Does my family know? What do they say about this?"

"John doesn't care about your affairs."

"And I don't care about his. I mean my father."

"Joshua, listen carefully." She placed her hand gently on my forearm. "John didn't want this to come by telegraph, and I agreed. Your father is dead."

I don't know how I expected to react to such news, but I felt like something broke inside me. I reached for the railing to steady myself. I wished for ordinary tears of grief, but felt different emotions: abandonment, defeat.

"Your father developed a cough that just wouldn't go away. He was planning a trip to Bath when his doctors confined him to bed. He went quickly after that. There was no time to alert you to return."

I clenched my eyes shut, trying to escape. "So, he's gone before I could accomplish anything. He died an embarrassed father."

"No, Joshua, that's simply not true. I'd been at your estate just before, checking on Nike. Your father was raving to everyone about how his youngest son was an honorary Sioux Indian with a real Indian name. Flying Horse, I think."

"What the hell?" Now I was confused. "Did Wyatt write my father that?"

"Oh, no. The telegram came directly from the reservation, Chief Ohanze himself. The Chief said you saved women and children. Your father was so proud. I think John was jealous."

Despite myself and the circumstances, I almost smiled. I imagined Ohanze laughing the whole time he dictated that cable. Wyatt must have put him up to it. Wyatt knew about the estate in Yorkshire and how to reach my father. Ohanze decided to lay it on thick. Nice touch, elevating himself to chief. There was no sense in disturbing such a lovely fable with truth. I simply moved on.

"Listen Margaret, John wanted to settle everything before I knew. He's in possession of the estate, and all holdings, I assume."

"Yes, of course."

"Nike as well?" My voice broke on her name.

"She is part of the estate. Really, I'm sure John would be charitable as to Nike."

"Charity is precisely what I wish to avoid. If I submit to John's forbearance, I'm no better than an inmate spending his days measuring his cell."

"My God, no man can lecture me of cages. You're asked to trim your sails, I'm cloistered in the harbor. No one ever died of eating bread instead of cake. Your family wants no pariahs. They'll provide some position."

People speak of falling in love as an unexpected, sudden occurrence, but for most, it's incremental, but undeniable once achieved. When should I have known? Wind River Reservation for sure, Yellowstone, confessing to Wyatt over the roar of Niagara Falls, branding my flesh with Lady Liberty's torch, or could it have been that first moment rounding Sandy Hook into New York Harbor? No matter, I was sure now—I was in love—with America, and I would never leave her. If America failed to always achieve her promise, it was because her promises were so profound. Blood and soil were primitive instinct. Americans strived for something nobler. Even if they fell short, the experiment continued. In my own small way, I might help that experiment succeed. Here I'd drop all pretense, no longer almost, but actually me.

"Margaret . . . I'm not going back."

Margaret face reddened. "Have you gone mad? Of course you are. I have two steamer tickets, for me and you. We leave tonight."

"I don't expect you to understand," I said. "I've met so many people, seen and felt so many things. Back there, I'm an empty vessel, a mere imitation of life. In America, I have a purpose. I can make a difference."

"You're not making any sense. You know you're starting to talk like a bloody American, but you're not American. No, you're only sleepwalking in a dream. I look at you and see Joshua Clarke Banks of Yorkshire and the Fens. When you get back to England, you'll awaken to life as it is, a continuous thread."

I found myself fighting back tears. "You see only my same brute form, but my memories are changed, and my story has just begun."

"Am I in this story, Joshua?" Margaret's face showed no tears, only fierce determination.

"You still may be, but I doubt you'd like its premise. First, would you stay here in America?"

"What a preposterous idea. You'd have me leave my family, my friends, my history, all I've ever known, to live here in this nation of impostors? How unfair of you."

"Well, then, the second question hardly matters, but I owe it to you to fully explain my actions. Could you marry a man who has one-eighth African blood coursing through his veins?"

Margret drew back and peered at me as if I were babbling in tongues. "You're talking rubbish again."

"No, I'm not. My father's father was mulatto, the product of my great-grandfather and a Black woman on the Island of Montserrat."

"That can't be true. Look at yourself. You're like Princess Caraboo claiming to have escaped pirates by swimming the Bristol Channel, only to be found out a cobbler's daughter from Devonshire."

"I assure you, this is no such fiction. I intend to live openly and proudly as an octoroon."

Margaret waged a finger at me. "How can you treat me so viciously? I've sacrificed precious years for you. You've been running from Yorkshire your whole life. Now you're running from Britain, and me. Joshua, I've seen these colored men, and you are not them."

"Of course I'm not them, nor are they me, but each of us makes up the whole. I grant that I exist in a paradox. I'm both White and not White, Black but not Black. I've stepped into the fiendish crucible of blood and law and emerged disrupted, new. I become what I do, and that is to apply all my will to rid this country of the vile obsession with race. If we're to overcome this as a species, it will not be in France or China or Egypt. It must start here."

Margaret placed a hand on my cheek and spoke as if comforting a child. "You've caught a fever in this barbaric land, but fevers can be broken, then forgotten. You saved me once, and I loved you for it. Let me save you, Joshua."

Her touch was warm and soothing. For an instant I imagined home and hearth, the playful chatter of children—for an instant—then pulled back my face.

"I'm sorry."

I expected the slap, and Margaret did not disappoint. I regretted sending the Indian clubs.

"Margaret, you're the finest woman I shall ever meet. The man who finally woos you shall be the luckiest man alive."

"Spare me such twaddle. I think I'm quite done with men for the time being. I prefer the company of women to such unfathomable creatures as men."

"What about Lord Merryman?"

"That insufferable popinjay? Please give me more credit than that.

He desires only the adornment of a wife. That, I will never consent to."

"Can you forgive me?"

"No, Joshua. I will never forgive you. I will instead try mightily to forget you."

She walked slow and stately back to her coach. She didn't look back but lingered before mounting so that I might fully realize my folly, might run and spin her around, cover her with kisses and beg her forgiveness. My heart beat hard in my chest. I stood rooted until her coach was gone.

My feet led where my heart piloted. I'd kept up steady communication with Miss Moon, but it had been years since I'd held her in my arms as we danced at the Bradley-Martin Ball. I yearned to hold her again. Still shaky from the courthouse encounter, I nearly stumbled, taking two steps at a time to enter the organization where Miss Moon worked. The staff, all women, bustled about, mailing off publications and newsletters, receiving and processing donations, and planning rallies. Miss Moon struck her usual business posture with me, but I finally persuaded her to accompany me to a location where we could speak in private.

The staging room was knee-deep in placards and banners. I needed to fully explain my African lineage. It didn't go easily. Miss Moon pushed back and prodded on each and every detail. She made me admit how much I still didn't know. At last, she accepted, at least, the possibility of my reality. After all, her family tree was touched with Whiteness somewhere along its growth.

"What do you wish me to say, Mr. Banks?"

"First, would you please, please call me Joshua? We're not strangers." She gave me a reluctant nod. I went right to it. "What I really want you to say is that you'll allow me to court you."

"Oh . . . oh." She clutched her hands.

"The major impediment to marriage is now removed."

"Mr. Banks—Joshua. I'm not sure that is wise. You may tire of your dark excursion. Then what?"

"My course is set, but I don't think I can do it alone."

"I'm not some jungle guide."

"Not a guide, a partner, in all things."

"I don't know." She pointed a finger at me. A bit friendlier than Margaret. "I will not be an exotic frolic, some fetish trophy."

"I promise you my affection, my admiration of you, is more than skin-deep. And may I finally say, I find you beautiful."

"You are easy on the eyes as well." She said it softly, then stiffened. "You will find me a strong-willed woman."

"I've known nothing but."

She gave me a stern look. "This is a big step. You understand, we are a long way from carefree canoodling."

I gave a slight bow. "You are worth the wait, but I will admit, I hope the way is not so long."

She paused and placed her finger on her lips, making judgment. "On one hand, I must admit, I've enjoyed your attention. On the other, I don't think you realize, or are prepared for, the path you've chosen."

Starting to worry the case was going against me, I fished around in my vest pocket and, while Miss Moon watched, revealed the ring with its constellation of diamonds. I'd been carrying it as a good-luck charm.

"I have a proposition. Let me lend you this ring. Of course, that means you have to meet me again, if only to return it. Have you ridden much?"

Her eyes on the ring, she answered nonchalantly, "Horses? Not really."

"Would you like to learn?"

"I think so."

"That settles it. I'll find you a good palfrey horse. The Tennessee Pacer is good. We can set up a lesson."

She trembled slightly as she slipped the ring on a finger of her right hand.

"It is grand, isn't it?" she said.

"Yes. Royal, I've been told."

"I will see you this Wednesday for luncheon."

"Splendid. And, Miss Moon, may I call you—"

"You may call me Hope."

I finished writing about George's trial during the cab ride to the *Journal*. I wanted to make the evening edition, but mostly I needed to confront Nowak. With my father dead and my life decision made, Nowak had little to hold over me. Brother John could fend for himself. Only Aubrey restrained me. My sister didn't have the independent fortitude of Margaret. Aubrey pinned her future on an elevating marriage. I wished not to be her undoing.

On the way to Nowak's office, I made a necessary detour. I'd only promised the former Lady L a partially broken Hammond No. 12, but even in disrepair, it still belonged to Hearst. I didn't want to end my first day as a somewhat-Black man with a theft. Making pains not to be seen, I unlocked the storage room and slipped in. The Oliver sat on the desk in full glory, a stack of paper to its left, Polish poems neatly typed.

After packing it into its carrier, I retraced my steps to stash the typewriter so I could grab it on my way out. L would learn to type in style.

I didn't knock before entering Nowak's office.

"What the hell you barging in for?"

"I have the George Johnson trial story. Not guilty, by the way."

Nowak laughed a hard little laugh. “Got away with it, huh? Listen, you can throw that story on the slush pile. I don’t know if it’ll ever see print. In case you haven’t noticed, we got a goddamn uprising in the Philippines.”

The conversation immediately stalled, and I noticed a new addition to Nowak’s spartan office. A second flag framed on the wall. On it, a peasant cloak and cap with crossed spear and scythe were surrounded by a circle of laurel leaves. Above a legend, **ZYWIA Y BRONIA.** *They Feed and Defend.* Ever since the humiliation at the restaurant, when Nowak used Polish as a weapon, I’d been studying a little Polish-English phrase book.

“Look,” said Nowak, “shouldn’t you be booking a steamship ticket? Trial’s over.”

“I’m staying.”

“What, are you nuts? Don’t think I won’t ruin you and your family.”

“There’s no need. I’m leaving the paper. I’m accepting my past. I intend to live openly as mixed race, a Mustee.”

Nowak furrowed his brow and shook his head. “What do you know about being a Negro? Your life is all talley-ho and release-the-hounds.”

“I’m sure I’ll learn.”

“Doing what?”

“The Negro organizations. They will want members who can walk freely through the White world.”

“You mean a spy.”

“If need be. And I thought I might take up preaching.”

“Ha. No offense, but you never struck me as particularly righteous, especially hanging around that reprobate Wyatt Brown.”

“Not that you care, but Wyatt’s a reformed man since Denver. Anyway, a Chinese American preacher showed me that religion can reach men’s souls, can make them change heart. I have a feeling that any progress for the Negro race is going to come wrapped in religion."

"Frankincense to the dead. You know I don't mean anything against the Negro, but come on, look around. You think you're going to change America?"

"It's always changing. It's the ship of Theseus. Each day a new plank, new mast, sail and crew, eventually a new America. The ever-new world. The question is, in which direction does it sail?"

"You'll still be a scandal to your family, without me lifting a finger."

"I'll change my name, embrace my new identity. I hear that's a very American thing to do."

"Oh, now you're an American?"

"Yes, I'm just like America. I woke up one day and discovered that I had Black blood in my veins from the start. That African stain makes me all the more American. You can stop your vendetta against me and leave my family alone."

"Me? I just wanted your highfalutin ass out of my newsroom. You've got bigger enemies than me. How do you think I knew to go looking in Montserrat? Sir Covington put me on the lookout."

"He has the report?" I felt myself deflate.

"Hell, no. He's even more insufferable than you. Kept it to myself. Told him it was inconclusive. All he has are rumors, and he doesn't have my contacts. He can pound sand."

"So, you will save my innocent sister from the knowledge that her great-grandfather raped a slave?"

"Damn, boy, I never said rape. Actually, the report says she was some kind of island royalty, Carib from St. Vincent. Here, Banks, or whoever you are now."

He reached in a cabinet and produced the dreaded file.

"You never actually studied this. I think you'll find it a fascinating read. For starters, it looks like your grandfather, the mulatto, was murdered. Maybe others too. Something of a mystery. That's why they shipped your father back to England."

I opened the file. There were pages of notes, and pictures of buildings, court records, and photos of illustrations of people both Black and White. I turned a page, a portrait of my great-grandmother.

Some kind of royalty, eh? That would be it. My name, Joshua Clarke Royal.

"Hey, you can read that on your own time. And by the way, I guess you know this means you're fired."

I thought to curse him, but the anger drained out of me. His part in my story was over. I felt free, scared, eager. I heard Nowak mutter.

"Good luck, jackass. Co ma wisieć, nie utonie."

I smiled. *He who will hang cannot be drowned.*

Acknowledgements

Authors often thank their editors, but rarely give the public any inkling of what the editor did. Danelle McCafferty did the heavy lift of turning 123,000 words of a first draft into proper prose, and getting me to cut the word count to 118,000. The next three editors worked on the first fifty pages used in agent submissions, but their comments changed the whole book. An unnamed Yorkshire editor from Farber Academy did not care much for the original version of Joshua, calling him "something of a privileged prig." I made Joshua more likable, more thoughtful and vulnerable from the start. Michele Rubin pushed me to convert any ornate, overly literate, period prose into more modern, readable English. I took her warning, "it's a novel about the 19th century, not a novel of the 19th century," to heart. Readers should thank her. Janet Reid was mainly focused on the query letter and synopsis, but her questions about the beginning pages led to rearranging the opening to accelerate Joshua's meeting with Doctor Qabash, as well as adding a physical manifestation of Joshua's psychosomatic injury.

I want to thank my copy editor, Andrea Vande Vorde, for always keeping the reader's needs as her priority. Several characters should thank her for making them more eloquent than I had originally portrayed them.

That leads me to Caleb Guard, who worked on the last structural edit. I cannot thank Caleb enough. He was presented a diamond in the rough, but the final cut and polish would either produce a glittering jewel or a dull stone. He pushed me to cut an entire subplot (really did not advance the plot, but I do miss the hand wrestling nun), condense narration, and tighten scenes. His attention to detail was inspiring, down to single word choice. The novel reads faster and flows smoothly because of his (and Andrea's) fine direction. I like to think we got a diamond with fire, but that is ultimately for each reader to decide.

Naming all the sources for the historical research, from scholarly texts and articles, to collections of news clippings, would take its own book (you can find some of the bibliography elsewhere). I will mention three that were particularly helpful in supplying the period detail to immerse the reader in the turn of the century. *Unspeakable Awfulness: America Through the Eyes of European Travelers, 1865-1900* by Kenneth D. Rose (Routledge 2014) and *Bad Habits: Drinking, Smoking, Taking Drugs, Gambling, Sexual Misbehavior, and swearing in American History* by John C. Burnham (New York University Press 1993), were both fun and informative, but more importantly were thoroughly footnoted back to the original sources. For the history of the early recording artists, I would have been lost without Tim Brooks's definitive work, *Lost Sounds: Blacks and the Birth of the Recording Industry* (University of Illinois Press 2004). Especially helpful was Brooks's reprinting of the trial transcript of George Johnson's murder trial. In a side note, Brooks wished that someone would tell Johnson's story. I did my best.

I also thank Terri Leidich, my publisher. She saw something in my novel that many had not, and helped me let it live in the world.

Lastly, I thank any of you who take the time to read the novel. I hope it will continue to live in your head and your heart.

About the Author

Jay G. Grubb is an entertainment attorney working in music, film, and publishing. As a professor teaching the history of jazz, blues, and pop he has confronted the complexities and contradictions of American culture that are at the core of *Land of Sins and Promise*. He was a columnist for *Script Magazine* (now merged with *Final Draft),* and received an Achievement Award in Writing from the National Council of Teachers of English. He is a frequent speaker, including lectures at Peabody Institute and the Maryland Institute College of Arts. He loves to travel, especially to scout the locations used in his writing.

Bibliography

Anderson, April J. "Peremptory Challenges at the Turn of the Century: Developments of Modern Jury Selection Strategies as Seen in Practitioners' Trial Manuals." *Stanford Journal of Civil Rights & Civil Liberties* 16, no. 1 (2020).

Brooks, Tim. *Lost Sounds: Blacks and the Birth of the Recording Industry, 1890–1919.* Champaigne, IL: University of Illinois Press, 2004.

Burnham, John C. *Bad Habits: Drinking, Smoking, Taking Drugs, Gambling, Sexual Misbehavior, and Swearing in American History*. New York: New York University Press, 1993.

Creelman, James. "The Atlanta Compromise Speech." *New York World.* Sept. 19, 1895.

Devere, Sam. "The Whistling Coon." qtd. in *Lost Sounds*.

Fagan, Barney. "My Gal is a Highborn Lady." Chicago: M. Witmark & Sons, 1896.

Fraser, Rae W. *Westward by Rail: The New Route to the East.* New York: Promontory Press, 1874.

Gershoni, Israel, and James P. Jankowski. *Egypt, Islam, and the Arabs: The Search for Egyptian Nationhood, 1900–1930*. Oxford University Press, 1987.

Gifford, William. "Probably a Mormon Trick.; Gen. Miles's Investigations Into the Crazy Among The Indians." *New York Times*, Nov. 8, 1890.

Johnson, George W. "The Laughing Song." qtd. in *Lost Sounds*.

Lyte, Henry Francis (lyrics). "Abide with Me." Music by Dr. William Henry Monk. 1861.

Muir, John. "The American Forests." *The Atlantic Monthly* 80, no. 478 (1897).

Nasaw, David. *The Chief: The Life of William Randolph Hearst.* Boston: Mariner Books, 2000.

Rexford, Even E. (lyrics). "Silver Threads Among the Gold." Music Hart Pease Danks, 1873.

Rose, Kenneth D. *Unspeakable Awfulness: America Through the Eyes of European Travelers, 1865-1900.* Routledge, 2013.

Spencer, Williams, and Quinn's Imperial Minstrels. "Minstrel First Part, Featuring 'The Laughing Song.' " Ca. 1894.

The People, et al v. George W. Johnson. Court of General Sessions of the Peace, City and County of New York, Part IV. New York, November 20, 1899. Transcript in the Special Collections Department, John Jay College of Criminal Justice, New York, NY.

Wagner, Bryan. "Disarmed and Dangerous: The Strange Career of Bras-Coupé." *Representations* 92, no. 1 (2005).

Washington, Booker T. *The Booker T. Washington Papers, vol. 3*. Edited by Louis R. Harlan. Urbana: University of Illinois Press, 1974.

Wellman, Francis Lewis. *Day in Court, or the Subtle Arts of Great Advocates*. New York: Macmillan, 1910.

Wilde, Oscar. *House Decoration*. Lecture delivered at the Art Institute of Chicago, Chicago, IL, March 1882.

Further Reading

Abbott, Lynn, Doug Seroff. *Out of Sight: The Rise of African American Popular Music, 1889–1895.* University Press of Mississippi, 2002.

Abbott, Lynn, Doug Seroff. *Ragged But Right: Black Traveling Shows, "CoonSongs," & the Dark Pathway to Blues and Jazz.* University Press of Mississippi, 2007.

Blum, Deborah. *The Poison Squad: One Chemist's Single-Minded Crusade for Food Safety at the Turn of the Twentieth Century.* New York: Penguin Press, 2018.

Brundage, William Fitzhugh, editor. *Beyond Blackface: African Americans and the Creation of American Popular Culture, 1890–1930.* University of North Carolina Press, 2011.

Chudacoff, Howard P. *The Age of the Bachelor: Creating an American Subculture*. Princeton University Press, 1999.

Drew, Sidney, dir. *A Florida Enchantment*. 1914; New York: Vitagraph Company of America, 1914.

DuBois, W.E.B. *The Souls of Black Folk*, Signet Classics, 1903.

Erbsen, Wayne. *Manners and Morals of Victorian America.* Charlotte, NC: Native Ground Books & Music, 2009.

Gates, Jr., Henry Louis. *Stony the Road: Reconstruction, White Supremacy, and the Rise of Jim Crow*, New York: Penguin Press, 2019.

Gates, Jr., Henry Louis. *Life Upon These Shores: Looking at African American History 1513–2008*. New York: Alfred A. Knopf, 2011.

Gilfoyle, Timothy J. *City of Eros: New York City, Prostitution, and the Commercialization of Sex*, 1790–1920, New York: W.W. Norton & Company, 1992.

Hoffmann, Frank, B Lee Cooper, Tim Gracyk. *Popular American Recording Pioneers 1895–1925.* Philadelphia: The Haworth Press, 2000.

Kang, Lydia, Nate Pedersen. *Quackery: A Brief History of the Worst Ways to Cure Everything.* New York: Workman Publishing, 2017.

Kasson, John F. *Rudeness & Civility: Manners in Nineteenth-Century Urban America.* New York: The Noonday Press, 1990.

Lott, Eric. *Love and Theft: Blackface Minstrelsy and the American Working Class.* Oxford University Press, 1993.

McCutcheon, Marc. *Everyday Life in the 1800s: A Guide for Writers, Students, and Historians.* New York: Writer's Digest Books, 1993.

McKay, Brett, Kate McKay. "When Christianity was Muscular." *Art of Manliness*, accessed Dec 30, 2019. https://www.artofmanliness.com.

Muirhead, James Fullarton. *The Land of Contrasts: A Brition's View of His American Kin*. Lamson, Wolffe and Company, 1898.

O'Neill, Therese. *Unmentionable: The Victorian Lady's Guide to Sex, Marriage, and Manners.* Little, Brown and Company, 2016.

Richardson, Heather Cox. *West from Appomattox: The Reconstruction of America after the Civil War:* New Haven, CT: Yale University Press, 2007.

Somerville, Siobhan B. Queering the Color Line: Race and the Invention of Homosexuality in American Culture. Durham, NC: Duke University Press, 2000.

Taylor, Elizabeth Dowling. *The Original Black Elite: Daniel Murray and the Story of a Forgotten Era.* New York: Harper Collins, 2017.

White, Richard. *The Republic for Which it Stands: The United States During Reconstruction and the Gilded Age, 1865–1896.* Oxford University Press, 2017.

Wondrich, David. *Stomp and Swerve: American Music Gets Hot, 1843–1924*. Chicago Review Press, 2003.